Katharine **Wilson**

Sleathwaite

A book based on the lives of villagers living in and around the Tyne Valley in Northumberland.

novum pro

www.novum-publishing.co.uk

© 2022 novum publishing

ISBN 978-3-99131-204-8
Editing: Hugo Chandler
Cover photos: Gordon Bell, Victordenovan | Dreamstime.com
Cover design, layout & typesetting: novum publishing

www.novum-publishing.co.uk

Characters

The Macalister family

Jack Macalister. Parent and Grandparent, retired farmer.

James Macalister. Husband and Father, Farmer.

Rachael Macalister. Wife and Mother. District Nurse.

Scarlett Macalister. Daughter and Sister aged 9. School girl.

Cameron Macalister. Son and Brother aged 6. School boy.

George Crosby. Parent and Grandparent, retired Engineer.

Marian Crosby. Parent and Grandparent retired Psychiatric Nurse.

The Mayhew Family

Thomas Mayhew Reverend of Sleathwaite Methodist church. Husband and Father.

Emily Mayhew. Wife and Mother, District Nurse.

John Mayhew. Son and brother aged 11, School boy.

Jamie Mayhew. Son and brother aged 11, School boy.

The Turner Family

Matthew Turner. Husband and landlord of the Hadrian Pub.

Caitlin Turner, Wife and Landlady of the Hadrian Pub.

Philip Marsden. ICT Consultant.

Patrick Hunter. ICT Consultant.

PART ONE

Chapter 1

Set on the banks of the River Tyne sits the village of Sleathwaite, which is between Corbridge and Hexham in the Tyne Valley, Northumberland. Here and throughout this county you will find the most iconic countryside set within Northumberland National Park. It was here that the Roman Emperor Hadrian came and settled with his army and built the Roman wall across Britain, also known as Hadrian's wall, in AD 122, which still stands today, along with the ruins of the army camps.

Sleathwaite gets its name from a nearby slate mine which offers employment to the community and *thwaite* meaning settlement.

In the village is the local school which has now been turned into an academy, a pub called the Hadrian, a surgery, shops and a church. It also has a rugby club where a lot of the villagers play, from children to adults; and there is the most beautiful park with lovely gardens full of floral displays, a bandstand, playing fields and the village also has its own bowling club.

On the outskirts of the village sits Sleathwaite hall once home to a local landowner called George Hamilton. His family were upper-class and belonged to the gentry, as he was the Duke of Northumberland. He had lived there with his family since the beginning of the nineteenth century when the hall was first built. Unfortunately, he passed away in the late 1990s. His grandson David now dealt with financial matters regarding the estate.

The Hamilton family still owns the hall and grounds, but the estate is run by Camden Leisure Complex. It is now a hotel with a restaurant, a bar, a swimming pool, spa and golf course, including a range of sporting activities.

The hall and grounds are as beautiful now as they were then. Although the hall has been extended to allow for the hotel, they have still kept the new buildings, in keeping with the style of the original hall.

⁓

Set higher up on the edge of the village is Brookfield Farm, where the Macalister family live, and it is here where we begin exploring the lives of these villagers.

It was very early in the morning in the Macalister household and James had not been out of bed long. It was Saturday and he was having a quick breakfast, a bowl of cereal and a glass of breakfast orange. He was getting his coat and shoes on ready to go out to feed the animals. As it was only five a.m. he had to be quiet so as not to wake the others who were still fast asleep.

James had inherited the farm from his dad Jack who now lived nearby in a bungalow but still often came to visit and helped out when he could. However, Jack was getting on a bit now, he wasn't physically fit enough to do the heavy work. He was in his eighties and had a few health issues but still liked to do his bit,

James was a proud family man and believed in strong family values which came from his upbringing. He grew up on the farm and had helped since he was a small boy. He worked hard, and the farm was doing well. They got a lot of business supplying local businesses.

The farm had been in the family for generations. He wanted his children to have the same upbringing as himself and to grow-up to live independently and become well-rounded human beings.

James looked up. Suddenly, there was a noise on the stairs, sounding like buzzing?

"Brrrr, Brrrr, Brrrr, Brrrr."

It was Cameron his six-year-old son, standing at the top of the stairs in his pyjamas.

"Hi Pal, how are you doing or what are you doing?"

"I am a bulldozer ready to crash into everything, BRRRR," he said rolling down the bottom few steps.

"Shush you'll wake Mammy and Scarlett. It's very early. Don't you want to get back into bed where it's warm?"

"NO spells no," said Cameron. "I came to help you."

James thought for a moment.

"PLEASE!"

"Okay, just keep the noise down. Right first things first. Help yourself to cereal and then I want you wrapped up in a warm, hoody, jeans and coat. Oh, and put your wellies on. I'll get the quad bike out of the garage."

James headed out of the front door. He looked back at Cameron sitting and eating his Cheerios and watching the Simpsons on the telly. Bart was causing mischief with Homer.

He thought Cameron looked like a miniature version of himself with his blond curly hair. He suddenly thought back to when he was a boy sitting at the table having breakfast, getting ready to go out and feed all the animals with his dad.

He went into the garage and got out the quad bike. It was a big double garage, which he had built next to the farmhouse. He hoped to build above it one day and extend the upstairs of the house to make more bedrooms. Rachael had come up with the idea of doing bed and breakfast for holidaymakers, when they got nearer to retirement age.

He looked around the garage, gathered the feed he needed and put it in the storage area of the quad bike. He could hear Sammy banging the door of his kennel which he shared with his sister Kim. They were Border Collies and were kept as working dogs, but the children adored them, and they did go into the farmhouse, but they knew that their kennel was where their beds were and their own private place.

James let the dogs out and they wagged their tails in excitement and started to bark at the sight of their master. He gave a command and they sat up straight and became quiet. They were still quite young dogs and still got excitable, but also knew they had a job to do.

"Daddy, DADDY!"

"Okay, Cammy," said James, using his nickname. "I know you are excited but remember it is only five-thirty in the morning."

As he walked towards his son he couldn't help smiling. There stood his little boy with his hat perched on the top of his head like the arch-bishop of Canterbury's, his coat over his pyjama top. He had his jeans on, undone, and his wellies were on the wrong feet.

"I see you got ready then."

"Yes, and I did it all by myself!" said Cameron proudly.

"Well done but let me help you a bit and then we'll get off."

James sat him down, put the wellies on the right feet and helped him with fastening his jeans and straightening his hat.

"You still have your pyjamas on under there," James pointed out.

"I know. I want to be cosy when I get back, before my bath."

"Okay son," said James patting him on the shoulder.

Cameron felt his hand being licked and looked down and Sammy was there.

"SAMMY! KIM!" Cameron whooped for joy.

Kim nearly knocked him over in excitement.

"Right let's all get on the quad and get going, it has taken a little longer to get organised this morning. Good job it is Saturday, and you don't have school."

"Silly Billy Daddy, it's the summer holidays!"

"Of course, silly Daddy," said James, putting the key in the ignition. The quad roared into life, and they were off down the dirt track road.

"Where to first Dad?"

"We'll see to the sheep and lambs."

"Goody."

They arrived at the field where the sheep and lambs were. Some of the younger ones were in the lambing shed with their mothers in the next field, nearby.

James stopped the engine and turned around to Cameron.

"Right Cameron can you open the gate? You should be able to manage."

"Yes, okay."

Cameron jumped down from the quad and ran to the gate to open it to let his dad through but couldn't resist having a swing on it while closing it.

"Wheee!"

"You love doing that don't you?" said Dad.

"Yes, can we go to the park this afternoon, Please!"

"Well after your homework is done, okay?"

"Good."

Sammy and Kim jumped down from the quad and ran off to round up the sheep.

James and Cameron walked down the field. As he held the small boy's hand, he noticed he was skipping along.

'Such a happy little boy,' he thought.

James stopped and took out his whistle. "Come by!" Come by!", he shouted.

The dogs had rounded up all the sheep and Cameron ran to open the gate but struggled with the rope keeping the gate in place.

"Oh!" said Cameron struggling to undo it.

"Hey, it's okay, let me help," said James gently.

He opened the gate and Cameron helped to get the sheep in.

"Can I give them some food Daddy?"

"Yes, I'll lift the sack down and using the scoop you can fill the trough for them, but not too much."

"Like this?" said Cameron eager to impress.

"Yes, let's spread it out a bit, we'll make a farmer out of you yet."

"I like helping with the animals better than washing dishes," said Cameron.

"Well, we all have to help with the domestic chores, because we all have a lot to do," said James reproachfully. "However, I am glad you want to help and learn about farming."

"I don't want to be a farmer till I am older."

"No, well."

"I want to be an astronaut and live in space!"

James laughed. "I wanted to be a pilot."

"Really?"

"Yes. Right is that them fed?"

"Yep, what's next?"

"Lambs of course."

James let the sheep back out to graze, they were fine in this field for the moment. He got dogs and boy back onto the quad and they went down to the lambing shed.

"Ahh! They are gorgeous," said Cameron looking at the baby lambs.

"Would you like to help give some of the older ones their bottles?"

"Can I?"

"Of course, here give him this one. Tip it like this so he gets it all but not too much. We don't want him to choke."

"He's hungry," said Cameron laughing as the young lamb guzzled down the milk.

"Dad! Dad!"

James looked up and saw Scarlett running down the path towards them.

"Hello love, you're up early."

"I wanted to help; mum's still asleep."

"Oh, she's probably still really tired. She did the late shift last night. She wouldn't have got in till way past midnight."

"Can I give the lambs their bottles?"

"Well, you can help. Cameron's been doing a great job."

Cameron beamed, he adored his dad and used to follow him everywhere when he was smaller.

"Ohh! They're so cute," said Scarlett, taking a bottle from her dad.

"Now just a little bit at a time. They tend to guzzle it, and I don't want them to have wind."

"I know."

They finished off the feeding of the lambs and went off to see to the hens and collect the eggs.

"Right Cameron, you can do some counting. I want six eggs in each carton okay."

"D'oh!" said Cameron playing Bart Simpson.

"I can't open the carton!"

"Just try without ripping it, see," said James opening the lid.

"Surely you can open a box Cammy?" said Scarlett in a superior manner.

"I am trying, there I did it!"

"Scarlett! He has trouble with things like that. Give him a break, okay," said James quietly.

"Sorry!"

"One, two, three, oh sorry, I dropped one!"

"Don't worry, there's plenty more."

"Four, five, six, done it, all finished."

"We have six cartons to fill."

They all worked together and soon got the job done.

"Race you back to the quad!" Scarlett shouted, and sped off before the other two had a chance to get going. She reached the quad and shouted. "I won!"

"That wasn't fair!" wailed Cameron. He was starting to get tired and was ready for something to eat.

It was eight thirty when they walked into the kitchen where Rachael stood cooking bacon.

"Morning all, who's up for a bacon barm and a brew?" she asked, smiling.

"Yes please!" They chorused.

"Well sit down. How'd it go? Did you enjoy yourselves?"

"It was fun!" Cameron shouted.

"Mum, the lambs are gorgeous," said Scarlett.

"Aren't they just!" agreed Rachael.

"They've worked hard," said James proudly.

"Good, they'll have worked up an appetite then."

"How are you love after your late shift, still tired?" he asked, putting his arms around her and nuzzling into her neck, finishing off with a big kiss.

"Err! get a room!" shouted Scarlett.

"Hey, you!" said James laughing. "I don't know where she gets it from."

"I am still a bit tired; it was a busy shift last night with some difficult patients. Some also needed a lot of special care."

Rachael worked as a band seven nurse in the district. She was the sister to several community staff nurses and health care assistants.

She was originally from Hebden Bridge in West Yorkshire, where her parents still lived. She trained at Leeds for her first year but then she met James when she came for a weekend to Newcastle on a wild girl's night out, and they had kept in touch.

They met up every other weekend at either Hebden or Sleathwaite and eventually, she moved to Newcastle and transferred her training to Northumberland University, at Newcastle upon Tyne.

She worked at Newcastle Infirmary on the Cardiology ward, treating adults and elderly patients.

They eventually got married, settled down together and had a family.

They all sat down to a hearty breakfast.

"Right, you two," said Rachael. "Baths, then homework, please!"

"Ohh!" both children protested.

Although it was the summer holidays, the school had set some homework for the children which wasn't mandatory, but they had suggested that the parents encouraged the children to complete tasks and activities. Each child had received a list of suggestions. This was so the children didn't fall behind in the six weeks off. Scarlett was writing a journal about her everyday activities. This included what she did on the farm and days out with family and friends; and also her two weeks holiday to her grandparents in Hebden Bridge.

Cameron had to practice his writing and numbers and was collecting treasures to stick into his scrapbook. They had been to York for the day, and he had got leaflets, stickers and masks from the Jorvik Viking Centre and the railway museum.

The idea was that the children could then talk about what they did in the holidays when they were back at school.

"And then, lunch, park and cinema!"

"Yippee!" they shouted.

Chapter 2

It was Sunday, a day of rest, family time, Sunday lunches, walks and drinks in the pubs.

Reverend Thomas Mayhew stood on the steps of Sleathwaite Methodist Church and thanked his parishioners for attending his service; shaking hands with them and saying, "Goodbye."

"When they had all gone, he went back into the church, where it was cool and silent with a peaceful feeling. He slid into one of the pews and looked up at the altar trying to imagine it in times gone by. The church itself had been there since Saxon times.

He was always fascinated by the beauty of the church and its artefacts. The morning sun shone strongly through the stained-glass windows, making everything look like gold. The gold font seemed to glow as if on fire. There was a rainbow spectrum shining across from the stained-glass windows. He thought it such an awesome sight that he took out his phone to take some photographs of it. At home he had a digital camera with a telephoto lens and liked to dabble in taking pictures. He often took his camera when out on walks to get some good pictures. He had uploaded a lot of his work onto the internet and had had quite a lot of interest in them on Twitter. He had even sold a few prints in the local art shop.

He often liked to sit for a few minutes with his own thoughts and give himself time for reflection.

After leaving school, he had become involved in youth work and found that he loved to help people. For some time, he worked as a counsellor and people would tell him their problems. As he had always attended church and choir, he felt he must follow his faith and joined the church as a minister. He had also done missionary work in African villages. In Nairobi when he was helping at a village hospital he became reacquainted with Emily. She was doing voluntary work for UNICEF and gaining some useful and valuable experience.

After meeting Emily, the couple settled down and got married and she gave birth to twin boys. She was a district nurse, a Band 6 Junior Sister and worked with Rachael.

They had both met at university and worked at Newcastle Infirmary. Only Emily had worked on a children's' cancer ward. They now worked together out in the community.

It was a short walk home from the church as he lived practically next door to it. Their cottage was owned by the church and was made from stone and slate from the local slate mine, as a lot of the houses in the village were. From their back garden they had a beautiful view of open countryside across the Tyne Valley.

Tom was a tall gentle person; he loved his family very much and treated his parishioners with the upmost respect. He was well liked in the village and an upstanding member of the community. He often joined in on community events, especially with the rugby club, where he played himself, the school, the community centre and local pub fun nights for charities.

He entered the hallway; he could smell the lamb cooking in the oven, and it smelled delicious. Emily his wife was an extremely good cook and had won awards for cooking competitions. He walked past the kitchen and found her in the dining room laying the table.

She turned around as he came into the room.

"Hello Tom, how was church? Do you want a cup of tea?"

"Hello Ems!" he beamed at the sight of her. He had known her nearly all his life. They had grown up together here in Sleathwaite. They had played as children as they lived next door to each other. They had gone to the same schools and been together in some classes throughout school. They had been childhood sweethearts since the age of twelve.

"Church was good, the service went well, and a cup of tea would go down a treat. Have I walked into the wrong house, everything is spotless and tidy. Are we expecting guests?"

"No, I just thought it would be nice to have our meal in here as a family. It is pleasant looking out at the garden, rather than looking at dirty dishes in the kitchen."

"So, it is. Have the boys helped?"

"No, but they promised to do the dishes."

"What in the dishwasher?"

"Whatever; as long as they clean up and put the clean dishes away, it's all right by me."

"Okay sweetheart, you work too hard. We could have had Sunday lunch at the Hadrian."

"That costs money, but you can take me for a drink later when the boys are at rugby? It's a nice day and we could sit in the garden there."

"All right, we'll have lunch and then we can all take Charlie for a walk along the river. The boys can bring their bikes and then they can cycle up to rugby and we'll go to the pub."

Charlie their Cocker Spaniel barked at the sound of his name.

"Sounds like a plan, even Charlie agrees."

Just then, they heard cheering from the living room, John was walking around with his football shirt over his head. They were playing the football game FIFA on the Xbox. John's team Manchester United had won by three nil to Newcastle.

"Glory! Glory! Man United, Glory! Glory! Man United, and the fans go marching in, in, in!" he chanted. "I slaughtered you!" he continued.

"We'll see about that after a replay, and I am going to buy some new players!" shouted Jamie.

"Hello boys! A lot of excitement going on in here."

"I won Dad!"

"So, I hear. Well, done."

Emily shouted. "Lunch is ready!"

They all piled into the dining room.

"Oh, wine as well, we are pushing the boat out."

"I just want us to relax this afternoon for once."

"Can we have some?" asked Jamie.

"Certainly not. You're too young," said Emily.

"Yes, you want to get the ball in a straight line if you get a try," said Tom.

"There is only a week of the holidays left now and then you two will be starting school at the Academy. You might not be in the same classes like before."

"I'm sure they'll be fine Emily; they'll learn to adapt."

"Yes, we'll learn to adapt Mother," said John mimicking his dad's voice. "Don't worry, I will look out for little brother!"

"Shut up!" said Jamie.

John was three minutes older than Jamie and he milked it all he could.

"Mam, can I have new football boots and trainers? I want some like Messi's." asked Jamie.

"Well, we have to go into town or Metro Centre for new things for school. Anyway, you'll both have the same amount spent on you, so it depends on how much they are."

"I want some blue adidas ones," said John.

"Well, we will see what we can afford," said Tom.

They finished their main course of roast lamb, potatoes, parsnips, carrots, butternut squash, Yorkshire pudding and minted gravy.

"Right boys; can you clear up and then we'll take Charlie for a walk," said Tom.

"Hang on! Hold your horses. I've made Apple Crumble," said Emily.

"Ooh Crimble Crumble!" said John doing high fives with his brother.

"I hope you two are going to be able to move after this delicious feast. I am ready for a sleep!" remarked Tom, feeling his tummy.

"What! They're growing boys and we are all going out – sleep later, okay!"

"Woo!" said Jamie. "You going to be lucky tonight Dad?"

Tom blushed and squeezed Emily's hand and gave her a kiss.

"Err! Jamie it's Dad you're talking to. Do you want us to leave you alone?" asked John jokingly.

"There is nothing wrong with showing affection as you'll find out as you grow older," said Emily, hugging Tom.

"I am not getting married," announced Jamie. "Girls are yuk!"

"Thank you, Jamie," said Emily.

"Apart from you Mam."

"Oh, that's all right then."

The boys cleared away the dishes and put them in the dishwasher and Emily and Tom went and read the Sunday papers. After half an hour or so they were ready to go for their walk.

"Charlie, walkies!" shouted Emily.

Charlie came bounding towards her. He was still a puppy at six months old. She clipped the lead to his collar.

The boys got their bikes out of the garage and already had their rugby kits on.

It was a beautiful day and they walked along to Corbridge by the river. Everyone was friendly here and even strangers said, "Hello." Northumberland was considered a tourist attraction and they often had holidaymakers staying in the village and surrounding areas.

The boys went ahead on their bikes; Charlie chasing after them along the river side.

Emily watched her boys. How tall they seemed to have grown in the holidays but compared to their classmates they were still smaller than they were. John had grown an inch and Jamie half an inch. They may seem bigger now but once they start at their new school, they would be the smallest again and the youngest.

"You look thoughtful?" said Tom. "Are you okay?"

"Yes, I was just thinking of the boys and their new school."

"Look Ems, they'll be fine. You have to let them go and give them space to grow."

"I know, but to me they are still my babies."

"Of course, they know you love them."

"Even when I am shouting at them to do their homework or chores or to stop fighting?"

"Even then," said Tom.

They had reached the bridge and Tom bought them all an ice cream. They sat at the riverside, eating them, while the boys went off to explore for a short while. It was blissful in the late afternoon sun.

Time was getting on and they needed to get the boys to rugby, so they turned around and walked back.

When they reached the village, the boys cycled up the road to the rugby club and Tom and Emily walked along to the pub.

The Hadrian was quiet and peaceful on this late Sunday afternoon. The gardens outside were so inviting and relaxing. The flowers were out in full bloom. Emily found a table under a parasol in partial shade and sat down with Charlie at her side.

"Right Em, what would you like to drink."

"Erm, I don't know, something cold and refreshing after that walk. I will have a pint of cider please."

"Okay, coming up."

Tom entered the pub which was cool and quiet apart from a few people from the village. He nodded to a few and said, "Hello," to some of his parishioners.

The public house was an old Tudor style building with beamed ceilings, heavy oaked doors and woodburning stoves, which weren't used in hot weather.

The pub had a new landlord and landlady called Matthew and Caitlin Turner, a husband and wife team. They had only been there just over a month.

Matthew was drying some glasses he had just removed from the dishwasher.

"Afternoon Reverend," said Matthew. "What can I get you on this fine afternoon?"

"Hello Matt! Can I have a pint of cider and one of your special ales?"

"Yes of course we have golden plover by Allendale breweries, would you like to try a tasting?"

"No, actually it's okay, I already have, I'll have a glass of that please. It's quiet in here."

"Yes, I have just got rid of the lunchtime rush. It will soon start getting busy up towards teatime."

"You are doing well then?"

"Yes, it doesn't seem to have made a difference that we have taken over here. It is still just as busy."

"The Hadrian has always been busy and the village folk always welcome new people."

"The last owners had charity nights; do you think you would be interested? We had a committee, and everyone put ideas forward," said Tom.

"Well, we are still finding our feet, but we welcome ideas and as it is a community pub, why not."

"Good, maybe we could all get together later in the month?" asked Tom. "I was chairman of the committee, but we can put it to the vote."

"Yes okay, I'll supply the drinks and nibbles."

"Tara."

"Bye Tom, always a pleasure."

Tom turned and was about to go out when he spotted James and Rachael at one of the tables. They waved, and he walked towards them.

"Hello, you two," said Tom, genuinely pleased to see them both. He had known James since infant school and the four of them had been friends for a long time.

"Hi!" they both chorused in unison.

"Do you want to sit down?" asked Rachael.

"No, Emily is outside with Charlie, but you two are welcome to join us."

"All right," said James. And they both stood up and followed Tom out of the pub into the bright sunlight.

"Hello Emily," called Rachael.

"Hi Ems," said James.

"This is a nice surprise. Where are the boys?"

"Oh, they are at rugby," said Tom. "They really enjoy it, but they are starting to like Footy as well."

"How are the children?" asked Emily. "Where are they?"

"Oh, they're fine," Rachael replied. "James's mam and dad have got them for an hour. We decided to pop out for a bit of peace and quiet. I wouldn't be without them, but it is nice just to have some time to ourselves, even if it is just for an hour."

"I know what you mean. Not long till school now?"

"No, we went and got the uniform and other things the kids needed the other week; it is so expensive!"

"Yes, it is. We are going this week, of course Jamie wants the latest football boots, like Messi's. We'll see."

"So, how are the boys getting along with their rugby?" asked James.

"Oh, they're doing fine; learning contact now. They've scored a few tries."

"Have you thought about Cameron starting? He is at the right age."

"Well, they are going to be doing tag rugby when he starts back in year one. I have been teaching him to throw and catch with an ordinary ball, but he finds it difficult. The ball is big enough; it could be his eyesight."

Rachael looked up. "I am not sure I want my baby playing that rough sport. He might get hurt!"

Tom saw how worried she looked. "You sound like Emily. At that age it is all about playing games with them and them learning to be part of a team."

James said, "You can't wrap him up in cotton wool, Love. It might be good for him."

"That's just because you two play. That's why you're saying that," said Rachael. "But it would be good for his ball skills. I x "Lt's see how he gets on at school first and then we'll talk about it."

"By the way, the boys are playing at Hebden Bridge the weekend after next, Hebden Harlequin juniors. Be good to see," said Tom.

"Yes, well isn't that the same weekend us adults are playing at Hebden?"

"Oh yes. I had forgotten about that."

"We are going down to see Rachael's Mam and Dad anyway then perhaps we could all meet up after the games and go out for a meal?"

"Yeah, good idea," said Tom. "Sleathwaite Warriors are going to win though! Although it isn't all about winning. I of all people should remember that."

"I'll remind you of that if we lose," said James grinning.

The four sat deep in conversation for the next hour or so and then decided it was time to go and meet their children. Charlie had fallen asleep and was now glad it was time to go.

Chapter 3

Matthew locked the doors after the last few stragglers and was glad to be able to get cleared up and ready for the next morning. He was tired and ready for his bed.

Caitlin was collecting glasses and cleaning the tables; and Matt started to cash up. They were a good team and had worked well together both professionally and personally. They had been married for five years now but had been together for eight years.

Caitlin was thirty and Matthew was thirty-two. They had no children yet but now that they had found a nice village to live in with a nice house attached, they certainly wouldn't rule it out. When they had first came to Sleathwaite, they had decided that they wanted to move to a village that was well established with good schools for their future offspring.

They were both originally from Newcastle and had met in the licensing trade, working in a bar in Newcastle city centre. They had enjoyed the hustle and bustle of city life when they were younger. They became tenants of a public house just outside Newcastle in Throckley, but decided that they craved a more rural country life. Caitlin always knew that city life wasn't really her, especially now she wanted to settle down and have a family.

Matthew's grandparents lived in the Lake District and he loved to escape city life and go and visit them. They came from Newcastle originally and his parents still lived that way on the outskirts in Ponteland where Matthew had grown up. When he left school, he went to college to learn the chef trade and his dream was that one day he would open his own restaurant and public house, where he would do the cooking. He had earned his living working in different kitchens peeling vegetables, learning about preparation. He worked as a Sous chef, making sauces, and had worked in all areas of the kitchen before qualifying.

His parents were very proud and gave him some money in a trust fund, so he could start his own culinary business. They had been to see them and had enjoyed their stay at the Hadrian very much.

Caitlin was a university graduate; she had a passed with a BA honours in a history degree. She had specialised in the history of the Romans and their many artefacts. Her dissertation had been all about how the Romans left Italy and settled in England. Quite fitting that she lived in the Hadrian.

This was her favourite part of England and she loved to wander round the old Roman ruins and had taken part in archaeological digs. She was fascinated to come across some treasures.

She enjoyed working in the pub and meeting new people and wouldn't change her life for the world, but she had always kept up with studying history and was even writing a book on life in the Industrial Revolution in the North East of England. She considered herself as a historian but knew she had to be realistic and was thankful for their family business which would pay the bills and put food on the table.

Her parents had moved to Hexham a few years ago so she already knew the area but had not been to Sleathwaite. They didn't realise how beautiful the village was until they had been invited to a wedding reception at Sleathwaite Hall.

Her mam and dad were glad she was nearby and used to go to the pub for the odd Sunday lunch. It had always had good reviews and received five stars. Both sets of parents were proud when they moved in and took over.

"Well, it's been a busy day hasn't it?" said Caitlin yawning.

"Certainly, has love," said Matthew. "But then it is the weekend and the summer holidays."

"No doubt we'll get some hikers through the week or people on holiday."

"Yes, well I think we are on a winner with this pub, and we seem to have made the right decision. It's a gold mine, you are happy aren't you?"

"Of course, I love it here silly."

"I know but your history career never really got off the ground because of me did it? You wanted to be a curator."

"Yes, but I can still work from home, like I am doing, have you forgotten where we have moved to?" "I can't think of a better place to live than not far from the Roman Wall". "And I can still take part in organised digs".

"I just wanted to make sure, because you gave up a lot for me."

"And look what I have gained a lovely place to live, a thriving business and a gorgeous husband."

"Well, I can't argue with that."

"Plus, I wouldn't want to bring up our babies anywhere else."

"Well, we should get some practice in then!"

"Ooh! Up those stairs landlord," she said tapping him on the bottom.

They had finished their chores and were on their way to bed, Caitlin was tired and ready for some rest. She turned off the light and thought about her day.

She closed her eyes and seemed to be in the middle of a Roman army camp.

The ground felt muddy, and she looked down at herself, she was wearing a Roman dress and had bare feet and strapped sandals on. The camp was full of hustle and bustle, and she had her basket and was going out to collect ingredients off the land for the evening meal.

All around her men seemed to be building parts of the camp and it got bigger every day. The baths had just been built but a servant like her wouldn't get the chance to use them.

She worked in the kitchen and cooked on an open fire with a metal mesh over it. The walls were made of wattle and daub, made with sticks and mud to cover it. The floor was muddy with oil coverings on it.

Caitlin was now in a deep sleep dreaming about ancient times and Matthew was so tired that he fell fast asleep as soon as his head hit the pillow. The country air seemed to have that effect on them.

The next morning Matthew went into the bar and started on his chores. They had just had breakfast and Caitlin was doing the washing up.

He suddenly felt as if someone was standing behind him, he thought he could sense breathing on his neck. The hairs on the back of his neck stood on end.

'Must have had too much whisky last night', he thought thinking it was his imagination. But then he noticed one of the chairs had been placed in front of the fire. Almost as if someone had been warming their feet. It wasn't there last night he had checked everything and made sure everything was locked up. How could someone have got in? He went and checked the cellar door and noticed the lock was loose. He put it on his to-do list to get it fixed today.

Caitlin appeared and started putting out beer mats on the tables, and bar, getting out clean tea towels and setting up the tills. She then made a list of items she needed from the cellar.

"Matthew! Give me a hand with these bottles would you."

She had called up from the cellar. Matthew appeared at the top of the stairs.

"Right, what do we need?" he asked.

"The list is here; look I've already got some stock together. I'll take these boxes of crisps up."

"I'll bring these bottles then."

They walked up and down the stairs taking stock up to the bar. Caitlin went back down she had seen some boxes in the corner of the cellar and thought they needed clearing away. They had dumped some boxes in there when they had moved, and they were probably left over.

As she bent down, she looked into the cardboard boxes and realised they were not their things. They were too old to belong to the last tenants they must have just disregarded them as old junk and not got rid of them.

She put her hand into the boxes and found old fashioned toys, there was a wooden plane and wooden train set, an old rag doll and teddy and an old-fashioned spinning top along with story books and games. They were quite dusty.

The other box had old papers in them. She pulled a handful out and on top was an old booklet with a drawing of a house which looked strangely familiar. It had the writing on the cover, and it read Sleathwaite Orphanage, established 1912.

Chapter 4

She couldn't believe her eyes. It was the same address as the pub! It had information about how the orphanage worked and adoption processes.

Underneath was a black hardbacked book and it had names of children who had lived there. Admissions and discharges. There was also another book underneath that had children's names, dates, crimes and punishments. The pages in these books were yellow with age.

One boys name was mentioned regularly, Jakob Schmidt, sounded German. He was five years old, and his punishment was the cane for stealing chocolate.

Caitlin was fascinated by all the books and items. She got out a cloth and polished and cleaned them all up.

"Caitlin! Caitlin!"

Matthew was calling her. She stood up and put the items back into the boxes and carried the ones with the books in it up the cellar stairs.

"Matt!"

"What have you been doing down there; I need to do some prep in the kitchen ready for Ian when he comes in."

Ian was also a chef and did a lot of the cooking but Matthew still prepped and cooked dishes every day as well, depending on how many bar staff they had.

"Can you finish the bottling up?"

"Yes, erm."

"What have you got there?"

"I found them in the cellar, I thought the boxes belonged to us."

"What there's more?"

"Yes, here Matt, look at this picture," she said, showing him the book.

"What, looks like an old house, which must have been here in the village."

"It is this place! Look closely."

"Blimey!"

"It was an orphanage! Look at these books, information, admissions, discharges and punishments. There is a box of old-fashioned toys, games and books as well."

"Really? Right well put them away, we need to get on for now."

"Okay."

"I need to put a new lock on that cellar door, it's loose," said Matthew.

"Right, we had better get on then," said Caitlin, putting the books to one side and resuming her duties. She put it to the back of her mind, but she was going to look into this discovery.

They had a busy day serving walkers, holidaymakers and locals' refreshments.

It was now 11:30 at night and they were tucked up in bed. Caitlin was looking at some of the books.

"I am really interested in this Matt. I can't wait to find out about it!"

"You and your history," muttered Matt sleepily.

"Aren't you interested?"

"What? Well yes but it is very late."

"This orphanage was here in our new home," said Caitlin incredulously. "I am going to our local library and see what I can find out, there may be some local records on it, or I could go to the City library in town."

"All right but just be careful."

"Why? They were meant to be found by us."

"Well, you hear of people discovering things and strange things happen."

"What, like ghosts!"

"Well, you never know. Woo! "Wooo!" said Matthew. "It all started with the box of things and then whoosh out popped the ghost! Aargh!, Aargh," said Matthew pulling at the duvet and lunging at her.

"Aargh!" screamed Caitlin laughing.

"Now can we please go to sleep?"

"Yes!"

They were just settling down when Caitlin felt a tugging on the duvet.

"Matthew! That isn't funny."

"What? I didn't do anything."

"You pulled the duvet from me."

"No, I didn't."

"Strange."

"It's your imagination working overtime."

But Caitlin did feel something. She was going off to sleep again when she thought she heard the pitter patter of footsteps. It could have been just night noises. It was a very old building, and she was still adjusting to sleeping there. They hadn't been here very long. She tried to put it to the back of her mind but ended up having a very restless night.

Next morning when Matthew woke up, she was sound asleep, and he thought he would let her have another hours rest before waking her. It was quite late when he eventually drifted off and he still felt quite tired himself.

He pushed his feet into his slippers and pulled on his dressing gown. He saw the books Caitlin had found and had a look. It really was a miraculous find but he felt there was something amiss here. He had felt breathing on his neck yesterday, the chair had been moved and the cellar door was open when he knew he had shut it.

Before he made breakfast, he thought he would check on the bar downstairs. He entered the lounge and noticed that a glass had been left on the bar top, which hadn't been there last night. Strange because he thought he heard glasses clinking through the night.

He went behind the bar and saw that the cellar door was open wide, he had definitely closed and locked it. He felt for the light switch, but the light wouldn't turn on.

"Damn it, bulb's gone."

He fetched a torch and turned it on and went into the cellar to see if they had left some bulbs there. He noticed the box of toys Caitlin had been looking at.

He could see how she would be interested in this, but he hadn't yet told her about his own experiences.

When he had been putting things away in the attic, he had found some old looking bunkbeds stacked up on top of each other. He would have to talk to her today, it was only fair. At the same time, he didn't want to scare her. It was an old building he told himself and they just had to get used to it.

Even if there were such things as ghosts, they couldn't harm you, could they? Matthew still remained sceptical about this sort of thing.

He got a bulb and replaced the old one. He went upstairs and started making some breakfast for himself. He would heat a croissant up and take a cup of tea to Caitlin in half an hour or so.

The pub was quite busy the next few days it was the last week of the six weeks holidays and things would be a little quieter but from what the locals had told them the pub always did well, even when it was not peak season.

The unusual occurrences had settled down and it being Friday it was Caitlin's day off, and she was all fired up to do some research on their pub which used to be an orphanage.

Matthew had some spare time and thought this was as good a time as any to have a talk about their discoveries and what they each thought about it.

Caitlin was upstairs putting a notebook, pens and laptop into her backpack.

She seemed quite upbeat and eager to do some research.

Matthew appeared in the doorway.

"Oh Matt, there you are. You've remembered I am going to the library?"

"Are you really, I didn't know," he said mockingly.

She hit him playfully with a cushion off the settee.

"I know, it's all you have talked about for the last few days, but if I can get a word in edgeways, there is something I have been meaning to talk to you about. It has been so busy lately we haven't had a chance to catch our breath."

"Yes, I know what you mean, it has been mad recently. Just the other …"

"Okay, let me speak please, this could be important."

"Yes, what has happened?"

"Well, you know how you have found the box of toys and books about the Orphanage?"

"Yes."

"Well, I have made a discovery of my own and had a few unusual occurrences.

"Like what? I'm getting worried now."

"The last thing I want to do is frighten you but when I was in the bar earlier in the week I felt breathing on the back of my neck, it was early in the morning before we opened. A chair had been moved and a glass was left on the bar even though we had cleared up the night before. Two mornings in a row the cellar door was open even though I had shut it, and the bulb had fused even though I knew I had replaced it not so long ago. I put a new lock on the cellar door and things seem to have settled down."

"Oh God! The other night when I accused you of pulling the duvet, I heard footsteps on the landing. I thought it was my imagination."

"Look this all can't be down to our imaginations, maybe there is some unrest here."

"Well, what can we do about it?"

"I don't know, I think we should just carry on here. I mean nothing bad can happen really can it. It is just an old building, and we are still adjusting but there is something else that you may wish to see before you do your research?"

"Well, I am happy here and I don't want us moving out because of this. I think we should just stick with it, but what do you want me to see?"

"You know when we moved in about a month ago and we put some boxes in the attic?"

"Yes."

"Well, I found some old metal bunkbeds folded down under some old grey blankets."

Caitlin's eyes widened. "Can I go and look? I haven't even been up there yet. Why didn't you say something?"

"I didn't make the connection until you found those boxes. Let's go up there."

Matthew and Caitlin made their way up the attic steps and went in. It was cold and a little dark, apart from some light coming through the sky light. Matthew turned on the light and walked over to the bunkbeds, pulling back the blanket.

"Wow, they look old but still intact, obviously being metal they would not wear with age. I wonder what else there is?"

They had a quick look around but couldn't find anything of great significance apart from an old school cap, an exercise book and a metal hula hoop with a metal stick.

"These must be very old; I have seen these in museums," said Caitlin.

Chapter 5

It was quiet in the library when Caitlin arrived. She had decided to start her mission on finding out about the children's orphanage at Hexham library.

The library was an old, listed building dating back to the early nineteenth century. It was built in stone and its interior had beautiful wood panelling with paintings by local artists. Some sections had more traditional style paintings and others had contemporary designs.

Caitlin sat down at a computer next to a painting of Hexham Abbey on the wall.

Normally when she went it was quite busy with students and school children.

She logged onto her library account which had links to various menus of the library's website. There were two she could start with which were the archives and local history. She clicked on the link for archives and entered the name Sleathwaite Orphanage. A list of former businesses came up under different dates.

She scrolled down the page and scanned the list. She noticed next to the search button there was a section where she could put in dates. She entered 1912. Another list appeared. She looked down the A–Z of past local businesses found S and there, lo and behold, was Sleathwaite Orphanage. She clicked on the link. She had an adrenalin rush and felt excited about what she could find out. This was the historian in her and she loved to find out about past events and compare them to how things happened today.

The page began to load, up popped pdf files of the old orphanage. She rubbed her hands together excitedly. The list of pdf files was:

Sleathwaite Orphanage established 1912.

The Sleathwaite Orphanage Handbook.

Sleathwaite Orphanage Admissions Process.

Sleathwaite Orphanage Adoption Process.

Sleathwaite Orphanage Prospectus

Sleathwaite close of business 1948.

She set about going through each of the files; writing down information in the A4 paper pad. The first file showed all the architectural designs and plans for the building, and legal documents from the local parish council.

She opened the next file and it had been opened on 14 April 1912 by a married couple called Thomas and Emmeline Mayhew.

'My goodness me.' she said under her breath thinking of their local vicar Tom Mayhew. "I wonder if they are related."

Using her mobile phone, she took a photograph of the pdf file to show Tom when she next saw him. She finished making notes and going through the files.

'Right, I am going to find if there are any actual books and documents to look at.'

She walked around to the archives section of the library with her list of pdf files. The shelves were all labelled by subjects and filed alphabetically. Each shelf had codes on the books. She looked at her list she had printed and there was a code next to the file Sleathwaite Orphanage 1912. She scanned the shelves for the code and found the actual book which had been written about the history of the building. She excitedly opened it and there was an old photograph of her pub in its former glory! It looked much the same, only the building looked newer, even though it had been updated with a conservatory on the back, which led out to their gardens.

The next page showed the photograph of all the staff and children. The couple who ran the orphanage looked stern and the children looked almost scared.

'I wonder if I can take this book out,' she thought. She looked at the side of the book and it said for reference only. She took it back to the table and read it.

She walked up to the lady standing behind the desk she was checking through books.

She looked up when Caitlin approached her.

"Hi can I help?"

"Yes please, I am interested in local history and wish to find out about a past business called Sleathwaite Orphanage established 1912."

"Right."

"I found this reference book and wondered if you had any books I could lend?"

"You may find some books on Sleathwaite Village in our local history section."

"Okay thanks."

"Are you writing an essay?"

"Not exactly, I am a historian though, but I have just had the most amazing find."

"Do you want to tell me? You look like you are about to burst with excitement."

"We moved into the 'Hadrian Pub' at Sleathwaite about six weeks ago and I was clearing out the cellar when I found this old box containing old fashioned toys. I then found another box with books about Sleathwaite Orphanage, and when I looked at the photograph it was of our pub in its former days."

"Really!"

"Yes, I came here and found pdf files stored on the library's archives and the first one was a file based on this book. The orphanage was established in 1912 by a Thomas and Emmeline Mayhew."

"Flippin heck!" she gasped.

"There is another curious find though I think the people that ran the orphanage could be related to our local vicar. He has lived in Sleathwaite all of his life and his name is Thomas Mayhew and even stranger his wife is called Emily."

"Well, I never!"

"So, obviously I am interested to find out about these people and their relationship to Tom the vicar."

"Right," she said recovering from the shock. "That's amazing!"

"Isn't it …"

"My name is Lauren by the way, we do have some local books over here in our local history section," she said leading the way. "As for information on those actual people you may have to go to the City Library in Newcastle. They have a larger archive section than us and an ancestry section on local pioneers."

"Thank you."

"Of course, you could just ask your friend if they have a family tree?"

"Yes, I was going to mention it to them anyway."

"Well done with your find. You know it is quite amazing what you have uncovered. The BBC might be interested in your story once you find out about the link between the founders and your local vicar's family."

"Really, do you think I could contact them?"

"Why not? It will be good publicity for your pub and the village. I think a lot of people would be interested."

"Do you know, yes you're right why not, but I have more research to do first."

"We do have some information on the history of the pub from 1952 that the solicitors sent, but nothing this far back."

Caitlin suddenly remembered about the strange occurrences that had happened and went on to tell her about what they had found in the attic and the strange activity about the place.

Lauren couldn't believe her ears. "Look I hope you don't think I am being pushy, but if you need any help with all of this, I would be glad to offer my services. I too have an interest in local history."

"No, not at all and yes if you're interested we could do some work together."

They exchanged telephone numbers and email addresses and Caitlin said she would be in touch.

"Good luck with it," said Lauren. "And I will help where I can, okay?"

"Yeah, cheers and thanks."

Caitlin had a quick look at the local history section and borrowed a book about Sleathwaite Village. She didn't have time to look at it. The time had passed so quickly.

She walked out of the library feeling triumphant at her discoveries and even more so that she seemed to have made a friend. Working in the pub she didn't have much time for socialising herself even though she saw regulars most days; but she hadn't had time to make many friends in the village in the short time they had been there.

Chapter 6

It was Monday morning. The summer holidays had ended, and it was the first day of term. The family were in the kitchen having breakfast.

Rachael Macalister felt harassed to death as she was trying to get the children organised for school. She had to do the drop off and then go to work and go back to school for pick up. They were in after school club, so they would be ready an hour or so later, when she got finished with her shift. Scarlett sat quietly eating her cereal.

Rachael looked at her daughter. "You okay love?"

"Yes."

"You're quiet, you nervous?"

"No, I am fine, anyway it's hard to have a conversation with noisy over there."

Cameron had finished his cereal and had grown restless. He started running around the kitchen fiddling with electrical things. His eyes settled on the stereo, and he shouted.

"Moosic! Moosic!"

He pressed play and a CD started playing. It was Queen and Freddie Mercury's voice came out of the speakers singing 'We are the champions'. Cameron turned up the volume full blast.

Rachael went over to him. "No, Cam not now, we have to get to school," she said turning it down.

"Moosic! Moosic, I want Moosic!" shouted Cameron.

"It's too loud, I am turning it off!"

"NO!"

"Yes! Now get your book bag and you can put your lunch in it."

"Ahh!"

"For god's sake! Scarlett have you got your book bag?"

"Yes Mum." Scarlett got up from the chair and got her lunch.

Cameron came back into the kitchen, trailing his book bag behind him on the floor. It was open, and the contents were falling out.

"Cameron pick it up, look everything is coming out. Give it here," said Rachael trying to be patient with him. "Go and get your shoes on please."

He went into the hall and put on his new school shoes; they were strap shoes from Clarks. When Rachael went through to the hallway Cameron was sitting on the stairs with his shoes on the wrong feet again.

"Well done for putting them on. Here let me help you. Right, you ready Scarlett?"

"Ready."

Cameron reached for his beloved headphones.

"No Cam not for school."

"But I want them."

"School rules Cam," said Scarlett.

"Oh, I haven't got ttime or t'energy to argue with you, come on in ter car you two, I have to get to work."

They got in the car and Scarlett helped Cameron with his seatbelt.

Across the village at the Vicarage, Emily was getting the twins organised.

"Right, you two, have you got everything you need?"

"Yes Mam," said John.

"I haven't got my dinner money," said Jamie.

"I left it there on the bookcase, I did tell you."

"Oh right, sorry."

"You both look very smart and grown up in your ties and blazers. I want to get a photograph of you both?"

"Oh! do we have to!" said John.

"Yes, please come on, it will only take a minute."

"All right then," they chorused.

"I am walking your way to work do you want me to walk with you?"

"No Mam. It would be embarrassing. We are eleven now, we're not babies," said Jamie.

"Okay, see you later, have a good day!"

"Bye!" They shouted, running down the path.

They arrived at the school. Rachael parked the car in the car park.

"See you later Mum," said Scarlett.

"Okay sweetheart, have a nice day."

"Bye."

Rachael turned to Cameron. "Right, come on trouble," she said smiling, holding his hand while they walked through the carpark

"Mammy can we go to Macdonald's after school?"

"It depends what time I get finished at work. Remember, you are at after school club."

"Yeah!"

They entered the yard, time was getting on and the children were starting to line up, ready to go into class. Rachael found his line and they stood at the end.

"Cameron you'll have to give me those headphones."

"NO!" said Cameron holding onto them. He looked up at her tearfully.

"Cammy you aren't meant to have them in school," she said gently.

The teacher saw them and came up and said, "Hello, I am Miss Haslem," she said, shaking Rachael's hand.

"Hi, I am just trying to explain ter Cameron that he isn't allowed his headphones in school."

"Oh, it's okay, it's his first day back. Listen Cameron we can put them in my special box that I keep for children's favourite things."

She turned to Rachael. "I'll keep them safe when he is distracted."

The other children were going in with a teaching assistant and they were the only ones left in the playground.

"Right come on Cameron," said the teacher. "Say bye to Mummy."

Cameron grabbed a hold of Rachael's legs and wouldn't move.

"Ohh, come on Cammy you'll be fine," said Rachael soothingly.

"Cameron we are doing some special activities today, do you want to come with me and see? I will show you where your peg is to hang your coat. It has a special picture above the hook, and you are going to sit next to your friend Bill."

"Bill! Yes. Bye Mam!" he said still looking tearful.

"Bye Cam."

The teacher held his hand. "He'll be fine once he gets settled. Any problems and we'll ring you."

The teacher led Cameron away into class.

Emily was already in the office at the Medical Centre when Rachael walked through the door.

"You look shattered," said Emily cheerily, pleased to see her friend.

"Oh, I feel exhausted," said Rachael, making a cup of tea.

"Sorry, do you want a brew?"

"I have one thanks; kids get off to school okay?"

"Yes finally. Scarlett's no bother now she's getting older, but Cameron can be a handful at times. He is lovely but he's obsessed with his music and headphones, and he does struggle with things. He seems to have behavioural problems. When there's anything he finds difficult, he puts his headphones on."

"Well, it is lovely that he likes music. Maybe you could encourage him to learn an instrument."

"Maybe when he is older. I want to try and get him to concentrate on things for more than five minutes."

"It will come. He is only six."

"Yes, but he is behind in his development."

"Rachael all kids are different and develop at different paces. Look at my two. In some ways they are like a carbon copy of each other and in other ways they struggle with certain things."

"Sorry. I never asked how they were this morning at their new school."

"They were fine, as cool as cucumbers and looking forward to their days."

"Good."

"Are you okay you still seem a bit preoccupied?"

"I think Cam is autistic," she said worriedly.

"Ahh Rachael, try not to worry."

"Well, I think he has a communication disorder."

"Look if you're really worried talk to the school about it, they will refer him to Psych-Ed if they think something is wrong, or talk to one of the doctors here."

"I will give him time to settle into school, they have a parents evening in a few weeks' time just about how they have settled in, I can discuss it then."

"Have you mentioned this to James about how he could be on the Spectrum?"

"No, I have only started to think it these last few days. We both know he struggles at some tasks, and we try to encourage him to be independent."

"Well, that's good isn't it? But you need to talk to James about your fears. It may not be autism at all."

"Well, I really hope not. He is our beautiful boy and I hate to think of him being faulted".

"Rachael, on the surface he seems a contented little boy who is as bright as a button. He seems to bring you a lot of joy."

"Oh, he does, he really does. Thanks Emily. We had better get on with our rounds."

"Yes, come on," said Emily, standing up. "You know you can talk to me about things whenever you like. Don't bottle them up."

"I know thanks, it can be hard though."

"I know, when my two were babies it was double trouble when they were both hungry at the same time, but I got through it. They've had some problems, but we got through it, and you will with Cameron."

"Thanks."

"Stop saying thanks."

"Thanks." They both laughed.

It was a beautiful September day and Rachael had opened the sunroof of the car as they drove along the road. It was quite warm, and they were enjoying the autumn breeze.

The sunshine just made the local countryside even more stunning. They were driving along to Corbridge to see their first patient. The River Tyne looked idyllic in the sunlight as they drove over the bridge into the village.

They were seeing an elderly lady called Mrs Taylor.

Rachael pulled into the side of the road and parked the car. They both climbed out and Emily got their medical bags out of the boot while Rachael locked up the car.

They walked up the drive to the couple's bungalow and rang the doorbell.

Having recently had a fall in their street and broken her hip, she had sustained some injuries to her legs from her fall. She was obviously becoming more dependent on her husband. She didn't like to sit still and take it easy, so she was finding it frustrating not being able to do things for herself.

Her husband Bob was also in his late eighties, and he had heart failure and other serious health conditions. He was in the kitchen washing the breakfast dishes when he heard the doorbell ring.

He was slow and like Elsie was also a falls risk patient. He was slow in his mobility and took a while to answer the door.

"Oh, good morning."

"Hello Mr Taylor," said Rachael.

"Come in, come in. Elsie is in the living room."

"Good morning," said Emily. "Beautiful day."

"Isn't it, here she is."

"Hello Elsie. How are you?" asked Rachael.

"Oh, hello girls. I am fine. I suppose but I'm sick to death of sitting around with my feet up, but the doctors said that I have to rest."

"Well, you have only been out of hospital a few days, you need to give yourself time to recover," said Emily.

"We've come to change the dressings on yer legs Mrs Taylor. Is that okay?" asked Rachael.

"Elsie, and yes of course it is pet."

"Is that a Yorkshire accent I detect?" asked Bob.

"Aye it is that Yorkshire born and bred."

"Can I ask where you are from dear?" asked Elsie.

"Yes, Hebden Bridge."

"That's near to where the Bronte Sisters lived and quite a literary village if I am not mistaken," said Elsie.

"We are just being nosy you know," said Bob.

"That's okay. Right Elsie these wounds seem to be healing well. We'll give them a clean and put a fresh dressing on, okay?" said Rachael.

Emily started to clean the wounds and Rachael got out the dressings.

Rachael asked, "I don't suppose anyone has been here from Occupational Health or Physiotherapy, yet have they?"

"No, not yet love."

They finished and washed their hands. Emily looked around the kitchen and tidied up a bit. She went into the living room.

"Can I get you two a cup of tea before we leave?" she asked.

"Oh yes that would be lovely, thank you," said Elsie.

Rachael was filling in some forms and turned to Bill. "How are you coping?"

"Aye, fine pet."

"Because we can arrange for a community health care assistant to come in to help with personal care and help in the house; and maybe to prepare some meals?"

"Well, that would be a help wouldn't it Else?"

"I can get myself washed."

"It is just to help you with things you may find difficult at the moment. They will encourage independence and respect patient dignity," said Rachael.

"Well okay just till I get on my feet and feel better mind," said Elsie.

"Good, I'll arrange it when I get back t'office," said Rachael.

Emily appeared in the doorway with a tea tray, two cups and biscuits.

"Tea's up!" said Emily and set the tea tray on the table.

"Thank you," said Bill. He looked at the tray. "Why don't you get yourselves a cuppa?" he asked.

"We have to be getting onto our next client," said Emily.

"Go on Ems, I wouldn't mind a brew. I am parched," said Rachael.

"Okay then, thank you," said Emily. And went off to make two more teas.

They both got into Rachael's car and drove to their next patient; a young man who had been involved in a crash on the A69 Dual carriageway. He had been riding his motor bike when a car crashed into him as he was going around the roundabout. He was knocked off his bike and ended up getting his legs trapped under the wheels of the car. The driver had been drinking and had been under the influence of drugs. He had been driving very fast.

Now an amputee, David Thompson was now wheelchair bound. He lived in a terraced house in Hexham and Occupational Therapy had had his house adapted with equipment to help him live safely.

Rachael and Emily had come to check on his progress and well-being as well as to tend to his injuries.

"So, Mr Thompson, how are you managing?" asked Emily.

"All right, I guess."

"How do you feel after your accident?" asked Rachael.

"Some days I feel really upbeat and think I am going to beat this and move on with my life. On others I feel so angry that I have lost my legs because of some maniac. I loved my bike and now I can't ride anymore because of that lunatic or more importantly, even walk!"

"Well, we can help patch you up and try and make you comfortable, but maybe you could do with some counselling after such a traumatic event," said Rachael gently patting his arm.

"I am not really into all that, talking about my feelings."

"Well, you don't have to rush into it. Think it over and talk to your partner," said Emily.

"I will. He does his best and tries to help, but I want to do it for myself."

"Has the physio been to see you yet?" asked Emily.

"No, but they have been in touch. They are coming this week to do some exercises with me on my upper body. They have said my wounds have to heal first before they will think about prosthetics, obviously."

"Well at least they are making a start, but it will take time," said Emily.

Rachael nodded in agreement. They made him comfortable and saw to his injuries.

"We will call back and see you soon, just to make sure that the open wound is healing all right?" said Rachael.

"Is your partner at work today?" asked Emily.

"Yes, he is. His boss has been really good. He goes in for a couple of hours every day and brings work home with him. I am hoping to get back myself soon, they are wheelchair accessible. That is where we met at work," he said.

"Well don't rush back too soon. You have been through a big ordeal," advised Rachael. "It could take a good few months."

"Yes, I realise that. It is just I am eager to get better."

"Just one stage at a time," said Emily.

They finished the rest of their rounds and went back to the office to do paperwork and make some phone calls.

Chapter 7

James was walking Sammy along the road down to the field where the sheep were grazing. He opened the gate and Sammy sped off into the field barking. James thought that it was unusual for him to make a fuss. He looked towards the far end of the field and saw some sheep gathered together, bleating loudly. He started running and could hear Sammy barking frantically and jumping up and down.

Sammy saw his master and ran towards him, whining.

"What's up boy? Oh god!"

There were two sheep lying on the grass, both covered in blood. He reached out to the first one which was unresponsive and felt for a pulse. He was dead. The second was breathing, but had its eyes closed, presumably unconscious. He took out his phone and phoned the police and the vet for assistance. The police said that they would inform the RSPCA.

James took off his jacket. It was getting really warm anyway and put it on the wound of the unconscious sheep to suppress the blood. The time seemed like an eternity until help arrived.

The police came first, followed by the vet and then the RSPCA.

"Hello James." It was Sergeant Jones. "I'll just have a look around. You didn't leave the gate open or could there be a hole in the fence or the hedge?"

"I didn't leave the gate open, and I don't know of any holes. Could they have been savaged by another animal or do you think this is the work of some evil person?"

"I don't know. Is that a public road?"

"No, it is private, but at the bottom it leads onto public access."

The vet looked up and said, "These wounds aren't bullet wounds. Look at the edge of the wounds. That looks like it could be teeth marks."

The RSPCA officer said that there had recently been a few offences of dogs being let off leads near private property and damaging livestock.

"Do you see any dog walkers around here?" he asked.

"No."

"Right, well for the protection of these animals, we need to make sure that they can't get out and that dogs can't get in. We need to make it secure and put notices up about trespassing."

Sergeant Jones was having a look along the fence. He reached the bottom where the fence met the bushes and hedges. There was a gap big enough for a large dog to get through. He looked down at the ground and there were spots of blood on the earth. He shouted up to the others. James and the RSPCA officer whose name was David walked down.

"It looks like an animal or a dog got through."

"I try to keep on top of maintaining the fences and hedges. I put up chicken wire, so they couldn't get through."

The policeman looked at the bottom of the hedge where the hole was.

"Look! See the chicken wire there. That has been cut. An animal couldn't have got through unless it dug a hole and there is no hole and no signs of earth being turned over, to cover their tracks."

"So, it has been deliberate. How can people be so evil to treat animals like this?" said James angrily. "Not to mention how much it is going to cost me. Luckily, I have insurance against this sort of thing, but my premiums will go up."

The policeman and the RSPCA officer looked at each other, shaking their heads.

"Well, we shall start making enquiries and get to the bottom of this," said Sergeant Jones.

"Have you seen anybody acting suspicious, hanging around?" asked David.

"No, I don't usually see people walking their dogs up on this road and the bottom gate onto the parallel road is always locked. I always use the farm entrance and so do visitors, like you lot have," said James.

They walked back up the field to see how the vet was getting on. Sammy was keeping watch, supervising him.

"How are you getting on. How is he?" asked James.

The vet looked up.

"I have cleaned up the wound and put in some stitches. The wound is quite deep. I have tranquilised him but I would like to take him in for surgery so I can check the extent of the injury. I am hoping we found him in time. It is unfortunate about the other one. Unfortunately, he is long gone."

"Oh, well, I suppose that is the best thing for it," said James.

Sammy grew restless and started licking his hand.

"Okay boy, not long now."

The vet brought his land rover along the road and they put both sheep on the trailer at the back. James watched them drive away, feeling sick to his stomach.

"Right James; we'll be in touch as soon as we have some news," said David.

"Rest assured whoever instigated this will be imprisoned for such cruelty, not only about your sheep but training dogs to be vicious makes my blood boil."

"Thanks for coming."

They walked up to the top road with Sammy running on ahead. After all the commotion, James decided to get some lunch before seeing to his afternoon jobs. Not that he felt especially hungry, but he needed to keep his strength up.

As the week went on the weather was getting exceptionally warm. It was baking hot, about twenty-five degrees Celsius. It was Wednesday afternoon and Patrick was enjoying the freedom of being outside. He stretched out on the sun lounger and breathed in the fresh air. His partner Philip was inside making afternoon tea.

They had been living there for about six weeks now and had moved next door to Tom and Emily, the reverend and his wife and boys. The garden was well secluded, could not be overlooked and had a beautiful view of the open countryside. The house next door was set further back than theirs. They had invited them round for a cup of tea when they had first moved in. They were a friendly family and had welcomed them into the area. They seemed quite accepting of their relationship and lifestyle. It was their choice after all, this being the twenty-first century.

Philip and Patrick were both naturists and enjoyed living at home without having to wear clothes unless it was too chilly, but this weather was ideal. They always wore clothes when they had guests, especially those who didn't practise naturism and they respected that not everyone approved of this kind of lifestyle. There were individuals who were very judgemental. It seemed almost as if they had to be ashamed of their bodies and that nudity is a sin; but as a matter of fact, a lot of tribal communities practiced naturism in their everyday lives and celebrations. The ancient Greeks didn't wear clothing when practising sport such as Gymnastics. They called it gymnos, meaning naked or bare.

They were both I.T consultants and wore suits to the office all week. It was nice to come home, shake off the days' worries and be able to shed the suits and relax in the sun. They had both finished work early and were enjoying the peace and quiet of the garden.

Patrick had never liked wearing clothes for long, right from when he was a toddler. His parents gave up trying to keep him dressed inside the house when he was little and just let him play in the paddling pool and round the house in the nude, as nature intended. As he grew older though he became more private about when he was naked in the house. He grew up to accept that not too many people approved, and he didn't want to be known as a freak.

When he first met Philip, it was at a naturist event; some art weekend that offered the opportunity to join British Naturism, where they became members and quickly became friends. Philip enjoyed being in the buff, so to speak, and had always been curious about naturism but had felt shy and a little reserved about it. Having got to know Patrick and seeing how free, relaxed and happy he was, he couldn't help but fall in love with him. Neither had ever realised that they were gay until then and it just sort of happened. They had been blissfully happy since.

Philip finished making the sandwiches and stepped outside into the sunshine. It felt refreshing feeling a slight breeze. He walked into the middle of the lawn and put the plates on the table.

"Come on Patrick, tea is ready," said Philip. He walked back to the kitchen for the teacups.

Philip placed a towel on the chair and sat down.

"There you are sleepyhead, you nodded off in the sun," said Philip, giving him a kiss.

They both sat down, Philip took his flip flops off and stretched his legs, the grass tickling his bare feet.

"I hope this weather lasts," said Patrick.

"I was reading that we are going to have a heatwave for the next two to three weeks," said Philip.

"Suits me!"

"Why so you don't have to wear any clothes?"

"Why else, less washing," said Patrick, grinning.

"The office will be scorching, and we still have to wear a tie; pity it isn't clothes optional," said Philip.

"Yes, I bet we would have a lot of surprised faces if we turned up with just our Lanyards on."

"We wouldn't have any pockets," said Philip laughing. "We would have to carry bum bags!"

They finished their tea and Patrick took in the dishes.

He came out and got the hose out to water the plants.

"What are you doing, just relax," said Philip, stretching his long bare body in the sun.

"They just need some water like us," he said, turning the hose onto Philip and laughing.

"I am going to get you!" Philip screamed with the shock and Patrick chased him around the garden. They were both laughing and were drenched. Good job there were no clothes to dry.

"Let's get in the hot tub," said Patrick.

"Okay, just one thing Patrick."

"What? ahh!"

Philip soaked him again with the hose.

"You little …!"

They relaxed in the hot tub, enjoying the warm bubbly water on their skins. Patrick snuggled into Philip in the water.

"I love you!"

"Me too, I can't think of anyone else I would rather be with than here in our private retreat with you."

"Aah bless!" said Patrick.

They stayed in the garden until about seven p.m. and then went indoors for the rest of the evening When they went into the sitting room to watch television.

"Come on Philip, bed now. We have to be up for work in the morning," said Patrick, grabbing his hand.

"Okay bossy, I was comfy," he said, moaning.

They went up to bed and snuggled down together, enjoying the feel of each other's bodies between the clean Egyptian sheets. Within minutes, they were both fast asleep.

Patrick was up early in the morning making breakfast and packed lunches for work. He had the back door open to let in some air. It was still warm, even at such an early hour. He was making soft boiled eggs when Philip came in with his hair all stuck up.

"You should have woken me," he said yawning.

"You looked so peaceful."

Patrick served him his breakfast and sat down to his own.

He opened his tablet to check his work emails.

"Can't you do that at work."

"Not really, good job I checked, we all have to go for a staff meeting at ten o'clock and have to reschedule any appointments with clients."

"Why?"

"It says there has been a breach of conduct in security."

"Oh God, I wonder what that is about."

"I don't know. All of my files are backed up."

"So are mine."

"We had better get some clothes on and hurry up. The traffic will start getting busy soon."

"I'll drive," said Patrick.

They were soon suited, booted and looking smart. They both took a pride in their appearance and liked to look smart for work, even though they couldn't wait to get out of their suits by the time they got home. They got into the car and Patrick reversed their Audi out of the drive.

Chapter 8

Caitlin walked along the road in the sunshine. She had arranged to meet Tom Mayhew. She had told him about her discoveries about the pub being a former orphanage and about the proprietors having the same names as himself and Emily.

She had armed herself with all the information she had collated. Tom was amazed about the pub and said that they could have been his great grandparents or aunt and uncle. He was going to check on the family tree.

She walked along the long drive and rang the bell. Tom answered the door. Emily was at work and the boys were at school.

"Hello Caitlin, come in," he said, shaking her hand.

She told him about the librarian she had met and her idea of contacting the BBC local news and he thought it was a brilliant idea.

"I'll make us a brew. Do you want a cup of tea?"

"Yes okay, thanks."

They settled down at the dining table and Caitlin took out her work from her backpack. She showed Tom everything and told him what she had found at the pub.

"Could I see them next time I come?"

"Of course, and the attic."

"What's in the attic?"

"Matt found old trestle bunk beds, a school cap, an exercise book with old fashioned cursive handwriting in it and a metal hoop with a metal pole to control it."

"This is amazing," said Tom, taking out the family tree and spreading it across the table. "Right, this is the Mayhew side of the family. I have traced it back from my immediate family now. That's us there in that box, then to my parents and then my grandparents and great grandparents and there are aunties and uncles, as well as cousins and brothers and sisters."

"Did your parents mention anything about your ancestors owning an orphanage in Sleathwaite?"

"No, but they did say that my grandparents and great grandparents were educators."

He traced his finger along the lines of relations and saw a Thomas and Emmeline Mayhew – Thomas Mayhew born 29 May 1887 and Emmeline Parkin born 30 June 1887. Married 25 June 1910.

Thomas Mayhew died 4 April 1970 aged 83.

Emmeline Mayhew died 25 May 1971, aged 84.

He traced his finger from his parents, to his grandparents to check the relationships, and worked out that Thomas and Emmeline Mayhew were in fact his great grandparents.

"Look Caitlin, they were my great grandparents; see they are the parents of my grandparents!"

"Well, I never! I did wonder if there could be a connection. We could check where they were located, if that is possible."

"I'll put their names into Google," he said, turning on his laptop.

"Right, there are a number of links. I will click on this ancestry one. It mentions their names."

"Okay. It says, Thomas and Emmeline Mayhew were born, raised and married in Sleathwaite. They were proud educators and ran an orphanage in Sleathwaite which closed in 1948. They lived in the village until their deaths in 1970/71."

"Really, are there any more links for information?"

"Yes, for a more detailed report you have to pay a small subscription to Ancestry U.K."

"Well, it's worth doing," said Caitlin, taking out her purse.

"No, I will pay. I don't mean to sound rude, but they are my family and I thank you for discovering it and for the work you are putting in. Right it's £45 and I will receive the full report in 7–14 days."

"Can I borrow it, when it comes?"

"Of course, what are your plans?"

"I am going to write an article and get it published and contact the BBC, with your permission, if you are on board?"

"Of course, we could end up being famous, and who knows where it could lead?"

"I know it may lead nowhere or it could end up being successful, but we won't know if we don't try."

"What about your dissertation?"

"Oh, I have nearly finished it, and besides; it's nothing compared to this."

"Well, let me know if I can do anything? I am very interested."

"Thank you for your time and for getting involved."

"Not at all, thank you!"

"So, how are the new neighbours settling in?" asked Caitlin.

"Oh, they seem a friendly couple, quiet, and they keep themselves to themselves. They seem to have settled in well though. We invited them for tea and cake not long after they moved in, and they have had all of us round for a drink."

"Good, you'll have to tell them about our pub. We are always happy to welcome new people."

"Of course, yes, no problem."

"Bye then."

"Bye Caitlin."

It was a rainy afternoon in Sleathwaite. Rachael and James had come up to the school for Scarlett and Cameron's parents evening.

They had already seen Scarlett's teachers. They had received an excellent report, saying she was doing exceptionally well for her age and was well above target. They said that she was more on the level of a child who is a year older. They were both very pleased with her.

"Well done Scarlett!" said James.

"They say that you are doing really well. You are well above target and more on the level a child in the next year above you should be," said Rachael smiling.

"Thanks, I know that I have to get on with it, so I work hard. I may as well make the most of it and try to enjoy it, which I do," said Scarlett.

They were sitting in the book corner waiting to see Cameron's teacher. Cameron was looking through the books.

"I can't find it," he said.

"Which book are you looking for?" asked James.

"The Harry Potter book, ah here it is." He pulled it out from under a pile of books and they tumbled onto the floor.

"Cam!" said James, frustrated.

"Read it Mammy," said Cameron, pushing it onto Rachael's knee.

"Please," said Rachael.

"All right please," he said as he climbed onto her knee and bumped her cheek with his head.

"Ow!" said Rachael.

"Sorry."

Miss Haslem came to get them.

"Hello Mr and Mrs McCalister. Hello Scarlett; you have grown since I last saw you."

Scarlett smiled and said, "Hello."

"Right shall we go through."

They went through to the classroom and sat down at one of the tables. The teacher looked down at her notes and looked up smiling.

"Well, Cameron's a lovely boy isn't he, very gentle and always cheerful."

They both looked at each other and smiled. The teacher showed them some work he had done. They all looked down at the pictures he had drawn.

"However, I do have some concerns he does seem to have problems in forming his letters, his pencil control is quite shaky, and he seems to find activities difficult that involve fine motor skills. He does try hard but then gets frustrated. He seems to find it difficult to follow instructions. We don't overload him, and we adapt activities to his needs."

"Yes, we've noticed that, and we do try to help him, but we also try to encourage him to do things for himself," said James.

"Good, he is very proud of you all and seems to enjoy living on the farm."

"Yes, he helps James with the animals," said Rachael. "I was wondering how he gets on with the other children? We are concerned that he might have a communication disorder and could be on the Autistic Spectrum."

"Well, if you are concerned, I can refer him to Psych-Ed but this is more to do with his co-ordination and fine motor skills. He could have Dyspraxia and children get frustrated and have poor communication problems when they have that disability. He cannot cope with too many instructions at once, and he seems to have problems with Sequencing and Ordering. That is why he is struggling with multiplication. He does try to get on with the other children and seems to like the company of his two friends, Bill and Oliver, who have similar problems."

"I think we should have him referred to someone," said Rachael looking at James worriedly.

"I agree," said James sadly.

"I am a nurse why didn't I think of Dyspraxia?" said Rachael.

"Sometimes we don't like to admit what could be happening to those closest to us because we want to protect them," said Miss Haslem. "Right; well in that case I will refer him to Psych-Ed but they may also suggest that you take him to see a physiotherapist and an occupational therapist."

"Would that be at Hexham Community General?" asked James.

"I think it would be at The Great Northern Children's Hospital in Newcastle. We have had children attending there before."

"Well, if it is going to help him," said Rachael.

"Try not to worry. Has he had his eyes tested recently?"

"No, why?"

"Well, I think he may need glasses. I have put him at the front of the class, but I think it may make things easier for him when it comes to close up work and work we do on the white board."

"Yes, we'll sort it out," said James.

"Now there is one more thing I would like to discuss which I think would be nice for Cameron and good for his confidence."

"Yes?"

"We often have school trips to farms. It is good for numeracy and social aspects. Cameron obviously has a good upbringing living on a farm and joining in with the work there. I was wondering if I could bring his class to the farm and if you have time you could show us round and talk to the children about farming."

"I would be glad to," said James. "We can do some activities."

"Good – thank you, I will be in touch to make arrangements and let you know how I get on with Psych-Ed. You will probably receive a letter."

"Thank you for your help," said Rachael.

"Oh, it's a pleasure. He is a lovely boy, very attached to his headphones. We have been having music classes and he loves joining in with that. He hands out the instruments and collects them afterwards, and then he feels important."

James said, "Yes, we have trouble getting him to take off his head-phones. I sometimes wonder if he is trying to block out situations, he finds difficult."

"Well, he could be, but it is good that he likes music," said the teacher. Well goodbye. Nice to see you both and don't worry too much. He is a trier and a pleasure to have in my class."

"Bye."

Chapter 9

They were in car on the A1 going passed the Metro Shopping Centre. It was teaming down with rain. Cameron was getting restless.

"I want my moosic on!"

They were listening to the news on the car radio. He started kicking the back of the passenger seat with his feet.

"Cam that hurts. Stop it!" said James.

"I am trying to drive!" said Rachael. "James turn on the music please and let's have some peace and quiet."

"We can't just give in to him all the time. I am trying to listen to that."

"Right Cameron enough!" said Rachael. "Dad will put your music on if you promise to sit in your car seat sensibly and quietly?"

"Okay."

James looked at Rachael but rather than start a row he turned off the news and turned on the music to Jungle Book.

"I want my Queen CD."

"Let's just have something quiet," said James.

They all sang along to the 'Bare Necessities' and then listened to the rest of the story. Cameron settled down with his thumb in his mouth and was soon fast asleep.

"Thank God for that," said Rachael seeing him in the car mirror.

"How are you doing back there then Scarlett?" asked James.

"Okay, a bit tired."

"Well close your eyes then, have a snooze."

They were in North Yorkshire going through Barrow Bridge on the A1. Both children were fast asleep.

"Are you okay love after parents evening?"

"Yes, but I am a bit annoyed with myself for thinking he was on the Spectrum. I suppose we won't know anything until he has been diagnosed."

"Don't beat yourself up Rach. We are just going to have to try and be a bit more patient with him."

"I can't believe I didn't think of Dyspraxia though. I suppose I didn't really want to believe anything was wrong."

"Me too, but once we know what we are dealing with, we can try and help him."

"I know – it can be exhausting though."

I know, let's just take one step at a time."

They joined the slip road for Leeds and continued their journey. It was dark by the time they pulled into the driveway of Rachael's parents at Hebden Bridge.

"Hello! Hello!" George, Rachael's Dad came out of the house waving, followed by his wife Marian.

"Hi Dad, Mum," said Rachael, kissing both of them.

The children woke up and got out of the car.

"Grandma!" Scarlett ran up the drive and gave her a big hug.

"Grandad! Grandma!" Cameron flew at them excitedly, nearly knocking them over with excitement.

"Right, you all must be hungry. I have cooked us some tea," said Marian.

"Thanks Mum," said Rachael, following her into the kitchen.

"You look a bit subdued love, you all right?"

"Yes, a bit tired I suppose. We went to the parents evening."

"Oh, how did that go?"

George came into the kitchen and joined in the conversation.

"Are you helping your Mam? Sit down and relax for once."

Rachael put the pan on the hob and sat down at the kitchen table.

"Scarlett is doing exceptionally well; well above target and hitting targets for the year above her."

"Brilliant, I always said she was a brainbox," said George triumphantly.

"That's fantastic news," said Marian. "I know that look and I know when something is worrying you. Out with it lass," she said, gently.

"It's Cameron."

"Well, he's fine, bright as a button."

"Hush George, let her speak."

"He's struggling at school and at home he is finding it hard to do activities which involve co-ordination, fine motor skills and communication."

"He's just a bit shy with those he doesn't know," said Marian.

"It's more than that. He is battling with ordering, sequencing and following simple instructions. It's having an effect on his writing and numeracy."

"Well, what is it then?" asked George.

"They have asked us for permission to see Psych-Ed and he may have to see a physiotherapist and an occupational therapist; just to help him with his co-ordination and fine and gross motor skills."

"Well, if it is going to help him then go for it, take all the help he needs," said George.

They went into the dining room and had a hearty tea of Lancashire hotpot. The lamb melted in their mouths it had been slow cooking on a low heat for four hours. Followed by Apple crumble.

"That lamb was to die for," said Scarlett clearing her plate.

"Apple Crumble next wi' custard, come on Cam give us a hand in ter kitchen," said George gathering up the plates.

They went into the kitchen and Cameron put some dishes by the sink.

"Right then lad, what does we need?"

"I don't know Grandad?"

"Well, I does, how many people do we have?"

"Grandma, you, Daddy, Mammy, Scarlett and that's it."

"Haven't you forgotten someone?"

"Who?"

"You dafty!"

"Oh! Silly me!"

"Right, so how many bowls do we need?"

"One, two, three, four, five and six. Six bowls," said Cameron counting on his fingers.

"Right, you get the bowls, and you need how many spoons?"

"Erm! Don't know."

"Well, how many bowls has tha got?"

"Six."

"So, tha need six spoons."

Cameron looked in the kitchen drawer and counted out six spoons.

"Look Grandad."

"Good lad! Let's tek through what we needs."

They went into the dining room and Cameron put the bowls and spoons on the table and went to sit down.

"Isn't our waiter going to give us our bowls and spoons then?"
asked Marian.

"Sorry!" Cameron set about giving each person their bowls and
spoons, and George started serving up the food.

"I love my custard," said Cameron.

"So, Cam your Mam and Dad tell us you've done some nice pictures of you all on the farm," said Marian. "I bet they're good!"

"I can draw one of me, with you and Grandad in it," said Cam.

"We can put it on the wall," said George. "Are you enjoying your
new class Cameron?"

"It's the same class but a different teacher, she makes lessons fun."

"The teacher said that he is a delight to have in class and is always
willing to try," said Rachael, stroking his curly hair lovingly.

"Well always best ter try, God love's a trier," said Marian.

"And how long have you had God's number?" asked Rachael.

"Well, ya know."

"And Scarlett we hear you're doing really well at school, a brainbox like your Mam is," said George.

"I want to be a surgeon," said Scarlett.

"You've never said that before," said Rachael.

"No harm in having ambition," said James.

"I could work on the brain and be a brain surgeon."

"Well, you will have to spend seven years training to be a doctor
first. You don't just become a surgeon," said Rachael.

"I am not afraid of hard work," said Scarlett.

"So, you're going to follow in your Mam's footsteps?" asked Marian.

"Yes, only I am going right to the top."

"Well, there's no hurry, you are only nine and you may change
your mind several times over. But I am glad you want to do medicine," said Rachael.

"I wanted to be a train driver at that age," said George.

"I want to be an astronaut and live in space," said Cameron.

"Really cam?" said Marian.

"Yes, I will come to earth just for holidays and you and you
and you and you two can come and visit, and we'll have a float-
ing tea party."

"Do you know why things float in space Cammy?" asked James.

"Because the spacemen have springs in their shoes and underneath the furniture, so everything is bouncy!"

Everybody laughed.

"It's because there is no gravity."

"What's that thingy? Gravty."

"Gravity," corrected James. "Gravity is a force that we have on earth which keeps objects still and level. In space they don't have that and everything floats."

"Oh! Maybe I'll stay on earth."

"But it is really interesting. The life centre has an exhibition on space. I could take you, we could all go."

"Can I go up to space there?"

"No, but they have a special simulator ride that gives you the experience of what it is like to go into space."

"Will I have to wear a seatbelt?"

"Possibly."

"I could collect things for my school project," said Scarlett. "They are talking about taking us to the planetarium at the Great Northern Museum," she said.

"That will be interesting, aren't you two lucky? We didn't have such opportunities in my day," said Marian.

"I can't remember going on school trips," said George.

"Well, we had better get cleared up then it's off t'bed for everyone I think," said Marian. "Rugby tomorrow."

Chapter 10

The next morning Rachael opened her eyes to a bright sunny morning and for a moment wondered where she was. Of course, back in her old stomping ground Hebden Bridge. It was already quite warm, and it was only 7.30 a.m. it was going to be a really hot day. She left the school while it was pouring with rain. It had followed them down to Yorkshire. There had been thunder and lightning during the night.

James stirred and she gave him a playful shove.

"Err, what? I'll take Sammy out soon," he muttered dreamily.

"James, you don't need ter".

"Err, what?" he opened his eyes and sat up. "Oh, I forgot where I was."

"So did I for a moment."

"I can smell breakfast cooking. Come on, let's go down ter kitchen, be ready soon no doubt, bet kids are up."

"Your accent gets stronger when you're here."

"Does it?"

They walked into the kitchen which was bright and airy, and found George cooking bacon. The others were sitting outside at the table under the parasol on the patio.

"Ah morning you two, sleep well?"

"Yes, thank you," said James.

"That bed is so comfy that James didn't know where he was and said he was going ter tek Sammy out."

George laughed.

"Well, you forgot as well," said James, tickling her.

They walked through the conservatory to the garden.

"Hello you two. Sleep all right?"

"Yes Mum, thanks."

"You never call me Mam anymore."

"Well Scarlett calls me Mum. I think it's because some of her classmates call their Mam's Mum."

"Oh well, doesn't matter, glad you're here, love," she said, standing up to give her daughter a hug. "We miss you all, but at least you can get to us within a few hours."

George came out with a plate full of bacon croissants and they all helped themselves. There was fresh orange juice, freshly squeezed from an orange, fresh from a tree, not just from a carton. There was tea to drink and cereal and strawberries.

"So, how's t'farm going then James?"

"Oh, okay, hard work but it's worth it."

"Tell him. James has had a bit of trouble," said Rachael.

"Oh, what's happened?" asked Marian, concerned.

"I took Sammy out on Monday down to the field where the sheep are. He ran off as usual and started barking sharply. I went down to him and there were two sheep that had been savaged. One was dead and the other one unconscious."

"Oh God, was it deliberate?" asked George.

"Well, there are dog walkers on the path running parallel with the bottom of the field. The policeman found that the chicken wire I put up had been cut with wire cutters."

"The RSPCA officer said that there had been quite a few offences recently where owners trained their dogs to be vicious and set them on defenceless farm animals."

"That's terrible. No doubt they are mekin' enquiries inter this?" asked Marian.

"Yes, they are investigating it. They said whoever did this will be facing charges. Luckily I have livestock insurance, but it means my premiums will go up, but besides that, it is wicked and evil," added James.

George and Marian both looked shocked.

"They should be locked up," said Marian.

"And throw away t'key," said George.

James looked at his watch.

"We'd better get ready for rugby. Are you two going to come and watch Daddy and Tom play? His boys have a game as well, which I said we'd watch."

"Rugby's boring!" said Cameron. "Can't we go to the park to play? I want to go on the big slide and climbing frame," added Cameron.

"Yeah, I want to go to the park," said Scarlett.

"Well, we can go to the park for a bit and then on to rugby," suggested Rachael.

"Yay!" they both cheered.

"We are meeting Emily and everybody for a meal later on as well," said Rachael.

"After match booze up first," said James.

"Not too much, we don't want you and Tom pie-eyed, specially the Man 'o' ter Cloth."

James grinned. "For you my dearest, anything," he said, planting a kiss on her lips.

"Urgh, get a room!" said Scarlett.

"You two are mushy, mushy," said Cameron.

"Nothing wrong with showing affection," said James, giving them both a kiss.

"Eeeuuw! Get off!" said Scarlett.

Emily stood with the boys watching Tom and James play rugby. The seniors were playing in that morning and the boys were playing in the junior league after lunch.

They had just kicked off. James ran down to the touch line with the ball and passed the ball to Tom. Tom caught the ball and scored the first try of the game.

"Oh well played," said Emily, clapping and cheering.

Jamie whooped for joy and wolf-whistled.

John yelled, "Wicked! Good on yer dad!"

Rachael walked along the path with the two children and her parents. She saw Emily and boys.

"Hi Ems, have they scored a try yet?"

"Yes, James passed the ball to Tom, and Tom scored the first try."

"Oh well done them. You remember my Mum and Dad?"

"Of course, hello Marian, George, how are you both?"

"Oh, very well," said Marian. "Yourself, how are you?"

"Good thanks."

The boys are getting tall, nearly taller than their Mam," said George.

"Do you like rugby or footy best?" asked John.

"Oh, I am a rugger man myself. I've played more rugby than football, course good luck to both teams but I am Hebden born and bred and I hopes e t'Harlequins do well."

"No chance," said John, laughing.

"Well, we'll see," George said, smiling at him.

"You two talk funny," said Jamie.

"Oh, that's just our accents," said Marian.

"Jamie! Sorry," said Emily, embarrassed.

"S'all right," said Marian, smiling. "We all have different dialects. Anyways you two sound funny as well when you start speaking Geordie slang. We're all different tha knows".

"It would be a boring world if we were all the same," said Rachael.

"And how are you two, are you having a nice time at Grandma and Grandad's?"

"We went to the park, and I went on the big slide!" said Cameron.

"He got stuck on the climbing frame at the top, and I helped him down," said Scarlett.

"How did that happen?"

"He just got a bit scared at the top," said Rachael.

"Can we get hot dogs Mam?" asked John.

"Yes, but aren't you going to wait until half-time?"

"I am hungry," said Jamie. "We only had cereal for breakfast."

"How is the bed and breakfast?" asked Rachael.

"Oh, it's nice, we went there, last time we came down, remember, but that must be a year ago now."

"Mam!"

"Oh, all right. Are you going to take Cameron and Scarlett with you?"

Cameron hid shyly behind Rachael's legs.

"Oh, they've had bacon croissants," said Rachael.

"Mum could we get some crisps?" asked Scarlett.

"Yes okay."

"Crisps, come on Mammy," said Cameron, grabbing her hand.

"You can come with us Cam," said Jamie gently.

"Okay," he said, shyly.

"Jamie hold his hand," said Rachael.

"Okay," said Jamie. "Crisps yeah, what flavour do you like?"

"Cheesy quavers."

"Me too, that's my favourite."

"Here get what you want with that," said Marian, taking a ten pound note out of her purse.

"Oh no I can pay," said Emily.

"No, I don't see tkids often. I'd like ter treat them."

"Thank you," said, John taking the money. "I'll bring you your change."

"Oh, no. Share it among yoursens for snacks for t'day," said Marian.

"That's very kind," said Emily. "Thank you."

The children set off to the shop. Cameron took one last look at his Mam, waved, and set off skipping while holding Jamie's hand.

They soon returned with their food. Cameron handed his packet of crisps to Rachael.

"Open them," he said

"Cam you try to yourself."

"No, I can't."

"Look I will start you off and then you open it," said Rachael.

Cameron managed to open the packet and took out a small crisp for her and gave it to her.

"Oh, thank you, is that my payment."

"Yes."

Hebden Harlequins were beating Sleathwaite Warriors. They started off well and then Hebden took the lead before half time.

The players came off the pitch for refreshments. Tom and James caught up with the rest of them.

"Well done on your try," said Emily to Tom.

"Thanks, we're losing now though," answered Tom.

"We'll pull it back in the second half," said James.

"Daddy, hug?" said Cameron, putting his hands out to be picked up.

"Daddy's all dirty son," said James, kneeling down. "Can I have a crisp then?"

"Yes, but I'll give it to you. You are a dirty man," he said, handing James half a Quaver.

"Oh, thanks Cam," said James, looking at it. He opened his mouth and Cameron popped it in.

"We're going in for refreshments," said Tom, and off they went.

In the second half Sleathwaite pulled it back and took the lead again but then Hebden won the match. It had been a hard game, but the lads came off feeling like they had had a good game.

After James and Tom had their showers, they went to the bar for a couple of pints. They then caught up with the others who were having a picnic in the park.

The children tucked in and then went off to play, but stayed in sight. It was getting really hot again. But luckily, by the time the boys started playing their game, there was a bit of a breeze.

The junior league team were aged 11 to 16 years. They had a good match. Jamie scored a try in the first half and John one in the other half. Sleathwaite Warriors won the match. John was awarded man of the match and went up to receive the trophy. The other players picked up the twins and carried them around the pitch chanting.

"We are the wanderers, we are the champions, no room for losers in the world!"

They were led into the bar where the barman had set up drinks of juice or water. There was fruit and a few bar snacks.

Tom and John caught up with the boys and congratulated them.

"Well done boys," said Tom, patting them both on the shoulder.

"Well played lads," said James.

"Thanks." They both said in unison.

"Right, I think this calls for another pint," said Tom.

"Well of course!" said James.

Rachael and Emily caught up with them.

"Well done boys." They both congratulated them.

"We're just going to have another pint," said James.

"You two already look the worse for wear," said Emily.

"Well, there is important drinking time to be had," James told her.

"Hey, we are going out for a meal remember," said Rachael.

"I know dearest," said James.

Jamie asked James. "Can we have some beer?"

"No, you are far too young."

"Nice try son," said Tom.

"Dad we're going for a shower," said John, dragging his brother away.

"See you outside!" shouted Emily.

"Look, it's such a nice day. Why don't you both come outside while we wait for them," said Rachael, "and mines a voddy!"

"Mine is a peach schnapps. We'll be outside," said Emily.

"Hang on a minute. You two have the kids to look after," said James, slurring his words.

"Well, if you two can, so can we," said Rachael, heading out.

They stayed at the rugby club for another hour and then headed back to get ready for their meal out. They were going to Gino's, an Italian restaurant.

They all enjoyed the food, and the wine was flowing between the adults. They were all a bit drunk. They agreed to meet up for Sunday lunch the next day.

The weekend seemed to be flying past. They all brought their cars to the pub so they could head off home afterwards.

After sitting out in the beer garden for another hour or so, it was nearly four o'clock and would be nearer seven by the time they got home. The kids had school the next day and were starting to get tired.

"Well time for us to say goodbye," said Rachael, hugging both of her parents.

"Hope to see you all soon," said Marian, giving hugs all round.

Rachael looked at James and he nodded in agreement.

"Well, why don't you two come up for the week at half term? We would love to have you."

"Oh, that would be lovely," said Marian.

"Great, I'll give you a ring when we get back," said Rachael.

"Grandad, you can sleep on my bottom bunk," said Cameron.

"Oh, thanks Cameron, but Grandad's getting a little old for bunkbeds."

"You can have the spare bedroom," said James.

The journey back was hot and stuffy. Both children fell asleep. Scarlett didn't wake up until they joined the A69, the bypass to take them home. Normally they would stop off for a drink at Scotch Corner, but they didn't want to wake the kids and time was getting on.

Cameron was fast asleep, and James carried him out of the car and up to bed.

"James I am mekin' a brew, does tha want one?" Rachael asked.

"Yes please love."

"It was a good weekend wasn't it."

"Yeah, really good. I enjoyed the break although my head is starting to feel sore!"

"Too much booze, I feel a bit like that too, but it was nice to unwind."

"Let's take these teas up to bed," said James wearily. "I have an early start tomorrow."

"Oh, I am on earlies. Got ter be up at five, just remembered."

"Well, I can see to the kids and do the school run then, but I will probably be finished later in that case," said James, climbing the stairs.

As soon as their heads hit the pillows, they were both out for the count.

Chapter 11

It was Monday teatime and Patrick and Philip had just arrived home after a tiring and stressful day at work. On Friday morning it had been announced that there had been a serious breach of security involving clients' data.

Some confidential files had become encrypted and a few important clients' data had been leaked to an unknown source. The information which had been leaked was account details, email addresses and company details. A serious investigation into fraud was being carried out. The crime squad had been there, along with forensics, looking at computer files and security cameras. Every member of staff who had dealings with these clients had been interviewed by the police.

"Well, I am glad that day is over," said Patrick, undoing his collar and tie and rolling up his sleeves.

"I know," said Philip. "I hope they get to the bottom of it. It could ruin the company. They could end up closing if they lose those clients'. They do the most business with us."

"Well let's hope it doesn't come to that. I need to unwind," said Patrick, filling the kettle.

"Ooh that's a good idea," said Philip, throwing his jacket on the chair. He came up behind Patrick and put his arms around his waist, nuzzling into his neck.

"Don't you think of anything else," said Patrick, turning around and giving him a hug.

"Not when you are in my sights, and you are never far from my thoughts."

"Well, I am a god!"

Philip started laughing and tickling him.

"Tell you what. After tea, why don't we go for a swim and a jacuzzi."

"Yeah, all right, good," said Patrick, pleased.

They sat down at the table and drank their tea. It was four p.m. Patrick stood up and started peeling and chopping vegetables for a stir-fry.

He turned around. Philip was sitting at the table reading the news-paper. He was on dish-washing duty.

"Hey Phil, I was talking to Tom yesterday and he says he often pops into the Hadrian for Sunday lunch or the odd drink during the week. He says that they have got to know the new tenants quite well. He was asking if we would like to pop in for a complimentary drink, to welcome us to the area. They are relatively new themselves."

"Oh, that would be nice, we could arrange to meet up with Tom and Emily."

"Yes, how about the weekend. It would be a nice break after the week we are in for."

They sat down to have their dinners. It was nice to be out of the office. It had been another scorching day. Philip had opened the French doors to let some air in, but it didn't make much difference.

After clearing away and dishes were done, they went upstairs to change.

"Right, shall I drive?" asked Philip. "Give you a break from driving."

"Yes okay."

They arrived at Sleathwaite Hall and walked towards where the pool was located. The hall had special events for Naturists, this hot evening being one of them.

Patrick and Philip had season tickets for which they had paid. They showed them to the receptionist who gave them tokens for the lockers,

They went to the changing rooms to get undressed. They decided to have a swim first and then a Jacuzzi.

Patrick dived in and started swimming up and down the lanes. He was a strong swimmer and had often taken part in swimming galas and competitions. He liked the pool at this time before it got too busy.

Philip was a good swimmer too. He used to be more into scuba diving, but didn't get a lot of opportunities for it.

Patrick must have swum sixty lengths and went and stood at the side of the pool.

Philip joined him when he finished fifty lengths.

"You okay?" he asked, giving Patrick a kiss.

"Yes, I enjoyed that," he said, putting his arms around his neck and kissing him on the lips.

"Shall we go into the jacuzzi before we get cold?"

"Yes."

They got into the jacuzzi. Another couple was in there. They all smiled and said, "Hello."

"Do you come here often," asked Philip.

The young woman looked at him and laughed.

"That's a funny thing to ask in the jacuzzi, sounds like a chat up line."

"Oh, I assure you it isn't. Sorry I didn't mean that in the way it sounded. It's just that we have recently moved to the area and are new members."

"Right, well welcome to Sleathwaite. I am Gemma by the way, and this is my partner Karl."

"Hi, I am Philip, and this is Patrick, my partner."

They sat in the jacuzzi, making pleasant conversation, talking about the sports and facilities Sleathwaite Hall had to offer. Gemma told them about the spa, and they were going to go for a massage the next time they came.

After half an hour they all got out and headed to the showers and then to the changing rooms. They met Gemma and Karl for a coffee afterwards.

Philip drove home and thought Patrick seemed unnaturally quiet. He was normally a chatterbox once he got started, but after the day they had had, he thought he must be tired.

"You're quiet?" said Philip. "Hello! Earth calling Patrick!"

Patrick was staring into space, miles away.

"What! Oh I was just erm…", he said getting out of the car.

They unlocked the house and Patrick headed straight for the stairs.

"Night Philip."

"Err night, have I done something wrong."

"No, I am just tired that's all. Don't be long."

"No, I won't, just going to put the bin out."

"Okay!"

Philip went into the back garden and retrieved the bin to put out to be emptied the next morning. He didn't understand it. They had had an enjoyable night and always got on like a house on fire and then Patrick ended up being in a strange mood.

"Hormones," he said to himself.

He went into the bathroom to clean his teeth. When he came into the bedroom Patrick appeared to be fast asleep. He gave him a kiss on the head and turned over and tried to get to sleep, worried about what was troubling him.

The next morning, he awoke to an empty bed. He padded downstairs in his slippers and dressing gown. Patrick was all dressed and ready for work.

"You're up early," said Philip cautiously.

"Yes, I have a lot to do. I am taking my car and going in early. I am finishing early at 11:30. Got things to do," he said, patting Philip on the shoulder and heading for the front door.

"Anything you'd like to share?" asked Philip, curiously.

"No, top secret," he said.

"Oh!"

"See you later."

Patrick kept his head down all morning buried in his work and didn't take a break. He only had time to say a quick hello to Philip when he arrived at work.

The clock reached twelve o'clock and Patrick packed his things up. Philip was busy on the phone, so he just clocked out and left the building.

He drove into town and bought engagement rings, flowers and then popped into Marks and Spencer for some nice food and wine. His intention was to surprise Philip. They had been together for a long time, and he had been thinking of marriage for the last couple of weeks and had only just built up the courage to ask him.

Patrick entered the front door of his house. His tabby cat Tabitha came to greet him.

"Hello, tabs, all right sweetheart?"

The cat mewed and leant against his legs. Then she rolled onto her back to have her tummy tickled. At three years old, she was still a young cat and was quite playful. Patrick tickled her tummy.

"You, tarty kitten," he said smiling.

He stood up, grabbed the shopping bags and entered the kitchen. The house seemed really hot. He put away what needed to go in the fridge and went upstairs. Normally he could cope with heat, but it was starting to get to him. The heat was soaring into the early thirties.

He opened some windows wide, but it didn't make much difference.

He took all his clothes off and went into the shower. The water felt lovely and refreshing. After ten minutes he got out and dried himself. He lay on top of the bed with the window open and relaxed for half an hour. He had plenty of time, it being only three p.m. Philip didn't finish work until five p.m. today.

He padded downstairs in just his slippers, relieved to be out of his suit. He went into the kitchen and started preparing dinner.

He put on his stripy butcher's apron and got out the ingredients.

He whistled cheerfully and started chopping vegetables.

"I am the naked chef I am; I am!" he started singing. "Huh, I'd give Jamie Oliver a run for his money."

He had decided on Salmon Croissants with poached egg and rocket with a touch of mayonnaise on the side for the starter.

For second course they were having slow cooked lamb in a red wine sauce with Mediterranean vegetables and Dauphine potatoes.

For the third course, there was creme Brulee and tea or coffee to follow. Patrick had bought a bottle of Pinot Grigio and a bottle of Prosecco in case they had something to celebrate.

They weren't big drinkers; only on special occasions or the odd time they went to the pub. They liked to try and lead a healthy lifestyle, by eating sensibly, having a low alcohol intake and taking regular exercise. However, it was nice to relax with a glass of wine once in a while.

They both enjoyed the odd craft beer as well, 'Golden Plover' being a favourite.

He set the table after putting the lamb in the oven on a low heat and saw to the flowers he had bought.

The house was always clean and tidy. He wanted it to look nice for when Philip came home. He put the vacuum cleaner on and did a bit of a tidy up.

He wanted to wear his very best clothes, so he went upstairs and picked out his suit, a blue silk shirt and a dark blue tie. His shoes were already polished, Italian leather. Patrick liked to dress smartly.

"Oh, but it is so hot." He put the tie and jacket back in the wardrobe and started getting dressed.

"Some aftershave, I think," he said, reaching for a bottle of Autograph.

He looked at his watch 5:30 p.m. Philip would be arriving soon. He double checked everything; the lamb smelt delicious. Fifteen minutes later he heard the front door shut.

Philip didn't look in a particularly good mood, which was unusual for him. He looked at Patrick all smart in his best clothes.

"You off out?" he asked, throwing himself onto the settee and folding his arms.

"No, I erm," said Patrick uneasily, starting to point towards the dining room.

"Look, Patrick if you are leaving me, just say so. No point in standing on ceremony."

"What gave you that idea?" asked Patrick with his hands on his hips. "Why are you in such a bad mood?"

"Well, it's you. You have been so cold and distant."

"No, I haven't. I'm sorry if I came across that way. Come with me please," he said, gently grabbing Philip's hand.

"What for?"

"Come please."

Philip didn't hold his hand and followed him into the dining room.

"What's that smell, are we expecting guests?"

"No look, sit down please, I have gone to a lot of effort just for you."

"Sorry, you have cooked me dinner. It looks like you have gone to a lot of trouble just for tea."

"Well, I wanted it to be special."

"It smells delicious. You look lovely by the way, and so does the house. I like the flowers."

"Thank you. Now sit down and relax, I am at your beck and call."

"I haven't forgotten an anniversary, or anything have I?"

"No."

"You're up to something my lad. Look, I had better go and get washed and changed. I feel like a right scruff standing next to you in your best clothes."

"No, you don't, you look fine. Now, would Monsieur like some wine?"

"Yes please. I don't know what I have done to deserve all this special attention, I was just horrible to you back there."

"It's all right, I suppose I have been a bit distant, but in a good way."

"What do you mean by that?" enquired Philip curiously.

"I told you, that's top secret. All will be revealed in good time. Don't worry and try and relax."

"Now for the first course, we have Salmon a la croissant," he said, carrying the plates through.

They enjoyed the first course and then moved onto the second course.

"Now, we have slow cooked lamb in a red wine sauce, Mediterranean vegetables and Dauphine Potatoes. Dive in."

They enjoyed their meal and wine. Philip got up and put some soft music on and Patrick carried in the dessert.

"Crème Brule for Monsieur," he said.

"I must say you have gone to a lot of effort."

Patrick suddenly dropped to the floor.

"Oh God, are you all right?"

Patrick was prone to having Epileptic Seizures and Philip was immediately concerned for him. He had to be careful of his alcohol consumption because it affected his medication. Patrick looked up with a silly look on his face.

"Get up you silly sod, you can't be that drunk. We have only had a couple of glasses of wine."

Patrick went down on one knee and took out the ring box.

"Oh, my God," said Philip, putting his hands to his face, smiling.

"Philip, would you do me the honour of becoming my husband. I love the bones of you and love you to the moon and back. I want to spend the rest of my life with you and for us to grow old together. Well, what do you say, I am getting cramp."

"Yes! yes of course. I'd love to, what a lovely surprise!"

"Get in, I can get up now," he said standing.

Philip stood up and put his arms around him. "Thank you for a lovely evening and I would like nothing more than to marry you and grow old with you," he said kissing him on the cheek.

"Let's dance, can I have the pleasure sir?" asked Philip taking his hand.

"Why yes kind sir," answered Patrick.

They danced around the dining room and Patrick grabbed a hold of his waist and whooped for joy.

"Wa hey! Feel like I have won the lottery."

"We both have, I think this calls for champagne."

"All taken care of," said Patrick heading for the fridge.

"You've thought of everything."

"Well of course, nothing but the best."

"Let's take our drinks into the living room, the dishes can wait," said Philip leading his fiancé into the other room.

Patrick showed him the other ring he had picked out for himself.

"I should have got that for you," remarked Philip.

"That's okay, they fit perfectly."

"Well let me plan a holiday for us. I won't tell you where we are going or what we are doing till the last minute. I want to surprise you."

They talked about where to have the ceremony and decided to book the Registry office.

"What about asking Tom to give us a blessing in church. It would be nice for our parents, them being church goers," asked Philip.

"Yes, okay that would be nice," said Patrick. "Now how about I make a brew, tea, coffee?" he asked.

"You sit down. I will do that."

"No, I will, tea?"

"No, can I have an Americano. There is some Costa coffee in the cupboard."

"Okay."

Patrick went off to the kitchen. He was standing looking out of the window waiting for the kettle to boil. He didn't hear Philip come in.

He suddenly felt his trousers falling down to his ankles, and his shirt being lifted up. He didn't wear underwear and was just about naked.

"Oh," he turned around in surprise.

Philip started undoing Patrick's shirt buttons and Patrick let him undress him. He looked up with adoration painted all over his face. Philip put his hands on Patrick and pulled him towards him. Together, they became one.

Patrick hadn't needed to undress Philip; he had already done it. He kept penetrating until Patrick came with pleasure.

Patrick lowered Philip down to the floor and they started to make love. They started kissing and stroking each other all over. They were riding on a tide of ecstasy.

They rolled around the kitchen, stroking and caressing each other. They were both well aroused. They lay in each other's arms, for what seemed like ages.

"They carried on with their lovemaking and then proceeded upstairs.

Philip led Patrick into the bathroom and let Patrick soap him down in the steamy shower. Patrick kissed him passionately and Philip held him close under the shower.

When they had finished showering, they gently dried each other and walked hand in hand to the bedroom.

"Well, I wasn't expecting that quite so soon. We have certainly christened the house," said Patrick smiling. "We didn't have time for coffee," he said, smiling.

They lay on top of the bed chatting about their day and then Philip went down to load the dishwasher. There wasn't much clearing up to do as Patrick had cleaned and tidied as he had prepared the meal.

He went back upstairs, and Patrick was snuggled under the duvet, fast asleep. He kissed him good night and sat thinking over the last twenty-four hours. He could well have blown it with Patrick, but Philip didn't know what he was planning. When he had walked into the hall and saw him all dressed up, he honestly thought he was going off to meet someone else. He felt a pang of guilt for even having had doubts in the first place.

He snuggled under the duvet and thought of ideas for a surprise holiday and honeymoon.

Chapter 12

Rachael was driving Cameron to his first appointment at the hospital. They were meeting the physiotherapist. She found a parking space outside the children's hospital. They went through the swing doors. Cameron loved the swing doors and went around twice. On the third time she had to grab his hand and gently lead him into the hospital. They would have been there all day.

They entered the children's outpatient department and checked in for their appointment. The department was brightly decorated and had murals of cartoon animals painted on the walls.

"Look at that one Mammy," said Cameron pointing at a monkey swinging from a tree with a banana in his mouth. "He looks funny!"

"They're lovely, aren't they? Look, there's one of 'Bob the builder' on the other wall with 'Scoop'."

Cameron spied the play area near the waiting area.

"Can we go and play?"

"Yes, go on."

"You have to come!"

"Okay. Cam you still have your headphones on. Give them to me, you don't need them."

"NO spells no."

Rachael sighed but didn't press him. He had enough to cope with at the moment.

Cameron found the box of cars and started playing.

"Mam you can have the red one and I will have the sporty blue one. Brum! Brum!" he said, pushing his car along a wooden track.

Rachael set hers off and they played racing games.

"Cameron McAlister!"

Cameron looked up at the sound of his name.

"Come on Cammy," said Rachael taking his hand.

"Hello, you must be Cameron?" said the lady smiling. "Are you his Mum?"

"Yes."

"Right, welcome both of you, my name is Lisa, and I am going to be working with you Cameron. Shall we go through?"

She showed them through to a well-equipped gym.

"Are you a nurse?"

"No, I am what is called a physiotherapist and we are going to play games and do exercises and activities."

"Oh, a Physiowhatsit."

"Yes," she said smiling.

They sat down at the table.

"I am just going to ask you some questions Mrs Macalister, if that's okay?"

"Yes, sure and it's Rachael."

"Right, can I ask was Cameron a normal delivery, no complications. Did you carry him full term?"

"No problems at all, I carried him full term and it was a normal birth."

"Good, and how about his development, did he learn to use the potty and walk and talk round about the right times?"

"Yes, in terms of that he was fine, but he was still having some accidents wetting himself when he started school, but it soon settled down, but that is fairly normal."

"Of course, it is a big transition, starting school."

Cameron yawned and promptly put on his headphones.

"He is in year one now?"

"Yes."

"And how do you think he is getting on?"

"Well, he does find certain tasks difficult that involve fine and gross motor skills, ordering, sequencing, communication, following instructions. He is behind in his learning attainment. They have put together an educational plan and adapted lessons to his needs, but they are interested to find out what happens here. His handwriting is very shaky as well. At first I thought he was on the Autistic Spectrum because of his communication problems."

"Well, I have a report from Psych-Ed and they agree about the communication problems, but they have ruled out autism, from their findings in the testing they have done with Cameron."

"Good. If he wants to avoid something, he finds difficult, he puts his headphones on."

"To block out the world. Cameron do you like school?"

Rachael signalled him to take his headphones off.

"Cam, Lisa is talking to you."

"Sorry," she said.

"That's okay. What are you listening to Cameron?"

"Human League, Don't you want me? 1982!"

"You are well informed. You must love your music, can I have a listen?"

"Yes," said Cameron, passing over the headphones.

"That takes me back," she said smiling. "Cameron do you like school?"

"Yes."

"What is your favourite thing you like to do?"

"Playing in the water and the sand."

"They all like that don't they?"

Rachael nodded in agreement.

"Do you have anyone you most like to play with?"

"Bill! he is my best friend; I want him to come to tea."

"That would be nice. Now, you like music. How about I plug your iPod into the speakers and we can dance along to the music?"

"Yeah!"

"Mummy can join in."

"You'll be his friend for life!"

They danced to a couple of songs and then played throw and catch which Cameron found difficult. She showed him the hopscotch and he had a go on the balance board.

"Whee, this is fun!" said Cam.

They finished off with some games and puzzles.

"Right, well I will be running these sessions twice a month for the next six months. There are tests I would like to do with Cameron before we come up with a diagnosis. Have you heard from occupational therapy yet."

"No."

"I suspect that they are waiting to hear from me about my first session with yourselves. I will chase it up."

"Thanks."

"I will send out the next appointment in the post and it was a pleasure meeting you both. He is a lovely boy."

"Right Cam, time to get in ter car".

"Are we going home?"

"No, you are going to school."

"Ah, can't I stay here?"

"No, you can't, Lisa has other little boys and girls to see."

"Can we go to MacDonald's?"

Rachael and Lisa both laughed.

"Are you going to come and visit me again Cameron?"

"Yes! And you can call me Cam."

"High five Cam?" said Lisa, holding up her hand.

Cameron did the same. "High five!" he said.

"You have a friend there," said Rachael. "Right come on Mister, time to go."

"Thank you," she said to Lisa.

"I will be in touch, goodbye, bye Cam, see you again."

"Bye!"

They headed out towards the car.

"Well, you seemed to have a good time with Lisa?"

"It was brill!"

End of part one.

PART TWO

Introducing new Characters

The Seddon Family

Rick Seddon. Husband, Father, Grandfather, Site Manager.

Sally Seddon. Wife, Mother, Grandmother, Stay at home parent.

Sarah Seddon. Daughter, Mother, Sister, aged 16.

David Seddon. Son, Brother, Uncle, Schoolboy, aged 14.

Max Seddon, Son, Brother, Uncle, Schoolboy aged 11.

Charlotte Seddon, Baby Daughter, Grand-daughter, Niece.

The Patel Family

Sanjay Patel. Husband, Father, Cardiologist.

Aisha Patel. Wife, Mother, Neurologist.

Shireen Patel. Daughter, sister, schoolgirl aged 14.

Aadi Patel. Son, Brother, Schoolboy aged 12.

Chapter 13

Sleathwaite village looked idyllic in the Autumn sun. It was still quite warm for the time of year. The trees, plants and hillside were gradually turning russet brown, orange and red. The trees almost looked golden in the sunlight.

It was Saturday and a month since Patrick had proposed to Philip. The wedding hadn't taken much organising as they wanted just a simple affair, but obviously they wanted it to be a special day.

In the morning they had been along to the Registry office at Hexham, where close family had been invited for a civil partnership.

They all then assembled at the church at Sleathwaite where Tom was giving the couple a blessing. Friends and neighbours, villagers they had got to know, and family of course had been invited.

Tom stood at the top of the altar waiting for the couple to walk down the aisle. Classical music played in the background.

The congregation stood when the couple entered the church and proceeded to walk down the aisle.

Tom raised his arms in welcome.

"You may all be seated. Welcome to everyone, including our happy couple, who with my blessing are going to commit their love for each other. We will start with the hymn 'Oh perfect love'. Please stand."

The congregation stood and everyone started singing. They could have raised the roof with the volume of the singing. It sounded wonderful.

After the hymn had finished, Tom said, "Please be seated, Philip, Patrick please remain standing. Your relationship is a partnership, the joining of two parties ready to make a commitment to each other, to respect one another, to cherish each other and have fulfilment; to show love and affection for each other in a secure loving home."

"Patrick, are you ready to commit to Philip, will you love him and cherish him, say 'I do' when you are ready."

"I do."

"Philip are you ready to commit to Patrick, to love him and cherish him, say 'I do', when you are ready."

"I do."

"Now, I believe that you have some vows that you would like to say to each other. Patrick, would you like to start?"

"Yes." He turned to Philip. "Philip, I promise to look after you through sickness and in health. I promise to be a faithful loving husband. I really liked you when we became friends and always felt we had a special bond. I was the happiest man on earth when we first got together, and we moved into our first flat. I love you to the moon and back."

"Now Philip, are you ready to commit to Patrick?"

"Yes. Patrick, I have loved you for such a long time and have cherished and enjoyed every day with you since we got together. I love you and want to spend the rest of my life with you. I promise to love you, respect you and look after you in sickness and in health. I love you right round the moon, the galaxy and back to earth. You are my world."

Then they both said together, "For acres and acres." This was something they always said together.

"Aah!" Someone said in the congregation

They hugged and kissed each other, and everyone clapped and cheered.

"Please be seated, I would like the congregation to join us in prayers."

Tom closed his hands and said, "May you receive love and happiness from each other as well as guidance from God, through your journey of life together. With God's blessing may this special friendship be a long and happy partnership together, be kind to one another through sickness and in health. God bless you both."

"God bless," said the congregation in unison.

"Now the Lord's prayer, Our father who art in heaven …"

The classical music started playing and they shook hands with Tom and thanked him for the ceremony.

They had booked a photographer who took some photographs inside the church with just Patrick and Philip. The rest of the congregation and Tom had stepped outside. When the photographs had been taken inside, they then went outside for some more photographs to be taken with family and friends and just with each other.

They came out of the church and there was a lot of cheering and confetti being thrown. Family and friends congratulated them and wished them well.

They all headed for the cars, there was an old traditional car to take Patrick and Philip to their wedding tea at the 'Hadrian'. There were two limousines for immediate family.

Philip and Patrick entered the pub. Matthew and Caitlin had decorated the dining room which had been hired for this happy day. There were only about forty guests which included both families, friends and some work colleagues.

"Congratulations!" said Matthew, shaking both their hands.

"Looks like you have done a fantastic job," said Philip.

"Well only the best, congratulations both of you," said Caitlin, giving both of them a kiss and shaking their hands.

The dining room was decorated with fresh flowers and balloons. There was a choice of Prosecco, grape juice or fresh orange juice. There were waitresses walking around offering guests refreshments.

People were standing in huddles chatting cheerfully and enjoying the day.

Matthew stood on a chair and gently clinked a spoon against a glass.

"Could I have everyone's attention please. We are ready to serve the wedding tea, could all guests please come into the dining room and be seated!"

Everyone started to file into the dining room. Amongst them were Tom and his family and James and his family who were seated at the same table.

Patrick and Philip were last to enter the room.

"Caitlin clinked a glass for silence, everybody hushed.

"May I present the newlyweds Philip and Patrick!"

Everyone clapped as they found their seats. The wedding tea consisted of a choice of pates, garlic mushrooms, melon or prawns for the first course. The second was a roast dinner with a choice of meats, such as lamb, pork, beef or chicken with vegetables. Any special dietary requirements had been taken care of.

For dessert there was Crème brulee, Belgian chocolate brownies, Belgian waffles, apple crumble, ice cream or custard.

Everyone seemed to be enjoying themselves and having a good time. Philip had booked a jazz band as a surprise to Patrick for the occasion. They were playing soft music in the background.

After dessert it was time for some speeches. Matthew clinked a glass and said, "Ladies and Gentlemen I give you the two grooms!"

Patrick was first to stand.

"I won't take long don't worry. I would like to thank you all for coming and special thanks to our parents to help organising this happy day. When I first met Philip, we were both college students studying ICT. We were just friends at first going out in groups with other students. We were both going out with these twin girls, nothing serious just a bit of fun, neither of us realised that we liked the same sex. It wasn't until we started sharing student accommodation that we realised we were more than just friends. The girls realised our attraction to each other and gave us their blessing, and from then on, we have been there for each other, we've had a ball. Now I hope you are all enjoying yourselves, eat and drink as much as you like, it's all free, now it's Philip's turn."

Patrick sat down and then Philip stood up. "Well as Patrick has said I would like to start off by saying thank you to our parents for today, and to our best man, I dread to think what he is going to come out with."

Laughter round the room.

"Now, as you know Patrick and I have known each other a long time. I could tell you a few stories, but I would be here all night. When I first saw Patrick, I was impressed by how easily he seemed to charm everyone. To me, he seemed to light up a room when he came in. He wasn't cocky or overconfident but had a pleasant manner and always presented himself well. I guess I was a bit envious of him. As he says, we were seeing these twin girls when we were at college. Unfortunately, they got the boot, but they were good about it. The day Patrick proposed I wasn't in the best of moods. He had seemed so distant at times. When I arrived home and he was all dressed up, I thought he was going off to meet someone else and he was leaving me. How wrong I was, and I must admit I felt guilty about it. He surprised me with a lovely meal, flowers, Prosecco and a ring! Now I would like to surprise him. Patrick, I have booked us three weeks off work and tonight we are off to the airport, I am taking you to Australia and you can teach me how to scuba dive!"

"Really, fantastic, thank you!" said Patrick, standing up and giving him a kiss.

"Now I think our Dads want to say a few words."

"Dad?"

Patrick's dad Derek stood up. "I would just like to welcome Philip into our family. I always try to treat you like my own and now you've sealed it. I think we have gained a son! Please raise your glasses to Patrick and Philip."

"Patrick and Philip!" "

"Now Bob has something to say."

"I just want to say to Patrick, I have always thought you were a great lad, and you are always good to Philip. Welcome to the family, you are like a third son, good on you both. Now it's the best man's turn, Pete?"

Pete stood up. "Oh well, where do I start. First of all, I would like to raise a toast to Patrick and Philip," he said taking a slice of toast out of his pocket and waving it in the air.

Everyone laughed.

"Now I did write down some ideas," he said taking a wad of paper out of his pocket. "Oh, sorry, mam why did you give me your shopping list?"

Laughter again.

"Right, well I went to the same college as my little brother Patrick, and we all went into town together on the lash, so to speak. I could tell you the time Patrick got chained to a lamp post on April fool's day with his pants round his ankles. Sorry you won't want to hear about that or the time Philip got stuck on Saint Mary's Island when the tide had come in. He didn't have a phone with him and was stranded. We thought he'd gone off to the pub! but luckily, we realised that he must have been left on the Island. When we ran out of options as to where he could be, we had to phone the coast guard. Patrick was a little devil as a child. He once collected worms in a jar and said that he had made me a sandwich, luckily I saw the worms wriggling between the two slices of bread before I took a bite. He was a right joker was our kid."

"Urgh!" someone said and there were a few chuckles.

"But seriously though, they are a good couple of lads and are great together. I wish you all the best and health and happiness. Congrats bros."

He sat down and chatter sounded through the hall. Half an hour later Matthew clinked a glass again. "Could everyone please assemble outside, where the happy couple are about to leave and go on honeymoon."

Outside, there were hugs all round.

"Bye Mum, see you soon," said Philip. "Dad."

"Have a nice time son."

Patrick's parents gave them both a hug and wished them well.

"Take care of yourselves."

"Thanks, Mam," said Patrick.

Steve and Pete drove up in Patrick's car and got out.

"Well do you like it?" asked Steve.

"Yeah, we have done some artistic work," said Pete.

"So I see," said Patrick, looking at his car. There was just married sprayed across the bonnet done in shaving foam, tins on string hanging from the bumper with a cardboard just married sign and balloons attached to the wing mirrors.

"God!" said Philip, laughing. "We have to go to the airport in that!"

"Just a little going away present bruv!" said Steve, smiling.

They got in the car and drove off and everyone cheered and shouted goodbye.

Chapter 14

The pub seemed to get a little quieter after the happy couple had departed. They had left at about 6.30. Matthew and Caitlin had done very well out of the wedding and the extra drinks that were bought at the bar. Most of the wedding guests had gone home, apart from a few. Steve and Pete had stayed for a couple of more drinks, and some friends of Philip and Patrick's.

The dining room was closed tonight, the waiting staff were clearing up afterwards. Any meal orders were being served at the bar.

It was 11.30 and Caitlin, Matthew and two of the bar staff, Adam and Simon were clearing away glasses and tidying up, ready for the next day. They had quite a few Sunday lunch bookings. The pub was doing really well, considering they were new tenants but then it had always done well and was at the heart of the community.

Adam and Simon said their goodnights and off they went. They weren't due back until Tuesday. They had been asked to come in extra as the BBC news were coming to make a film about the discoveries that had been uncovered.

Matthew was tucked up in bed and out like a light when Caitlin got into bed beside him. They were both really tired. She lightly kissed him on top of his head and lay down. Strangely enough, they hadn't heard any sounds for a few nights. Caitlin was just closing her eyes when she thought she heard singing.

'Ring-a-ring-rosies a pocket full of posies'.

She looked up at the ceiling and there was a sound of a pitter patter of feet.

'Ha, ha, ha!'

The attic was directly above their bedroom. That was where the old bunk beds were, which must have been where the children had slept.

Caitlin knew she wasn't dreaming. These occurrences had happened to often; nothing frightening had happened so far. Ghosts couldn't hurt you, can they?

Caitlin closed her eyes and when she opened them, she was lying in an old-fashioned bunkbed bundled with blankets to keep her warm.

She sat up and she was in an attic dormitory with other children. She felt her hair and ran her hands down her chest where her breasts would have been but were no longer there. She looked at her hands in the moonlight and they were those of a child. There was a mirror on the wall, and she got down and looked at herself. She was a child again.

"You'll get into trouble if they realise you are out of bed Caitlin," a small voice whispered quietly.

"Who are you?"

"What do you mean who am I? I am your friend Emily."

"Emily?"

"Yes, why are you acting weird, you look like you have seen a ghost?"

"What am I doing? Where am I?"

"Well, where do you think you are? You are in the dorm with all your other friends."

"Dorm?"

"Yes, in the orphanage!"

"What orphanage?"

"Sleathwaite silly, we were playing 'ring-a-ring-a-rosies' half an hour ago. We got into trouble because it was after lights out, remember?"

"No."

A boy looked up from his bunk.

"What's all the whispering?"

"Who are you?"

Matthew looked at her in disbelief.

"What? Matthew."

Emily looked up at him. "Ignore her she is being weird," said Emily.

"Matthew, err, what?"

"Caitlin, get back into bed and stop being silly. We don't want them coming up again or we could get the strap!"

"Who, the what?"

"Mr and Mrs Mayhew. Now lie down and be quiet."

"Emily, what year is it?"

"1914, now go to sleep."

"Can't be," said Caitlin, confused and climbing up to her bunk.

"It is. Be quiet and stop being silly," another voice answered.

They heard footsteps on the attic stairs. They lay down and pretended to be asleep.

Thomas Mayhew sighed and quietly opened the door. The children seemed to be asleep.

'I must be hearing things,' he thought.

He had the cane in his hand. He wasn't being mean to the children but it being 1914, it had been drilled into him that children should be seen and not heard, and that bad behaviour should be met with discipline.

Caitlin tried to get to sleep but her blankets and sheets were scratchy. She finally drifted off. Strangely, the attic room looked surprisingly familiar.

The next morning, she awoke to a bell being rung.

"Must be the burglar alarm," she said to herself sleepily.

"Matthew?"

"What now? It's breakfast time. You had better get dressed quick."

"Into what?"

"Your school pinafore and smock."

"What, I am still here?"

"Course you are. Where else would you be, until someone comes for you?"

"What do you mean?"

"Future adoptive parents," he said, handing over her clothes.

They walked down the stairs to the dining room. Caitlin thought she must be dreaming. The place did look very familiar and Matthew and Emily, well she knew them from somewhere else.

Emmeline Mayhew was ushering the children into the dining room.

"Come along children, you all have morning prayer and Sunday school to go to, hurry please."

There were long trestle tables with seating either side. And bowls and spoons were placed along the centre of the table.

"What are we having Emily? What is in those jugs?"

"Porridge shush."

"Less talking please."

A teenage girl was serving the porridge to the children.

"Urrgh, looks like slop!" said Caitlin. "Excuse me miss. I don't like this; I want some honey in mine at least."

Emmeline Mayhew came along and stood opposite Caitlin.

"Miss Caitlin, eat your breakfast. We don't have honey. Don't you know there is a war on?"

"I always have honey on mine. I am not eating it and why are
you calling me 'miss'?"

"You don't and you are! We can't afford to waste food and do not
answer back to me!"

Thomas wandered over. "And what is going on here?"

"Caitlin, she's playing up and won't eat her food."

"Caitlin do what Mrs Mayhew has asked you or you will be sent
to the dorm for the rest of the day, with no food."

Matthew whispered to her. "Do as they say."

"I won't and I am not eating that yuk!"

"Right quite enough from you Miss Caitlin, up to the dorm," said
Thomas. She leaned towards Matthew.

"Just go, or it will get worse," said Matthew.

"You had better listen to your friend, thank you Master Matthew."

"I won't!"

"Won't what?"

Caitlin opened her eyes.

"Master Matthew," she said sleepily.

"Master what? well, you can call me 'master' if you like?"

"What weren't you going to do? You've been tossing and turning all night.

"I had a very strange dream."

"Oh, are you going to tell me about it?"

"I was going to sleep last night; this bit is reality; and I heard singing."

"Singing?"

"Singing, yes, it was children singing ring-a-ring-a-rosies and there
was a pitter patter of feet above us," she said pointing to the ceiling.

"You had too much Prosecco yesterday."

"No, I didn't. Anyway, I lay down and went to sleep and when I
woke up, I was in an attic dormitory with other children, and I was
a child again. I got up and looked at myself in the mirror, and there
was a girl called Emily saying that I would get into trouble if I didn't
get back into bed. I didn't know where I was and then this boy called
Matthew, told me to be quiet. Apparently we had got told off for playing ring-a-ring-a-rosies after lights out."

"Matthew, Emily?"

"Yes, they looked like you and Emily Mayhew only about six years old. I didn't know where I was and kept asking questions, they said I was in an orphanage, and it was 1914. I couldn't get to sleep because of the scratchy blankets. And when I finally woke up, I was being woken up by a school bell, I thought it was the burglar alarm. This boy Matthew was my friend and he told me to get dressed quickly, I didn't know what I was to wear, and he said my pinafore and smock.

We were ushered into the dining room and told to sit down. Emmeline and Thomas Mayhew were supervising. We were going to have breakfast and go for morning prayer and Sunday School.

There was a teenage girl serving watery porridge and I said I wouldn't eat it and not without honey in it. Mrs Mayhew said we didn't eat honey and that there was a war on. I said that I would not eat it and that it was yuk. She said not to answer back. Matthew told me to do as they said. Mr Mayhew was going to take me to the dormitory in the attic to be alone all day without food and that is when I said I wouldn't eat the porridge."

"Well, that was quite a dream. You have a very vivid imagination."

"I did hear the singing though."

"Course you did, *cuckoo*!" mocked Matthew.

"Look, I know that that bit probably was true as I too have heard voices and singing."

"Really?"

"Yes, as for the dream, it was just a story in your head based on the events that have happened."

"I was here, in my dream."

"Yes, and now I have made you breakfast," he said, grinning.

"What have you made and why are you grinning?"

"It's porridge!" he said, laughing, and before you ask. "Yes it has honey in it."

They went into the kitchen and Matthew spooned the porridge into bowls, he had kept it on a low heat.

"Yum! This is delicious Matthew."

"It's homemade."

"I have a very clever husband."

"Not as clever as you academically, but I can cook."

"I should hope so, given that you are a chef."

Chapter 15

It was Tuesday afternoon, and the pub was filled with noise and activity. The BBC had come to film about the old orphanage, and it was going to be shown on national and local news.

There were a lot of visitors in the garden and conservatory; having got wind of the BBC coming. It was a good thing that they had brought in extra staff.

The production team was there, setting up equipment, making sure the lighting and sound was right and that the cameras were all set up.

Matthew and Caitlin were behind the bar when news reporters turned up from Look North and the Six O'clock News.

They had been taken through what was going to be discussed and where they were going to film. They were going to film in the bar, cellar, up in the bedroom and landing and the attic. All the old memorabilia which were found in the attic were on display on a table in the bar.

It was four o'clock and filming was ready to begin.

"Ready to roll in one, two, three, lights, camera, action!" someone shouted.

"Good afternoon, I am standing in the Sleathwaite Arms in the village of Sleathwaite. The village sits in the Tyne Valley between Corbridge and Hexham in Northumberland. The reason we are here today is that the tenants of this pub have made some fascinating discoveries. In fact in 1914 this building was opened as an orphanage by a Mr Thomas and Emmeline Mayhew. Right, first can we start with Matthew, Landlord?"

"What were the first curious happenings you discovered?"

"We had only been living here for a few weeks and nothing strange had happened, but then one Saturday morning I came down and a chair had been moved in front of the fire, as if someone had been warming their feet. A glass had been left on top of the bar and the cellar door was open. The bar hadn't been left like that the night before and nobody could get in as it was all locked up. Anyway, I went to close the cellar door but then thought we needed some stock for the bar, so I tried the light switch, and it didn't work, so I replaced it. The next morning, I came down and the door was open again, we have both heard noises, but Caitlin heard more than I did."

"Caitlin, what can you tell us?"

"Well on the weekend Matthew was talking about, we went into the cellar to get some stock out. I took longer, and Matthew was wondering what I was doing there?" She paused.

"What were you doing?"

"I had found some old dusty boxes in the corner of the cellar and thought that we must have missed some boxes, because we just piled everything in there when we moved in."

"And what did you find?"

"They are over on this table."

"This is very interesting. There is an old admittance book for all of the orphans, a prospectus and a punishment book, as well as all of these toys, an old doll, a plane, a teddy bear, games, books etc."

The cameraman moved in close to film all of the items.

"I see an old school cap, an exercise book and a metal hula hoop with a stick to control it, I saw one of these at Beamish."

"We found those in the attic, along with a load of bunk beds. We think that is where they slept. I have heard footsteps across the landing and above our bedroom the other night I could hear laughing and singing 'a-ring-a-ring-a-rosies'. I fell asleep and the next moment I found myself in a dormitory with other children. In my dream, Matthew and Emily were there. They looked about six years old! I am a historian and so, I was immediately interested. I have been to the library at Hexham and the city Library in Newcastle to discover more information. I have made a report on my findings which I hope to get published. It turns out that our local vicar Tom Mayhew is the great grandson of the founders. He and his wife Emily are here."

"Hello Tom, Emily, so how did you feel when this was discovered?"

"Well, I knew my ancestors were educators in some way, but I didn't see the connection, Caitlin asked if she could come around and look at our family tree and lo and behold there they were listed -Thomas and Emmeline Mayhew! I grew up here and never realised that this had been an orphanage."

"And do you have your family tree here with you?"

"Yes," said Tom, unrolling it on the nearest table. He showed them the family birth line. The cameraman moved in for a closer look.

"And it is also a coincidence that you yourself Emily have the modern version of the name Emmeline?"

"Yes, curious, isn't it?"

"Do you think you could have a family connection in some way?"

"Not that I know of – I also grew up here and went to the same school as Tom. My family mainly came from a medical background, but I have not had my family tree traced, it might be an idea to do so."

The film crew filmed around the bar, talking to some of the more senior villagers but a lot of them were small children at around the time the orphanage closed in 1948. They then proceeded to the cellar, up to the landing and into the attic.

Matthew and Caitlin were up there with them.

"The attic is directly above our bedroom," said Caitlin. I heard the footsteps on this landing and up above us in the attic."

"And laughter and singing?" added the reporter.

"Yes, this is the way to the attic," said Caitlin, leading the way.

They climbed some steps. The reporter faced the camera.

"We are now standing in what we believe to be the children's dormitory."

Matthew lifted the cover off the old metal bunk beds.

"And you found these?"

"Yes, when I came up to store some of our boxes."

"Well, this has all been fascinating and thank you both for allowing us to come and film here."

"Thank you," said Caitlin. "It's been a pleasure."

"Yes, thank you very much," said Matthew. "How about a drink and some sandwiches?"

"That would go down very nicely thank you."

They went down to the bar. The camera was still rolling. Simon the barman was pulling some pints for the crew.

The reporter turned to the camera and said, "Well that is it from here in Sleathwaite, reporting for BBC news." He raised his glass.

There was cheering and clapping from behind him.

The crew cleared away their equipment and the BBC vans drove away.

At six o'clock Matthew and Caitlin were in the bar and turned on the news. There on national and local news was their pub and Caitlin and Matthew were on screen.

"This is so weird," said Matthew. "We are famous – autographs this way please."

"Shush, don't let it go to your head, but it is weird seeing our home and ourselves on screen.

At the vicarage, Tom and Emily also had the news on.

"You know Tom. I think I will look into having my family tree traced. We may have family connections."

"You never know," he said.

"Are you famous now?" asked John

"No, but you can address me as Sir if you wish."

"What?"

"He's pulling your leg John," said Emily.

"Did you get paid for it?" asked Jamie.

"No sweetheart," said Emily.

"Well, you should have had a fee for public speaking."

"They didn't say that much, you div," said John.

"Hey, enough," warned Tom.

The next lunch time they were busy with meal orders and serving drinks at the bar. Matthew had been up early preparing his specials; and they had proven popular as he had put them on a meal deal special of-fer. He only did this occasionally as a promotion. Caitlin was just about to walk into the dining room with some plates when the phone rang.

"Here, Si, take these through will you, while I answer the phone, table six."

"Sure, said Simon hurrying off with the plates.

'He's a hard worker that one,' thought Caitlin.

"Good afternoon, The Hadrian, do you have a reservation?"

"Oh, hello, no I don't, could I speak to Caitlin Turner please."

"Speaking."

"My name is Stephen Watkins and I work for the BBC."

"Oh," said Caitlin, surprised.

"Yes, I work for their archives and research department and organise contracts and freelance work for writers, historians, people like yourself."

"Yes," said Caitlin.

"After yesterday's news we have looked at your work that has been published and your dissertation which was posted online. Your work is exceptional, and we would like to meet with you at your local BBC TV Centre in Newcastle to discuss work possibilities."

"That sounds fantastic."

"I understand Romans and artefacts are your speciality. We are hoping to cover your area in a documentary. Would you be willing to help research and present some of the program?"

"I would love to."

"We will pay you per piece of work you do, and you can work from home, you don't have to come to London unless we have any future documentaries here."

"Great!"

"There is one other thing…"

"Yes?"

"I know that you have just had BBC news there, but we have a new series starting called "Historical buildings." They would also like to come and film, with your permission of course. Our archives team are interested in looking back at the building before the orphanage opened and see what other discoveries they come up with."

"It all sounds very good and will bring in a lot more trade. I am interested in the meeting and the work, but I will have to discuss this with my husband."

"That is absolutely fine, I understand."

"I am more than sure he will support me, but I need to run it by him first."

"Right if you give me your email address, I will send you the details."

"Okay."

She gave him the email address and hoped it hadn't been a hoax call.

Half an hour later her phone beeped with a notification from Gmail and there was the email. It also said some details would come by post once she had filled in the online application form.

Later on, when it was quiet, she looked at her emails. She and Matthew were upstairs having a break, sitting at the dining table.

"You look fit to burst – got something to tell me?"

She told him all her news.

"Wow, that is fantastic."

"You don't mind."

"Not at all, a lot of the time you work from home anyway when you have assignments, it won't be any different."

"It could be a lot of work."

"Well, you have never been afraid of hard work, and as for the documentary series thing it will bring in extra trade, especially when we get the guesthouse side of things sorted. The news bulletin has already brought more meal bookings."

"But when I do get work, I may not have a lot of time to help in the bar and restaurant."

"Just do what you can, when you can. This is too big an opportunity to waste, for both of us," he said, coming around the other side of the table and putting his arms around her. "Caitlin, your career was put on hold a bit when we came here."

"I didn't mind. We were trying to get this place sorted."

"Let me finish, history is your passion. It is what gets your adrenalin up with excitement. Go for it, you have my blessing; just as long as I am your passion too," he added, nuzzling into her neck.

"Ooh, well of course landlord."

"Fancy taking this to somewhere more comfortable?" she said, loosening his belt and undoing his trousers.

He stood up and took his top off and threw it over the chair and started undressing her. Minutes later they were standing stark naked in the bedroom, leaving a trail of clothes behind them.

Caitlin lay down on the bed and Matthew lay down, practically on top of her.

They kissed passionately.

Caitlin gave a moan of pure excitement and relaxation. He had reached a very sensual part. The next thing they were combined as one interlocked and not wanting to let each other go.

Chapter 16

James was feeling exhausted. He was worried about Cameron, even though he was making some progress and was relieved a little bit, but for some reason he couldn't quite put his finger on, he felt tense and restless. He was finding it hard to concentrate and felt he was snapping at those who were most dear to him.

He stood staring out of the sitting room window, not really looking at anything in particular. The views were majestic; open countryside for miles and miles. Yet on this occasion he didn't see it.

It was the day of Cameron's class coming to visit the farm and he thought he had better pull himself together. It gave him a focus and he enjoyed conducting visits with students and school children, especially little ones.

He was expecting them for about ten thirty that morning and he had got everything prepared and organised. It was a lovely sunny morning and that raised his spirits.

They had a busy week ahead and Rachael's parents were coming up to spend half term with them. They were going to help out with the children, and they were all going to get together for a meal with James's parents.

The school visit was a nice ending for the children ready for half term.

He heard tyres on the road outside, the school bus was pulling up.

The teacher was accompanied by two teaching assistants and two parent volunteers.

"Hello Mr Macalister, nice to see you again."

"Oh, James please."

"James, Cameron has been excited all morning. He is very proud we are coming here for a visit."

"Hasn't been too boisterous, has he?"

"No, not at all."

"Daddy!" said Cameron, rushing up to him.

"Hi Cam, are you going to help me with my talks and tours?"

"Yes."

"Just as long as you realise that the other children haven't been here before, and they need to have the opportunity to try some of the things you do."

"I know dad, I promise I'll be good."

"Right Miss Haslem, I thought I could give a tour of the farm on my trailer first and then we can go and feed the lambs and the hens. We can have lunch in the orchard and then they can see how Cam and I round the sheep up. How does that sound?"

"Sounds good to me; gives them a chance to do some numeracy."

"That's what I thought. That's what we do with our two." The tractor is parked over there if you want to get them organised and follow me."

The children were organised into pairs and had to hold hands down the road.

"Right children, up onto the trailer and sit in your pairs please."

"I normally sit in the tractor next to Dad," said Cameron.

"Just go with your partner Cameron please. You can show Bill your lovely farm," said Miss Haslem.

"Yes, come on Bill, said Cameron. "Sit next to me. I will be your guide."

"Cool," said Bill.

After everyone was seated James started the ignition. He took a deep breath. He had to do this for Cameron and his friends.

The tractor and trailer started to move down the road, he drove slowly around pointing out the animals, their breeds and where they originated from. They drove past the goats and the duck pond, past the horses and he pulled up by the lambing shed which was adjacent to where the hens lived.

"Right, everyone follow me to the lambing shed please," said James.

They all went into the lambing shed. The children and the adults gathered around the animals. They sat on bales of hay behind the barriers.

"Right children, my lambs are hungry and need feeding. Cameron and I will show you how we feed them and then each of you can have a go, okay?"

"Yes!" they all cheered.

"Right, we have some bottles of milk and some feed. Cameron you show them how much feed we measure into the cup."

"We only fill it up to the right level on the cup, the cup has numbers on, and I fill it up to 25 which is the same as 25 grams. I pour it into the cup like this, up to the mark and then I pour it onto my hand. I have to be careful not to spill too much," he said spilling a little. "Oh, no."

"Never mind Cameron," said Miss Haslem. "You are doing well, carry on," she said encouragingly. "Come around and show each of your classmates so they can see where to fill it to."

Cameron showed them the mark.

"When I feed the lambs, I keep my hand flat and upright, like this. Remember to keep your thumb in," he said, laughing. "They might think it is food!"

James held onto the lamb and Cameron held out his hand.

"He's hungry!" said Cameron.

The children laughed with pleasure.

"Right, you will find some sacks of feed on the other side of railings. You can each have a go at feeding them. Cameron, you can show them what to do and where the feed is please. I'll keep the lambs still as they are being fed."

"Bill, you're first in line. Cameron, you help him."

"Ooh! it tickles my hand."

"Now children, what do we have to remember when we are feeding animals?" asked Miss Haslem.

A show of hands went up.

"Yes Jasmine?"

"You aren't supposed to put your hands near your mouth or face, and you should always remember to wash them afterwards."

"Yes, very good, well done. Now remember you are measuring grams. The cup holds a 100 grams, and we are feeding them 25 grams. Who knows what the fraction is of the 100 grams?"

The children looked thoughtful. A boy put his hand up shyly. "Yes Niall?"

"Is it twenty-five?"

"Yes, good, but in fractions what is that twenty-five worth, imagine a cake cut into four pieces."

"I know, I know!"

"Okay, Daniel what do you think the answer is?"

"Is it a quarter?"

"Yes, well done, it is a quarter."

Each of the children had a go at feeding the lambs and were then going to have a go at bottle feeding them.

James stood in front of the children and tried to get their attention. They were very excited. The staff settled them down, Cameron sat down on a bale with his friends.

James clapped his hands together. "Right, children, next they need some milk. Why do you think that is?"

"To make them stronger!"

"Yes, what else."

"They are thirsty!"

"Yes, they get thirsty just like we do, but can anyone think of why they need this milk?"

All went quiet, and then a girl put her hand up.

"Yes, what's your name?"

"Jess. They need to have healthy bones."

"Bingo, well done."

"They need to have healthy bones. Now, when I stopped by the cows I asked if any of you knew where milk comes from, can you remember."

"Tesco's" said a boy.

"Well yes, but where does it come from before it gets to Tesco's?"

"The farm."

"Yes, and it comes from the…? Anyone?"

"THE COW!" They shouted excitedly.

"Yes! Well, done," said James.

He felt his hand being nudged.

"Oh!"

The lamb was trying to get at the bottle.

"He's hungry!" Cameron shouted and they laughed.

"Now, when we are feeding them, we don't tip it too much because we don't want them to choke or get wind. Just hold it like this but try not to let them guzzle it too much or they may get belly ache."

"This one's a feisty one."

Each of the children had a go at bottle feeding and then it was time to feed the hens and collect any eggs.

"Right children, we are going over to the hen shed. Now James here says that you can help feed them and any eggs will be put into egg boxes of six, (more numeracy). This way," said Miss Haslem.

They all filed out and over to the hens and Cameron showed them how he collected the eggs that were left and how they stored them in the egg boxes, being careful not to break any. They each then had a go with the feed.

After all that it was time for lunch and the children got back into the trailer and James drove them up to the orchard where they all sat down to a packed lunch.

The children enjoyed having a picnic in the orchard.

Cameron shyly sat down with Bill and a few others sat with them, with a teaching assistant.

"You're so lucky Cameron," said a boy called Reuben.

"Must be hard work though eh," said Matthew.

"I enjoy it, I don't think of it as work, it is where we live."

"Well said Cameron," said the teaching assistant.

"Don't you have the internet here or an Xbox, must be boring without that."

"We have the internet, and we also have a Wii."

"Oh, I have one of those," said Sienna. "What's your favourite game?"

"Sonic Hedgehog. Do you want to see it?" said Cameron, standing up.

"Err, not now Cameron, this is still a school day," said Jac the teaching assistant. "Sit back down please."

"Don't you have Call of Duty? Sonic is babyish," said Matthew.

"Enough thank you Matthew. You are too young for that game anyway," said Jac reproachful. "I am surprised you are allowed it?"

After lunch they let the children have a run around. They had brought a football and played some ball games.

After their time in the orchard, James returned and took them to see the sheep next.

"Right Miss Haslem, I am going to get Cameron to help me with moving the sheep like we discussed. I think the children would like to see it."

"Of course, yes, what do you want me to do?"

"I need you all to stand back, at the top of the field, you can see what is going on from there, just over by the gate."

"Okay, I will get them organised."

The class and teaching staff walked up to the fence and stood by the gate.

Cameron stayed with his Dad.

"Right, Cameron, just forget they are there and concentrate on the sheep, okay, just like you always do?"

"Okay Daddy," said Cameron, a little nervously.

Kim and Sammy were in the tractor and came bounding out. They nearly knocked poor Cameron over with excitement when they saw him.

James blew his whistle, and they knew it was time to work.

"Come by!" Come by!" shouted James, beckoning to the sheep, and the dogs ran around trying to gather them up. Cameron struggled a bit with the rope on the gate but then he realised that his Dad had loosened it a little. He held the gate open proudly and the dogs herded the sheep in. James shut the gate and put the rope over and pulled.

They heard clapping at the top of the field and walked up with the dogs. They were pleased to see the children, and they came and patted them.

"That was most impressive James, well done Cameron," said Miss Haslem. "Right children, I think you all have something to say to Mr Macalister and Cameron."

"Thank you, Mr McCalister, thanks Cam!"

"Thank you for a lovely day. The children really enjoyed it. The office will be in touch about the payment."

"It was all a pleasure."

"Dad, can't I stay here?"

"No Cammy, you have after school club, your mum is picking you up later, I have work to do."

"Okay!"

"You did well though son, see you later."

"Yes, very well done to you Cameron," said Miss Haslem. "I was impressed."

They all got on the bus, excited about their day.

It was finally Friday and the last day of term before the holidays. The children were excited for their last day and the week off school ahead of them.

James had been up with the larks and was sitting in the kitchen having a morning brew. Everyone else was out.

'Don't know why but I feel so tired,' he thought.

He had been working very hard lately, getting the farm prepared for harvest and the coming winter. He had a small team of farm hands to help him. There was himself and four others, one being a student who was doing agricultural studies who came one day a week from college and helped out during the holidays.

"Meow! Meow!"

"Hello Alfie." His cat jumped onto James's knee and nuzzled into him.

He cuddled him in, and the cat started purring and kneading his legs trying to get comfy. At six months old, he was still a kitten and loved to play. He saw the toggle hanging down from James' hoody and pulled with it.

He was glad to have a few moments to himself. He had found it stressful lately on the farm and it was taking its toll. At the beginning of September there had been the incident where his sheep had been savaged by a dog. The police hadn't found out who the owner was; but the boundary to the farm had been made secure with a new fence, so animals couldn't get in or out.

There had been another incident when some of his crops had caught alight from the burning September sun. Bush fires were popular abroad, but not so much in Britain. Luckily, the fire brigade was quick in responding. And he had tried to put it out himself before it spread right across the farm.

Obviously, he and Rachael both worked long hours, but they always tried to make time for the children. Apart from the long weekend they had down to Hebden to see Rachael's parents they hadn't been away for a family holiday for a while. The children had stayed there with their Grandparents for a couple of weeks in the Summer holidays.

He was glad they were coming up and that they were going to have some days out, and 'maybe go up to the Lakes for the day. The farm hands could manage on their own for a while.' He was thinking about taking on a relief farm manager, but this would depend on whether he could afford it. He would have to look at the accounts with his accountant. It would have to be someone he could trust, then at least he could spend some time away on holidays with the family.

His dad tried to help out where he could with the farm, doing light tasks and looking after the children. His parents helped when they could, but they were getting on in age and he didn't like putting too much onto them. They both had some health issues.

He finished his tea and thought he had better get back to work. He walked out into the Autumn sun. He felt a little better for taking a break. Often, he didn't bother and worked straight through till lunch time, but today he felt he needed it.

They were expecting George and Marian that afternoon. They were arriving at teatime.

He got on with his jobs and instructed the farm hands what he wanted done that afternoon. Before he knew it, it was time to get Cameron and Scarlett from school.

They piled into the car and Cameron struggled with his seat belt. James was feeling tired and a bit irritable.

"Oh! Cameron! just for once can't you manage to strap yourself in!" shouted James.

"I am trying!" said Cameron tearfully.

James immediately felt guilty. He knew Cameron struggled with this and was doing his best to complete tasks but sometimes when he was tired, he insisted, saying he couldn't do it, even though he had managed to do the same thing before.

"Oh Cam, I am sorry. I didn't mean to make you cry. Daddy's just tired and had a hard day. I am sorry, I shouldn't have taken it out on you."

"Dad! that was mean," said Scarlett, putting her arm around her brother.

"Look, I am very sorry, okay? Scarlett, can you help him please?"

"Yes of course."

Cameron wiped his tears away. He adored his Dad and didn't understand why he had shouted at him like that.

"I want Mammy!" he said.

"Let's get you both home, Mammy might be home when we get back and Grandma and Grandad are coming soon," said James. "Tell you what. Why don't we stop off and buy some ice lollies at the shop in the village?" asked James, feeling like he wanted to make things better.

"Okay," said Cameron, red in the face.

They got to the shop and Scarlett had the job of going to the counter and getting the ice creams.

"Right Scarlett, if I give you a ten-pound note and these two ice creams cost £2.50 each, how much change do I get?"

"Erm," said Scarlett thinking.

"Come on! What is £2.50 plus £2.50?"

"Oh, five pounds."

"Yes, good, so how much change do I get?"

"Oh of course five pounds."

"Yes! I don't know why you didn't work that out sooner! Now get served, quickly please!"

"Dad! Sorry, keep your voice down people are looking," said Scarlett.

Cameron had wandered over to look at the comics.

"Cam, come here please, you are not getting a comic as well."

"I want one!"

"Well, we can't always have what we want, and you just had one the other day. To the car please, Scarlett come on."

"All right I'm coming."

They stepped outside the shop.

"Cameron hold my hand."

"No!"

"Look you have to be careful and use your eyes. You nearly stepped in front of a car!"

"You're a meanie!"

They pulled into the driveway at home and two other cars were there. Rachael was standing talking to her parents. They had both arrived together. Cameron saw them and tugged at his seatbelt.

"Scarlett, help, please."

"Just press the red button Cam, see?" she said, gently putting his finger on the button.

Cameron pushed down.

"I can't!"

"Here let me," said Scarlett. "It's okay," she soothed when his eyes filled with tears again.

Scarlett was first out. "Grandma, Grandad!" she ran up to them for hugs.

Cameron stepped out the car with a pep lip.

"Mammy! Daddy was being mean to me!" he wailed, tears falling down his little face.

All three of them looked up at Cameron. Rachael ran up to him standing by the car.

"Oh Cam, what's wrong honey?"

"I couldn't do me seat belt and Dad shouted at me and then he yelled at Scarlett in the shop for not working out her sum quick xlyx enough! and he wouldn't buy me a comic!" he wailed.

She bent down and drew him in for a hug.

"How about some Juice and a biscuit? Grandma and Grandad are here, look."

He looked up at them tearfully and smiled.

"We have ice lollies. That's what I was trying to work out," said Scarlett. "Dad did apologise to Cammy but then I got yelled at as well."

"Take your brother in ter kitchen please Scarlett."

"Yes, come on Cam."

James got out of the car.

"Cam, Cameron, come here when I am speaking to you!" shouted James.

Cameron walked into the house holding his sister's hand.

"Look, I said I was sorry. Oh, I feel guilty now."

"So, you should," said Rachael glaring at him.

Marian and George looked shocked.

George stepped forward. "Look I don't know what is going on, but I don't like seeing t'kids upset."

"Don't tha thinks he has enough to deal with?" asked Marian.

"Mum, Dad, can you please go and see that t'kids are okay, I need to talk to James."

"Okay love," said George leading Marian into the house.

"So, what on earth was that all about? God knows what my parents are thinking!"

"I… I…"

"Well?"

"I am sorry! Okay?" said James rubbing his eyes and shaking his head in shame. Normally, he was such a gentle patient person.

"They are only kids and no it is not okay, so stop shouting. Now, are you going to tell me what has got into you?"

"I suppose I am tired, and everything is getting a bit much, what with the farm and us working long hours. We don't see enough of each other, we're like ships that pass in the night. I shouldn't have taken it out on the kids. Everything is just getting on top of me," he sighed.

"James, this isn't like you, I thought you were happy living here on t' farm with me and t'kids? Are you saying you want out?"

"No, of course not! I love it here and you and the kids, are all that matter to me."

"Well, what then? I have noticed that you have been quite tense lately."

"It's just what with the sheep being savaged and then the fire; but most of all I am worried about Cameron. I am so mortified; it won't ever happen again."

"Good, look maybe we need to spend more time together as a family. I suppose things have been hectic lately. Mum and Dad are here; they can help out and we can have some days out."

"Yes, I was thinking of the Lake District for an outing."

"You know I love lakes, but James you need to talk to me about stuff like this."

"I know, I didn't want to admit anything was wrong."

"Do you want me ter give up work?"

"What no, of course not, you love your work!"

"Well, I could help you out around here?"

"No, you are not giving that up for me, I won't let you, it's who you are, helping people."

"Family is more important."

"Yes, but no, we can work it out."

"Let's get this week over and then when Mum and Dad have gone, we can make some plans about the farm, okay?"

"Yes, I was thinking about taking on a relief manager, so we can have some holidays."

"That would be nice."

"If we can afford it, or one of the lads might be interested in a promotion, I need to speak to the accountant, but things are tickin' over quite nicely. It has been a bit full on lately. I guess it just tiredness."

"James, do you feel depressed?"

"No, No, but I do feel quite stressed at the moment."

"Do you want to talk to anyone professionally?"

"No, just you, I am not mad, if things are getting out of my control then I will, but hopefully we can make things better. I will make it up to the kids. Now come here for a hug."

"I love yer James."

"I love you Rach and our children and this place."

"We are lucky you know James."

"I know," he said, putting his arm around her and walking towards the cottage.

"God knows what your Mam and Dad think of me."

"Don't worry, I will talk to them. They were probably surprised, it isn't in your nature."

They entered the farmhouse and walked into the kitchen. Cameron was sitting on his Grandma's knee having a cuddle and eating his lolly. Grandma's cuddles were special. They looked up.

"Got everything sorted then, has tha?" asked George.

"We were worried, it isn't like you James," said Marian

"Yes, I know, I am very sorry," said James. "It won't happen again."

"Cameron come here please," asked James gently.

"No!"

"Hey, go and see Daddy," said Marian gently trying to move him off her knee.

"No!"

James bent down in front of them.

"Can I have a lick?"

"Only if you're good, you were naughty!"

"Yes, yes I was, Daddy was naughty," he said, smiling and gently tickling him. Cameron got off his Grandma's knee and let his Dad hug him. He stroked his curly head. And then stole a lick of his ice lolly.

"Hey, I haven't said yes yet."

"Cameron, I am so sorry, I love you and I should be supporting you instead of shouting at you. I won't speak to you like that again, am I forgiven?"

"Umm, well only if you buy me an Xbox. Daniel has one."

"Oh, bribery and corruption. We'll see."

Scarlett was sat at the table quietly devouring what was left of her ice lolly. James walked around to her and gave her a hug and stroked her hair.

"Sorry love, I shouldn't have embarrassed you like that in the shop."

"That's okay. Just don't shout at us, especially when we have done nothing wrong; and in public, it was embarrassing Dad."

"I know."

"Marian, George, welcome. I know that it wasn't the welcome you were expecting, and I am sorry."

"That's all right son," said George, shaking his hand. "Glad yer-got it sorted."

"It's fine, just as long as yer are treating my daughter and grankids properly," said Marian. "We realise yer must have had a hard day."

"Of course," assured James.

"He does Mum."

"Look, I am going for a shower before dinner," said James.

"Good idea, you stink!" laughed Rachael.

He padded up the stairs and felt ashamed of what had happened in the last hour. He was determined to put a brave face on it and en-joy half term.

Downstairs, Rachael was starting to prepare tea. The kids had gone off to the sitting room to watch television.

George and Marian looked at each other and nodded. After for-ty years of marriage, they knew each other well enough to work out what the other was thinking.

"Rachael, love," started Marian.

"Are you two having problems?" asked George.

"No, no of course not," she said, looking up from peeling vegetables.

"You can talk to us tha know," said Marian.

"We are fine, honest. I've got ter get tea on!"

"Didn't look that way when James arrived with t'bairns," said George.

"Look, that can wait. I'm yer Mam aren't I. yer can tell me any-thing. We're both here ters upport yer."

"Mum, Dad, you may as well know, especially since you are stay-ing for the week."

"What?" asked Marian concerned.

"Let the lass speak love."

"Over last few weeks I have noticed that James has been a bit tense, snapping at us and not being able to concentrate on things;

just little things, but he has never lost his temper with the kids, ever. Outside, he said that everything was getting too much for him and that he needed some space. I thought he meant he wanted out of our marriage but with past events on t'farm such as savaged sheep, t'fire and also being worried about Cameron, he thinks we aren't getting enough time together to do things and go on holidays."

"You both work hard love," said George.

"And long hours," added Marian. "Is he depressed?"

"No, he assures me of that, but he is very stressed. I asked if he wanted to talk to a professional about it, but he said he will do that if things get out of control."

"Poor James," said Marian, concerned for her son-in-law.

"Is there anything we can do to help? Wit t'farm or t'kids, ," asked George .

"Just offer support to James. The last thing he needs is being treated like an outcast."

"Rachael! We would never do that," said Marian. "We have always treated him as family."

"I know I just …"

"Are you okay love? We are concerned about you all."

"We are fine. We are going to take it one step at a time and work through things. We are thinking about getting a relief farm manager if we can afford ter, so at least it will take some pressure off James, and we might at least get ter go on holiday sometime, which is a rarity these days. James's Mum and Dad help out when they can, but they are getting on a bit now and he doesn't like ter depend on them too much."

"How are they," asked Marian.

"They're doing okay. They still have health issues. You will see them tomorrow night. We are going out for a meal with them."

"Well, none of us are getting any younger, be good to catch up wi' old Jack."

"You do all right Dad. You're in your prime."

"Yer as old as yer feels", said Marian. "Maybe you will let me, and your Dad babysit one night, so you and James can go out for dinner. I bet it's been a while since you've been out on yer own?" said Marian.

"Yeah, that would be nice. Let's see how t'week goes."

"It'll be our treat," said George.

Chapter 17

It was the middle of half term and the week was flying. It was still quite warm for October, and Autumn was definitely here, with the leaves falling off the trees and the gardens dying off.

The village was becoming very busy with holidaymakers, visitors and school children.

The village children were excited for Halloween and bonfire night. There was always a village Halloween party at the community centre, which catered for adults and children. The River Tyne at Hexham always had a firework display.

Winter would be on its way soon and then Christmas. The shops were already starting to promote Christmas. The village still had visitors even then. The pub offered bed and breakfast and the local farm rented out their small cottage which was on site.

Today the village was bustling with people. It was Market day which always did well. Brookfield farm provided stocks for local stalls and the local farm shop, which had just opened up as a coffee shop. Business was good and they sold cakes, scones etc; all sourced locally.

It was lunchtime and Rick Seddon was coming out of the fish and chip shop carrying the family's lunch. It smelt delicious.

Today was moving day for the family. They had moved from Manchester and had only just arrived that morning, along with a lorry load of belongings.

They had arrived at about eleven a.m. They had only been in the village a couple of hours, but unpacking was hard work.

He reached his Citroen and got inside the car. He put the chips on the passenger seat and then put the key in the ignition and started the engine. He was thinking of everything there was to do. He didn't start his new job for a couple of weeks so that gave him time to get the house fixed up.

They had moved into a terraced house across the road from the vicarage and obviously hadn't had a chance to meet the neighbours properly yet. But the people on the left of them had said hello and welcomed them to the street. On the occasions they had been up to see the house, the street seemed friendly, and the village was idyllic, a real country village.

It was a nice change from living in the hustle and bustle of city life. Their old house was only a few miles away from the Trafford Centre. It was a nice estate and the kids' school had been quite a good one. It was nice to breathe some country air instead of carbon monoxide fumes.

They had had a few problems, and this was going to be a fresh start, but he knew their problems wouldn't just disappear and not overnight; but they were here to try.

He pulled up outside their new house and sat looking at it for a few minutes. He didn't want to let the chips get cold. They were lucky to get a good deal on the terraced property. It had been a repossession and needed some work to be done on it. The surveyor had said that it was structurally sound. It looked smart from the outside but needed decorating throughout, new flooring and the kitchen and the bathroom needed to be renovated. It was a Georgian three bedroomed house with quite big rooms, with beams, and the sitting room had a wood burner housed inside an inglenook fire place. there was also one in the kitchen which had an agar. It was quite big compared to the small modern mid link they had owned in Manchester.

The front door opened, and his wife Sally opened the door and waved, prompting him to come in.

"Are you going to sit there all day or are you going to come in and give us our chips, kids are starving."

"All right Sal, coming."

"He entered the house. They had manged to clear some space to eat at the table. They couldn't find any plates, so they ate it out of the paper.

"Oh, my days! These chips are to die for!" said Sarah.

"Fish is good as well, melts in your mouth," said Rick.

"Is the baby hungry love?" asked Sally.

"Mmm, yes, and I am starving!"

Sarah was sixteen and due to give birth in six weeks' time. So, it was all hands on deck to get the house ready and habitable for a new-born baby.

She had been on a night out to their local cinema in town with her friends. They had got talking to a group of teenage lads who had asked them to a party. There was alcohol there and she had got talking to this one particular lad who came across as nice at first but as the night wore on, he became more and more drunk. He had followed her up to the toilet and barged in behind her. She tried to shove herself past him, but he had his full body weight against the door, and he had locked it. She started to panic he put his hand over her mouth and pushed her against the wall where he proceeded to rape her, ignoring her protests.

A full investigation had been carried out and it was found out that the lad was high on drugs which he had got from a dealer at the party. They were both charged and sent to a youth offenders centre.

She had just left the party without telling her friends where she was going. And when she arrived home, her Mum found her sitting in the kitchen in the dark sobbing. Rick wanted to go and punch the lad's lights out, but Sally managed to calm him down. With the help of SARC, The Sexual Assault Referral Centre, they got the support they needed.

Sarah was a clever girl and had just started in the Sixth form. The school had said that she was clever enough to get into Oxford. They had gone through all of the trauma about abortion, adoption, keeping it, not keeping it. Her parents were surprisingly supportive. They wanted her to do well and follow her dream of going to medical school to train to be a doctor.

Sarah had decided that it was her baby and not some rapist's and wanted to keep the baby and continue with her studies. Her parents went through all of the options with her, and it was decided that when she gave birth she could think about adoption. She was still very young to be a mother and her parents wanted her to have fun and to follow her dreams. If she kept the baby, it would be welcomed into their home and her parents would help with the upbringing, after all, it was their grandchild.

The school had been very supportive, but she was getting bullied for getting 'Up the duff, bun in the oven'. Those were some of the names she was being called. She could handle it at first, but then some troublemakers started posting inappropriate messages on social media. They called her a slag and the village bike. The police became involved and put an end to all of it.

They had always dreamt of moving further North and decided it was an ideal time to move. Rick had been offered a job as site manager at the local slate mine. He had left school at sixteen with no qualifications. He had messed about at school and got in with a bad crowd. He had always been at the bottom of the class at school but found that he was very good with his hands. He had enjoyed woodwork and metal work. He left school and managed to get an apprentice job as a bricklayer for a local building firm. The owner was a friend of his dad's and he had done some labouring jobs in the school holidays when he turned fifteen.

"Ooh."

"What's wrong," asked Rick concerned. "Is it the baby?"

"Nothing, I had a foot stuck in my side."

"He's just letting you know he is there love," said Sally.

David moaned. "Do we have to have baby talk every time we eat?"

David was the middle child and at the age of fourteen, he was just starting to show some interest in girls.

"What if I want to invite a babe around. It won't do much for my street cred with you sitting there, ready to drop."

"David!" said Rick.

"Listen to you, all of fourteen!" said Sally.

"What girl would be interested in you anyway?" asked Max the youngest, who was eleven.

"Why, what's wrong with me. You are looking at the Italian Stallion."

"You are not Italian, and can your head get any bigger?" asked Sally.

"Well at least I am not gay, Maxie?"

"Don't call me that. Girls are all right, as friends."

"Yeah, he's gay," mocked David.

"No, I am not!" he shouted.

"Boys, enough!" said Rick. "We are here to make a fresh start, not to squabble. Anyway now we have eaten, you two can help clear up, and then we need to sort out bedrooms."

"I am having the biggest. We had the smaller bedroom last time, and I don't want to share with Max."

"Well, you'll have to, we discussed this. We only have three bedrooms," pointed out Sally. "Can you clear up please," she added.

"Okay, I will do the washing up," said Max, scrunching up the chip paper, collecting the empty cans and putting them in the rubbish sack. They had yet to find the kitchen bin.

David put away the sauces and vinegar. "All done, can we eat off paper every night? saves on plates."

Ding Dong! Ding Dong!

"Well, I'll get it shall I?" asked Sally. The others plonked themselves down on the settees. She went to the front door and found an Asian family outside.

"Hello?" said Sally, smiling at them.

"Hello, we live next door and we have come to welcome you to the neighbourhood," said the man.

"Thank you, come in please and you are?"

"Mr Patel, Sanjay. This is my wife Aisha and our two children Shireen and Aadi."

"Well, I am Sally Seddon, and this is my husband Rick and our children Sarah, David and Max."

"Pleased to meet you all."

"And you," said Sally.

They all shook hands. Shireen and Aadi were the same ages as David and Max.

David sat there looking at Shireen with a dreamy look on his face. He smiled shyly. He wasn't as confident around girls as he made out.

"Please have a seat," said Rick.

They all sat back down.

"Holidays will soon be over, what school are you all going to?" asked Aisha

"Sleathwaite Academy," said Max.

"I go there. Clever clogs here goes to Hexham Community High School," said Aadi.

"Do you like football?" asked David.

"Yes, and rugby. We play in the rugby league with John and Jamie from the vicarage, they are about your age Max."

"Maybe we could all have a kick about sometime?" asked David.

"Yeah, well I'll see when the lads are free and we can go to the park some time, you as well Max."

"Oh, I don't like football much."

"But he'd love to join in, wouldn't you," said Sally, trying to be encouraging.

"Yeah okay," said Max.

"Ah before we go, I hope you like Samosas, bargees and Pakoras. I made them specially, there is always plenty," Aisha added, offering them to Sally.

"Oh, thank you very much," said Sally, accepting the kind gift.

"Maybe when you are settled you can come around for a curry?" offered Sanjay.

"That would be really nice," said Rick. "Thank you."

Shireen had been quiet; she was the shyer of the two.

"Mam's curries are the best," she said, looking at David and smiling.

He went red in the face, and stammered. "Maybe you can show me around the village, sometime?"

"Err, yes of course," she said, smiling.

Sarah stood up from the settee.

"Would you like a brew, tea? I am having one."

"Oh yes please," said Aisha, suddenly noticing her bump. "Would you like me to do it?" she asked.

"No, I need to stand up, oh my days, Mam where are the cups? Mam!"

"Oh, I don't know, somewhere in these boxes," said Sally

"Look we can see you are busy. We'll leave you to get on with it, if you need any help you just have to ask okay?" said Aisha.

"Oh, cheers, thanks. 'appen I have three strapping men here to help."

"Any time we're here okay. Thanks for offering us tea Sarah," said Sanjay.

"What accent is that?" asked Aadi

"Mancunian, we are from Manchester born and bred," said Rick.

"I love corrie," said Aisha.

"That is filmed in Salford, just on the outskirts of Manchester," said Rick. "How about coming around for a drink?" "when we are settled?" offered Rick.

"Well, we don't drink alcohol but yes that would be nice," said Sanjay.

Shireen was standing by the front door and David was leaning on the banister looking dreamily at Shireen, with his mouth practically open.

They said their goodbyes and Sally shut the door. She looked at her son.

"It's all right, they've gone now. You can put your tongue away and stop drooling."

Next door, the family entered their house. It was much like the Seddon's except the staircase and rooms were on the opposite side.

The kids ran upstairs making a lot of noise.

Aadi came running down the stairs with his football in his hands.

"Mam, can I go and see if the twins want to play football, I could ask David and Max to come."

"Well, that's very nice of you, but they are busy unpacking, I don't think they expected you to call so quickly, and if they see you out on the street, they may think you have left them out."

"Aah, but that's why I was going to ask them," he moaned. "Please!" He added.

"Well, why don't you go and call on the twins and go up to the park? You can always call on the boys in a day or so when they are more settled."

"Saturday?"

"Yes, okay."

"Great, I'll go and see John and Jamie then, laters," he added.

She walked down the hallway and into the kitchen. Sanjay was making some tea.

"Want some?" he asked.

"Yes please, coffee," she said, sitting down.

"Aadi gone out?" he asked.

"Yes, to play football, he wanted to ask the boys next door, I didn't think their parents would appreciate him calling round so soon, having just moved in."

"Well, it's good he wants to make friends; we should encourage it."

"I know, I put him off until Saturday, he has gone to call on the twins, they are going up to the park."

"They seemed like a nice family."

"Yes, I was a bit surprised to see Sarah heavily pregnant. I wonder what the story is there," she mused.

"Well, whatever it is, it's their business, and we shouldn't judge," he said.

"I wasn't, but she is very young."

"Yes, but I am sure she will have the support she needs. Maybe that's why they have moved here, to have a fresh start?"

"Maybe, hey, did you see David making eyes at our Shireen?"

"Yes, I think she has an admirer there and she seemed to like him."

"She needs to marry a good Muslim boy," she said.

"Don't be so old fashioned. She must be free to marry whom she loves."

"Yes, but it is traditional."

"Maybe, but I think we should encourage her to make her own choices," added Sanjay.

"Yes dear, maybe."

∾

Half term had gone so quickly, it was Friday night and Marian, and George were due to go back home tomorrow.

She stood staring out of the bedroom window at the fields.

'Hope, they are all going to be okay?' she thought to herself.

When they had arrived a week ago, they were quite shocked to see James shouting like that. It was so unlike him. She feared for his mental health and worried about Rachael and the children. She used to work as a senior psychiatric nurse at Infirmary Leeds Hospital and could see the signs starting to take root.

'I wonder if we should stay a while longer?' she thought.

"Maybe best to leave it to them. He is a lot calmer and relaxed."

"Who's more relaxed?" asked George, coming through the bedroom door.

"Oh, I was thinking about James. Do you think we should offer to stay next week, when t'kids go ter school?"

"Stop worryin' love, let them get on with it."

"I know, but ..."

"No buts, he seems a lot calmer now."

"Yes, but what about next week when our Rachael goes back ter work and the bairns are at school? What if he starts to panic over things again? They haven't made arrangements for tfarm yet."

"No, but listen we are only a few hours up the A1. If there are any problems, Rachael will let us know and we can come back. It's not as if we have work ter go to."

"Yes, I know, you're right."

"Let's go downstairs and enjoy our last evening with them," he said, putting his arm around her.

"Yes, okay but I can't help worrying and every time I think about it, I see our Cameron's upset little face."

"James was mortified by that, and things seem to have settled down for now, as you say, the real test will be next week, but we are just on the end of t'phone if they need us."

"Yes, let's go down. James is cooking and it smell delicious," she said, standing up and walking to the closed door.

They entered the farmhouse kitchen and James was stirring a chicken casserole.

"Hello." He smiled and turned around. "Hope you're hungry, there's plenty."

"I could eat a horse," said George, sitting down at the kitchen table.

"Let's hope not." James laughed.

"What are we having?"

"Garlic mushrooms which I grew, Chicken casserole and Apple and Rhubarb crumble."

"Sounds delicious," said Marian. "Should I lay the table?"

"No, you make yourself comfortable in the sitting room and I will fetch you a drink."

"I could get used to this," she said walking out of the room.

"Beer, George?"

"Oh, yes please."

Cameron and Scarlett came into the kitchen.

"Dad, 'Toy Story is coming on soon, can we watch it?" asked Cameron.

"What time is it on?"

"Six o'clock," said Scarlett.

"Yes okay, if we have finished dinner by then. Get your mam to record it."

"Okay, great!" she said, rushing off.

"Daddy."

"Yes Cameron?"

"Can we have popcorn when we watch the film?"

"Yes, okay, but you all have to help clear up and then we will sit down together and watch it."

"Yippee, to infinity and beyond!" he shouted imitating Buzz Lightyear.

"Grandad, will you take me to my swimming lesson tomorrow?" he asked.

"Depends what time it is. We are going back home tomorrow."

"It's at 09:30 George, like last week when we went, remember?"

"Ah, yes."

"You'll come?"

"Well Cam we can drop you off and get you settled into your lessons but then we have to go I am afraid; traffic will be busy, but we can watch you for ten minutes or so, will that do."

"Yes please, I want to dive in!"

"Not in the little pool Cameron," said James.

"Oh, never mind," he said running off.

George laughed. "He's a little cracker that one and our Scarlett, they are both as bright as buttons."

"Yes, they keep us busy."

"That's what you need James, the farm will get sorted and you have a lovely family. You've done well for yourself, and I know Rachael and the children will be well looked after."

"Yes," said James, looking a bit anxious.

"Marian wanted to stay and help out a bit longer, but I think you need some time to yourselves. She worries about yer as I do. James, anything you need, just, pick up the phone, okay lad?"

"Thanks, I am sure we'll get sorted out."

"Yes, that's the spirit, chin up."

They all sat down to their dinner.

"Ooh, James. You've excelled yourself love," said Rachael.

"It's lovely James, thank you," said Marian, patting him on the hand.

They had had a pleasant evening. The children helped with the clearing up and then they started watching Toy Story. By the end, the children were struggling to keep their eyes open.

"Gran, can I come back to your house tomorrow?" asked Scarlett sleepily.

"No, not this time darling, you've got school on Monday."

"Not boring school!" she said.

"You like school," said Rachael, surprised.

"Yes, I do but it isn't as much fun as being off," she said.

"Education's important," said Marian.

"Time for bed," said Rachael. "Scarlett you are struggling to stay awake."

"Oh, ten more minutes."

"Okay, but then time for bed," said James.

The children had changed into their pyjamas before the film. Cameron was fast asleep next to his grandad who had also nodded off.

"Look at these two," said Marian, looking at her husband and grandson.

"Shame to wake them," said Rachael taking out her phone and taking a photograph of them snuggled up together.

James walked over and lifted Cameron into his arms. He didn't even stir he was so shattered.

"George, George, wakey, wakey," prodded Marian.

"What, what, who goes there," he said sleepily.

Scarlett started to giggle.

"George, Cameron's going to bed and so's Scarlett in a few minutes and so should you."

"I'll put t bins out in t'mornin," he muttered.

Scarlett started to laugh, suddenly awake.

"Grandad, do you know where you are?" she asked, laughing and jolting him awake.

"Oh, God, I suppose you've all been gawping at me, hope I wasn't drooling?"

"Mum took a picture of you. She is going to put it on 'Instagram' you know."

"No, I am not," smiled Rachael. "Come on Scarlett bed, go and clean your teeth, be up in a minute."

"Okay." She kissed them all good night and followed her Dad and Cameron upstairs.

Next morning, James woke up feeling relaxed. He went out early to do the animal feeds and then came in for breakfast. The fresh air had done him good.

Rachael had made bacon barms for everyone for their breakfasts; and then it was time for Marian and George to start making their way home. They were going to see Cameron swim for a little while, and then Rachael was going in her car to bring him home.

They had enjoyed their week at the farm, they had had a few days out, one was in the lake district. The kids had had fun at an adventure park, and they all went on a tree top walk.

Marian was thinking about her week as George drove through some open countryside. She loved this part of the country, but Yorkshire would always be home to her and George.

They had decided they would try and come up a bit more often and that the family should try to visit them more often, but they all had commitments. At the end of the day though family was what mattered most to her and George.

They each had their hobbies. She liked indoor bowling and volunteered at a local dementia support group. She still liked to do her bit and it kept her busy. George loved his Golf and fishing. He was going to bring his rods up next time he came to visit, so the children could have a go at it.

George looked over at his wife sitting in the passenger seat. To him she still looked as young as she had when he had first laid eyes on her. Her hair was much the same, a blonde bob, although it was now dyed. She was going grey. He smiled and chuckled to himself. She had her head turned to one side, with her glasses perched on the end of her nose and was snoring softly.

He thought about when he had first met her. He was doing National Service in the RAF and she was a student nurse working on the base. He had injured himself during a parachute jump. He had landed wrongly during his training and had broken his leg. She nursed him in the medical wing. He was a navigator and was promoted to flying officer.

He had carried on his flying career with the RAF until his thirties. He had made it to squadron leader. When his flying career was over, he continued to serve the force but doing classroom-based training sessions with the air force. He came out with his flying pension and his regular work pension from the force. He had done well for himself.

Marian opened her eyes. They were on the A1 going past the 'Angel of the North', headed homewards.

She turned to George. "How long have I been asleep?"

"About forty-five minutes, you looked so peaceful love."

"Did I?"

"Yes, but your glasses were on the end of your nose, and you were snoring."

"Wasn't."

"You were though only softly."

"Your one ter talk, you could sleep on t washing line."

A couple of hours later, they stopped at Leeds Service Station for a coffee. George was glad of the rest. The traffic had been busy on the way down. All the motorists must be returning from the half term break. It shouldn't take much longer to get home, probably half an hour or so, but they were both ready for a brew and a snack.

A while later George was pulling onto their drive. Marian went to open the front door and to pick up the post off the door mat. She checked the phone for messages. There was one from the dementia support group where she volunteered, asking for help with their coffee morning that week and another one for George from the Golf club, reminding him to renew his membership. She played the message for him.

"Someone always wants money," he moaned.

"Oh, get away with you, you love it, it does you good."

" Aye, it does that and keeps me fit."

"Keeps your heart fit and healthy, as does my yoga."

Marian looked towards the phone. She was still apprehensive and worried about their family.

"Think I'll just give our Rachael a ring."

"We only just got back, we agreed we'd give them a bit of time to their sens

"I know but I am just letting them know we got home safely, Rachael will worry otherwise."

"And to check up on them."

"Well, there is that," she added, reaching for the phone.

She pressed their number on the phone's contact list.

"It's ringing."

The phone was soon answered. She could hear Bart Simpson in the background. The TV was on.

"Hello?"

"Cameron, it's Grandma."

"Grandma!"

"Hello darlin, are you watching telly?"

"No, Dad bought me and Charlotte a PlayStation. It's my new Simpsons Game."

"Well, you're both very lucky."

"Just got it, Dad took us into Newcastle, and we had a happy meal."

"You'd live off Macdonald's if you could?"

"It's sooo tasty!"

"Cam, it's your turn," said James.

"Oh, gotta go Gran," he said, and dropped the phone on the floor. James bent down and talked into it.

"Hi Marian, you made it home then."

"Yes, traffic was busy, it being half term. You all sound like you are having fun?"

"Ah that was good Cam."

"My turn!" shouted Charlotte, excitedly.

"Yes, it's good to have some time with them. We'll be busy next week though, when they are back at school and Rachael goes back to work."

"You'll be fine James, and if you ever need anything pick up the phone. You are like a son to us and we love you."

"Thanks Marian, that's nice. Same to you to … um do you wanna speak to Rachael?"

"Well, if she isn't too busy."

"No, she's just here," he said handing the phone to Rachael.

"You weren't doing jobs were you love."

"Hi Mum, no I wasn't. We're playin with tkids," she said, walking into the kitchen.

"Oh, good, is everything okay?"

"We're fine Mum, stop worrying."

"But I do. I always will just because you're all grown up doesn't mean that I stop worrying about yer, , yer knows".

"I know."

"I'll never stop being your Mam and if there's anything you need just give us a ring, okay? We love you all."

"And we love you. Things will settle down, they are doing so already, I hope, and if things do get on top of us, we'll sort it out; but it's good to know that you're not too far away."

"Well keep in touch love and let us know how things are goin? I will phone you next weekend, but if you need me before then pick up the phone."

"Bye sweetheart."

"Bye Mam," she said, using her childhood name that she had used when she was little.

"Blimey, you haven't called me that since you were ten years old."

"Yeah, well, I haven't forgotten, take care," said Rachael, putting down the phone.

She stood looking out the kitchen window into the garden. She admitted to herself that she was still worried about James. He had seemed much more relaxed this week, spending extra time with the family, but she reckoned he was in holiday mode. Come next week it would be back to normal and she would have to see how he would handle it and what she could do to help with getting a relief manager.

Chapter 18

Monday morning had come around quickly, and it was the start of school again and for the parents to return to work.

In the Macalister household, Rachael had been called out to work earlier, to call on a patient in need of some medical assistance. James was left holding the fort and trying to get the children organised for school. He was starting to feel stressed; the children had promised to be good but being children, they had no sense of time. It was 8:15 and they had to be out soon, or they would be late. He liked to be on his way by 8:30 and they didn't have a lot of time to spare. Luckily, everything had been organised the night before.

They had just finished breakfast and gone up to clean their teeth. James quickly cleared the table. Cameron was soon downstairs.

"I hope you have cleaned your teeth properly?"

Cameron didn't hear him; he had his headphones on and was sitting on the settee, about to turn the television on. He had picked up the remote.

"Cam!" Take your headphones off," he said, signalling for him to take them off his ears.

"Yes of course, telly time," he said, turning on the TV and putting his headphones down.

"No telly. We have to get to school," said James, trying to be patient. "Go and get your shoes on please."

Cameron stood up; he had his sweatshirt on back to front.

"You have your sweatshirt on the wrong way round, arms up."

"I put it on myself," said Cameron.

"I know son, you tried."

He clamped his headphones back on and went into the hall to put on his shoes.

Scarlett came running down the stairs and barged into Cameron.

"Hey, you nearly knocked me over!"

"Well, you were in the way."

"Was not!"

"Yes, you were, if you didn't have those things on, you would have heard me!"

Scarlett was normally very good with Cameron, but this morning she didn't especially want to go to school. She liked school but she just wanted to stay at home after the holidays. She hadn't liked being woken up when it was still dark. It felt like the middle of the night.

"You're not allowed headphones at school anyway!" she said superiorly.

"I want them!" Cameron said grabbing them as she was trying to take them from him. "They're mine!" he added tearfully.

James heard the commotion and entered the hall.

"What is going on?" he asked.

"It was him," said Scarlett.

"No, it wasn't. I was trying to put on my shoes and Scarlett barged into me and nearly knocked me over and then she tried to steal my headphones."

"Scarlett!" apologise to Cameron."

"Sorry," she said quietly.

"What's wrong with you?"

"Nothing, do I have to go to school?"

"Yes, what is this you are normally in a hurry to get there, you enjoy school."

"I know but I just want to stay here in the warmth."

"Are you feeling okay?"

"Yes."

"You'll be fine when you see your friends. Come on you two, we really haven't got time for this, we are going to be late. Cameron you will have to give those to me once we get there."

"I like my music and anyway Miss Haslem lets me put them in her special box."

"Okay, come on, let's get going."

They headed out of the door. James was feeling anxious again but was trying to be patient and not show it to the children. He was a little concerned about Scarlett. It was unlike her not to want to go to school. Maybe she had just got too cosy over the holiday break.

He locked up the house, he could feel his hands shaking and he didn't know why. Scarlett was still standing outside the car while Cameron had got in and was seen to be struggling with his seat belt again.

"Scarlett!" What are you doing, get in the car. We are definitely going to be late now!"

"I don't want to, stop shouting at me!" she said tearfully, her lip coming down. She started trembling.

"Scarlett, I am sorry, but I have to get you two to school. The traffic will be building up now."

"I am tired!"

"Look sweetheart, I am also tired, but that doesn't mean I can't work, and it doesn't mean you can't go to school. When you come back you can have an early night after tea."

"I wanted to stay with you and look after you. Mum said to be good for you because you are under the weather. I am not really tired; I just want to stay with you."

"Oh, sweetheart I am fine, don't worry about me. You are too young to be looking after me. I'll be okay, honest. Come on, get in the car and help your brother."

Cameron opened the car door. "Dad, are we going or not, because if we're not I can go and play my Simpsons game."

"You are both going to school, okay."

"Yes Dad," they said in unison.

James got inside the car and sighed. He had enough to do today and could do without any more delays. He put the key into the ignition and reversed up the drive.

He dropped the children off at school and gave each of them a hug. The farm staff were already hard at it when he got back.

He had a stressful morning and felt as if he was snapping at his farm hands which was very unlike him, and they had been surprised that he was acting out of character.

He entered the house to make coffee at 11:30 and saw the breakfast dishes lying on the bench. He just lost it.

"Aarrh!" he shouted and knocked the cereal packets onto the floor in a temper, which had also been on the bench. Some of the contents spilled onto the floor.

"Why do I always have to be left with the soddin' dishes?"

He sat on the floor and started to cry. He didn't know why or why he had even behaved like that.

"What is happening to me!" he said aloud.

He picked up the cereal boxes and put them away and started on the dishes it didn't take long. He calmed down and made himself a coffee. He sat nursing it.

'I need a proper drink,' he thought, reaching into the cupboard for a bottle of whisky.

He took out the bottle and reached for a glass. He looked down at the bottle and the glass. He needed to give himself a good talking to. He had responsibilities and couldn't allow himself to get drunk.

He left the bottle and the glass on the bench and walked out of the house, putting on his coat.

Some of the farmhands asked if he was okay and he said yes and apologised for snapping at them earlier.

He took himself off for a walk to clear his head. He wasn't gone too long as there was work to be done. He couldn't go on like this. He was starting to lose control.

If he didn't get sorted out soon, he would have to see his GP. He knew he should talk to Rachael. He had promised he would tell her when he felt stressed. He looked at his watch. He couldn't phone her at work, and he didn't want to worry her too much. He got into doing some jobs around the farm and working with the lads. He even felt better for it. They were a good lot and worked hard, he felt guilty for having a go at them. They cheered him up and they ended up having a bit of a laugh.

He made a promise to himself to try not to let things get on top of him. Little did he know that it was easier said than done.

It was 3:15 in the afternoon and school was finished for the day. The twins were walking home with Max. It turned out that they were in the same classes. They seemed to be getting along and making friends.

They had played football together at the weekend, along with David. The twins were football and rugby mad.

"So, Max, can we convert you into a Newcastle United fan," asked Jamie.

"Oh, I don't really like football that much, I play occasionally. David likes footy, he supports City."

"Well, what about rugby, we play every Saturday."

"I enjoy that a little bit more. I only really do sports in P.E. I did some football trials at school but that was more to keep my dad happy."

"So, what do you like doing," asked John, bewildered that no one could enjoy his beloved sports.

"Drama is more my thing; I was in some school plays. I had some lead parts. I used to go to drama school on a Saturday. We put some productions on at the Theatre Royal."

"Really?" asked John, surprised. "Was that in Newcastle?"

"No, Manchester."

They have more than one Theatre Royal John, I was the lead in the school play," said Jamie in junior school last year. "I enjoyed it."

"Yeah well, I hope to take it up again round here, I enjoyed drama school."

Suddenly, among the hustle and bustle of school children David ran up, followed by Aadi.

"We were shouting for you three," said Aadi.

"We never heard you," said Jamie. "How come you're out a bit later?"

"Oh, I had to see the teacher about my homework," said Aadi.

"Have you been a naughty boy then?" asked John.

"No, I just wanted to ask her some questions about it."

David turned to the other boys. "How do you fancy coming around our place for a bit, you can play my new FIFA game on the Xbox if you like?"

The boys looked at each other and nodded.

"Yeah, why not," said Aadi.

"Oh, Aadi, erm is your sister free later?"

"Why?"

"Oh, just wondered," he said, going a bit red.

"Oooh!" you fancy her!" said Aadi.

"He's been drooling over her, since she got here," said Max.

"No, I haven't, just being neighbourly."

"Yes, you have."

"You've got it bad mate," said Aadi.

They had reached the bus stop and Shireen was stepping off the bus.

"There she is bro; are you going to go and give her a kiss!" said Max teasingly.

David went bright red.

"He just wants to get into her knickers," giggled Jamie.

"Yeah," agreed John.

Shireen was in the same year as David but went to the high school although she would be fifteen in a couple of months while David was one of the youngest in his year. She turned around, saw the boys and then noticed David. She smiled at him shyly.

"So, Davy boy you like the older woman then?" said Jamie.

"Well, you know, more mature like," answered David.

"Oh, she's not mature, she still sleeps with her teddy bear," said Aadi.

"That's not all she wants to sleep with," said Max.

They had reached their street. The other boys rushed to drop their bags off at their houses and get changed.

Max and David went through the front door, slamming it shut.

"Don't slam that door," shouted Sally.

"So, how was school?" she asked.

"I had a good day," said Max. "Turns out I am in the same classes as the twins and Aadi."

"Oh, that's nice, are you all making friends."

"Yes."

"Actually, they're coming around to play a game of footy on the Xbox," said David.

"You and your football. How did you enjoy school David?"

"Yeah, was all right, the lads seemed nice."

"No friends yet?"

"It's the first day Mam."

"Oh, well he is making progress with Shireen. she smiled at him, and he went all gooey and bright red," said Max mockingly.

"Shut up!" said David throwing a cushion at his brother. "I'm going upstairs to put on my game. Send the lads up – laters."

"Are you going to join in Max?"

"Only if they play some other games as well."

"Look, I know it isn't your thing but just join in. They seem like a nice lot of boys."

"I will, it's just well, I can't help it if I don't like sport or shooting games is it?"

"No, I am glad you don't like shooting games. I just don't want you left out."

"I won't be. Jamie says he enjoys drama, so there's something we both like."

"Yes, okay son."

She looked at her son. He always was the gentler of her two boys. David was more rough and tumble. Rick was always wanting to toughen Max up, but she wouldn't change him for the world. He was always happy to play with Sarah's dolls when he was little. He used to play games with her Barbie dolls and the boys action men. He played with boys toys as well. She remembered he used to push a toy push chair round wh with his teddy bear in it, all of which was perfectly normal. But now since he had started at the academy in year seven she hoped he wouldn't get teased. There was nothing wrong with her boy but sometimes he could be a bit effeminate. Kids could be cruel. Still, they seemed to have moved to a nice village.

"You look deep in thought Sal," said Rick, coming through to the sitting room from the kitchen.

"Yes, was just thinkin," she said distantly.

"Where are the boys?"

"Upstairs with twins and Aadi."

"I am glad they're making friends."

"Yes, I just worry about Max. I don't want him left behind."

"Well, they seem to be including him."

"He says Jamie likes drama as well."

"Drama, he wants to get on the footy pitch, get some exercise."

"Well, he does at school; you know he isn't that keen on sport apart from tag rugby."

"He'll be learning contact in year seven. That'll toughen him up."

"I don't want him toughened up, as he has just told me he can't help what he likes. He needs our support."

"Yes, I know, I just don't want my boy to be picked on, that's all."

"I know, but he is different to David. We just have to accept that."

"At his last school he didn't have many friends who were boys. He seemed to do more things with the girls. I don't want that happening again."

"Well things seem okay at the moment. I would be happy for him to make friends with either sex, just as long as he has friends."

"Okay Sal, I do accept him. It's just that I was brought up that boys were boys and girls were girls; everything black and white."

"The world isn't like that anymore kids seem to go around in groups of both sexes these days, what with all of this gender equality."

"What, you don't think he's …"

"No, it's all part of growing up isn't it, experimenting."

"What are you trying to say Sal?"

"I am not saying anything. I am just talking about society today."

"I am not some kind of dinosaur you know. I do know about acceptance and equality. My old man wouldn't understand though."

Later that evening they were all tucked up in bed and the house was quiet.

Max looked over at his brother fast asleep in his bed, snoring. He reached for his headphones so he couldn't hear him. He had put on his lamp on a low setting so as not to disturb David. He reached under his bed and pulled out a fashion magazine of ladies clothing and cosmetics. He sighed to himself, he looked at the images of girls dressed up. He liked their clothes. He scanned through the magazine looking at cosmetics and perfumes.

'This isn't normal,' he thought to himself. 'What's wrong with me?'

He looked under the covers at his body. He felt down below at his privates.

'I shouldn't have this,' he thought. 'I don't know why, but I like girls things and doing girl things, do I want to be one? Am I a freak? I do like boys things as well.'

He pulled out his tablet and looked up on the internet about gender change. He didn't think he liked the sound of having things cut off and added to him. It sounded a bit drastic, but still he felt disturbed by the way he was feeling.

'My voice is going to change. I don't want it to. I don't want to hit puberty, because then I will have to accept that I will be changing into a man and I don't want to. I will have to borrow Mum's lady shaver or get my own,' he mused.

He was starting to feel tired and turned his light off and snuggled down under the covers.

In the next room his Mum and Dad must be fast asleep, no noises coming from there tonight. Sometimes he could hear them through the wall, the sound of mattress springs.

In Sarah's room she was trying to get some sleep but kept waking up, the baby was being restless in her tummy. She got up and padded downstairs in her slippers for a glass of hot milk to help her sleep.

She sat at the kitchen table drinking the milk. She thought about her brothers and how different they were. She had heard Mam and Dad discussing Max, growing up with him she knew he was different. She wouldn't want him any other way. He used to play dress up with her and she let him wear her fairy outfit. 'Dad went mad. He said that I shouldn't have done that, it would scar him for life. When people refer to him as 'he' I can see him wanting to correct them.' She had seen the magazines under his bed when she borrowed some of his art stuff. She hadn't told anyone.

She went back upstairs and got into bed and snuggled down. She was soon fast asleep and started to dream. In the dream she was in her new bedroom feeding her baby, when she saw this lad standing in the shadows. He had his arms stretched out towards her. She recognised him from the party in Manchester.

"Come on you know you want to."

"Want to what?"

He stepped towards her and started stroking her hair and trying to kiss her. He bent down and put her baby in the cot. The baby started to cry. He put his hand under her top and felt her breast and kissed it.

"Come on, one last time, for old time sake."

"No! Get away from me, I don't want this, and I don't want you."

"Oh, but you do," he unbuttoned his belt and pulled down his trousers.

She pushed him away. "Get out, get out, go!"

"All right, all right, I am going." He stood up and pulled up his pants. "Just one thing." He reached into the cot and took the baby out, who started screaming. "Okay, I didn't get to shag you again, but this is who I really want."

"Give me back my baby! Get out, go away!"

"Ah, But she's mine."

"Give her back to me!"

Rick and Sally started stirring.

"Rick, what's that noise? I can hear screaming. Oh God it's Sarah."

"Come on, let's see if she's all right," said Rick getting out of bed.

They went into Sarah's room she was sitting upright looking towards the window.

"What's wrong love? Is it the baby?"

"Is it time?" asked Rick going to grab her dressing gown and bag she had packed ready for the hospital.

"Don't you see him?"

"Who?"

"The boy. He wants my baby, go away!"

"Sarah there's no one there, love," said Rick worried.

Sally sat next to her on the bed. "You're having a bad dream love, come on settle down," she said, bringing her daughter in for a hug.

Sarah snuggled into her. She was shaking and sobbing.

"Mam, he was going to take her."

"There, there, it's all over now."

"What if he comes back?"

"He won't."

"I did see him you know; he was here. You don't believe me."

"I do, it was a bad dream, that's all. Come on love, you are safe."

"How did he get in? Has he followed me from Manchester?"

"No, it was a bad dream. Sarah, your pyjamas are soaked with sweat. Let's get you freshened up and into some clean ones."

"I'll go and check on the boys," said Rick. He didn't want them up, they had school in the morning. He stepped out onto the landing.

The boys' bedroom door opened, and a sleepy David stood there.

"Dad, what's goin' on? What's all the noise about. Is it ah Sarah? Sprogs not on its way is it?"

"No son. You go back to bed and it's a baby not a sprog. Is Max okay?"

"Fast asleep, can I go and watch Family Guy?"

"What? No, go to bed, you have school in the morning."

"Oh, but …"

"Davy go on, back to bed now. Let us see to your sister."

"Is she okay?"

"She will be."

"Night Dad, love you."

"Night son, I love you too," he said, patting David on the shoulder. He went back into Sarah's bedroom.

"You okay love?"

"Dad, I was frightened." She stood up for a hug.

"I know darlin'. It's over now," he said, hugging her.

"I think you need some sleep now sweetheart, the baby will know your upset and you don't want it distressed," said Sally.

"Will you both stay with me until I fall asleep?"

"Of course, love," said Rick.

"Get into bed Sarah. I changed the sheet when you were in the bathroom," said Sally.

It was a bit of a squeeze, but they settled on the bed. Rick and Sally watched their daughter finally drift off into a peaceful sleep. They stayed a few more moments and then slipped out of the bedroom and back to their own room.

"It was like watching over her when she was tiny," said Sally. "Rick I am worried about her."

"I know love, so am I. The nightmares have come back. Still, she has only got another week until her due date."

"She went through a traumatic experience with the rape. What if this has an effect when the baby is born?"

"Well, we'll have to give her all the support she needs." He yawned pulling the duvet over himself. "I am just glad I am not due at work this week, but unfortunately I start next week, which is round about her due date."

"I am sure they will understand."

"Yes, but I need to be careful it being a new job."

The next day, Max was the last one upstairs getting ready. Everyone else was sitting downstairs having their breakfast.

He stood looking in the mirror, posing. He thought about brushing his hair a few different ways. In the end, he decided to brush it with a side parting as opposed to spiking it up like he normally did.

He went into his Mum's room and gave himself a light squirt of perfume. He didn't want it to be noticed but he liked to smell nice. He put on some lip balm and reached for the lipstick. He put it on but then wiped it off again. He borrowed Sally's moisturiser and put it on his face.

He looked in her wardrobe and had a quick look at her clothes, he picked out a top and held it against himself, looking in the mirror.

Downstairs, Rick was looking at the clock.

"What is that boy doing, time is getting on and he hasn't had his breakfast."

"He was posing in the mirror when I went up for my bag. He didn't hear me," said David.

"Nothing wrong with looking smart," said Sally, looking at David with his tie askew, shirt sleeves rolled up and shirt not tucked in. "I hope you are going to tidy yourself up before you leave the house?"

"Yeah, yeah," he said.

Rick got up from the table and walked to the bottom of the stairs.

"Max! Max! What are you doing up there, you are going to end up late and you haven't had your breakfast yet."

"Coming Dad.'"

Rick walked back to the breakfast table and Max followed.

David wolf whistled at him.

"Looking sharp my boy, you will impress the ladies," said Rick. "You don't normally wear your hair like that Max."

"Fancied a change."

"Fancies himself more like," said David.

Max had put on a clean pressed uniform, his tie done properly. He even had his blazer on and buttoned up.

"Mam are my shoes polished?"

"I did the shoes last night," said Rick. "Even David's which were covered in mud. You been playing footy in the mud again in your school shoes?"

"I don't care what I look like. It's only boring school."

"I thought you liked your new school?" asked Sally.

"I do, but it's still just school. Hey Maxie, we aren't going to work in an office you know!"

"I just want to take pride in my appearance."

"You're a boy. You are meant to be covered in mud."

"Oh, shut up Davy."

Later that morning, when Sally was halfway through cleaning and tidying the house, she went into the boys' bedroom. They still had some cardboard boxes to unpack. The boys hadn't made their beds as they hadn't had time that morning.

She tidied up their room, pulled the sheet on David's bed straight and put the Duvet right; and then she did the same to Max's bed. She pulled the sheet straight and tucked it under the mattress. As she did, she saw a few magazines lying on the bed base faced upside down.

'Oh God, surely he isn't looking at pornographic magazines.' That seemed unlikely. 'Should I look?' she asked herself, not wanting to invade her son's privacy. 'No, he'll tell me if he wants me to know anything.'

She carefully put down the mattress and got on with her housework. She went into her own bedroom and looked at her dressing table. Her moisturiser, lip balm, lipstick and hairspray had been moved; as well as her perfume. They had all been put back in the wrong places. She knew Sarah had her own stuff. She sat down on the bed and had a think to herself. For some reason she got up and looked at her wardrobe door. She was sure she had shut it properly. She opened it and found one of her tops had been haphazardly hung up. Sarah couldn't have done it; it would never fit her. Curiosity got the better of her and she went back to Max's bed and lifted the mattress. She took out the magazines, they were all about ladies' fashions and cosmetics.

'There's more to this than meets the eye,' she thought; and put them back the way she had found them. She decided not to say anything just yet and wait and see if he came and talked to her about it. She didn't want to leave it too long, but she needed to know if he was okay.

'He could just be experimenting,' she thought worriedly.

Chapter 19

It was the following week and Rick had finished fixing up the house. They were all unpacked now after the move and he had even started some DIY jobs. They were beginning to feel more settled.

Sarah still seemed on edge and was scared about giving birth. She was trying to focus on being positive, but this was easier said than done. She had a lot to think about. Expectant married parents were anxious about giving birth; never mind a sixteen-year-old. With her being so young, they were worried about her but would support her in whatever she decided to do when the baby was born. They hoped that she would keep her baby and they would then help with its upbringing.

Rick was driving, on his way to work and having a think about things, he was worried about Sarah the most. The boys seemed to be settling down. David needed to focus more on his schoolwork though. He hoped that he would try hard at his new school. He seemed to be more interested in sport than anything else, but he would have exams coming up, and Rick didn't want him messing around like he himself had done.

He then thought about Max. He was a lovely lad, but he worried about the other boys picking on him. He didn't stand up for himself at his old school and got bullied a bit by some of the older boys. That was why he tended to make friends with the girls. Still, he seemed to be joining in with the twins and Aadi. They were all good kids and he loved spending time with them. He felt that his dad hadn't had enough time for him when he was a boy, and so he always tried to make an effort with them.

Sally was always very supportive of all of them. He didn't know what they would do without her. She kept the family strong and united.

He turned the car onto the site and drove through the entrance. He had only been on two occasions previously, once for his interview and once to show the family where he would be working, when they came for a visit before the move.

He parked the car and walked towards the site office.

The owner, the foreman and the secretary were waiting for him. Introductions were made. He had already met the owner and the secretary.

"Hello Rick, welcome," said Steve the owner. You've already met Maddie my secretary."

"Hi." she smiled at him.

"And this is Mike my foreman; he was on holiday when you came up for your interview."

"Hello there," said Mike.

"Pleased to meet you," said Rick.

"So, you found your way okay?" asked Steve.

"Oh, yes no problems," said Rick.

"Good, well how about me, you and Mike take a walk around the site, and you can meet the lads. They are good workers and are all friendly."

"Aye, they're a canny bunch," agreed Mike.

"Canny, you mean shrewd?"

"They're all friendly, canny it's Geordie. That accent of yours is Northern but you don't sound Geordie. Are you from the North East?"

"No, North West, Manchester."

"Well, we won't hold that against yer," he said, smiling at him.

"Yeah, well we've been living up here for a few weeks now."

"Certainly, it's all change for you," said Steve.

"Well, we are gradually getting the house sorted out and the kids seem happy enough."

"Good, well shall we?" said Steve.

They walked out of the site office, putting on their hard hats and bright coloured jackets.

There was a lot of hustle and bustle on the site and a lot of noise. He was introduced as they walked around, and he was told about each section of work and the process of the slate mining. He had worked on building sites before but none like this. He was looking forward to the change.

All the lads seemed friendly enough and he hoped this was going to be a good start; after all he was going to be left in charge of them.

They walked back to the office and sat down together with Maddie the secretary and went through the admin side of things, as well as the managerial duties.

He and Mike sat down and looked over the supplies list and the wholesalers they dealt with. He showed Rick how to order online and helped him set up passwords on the computer for different portals.

Steve the owner stayed until lunch time. Mike stayed in the office a while longer but after lunch he went back out to supervise the lads.

Rick had had a good day and he enjoyed his time there. Everyone had made him feel welcome.

James was getting on with his chores on the farm and trying to stay busy and focused. He was making an effort with trying to keep normal. He had decided to try and get himself sorted out. He didn't want the children distressed, and Rachael had enough to deal with. He promised he would talk about it with her if he felt stressed, but he was having enough time dealing with it himself. He had made an appointment to see the doctor; and that was a step in the right direction.

He walked around the farm, making sure all was well with the animals; all had been fed, watered, and shut up for the night.

He went into the kitchen to start dinner. Rachael was picking the kids up from school. He put the oven onto preheat and started making the sauce for the pasta and preparing the chicken to go in it.

"Daddy! Daddy!" shouted Cameron rushing through the front door. He nearly knocked James off his feet, he was so glad to see him.

"Hello, boy had a good day at school?"

"Yes, I painted you a picture."

"Let me have a look then."

"Look, that's me, Scarlett, Mam and you."

"Oh, that's lovely son, thank you," he said, giving him a hug.

"You have to keep it, it's for you."

"Yes, let's put it up here on the fridge, shall we?"

"Yeah."

"Take your shoes off and hang your coat up then please."

"Okay."

"Hello, love okay?" asked Rachael, coming into the kitchen.

"Yes, I have been keeping busy with the farm and have started dinner."

"Oh, good, I could get used to this," she said giving him a kiss.

"Hi Dad," said Scarlett going straight to the fridge.

"Hi sweetheart, have you enjoyed your day."

"Yes, it was good, we did a bit of Tag Rugby in P.E. It was well cool."

"You enjoyed it then?"

"Yes."

"We'll soon have you playing for the village."

"I didn't say I was that keen."

James got on with the dinner and they all sat down at the table. They had chicken in a mushroom sauce and penne pasta with garlic mushrooms. All freshly made, he was becoming quite the chef and for once the kids didn't complain about their food.

Rachael told him to go and watch the six o'clock news and she would clear up.

She came into the sitting room just as the news was finishing.

"I have made the packed lunches for tomorrow."

"Good, it will save time in the morning."

"So, how have you really been?"

James looked towards the door to see if the kids were about.

"It's okay, they're both upstairs."

"Fine."

"James, you promised you would be honest with me."

"I am honest okay. Look you have enough to deal with."

"James, you are my husband, it's my job to worry about you."

"Well, you needn't, I told you I am okay."

"So, it's just gone away, just like that," she asked, clicking her fingers.

"No, it hasn't, but I am trying to deal with it."

"How?"

"What?"

"How are you dealing with it."

"I have made an appointment for next week to see our GP."

"Doctor Mansfield?"

"Yes."

"Do you want me to be there? I can alter my rounds so I can fit it in."

"No, if you don't mind, I would rather see him myself for my first appointment."

"I just want to support you."

"I know you do, and I appreciate it, really I do. It's just that I want to get it clear in my own mind first. I don't know what is happening to me." He looked anxious again.

"Oh, James, I understand. Don't get upset again. I do have some experience in this field you know."

"I am not one of your patients."

"I know, just keep me informed on how you are doing. I can get you help."

"I am not seeing some shrink."

"No but psych may be able to help you. We have a good psychologist on the team."

"One step at a time," said James. "I looked online at relaxation techniques."

"Good."

"Will you be okay if I have a bath and an early night? I am shattered."

"Yes, go on, I will see to the kids. I don't need babysitting."

"I wasn't suggesting you did. Well just get them in the bath and they can have some milk and stories, is that all right? Sorry, to leave it all to you but it has been a stressful and hectic day."

"Go on love, I know how hard you work."

"Night Darlin', can I have a hug?"

"Of course, sweet dreams," he said, hugging his wife.

Rachael walked out of the room, She was still concerned about him but at least he was going to see the doctor. That was a start.

After Rachael had had her bath, he got Cameron and Scarlett organised. They both had their baths and came down for supper and stories. They were both soon yawning so he took them both up to bed.

He came back downstairs. He didn't feel tired yet, even though he had had a busy day himself. He turned on the television. There was a drama on about a murder at a farm. It probably wasn't something he should watch given his state of health, but he was soon engrossed in it.

As the drama unfolded it showed this daughter getting hold of a gun and shooting her whole family, which included her Mum, Dad, two young sons and husband. She had drugged them and then shot them.

She had put Cannabis in their teas and the boys' milk. James immediately became upset and turned off the TV, cross with himself for watching it.

'Christ almighty,' he thought shaking. 'Can't be real can it?' He picked up the TV Times and saw that it was based on a true story. "Bloody Hell," he said aloud. 'I need a drink after that,' he said to himself. He went to the kitchen and took out a bottle of whisky.

He filled the tumbler and took a large swig of it. So far, he had avoided alcohol, but he wanted to calm his nerves. He stepped outside with a glass and stood staring out at the darkness.

'Calm down, calm down, count to ten. One, two, three, four …' He took some deep breaths and then breathed more slowly through his nose. "Aah, panic over."

He went back into the kitchen and put the whisky bottle away. He didn't want to make a habit of that. He had enough to deal with, without that. He walked back into the sitting room and sat down in the chair.

The next morning, when everybody had gone off to school and work, he set about his tasks around the farm. He got everything done and then went into the barn. He sat down on a bale of hay and thought about how lucky they were to be living here. He had grown up here and had taken over the farm from his dad, when he became too old to manage it all.

But now the stress and responsibilities of owning a farm were getting to him. The farm hands were hard workers and one of them was acting as relief manager when James couldn't be there.

"Oh, I think I just need a break," he sighed to himself.

He sat a few more moments and then took himself off for a walk to clear his head. He looked towards the field where the sheep were and could hear loud bleating. 'Oh no, what's wrong?' He walked over towards a young lamb and its mother.

"James, James, come here quickly!" He ran over. Paddy was looking at the lamb. "James, it's struggling to breathe!"

Paddy laid the lamb down and tried to clear its airways.

"What's that round it's neck?" asked James.

"Barbed wire, oh no."

"I have some cutters, here," said James cutting away the wire. "Looks like it was restricting him from breathing. As he cut it off, the lambs neck started bleeding.

Paddy took out a clean hankie and pressed it onto the wound. The poor lamb was struggling to breathe, and her mother was trying to lick it better.

"She's cold," said James taking off his fleece and wrapping the lamb in it. He held it inside the fleece to get warm and massaged the lambs throat, gently blowing air into him. The mother started bleating loudly.

"Let's take them up to the barn and out of this cold," said James. "Can you prepare some feed and milk when we get there and then go and phone the vet please."

"Yes, of course." Paddy whistled and the sheep dogs came running.

They walked back and James sat with them, to make sure they were okay. Paddy prepared some milk for the lamb and some feed. He then went to phone for the vet to come and pay a visit.

James checked his neck where the barbed wire had been. The bleeding had settled down a little. The vet was due to come out, and it still needed stitches. He got out the first aid kit and tried to patch it up as best he could.

He tried to get the lamb to take some milk, but it only took a few sips. He didn't think it looked too good.

Paddy came back a while later. "James, the vet is coming in the next half hour or so, he says to keep it warm and carry on what we are doing; said he shouldn't be too long."

"Okay, thanks Paddy."

"Is it okay if I get off home now?"

"Yes, of course, we have done enough for today, thanks for your help."

"See you tomorrow."

"Yes, bye then."

The mother had some of the feed and kept coming to look at her lamb.

Half an hour later, he heard the sound of tyres on the gravel. He got up and went to the door. The vet had arrived.

"James, James! You about!"

"Here," said James.

"Oh, I didn't see you there, where's the patient?"

"Here in the barn."

"Right, that's a nasty wound," he said, looking in his vets' bag.

"I am going to anaesthetise her, so I can stitch that wound up, if you could keep her still please?"

"Yes."

"And then I am going to give the lamb an injection of antibiotics and clean and stitch up the wound. I will give you some cream to put on the wound, okay?"

"Yes."

"Your very quiet today James, sure you're all right?"

"Yes, just worried about the lamb, she was struggling to breathe."

"Well, we'll get her sorted, I know how much you care about your animals - and you did a good job too."

The vet got her all cleaned up, stitched the wound and carried out the necessary observations.

"Right, she should be okay now. Keep her in here tonight in the warmth. She should be fine with her mam in here, but I would check on her before you lock up for the night."

"Thanks a lot."

James saw him out and sighed to himself. He went into the house. Rachel and the kids had already arrived.

"Was that the vet? Is something wrong with one of the animals?" asked Rachael.

"Yes, Paddy found a lamb with barbed wire round its neck. It was awful, it was struggling to breathe," he said, his eyes filling up with tears.

"James is it okay now?"

"Yes, but I have to keep the lamb warm and check on it before we lock up, it's with its Mam in the barn."

"Okay, let me go and put the kettle on and we'll have a brew, okay."

"Daddy, can I see if the lamb's okay with you," asked Cameron.

"We'll look before you go to sleep."

"Dad is it going to be okay?" asked Scarlett.

"I hope so. The vet has made her comfortable."

"Let's go in the warmth James," said Rachael, steering him towards the sitting room. "I have turned the heating on."

They had a wood burner and James turned it on. The flames soon started to crackle.

After tea they went and checked on the lamb. It was snuggled up with its Mother, so they left them to it.

Later that evening James disappeared. Rachael looked all over the house, in sheds and barns but couldn't find him anywhere. She knew he had gone to check on the lamb, but she couldn't see him in there.

She went and checked again.

"James! James! Where are you?"

She looked behind the bales and found James sitting rocking and holding himself, he was sobbing his heart out. An opened bottle of whisky was beside him and a packet of painkillers.

"Oh, my God, James! No!"

"I can't go on Rachel. I have to go."

"Go where, James this isn't the answer. You can't what about the kids and me?" "If you want to move, we can, don't overdose with pills and alcohol."

"Be easier for me if I just killed myself."

"What no, no absolutely not. We need you," she stepped closer.

"Stay away!"

"James, I am going to get help."

"No, no help, that lamb was injured because of me."

"No, it wasn't."

"I should have checked the fencing."

"It's not all down to you."

"It is, it is, it's my farm; Aaah!" he screamed.

He reached for the packet of pills and opened them; he had had half of the whisky.

"No, you don't James Macalister. You're stronger than this!" shouted Rachael pulling out her phone. "No sodding signal! Right James, look at me and focus; deep breaths through your nose, in and out, in and out. That's it. Think about the lamb, you helped save its life, look she's cuddled into Mum, she's fine."

"Fine? – fine; no you're trying to trick me. I know what this is. They're all out to get me, all of them."

"Who?"

"Everyone."

"James, we are all here for you. We all adore you. I love the bones of you. The kids wouldn't be able to manage without you and you have your friends at rugby. The staff all have a lot of respect for you."

"Why do I feel so lonely!"

"You're having a rough patch, but this isn't the answer."

She bent down in front of him. "Now hold my hands. Ooh, they're cold. Now, your resps are high and your pulse is racing," she said, feeling the pulse on the inside of his wrist. "Remember to slow down your breathing. You are coming with me into the house." She bent down for the packet of pills and reached for the whisky.

"That's mine."

"That's not the answer, come on. I am going to phone 999, you need help."

"I don't want the paramedics here; they will take me away."

"No one is taking you away, but you are very distressed." James held back. "James, Come on!"

She managed to get him into the house and calmed down.

"Rach, no 999," he said sobbing.

"Okay, but let me check your blood pressure and temperature. Then you can have a cup of tea. I am going to phone Doctor Mansfield first thing in the mornin' and you are going to ask Paddy to run the farm for a while. You need to have a good rest."

"Okay."

She checked him over. His temperature was a little low, but he was cold. She made him a cup of tea.

"Just take some sips at first, otherwise you might be sick."

"I am sorry, so sorry, please forgive me. I love you!"

She managed to get him upstairs to bed. She lay on the bed next to him, watching him fall into a deep sleep.

She could feel the tears streaming down her face, wondering what had happened to her beloved James. He was such a gentle person; she knew he wouldn't be violent and cause trouble, but she knew he needed urgent help. There were a lot of farmers who suffered from mental health problems. She didn't think that he needed sectioning just yet, he needed help before it got to that stage. He used to be so happy and easy going, full of confidence, but recent circumstances had changed that. She just wanted her James back.

Chapter 20

It was lunch time and Rachael was taking a well-earned break. It was a cold day but bright and sunny. It was November and still quite chilly. She pulled her coat collar up round her neck and shoved her hands in her pockets.

She was walking up towards the church; she wasn't a religious person but felt she needed half an hour of peace after the last twenty-four hours. Before work, she had got the kids and James in the car to take them to school. She had phoned Paddy and asked him to take on the role of being relief manager until further notice.

She was dressed in her uniform for work but was not sure how long she would be able to work today given the circumstances with James. She had left him in the car and gone into work. She went to see Doctor Mansfield straight away before surgery and told him the circumstances. He agreed to see James with herself present, straight away.

They had talked at length about his problems. He prescribed some anti-depressants and suggested he went to see a behavioural councillor for therapy sessions. He also made him an appointment to see a psychologist from the psych team. James had become agitated and was worried he would be sectioned, but the doctor had assured him that that wouldn't happen at the moment and that it was paramount that he received the treatment he needed to help him before anything like that happened. But if it did it would be for his safety and those around him.

She had then driven him up to spend the day with his parents so she could get on with her rounds. She didn't wanted to leave him on his own.

She entered the church and sat down heavily on one of the pews and put her head in her hands.

'How has it come to this, not my James,' she thought to herself. She had been strong all morning, trying not to get upset. She got out her tissue and wiped her eyes and blew her nose.

Tom suddenly appeared out from the vestry. "Rachael, this is a surprise, how lovely to see you."

She looked up and tried to smile at him, but tears were streaming down her cheeks.

"Rachael, what's wrong, has something happened, are the kids all right, James, you?"

"No, we're not."

"Do you want to tell me, we have been friends, a long time the four of us and I have known James since school."

"It's James."

"Is he okay?"

"No, he's been having some problems lately, been very stressed. I think he is having a breakdown, he is suffering from mental health problems."

"Oh no, I am very sorry to hear that."

"That's not all," she said shaking her head with grief. "I found him in the barn with a half-drunk bottle of whisky and a packet of pain killers, he was going to kill himself."

"Oh, my gosh!"

"Rachael is there anything I can do. I feel awful now, I have been so busy lately. Can I put him on my list to see him or maybe it would be better to take him out for a coffee, I won't suggest the pub."

"He would like that. Be a mate to him like you always have been, not the local vicar."

"Okay, how about you?"

"I don't know. I feel so alone in this." She started sobbing again and he put his arm around her and kissed her on the cheek.

"Come here," he said, and she snuggled towards him. He held her close.

She sat up straight after a little while and blew her nose. "I have to be strong, for the kids and James. I can't just crumble."

"I know sweetheart, but you need support as well."

"I know. We saw Doctor Mansfield before my rounds and he has prescribed anti-depressants, to see a behavioural therapist and he is referring him to psych."

"Good, well at least he is going to get help."

"He was scared in case he got sectioned, but Doctor Mansfield assured him that if they start treatment straight away, hopefully it can be avoided, but if it does it will be for his safety and ours."

"Right, where is he now?"

"I took him up to spend the day with his mum and dad. I didn't want ter leave him on his own. I have asked Paddy ter take over the running of the farm until further notice."

"Did something happen yesterday to spark off him wanting to end it all?"

"It has been building up for a few months now, with different occurrences happening on the farm, but yesterday they found a lamb struggling to breathe with barbed wire round its neck. It's okay now."

She looked at her watch.

"I had better be going shortly, said I would only be half an hour, I am going to try and finish a bit earlier, and Emily is going to see some of the less complex patients later on. I haven't told anyone else about what is happening with James. My mum and dad know he has been distressed but they don't know about last night. Mum used to be a psychiatric nurse. She said she recognised the signs. But, oh no, what am I going to tell her now, they're both worried enough. They'll want me ter go back home and bring James and the kids, but we can't just run away." She started crying again and leaned into Tom.

"I think that you need to take the rest of the day off. You're not fit for work, Rachael, you have enough to deal with and your own health to think of as well."

"I just wanted to keep busy. I am trying to keep our heads above water, but I feel like we're drowning."

He stood up and grabbed her hand.

"Rachael, where is your car?"

"At work."

"I have an appointment at two, but I am going to walk you back to work. We will have a talk with your boss and then I am driving you to get James and then home in your car and then I will walk back to get mine. I don't want you driving today. You are too upset, I can pick the kids up from school."

"Oh, that's very kind but ..."

"No buts, no arguments."

"Right, okay," she said with a small smile.

"Okay, I'll just get my coat and then we'll lock up."

He led her out of the church holding her hand. She was still very upset.

They walked the short distance up to the surgery; afternoon practice hadn't yet started, and they went in and explained the situation to the practice manager. Emily had been surprised to see them both together. She had sensed something was wrong with Rachael and kept asking her if she was okay, but she kept saying that she was fine.

Rachael grabbed her bag and car keys and explained to Emily that she wasn't going to be able to continue with her rounds that afternoon and that they were going to send someone from the bank staff to cover her shifts. She told her she wasn't sure when she would be next on duty and that she was taking a few days off.

"Emily, I am going to drive her home in her car, and I will pick their kids up from school. I will explain later when I come home."

"Right okay, is she okay?"

"No, not really."

"She's been quiet all morning but refused to say anything was wrong."

"I can't tell you here."

Colleagues were wandering around,wondering what was going on. He kissed his wife and went and caught up with Rachael.

"I am driving," he said, taking her car keys.

"Okay."

Rachael sat in the passenger seat. She was shaking and shivering with the cold and probably had delayed shock. It had started raining.

"Come on sweetheart, things will get better you'll see, and James is going to get help now." He put the key in the ignition and started the engine. "Let's have some heat," he said, turning on the heater.

Rachael sat back, rested her head back on the head rest and closed her eyes for a while. She felt exhausted and hadn't had much sleep last night because she was so worried about James.

Tom turned the car around and they drove out of the surgery.

They were driving along the A69 heading for Haydon Bridge where James's dad lived. Rachael opened her eyes and found they were on the dual carriageway.

"Oh, I nodded off," she said rubbing her eyes, which were already red from crying.

"How are you doing?"

"Okay, I guess." She sniffed.

They approached the slip road for Haydon Bridge and came off the motorway, entering the village.

Tom parked the car in a lane and stopped the engine. "Do you want a few minutes before we stop outside the house?"

"Yeah, I suppose."

"Here's some clean tissues."

"Thank you."

She leaned towards him, and he undid his seatbelt and put his arm around her. "Rachael, I am so sorry this has happened. Maybe if I had taken him for some lads nights out and spent more time with him …"

"Oh Tom it certainly isn't your fault, you are a good friend you know."

"I have been so busy with work though. He is a parishioner, and I didn't realise something was wrong."

"He didn't like talking about it. He is still trying to get his head around it, as I am."

She looked up at Tom.

"I, I am scared about what is going to happen to us. It is part of my job. I have some experience in mental health, but I just feel as if I have let him down because it took last night for it to sink in as to how bad it had got."

"Rach, you haven't let him down. You are a good wife and a good Mam."

She tried to keep back the tears. "What if I hadn't got to him in time. He could have been dead by now. What if he tries it again? I love him, I don't want this to destroy us and our lives with the kids."

"Shush, sweetheart, me and Emily are here, and we will do anything we can to help, if you want the kids to sleep over at ours, that's okay, whatever you want you only have ask, okay?" He moved some of her hair away from her eyes.

She leaned in for a kiss. He started kissing her passionately but pulled away quickly. "What am I doing? No, Rachael. Sorry but I love my Emily and my boys. I am very fond of you but that is as far as it goes. You're very upset and you are missing James. Come on sweetheart, chin up, wipe those tears and put your seatbelt on." He reversed and turned the car around and headed up to Jack's house to pick up James.

Later after he had been to see one of his parishioners, which he was a little late for, and dropped the Macalister kids off at home, he headed home himself.

It was after 4·30 p m. when he arrived home and the boys were sprawled on the settee each with a controller in their hands playing 'Assassins Creed'."

"Hello boys, good day at school?"

"Yeah." They chorused together.

"Your Mam not back yet?"

"No, not yet Dad. What's for tea?" asked John.

"I don't know what your Mam has planned. I suppose I had better get something out of the freezer?"

"Can we have takeaway pizza?" asked Jamie.

"Oh no not on a weekday."

"We could have a chippy tea, just this once, please," asked John.

"Okay, as long as you two get it. I'll just text your Mam and see how long she is going to be."

'Bing'. His phone soon responded with a text.

"She's on her way, get your Mam her usual, in fact just get four cod suppers, beer battered."

"Okay Dad," they said in unison.

Ten minutes after the boys left for the chip shop, Emily drove her car onto the driveway behind Tom's.

"Hello, anyone home?"

"Hello love."

"You okay?"

"Not really, how was work?"

"Busy, been worried about Rachael."

"Ah, well, yeah, so am I."

"Is she sick?"

"No, but very worried."

"What about?"

"Look there's no easy way of saying this but she says James has been suffering from some mental health problems, he is having a breakdown and erm, well …"

He put his hands up to his face and shook his head. He looked at Emily with tears in his eyes.

"Oh, Ems, he tried to take his own life with whisky and pain killers. He had drunk half a bottle of whisky and was opening the pills in front of her. He didn't take them. She stopped him just in time."

"Oh, my God, poor James, poor Rachael and those poor children."

"She is blaming herself and feels guilty as do I."

"But she does what she can, she couldn't have known that that was going to happen, she is a good wife and mother, and you are a good friend"

"We both feel we haven't had enough time what with work and everything."

"How could I not have known something was wrong, she is my best friend?"

"I think they have both kept it well hidden, it has been going on for the last few months apparently."

"Hang on a moment, I don't understand, how do you know all about this, how long have you known?"

"Not until today, she came into the church for some peace and quiet, she didn't know I was there and when I came out of the vestry, she was there with her head down, sobbing her heart out."

"Oh no, I wish she could have felt that she could have talked to me."

"I think that she has been bottling it up, she really broke down."

"What did you do."

"Talked to her, calmed her down. What else could I do?"

"No, you have done the right thing. If it was the other way around, I would like to think that I could turn to my friends and also you, being a man of the cloth."

"That didn't have anything to do with it. She just needed to offload and obviously she didn't get the opportunity at work to talk to you, what with having to do the rounds."

"The colleagues were wondering what was going on. They were just worried about her."

"Well, if they ask, she just has personal problems to sort out."

"Yes, I know, I am not going to go into details. Oh my God, I hope this gets sorted."

"Yes, well he is being referred to psych and a behavioural therapist and has to take a course of anti-depressants."

"I must phone her, to make sure she and James and the children are okay."

"No, I said we would leave them be tonight. I said we are here and will do anything to help, all she has to do is ask. I even offered for the children to stay overnight here if needs be, but she said they were used to their routine."

"Still, I think I will text her, just to let her know that I am thinking of her."

"Right love, okay."

"Where are the boys?"

"Sent them out for chips."

Chapter 21

Sarah had an uncomfortable night and could not settle. She had very little sleep and the baby was restless. She had got up twice in the night to go to the toilet, to have some water and stretch her legs. She had gone downstairs, so she didn't disturb the rest of the family.

It was 06:45 a.m. and she finally decided to get up and make herself some breakfast, the baby was hungry.

She sat at the table in the kitchen having jam and toast and a mug of tea.

'I don't have long to go now and then we will be seeing you,' she thought patting her bump.

Rick came downstairs and entered the kitchen, surprised to see Sarah up and about so soon.

"Mornin' love, you're up early?" he said kissing his daughter on the cheek.

"I know, I couldn't get comfy. Baby was restless. I have been down here twice in the night."

"You should have woken me."

"I am fine, honest. Do you want a brew?"

"I'll get it, you just sit there and enjoy your breakfast. I think you should just take it easy today."

"Well, I wasn't going to compete in a marathon."

"I know that. I just meant stay at home, don't go off shopping or anything."

"Dad, it doesn't matter where I am, the baby is going to come."

"Yes, I know, I just want to make sure you are with one of us when it happens, your Mam is going to be around."

"Dad, I am fine, stop fussing!"

David came in the kitchen and started getting the cereal out of the cupboards and started making his breakfast, rather noisily, slamming cupboard doors.

"What's wrong with you?" asked Rick.

"Nothin' pops."

"Morning to you David, why are you being so noisy?" asked Rick.

"Sorry," he said, scraping his chair on the floor and slumping down on it, knocking the table in the process.

"David man!" shouted Sarah, steadying her cup and plate.

"Oh, what's all this noise about?" said Sally, coming into the kitchen.

"Just David being David," said Rick.

"Well can you do it more quietly?" said Sally.

"I think I will go up and have a bath, if everyone is finished in the bathroom?" said Sarah, standing up.

"I haven't been in yet and Max is hogging the bathroom," moaned David.

"I will go and hurry him up," said Rick. "I need to get to work and David, bathroom as soon as Max comes out."

"Oh, it doesn't matter. I'll skip a shower today."

"Err shower now," said Sally.

"Yes, go on scruff," said Sarah.

"Okay, I am goin."

"And not just a lick and a promise," said Sally.

Max was coming downstairs.

"Oh, so you're finished at last, poser!" said David shoving past him.

"You're looking smart love," said Sally. She was proud to see that Max was taking care of his appearance, but after her discovery last week, she was still a bit concerned about him.

"Max, what are you wearing?" asked Sally.

"Clothes."

"No, that smell. What is it. It smells familiar."

"Err, just some new Lynx."

"Right."

"So, Sarah, how about we sort through your hospital bag today, make sure you have everything?"

"Okay."

Later in the day, after lunch, Sarah was becoming more and more restless. She tried walking around, lying down, propped on the sofa but just could not get comfortable. Everything was organised for the arrival of the baby. She was pacing the living room floor when Sally came in.

"You okay Sarah?"

"Yeah," she said breathlessly.

She sat down on the edge of the sofa holding her bump. She had had Braxton Hicks a few weeks back. Maybe it was just that.

"Is this it, Mam?"

"Well, you are very close to your due date. Do you want me to phone maternity, see if they can take you in?"

"No, not yet, I am fine," she said standing up. "Ooh!"

"I am driving you to hospital, come on, this baby is on its way."

"Mam, I am scared about all this."

"I know, try not to upset yourself. We don't want the baby distressed."

"Will you help me, if I decide to keep her?"

"You know I will and your dad, but the choice is yours, love."

"There's always adoption."

"Well, if that's what you want, but that's my grandchild and he or she will be loved just as much as you and your brothers. We can always bring her up for you, until you feel ready to. You're going to have exams and your future to think about. There's no rush, we are here to give you support."

"Ooh, I have wet myself!" said Sarah, looking down at her jogging pants.

"Right, come on, to the car. No time to phone them," said Sally escorting her daughter out of the house.

"But I need to change, I can't go with wet pants. Ooh!" she said, very short of breath.

"No time," said Sally picking up the hospital bag on their way out.

Luckily, the hospital was only fifteen minutes away in good traffic. She parked the car and got a wheelchair for Sarah. They checked in and Sarah was soon shown to a cubicle, made more comfortable and put into a gown.

"Right. Have you been having many contractions?" asked the nurse.

"I have been uncomfortable all day but in the last hour I have felt short of breath."

"Right, I will check your blood pressure and then the midwife will come and examine you."

The midwife had just entered the room. "Hi, I am Gillian, the midwife looking after you. Has Charlotte been looking after you?"

"Yes, ooh, I want to push!"

"Well, your blood pressure is fine," said Charlotte.

"Mum!"

"I am here love; I won't leave you."

"Have you phoned Dad?"

"Yes, he's on his way."

"Err, ooh," said Sarah, starting to pant.

"Try to control your breathing, your resp's are rising," said Charlotte.

"Look at me Sarah, nice and calm, in and out, try to control it. That's it, good," said Gillian. "That's better, now I am going to examine you down below to see if I can see the head. You will feel my gloved finger, okay."

"Yes ooh!"

☙

Rick left as soon as he had turned his phone off after speaking to Sally. The traffic was getting heavy, and the roads were busier. School was due out soon and so it was slower trying to move along the road.

He eventually turned into the hospital and found somewhere to park. He thought he had better phone the boys. They would wonder where they were.

He tried both of them, but both phones went to answer phone, so he left some messages. He was going to let them know when they could go to the hospital to see their sister and the new baby.

He found the maternity wing and asked where his daughter would be? He was soon shown to the room they were in. He could hear Sarah shouting and screaming. A lot of noise was coming from that room.

Sarah was sat on the bed, knees up to her chest, taking in oxygen.

"Right, Sarah, I can see the head now, just another few pushes and then baby will be here."

"I can't, I'm tired!" she gasped.

"Yes, you can, come on, control that breathing like we said and push now."

"Urgh! Ooh! Urrgh!"

"Head and shoulders are out, you're nearly there," said Gillian, supporting the newborn.

"Aarrh! Ooh! Urrgh."

"Congratulations – you have a baby girl."

"Is, is she okay?"

"Just about to check her over," she said, cutting the umbilical cord.

"Why, why isn't she crying."

The midwife and the nurse were checking over the baby. The midwife listened to the baby's heart through the stethoscope and the nurse wrapped her in a towel and rubbed her back and the midwife blew into her mouth. The baby's chest started to rise up and down and she let out a loud cry.

"Here give her a cuddle."

Sarah looked at her baby and saw a beautiful baby girl. She felt anxious. She looked again and saw the baby's father's head on the baby.

"I, I don't know, take her away."

"Sarah?" said Rick.

"She's finding this difficult," said Sally.

"Would you like to hold her then?" asked Charlotte, holding the baby towards her.

"I'd love to," answered Sally. "Ooh, she's gorgeous!"

"Looks like I arrived just in time. Congratulations Sarah, she's lovely," said Rick, stroking the baby's head.

"I can't deal with this!" said Sarah, starting to cry.

Sally passed the baby over to Rick and stood by her daughter's bedside.

"Oh, love, come on, we said we would help you."

"Second time I looked at her face I saw him staring back at me."

"Ah, darling." She put her arms around her daughter and hugged her tight.

"You'll be okay, we're here to support you, okay, yes?"

"Yes, I suppose so," she said, wiping her eyes and nose.

"Right, Sarah, I will clean you up and we'll get you into a fresh gown or have you brought some night clothes?"

"In the bag, there's clean pyjamas and my wash bag. I have brought some baby clothes and nappies."

"Okay," said Charlotte getting organised.

"Well Sarah, you have a lovely, contented baby. I just want the paediatrician to check her over and do some preliminary checks," said Gillian.

"Why?"

"Is something wrong?" asked Sally.

"Everything seems fine as far as I can see. It is just a standard procedure with new-borns. I won't be a moment."

She arrived back ten minutes later with the doctor, and he checked the baby over and said that everything seemed to be normal.

"I think baby may want feeding; shall we try her on your breast?" asked Gillian.

"I don't know, Mam?"

"It's okay love, here give her a cuddle first, she needs to smell you and recognise you as her Mummy."

"Okay." Sarah sat up and Sally put the baby in her arms.

"She's yours and very precious she is too."

"Hello, you," said Sarah, looking down at her baby girl.

"Any idea what you are going to call her Sarah?"

"I'm not sure I want to name her yet. I am too young for this. Maybe I should just get her adopted."

"Is that what you really want?" asked Rick.

"I don't know, it is all too soon."

"We could adopt her if you wanted us to, that way she is staying with the family," said Sally.

"She's my baby!"

"I know sweetheart. I am not trying to take control; I just want to help you."

"I don't know if I can handle seeing her every day. What if every time I look at her, I see that rapists face?"

"I think you should try to think of her as your baby, after what he did to you he has no rights over her and when and if you need more professional help to deal with the trauma of what happened we'll get it for you," said Rick. "Okay love?"

"Yes, I know I have had nine months to think about it but now she is here, well?"

"We understand sweetheart," said Sally. "Now how about we try to get her latched on?"

"Err, yeah, okay."

Sally supported the baby's head and tried to latch her on to the breast.

"Oh, it's not working, I can't do this."

"You can," said Sally.

"I'll go and get the nurse," said Rick.

"Hi, Sarah, how are you doing?" asked Charlotte.

"Okay, she won't latch on."

"Here let me try, sometimes it takes a little bit of time, she is learning just the same as you are. There we are, she seems quite content."

"She does, doesn't she?"

"I can see this little one is going to be well looked after and you will have plenty of babysitters when you want to go out with your friends. Any names yet?"

"Your name is Charlotte, right?"

"Yes, that's right."

"I like that name, I am going to call her Charlotte, Sally."

"Oh, I am honoured," said the nurse.

"And Mam, her name is Sally."

"Thank you love," said Sally, looking pleased.

"Well, I'll leave you to it and check back later. You will be ready for some food yourself soon. Baby Charlotte seems to be doing fine."

"Dad, what about the boys, are they coming?"

"Well, they should have got my messages by now. I told them to get their own teas and I would let them know when they could come."

"Okay."

"I hope I still have a kitchen left and that they haven't burnt the house down," said Sally.

"You should have more faith in them Sal."

"Remember last time David tried to cook! He burnt the bacon and left the gas on."

The boys were walking along past the hospital, eating bags of chips.

"Do you think we should go in?" asked Max.

"Don't know, dad said he would let us know when."

"Yeah, but we're walking past now and that was a while ago."

David's mobile rang in his pocket.

"Dad?"

"Yeah, Maxie, sprogs arrived."

"Can we see it?" asked Max.

"Dad, yeah we have had some tea and no we didn't make a mess of the kitchen."

"Okay, yeah we'll come now."

They found their way to maternity and asked to see their sister. As it was now visiting time, they were allowed in.

"My that was quick," said Rick looking up.

"We were walking past, we had chips," said Max. "Is that the baby? It's nice."

"It is a she and she's called Charlotte Sally Seddon," said Sarah, feeling a little better in herself.

"Oh, it's a girl," said David. "I wanted to play footy with it."

"She, and Charlotte is only a few hours old."

"You can still play footy with her Davy," said Sally. "Girls do play football."

There was a lovely family atmosphere and although Sarah felt more relaxed at that moment, there was still a lot of adjusting to do in the transitional period and this was just the start of it.

Chapter 22

It was now December and with just a few weeks until Christmas everyone was busy, preparing for end of year celebrations.

The village looked very pretty. The big fir tree had fairy lights on it and there were lights strung across the main road leading through the village. Even the church was lit up, which looked magical in the moonlight.

By now, most families had their Christmas trees up. This made people feel more festive but not everyone felt that way. For some people who were on their own it could be a lonely period of the year. The Salvation Army had booked the church hall on 23 December and were going to have Christmas lunch and carols for the elderly and the homeless.

Tom had arranged for a carol service to be held that night and then they were going to go around the village carol singing. The Hadrian pub was going to lay on a supper.

There was only a week left at school and all the children and staff seemed to be in high spirits.

At Sleathwaite Primary School, arrangements were well under way. Class parties, Santa Claus and the Nativity play were planned for the final week. But this week the reception and year one children were practicing for their play and the other year groups were going around shops, old people's homes and the local hospital carol singing.

The reception and year one children were now in the school hall practising.

Cameron sat with Bill his best friend and the rest of the class. They were both feeling shy and nervous. Being in year one, and considered the slightly older children, they had all been asked to take part in narrating the Christmas story and singing the carols. Cameron and Bill had a couple of lines to read off cards. Matthew, one of the more confident class members had to introduce the play. He had more to read and one of the girls, Bethany was going to start the first verse of 'Away in a manger'.

They had all got dressed up in their costumes. Cameron and Bill loved dressing up.

"My mammy and daddy are going to see me Cameron and my gran. My Jack will be watching with his class," he said proudly, referring to his older brother.

"Well Scarlett will be watching with her class. My mammy is coming, and grandma and grandad are coming up from Yorkshire for Christmas, so they are hoping to be here. Grandad said he would record it, but he has to ask permission. I'm not sure that he will be allowed to do so."

"Isn't your daddy coming then?"

"I hope so, but he isn't very well at the moment."

"Ah, what's wrong with him?"

"Don't know. Mam says his brain is hurting."

There was a sudden loud clapping as the teachers tried to settle them down and get started with rehearsals.

"Right, hush now, hush, now Matthew, when you are ready stand up and say in a clear voice your lines to open the show please," said Miss Haslem.

Matthew stood up and looked around the hall at all four classes and teaching staff. 'It would be a lot more crowded on the day he thought.'

"Are you okay Matthew?"

"Yes, erm." He held up his card so he could read what he had to say and took a deep breath. "Welcome to Sleathwaite Primary School. We are going to tell you in our own words the Christmas story. We hope you will enjoy our play," he said, sitting down.

"Well done. Ready reception?"

They practised for a good hour or so to make sure everyone knew what they were doing.

Meanwhile at Hexham Hospital, Scarlett was standing with her classmates in the foyer by the entrance. Her year group were performing their carols this week.

"So, what did you ask Santa for?" asked her friend Olivia.

"For my dad to be better," answered Scarlett.

"What, is he still not well?"

"No, he has good days, some not so good days and sometimes bad days, but he is getting there, I hope."

"What is Santa bringing you?" asked Olivia.

"I don't know, I just asked for some new books and games. I did ask for an all-terrain snow board but that was a while ago now, I doubt I'll get it."

"Cool."

"I just want to have a nice Christmas with my family, grandma and grandad are coming up from Hebden; and my other grandparents from Haydon Bridge."

"Oh, that's nice. We are going to my grandma and grandad's for Christmas day."

"My grandad is so funny, he talks in his sleep," said Scarlett.

"My grandma keeps singing when she's in the kitchen and then when she thinks no one is listening, we can hear her swear, if she has dropped something. Course, she'll say that she never swears," said Olivia.

"Right, class have you've got your hymn sheets ready and hold out those collection buckets, all proceeds go to Macmillan cancer charity. Right, we'll start with 'Once in Royal David's City'. Nice and loud, we want to be heard, ready?"

The children started singing and the teaching staff joined in. A crowd was gathering; nurses, doctors, outpatients, inpatients, visitors and by the time they had finished their carols their buckets were nearly full.

They all got a standing ovation and cheers.

Back at the farm Rachael and James were wrapping presents. She was trying to keep him busy. Since his visit to the doctor, he had been having regular visits with the therapists and the anti-depressants seemed to be calming him for a short period but they made him tired and then irritable and so he had to rest up. The psychologist seemed to think that James has had a nervous breakdown, brought on by worry and depression. This was having a major effect on his mental well-being. He was shown techniques on how to control his panic attacks before the paranoia set in.

The psychologist had also talked to Rachael and the children because it was affecting them as well. Cameron and Scarlett drew pictures to express their feelings and Scarlett also wrote down her thoughts. That seemed to be helping.

Cameron being the youngest, didn't understand what had happened to his dad and Scarlett was also confused by what had happened. They tried to be well behaved, but this was especially hard, and they started to fight and express naughty behaviour when things got tough.

They were wrapping up a remote-controlled stunt car for Cameron. James started writing the gift tag.

"Is this one from us or Santa?"

"Santa; make the writing different. He asked for it in his letter to Santa, remember?"

"Oh, yes, what's Scarlett got from Santa then?"

"James, all of Santa's presents are what we are doing now, I told you earlier," she said patiently. "We'll finish Cam's first then get started on Scarlett's okay?" Rachael was feeling tired herself with all of the stress they had had lately. "Scarlett's pile is over there."

"Yeah, he'll love this car. The cat will chase it."

"Yes, he will."

"Has Scarlett got that snowboard? I hope we get some snow, so she can use it?"

"Well, it's what she asked for, it's an all-terrain one, you can use it on grass."

James started yawning. "Are we nearly done; we've been doing this for ages now."

"Yes, just a few more, why don't you make us a brew?"

"Okay," he said still yawning. "James, those tablets make you sleepy. You haven't had a lie down yet."

"I am okay love, honest."

"You look dead on your feet. Have your tea and go and have a sleep."

"I think I might."

She looked at him. The last thing she wanted was him getting irritable. He needed his rest at the moment and to stay calm.

The kettle boiled and he filled the cups up with hot water, but then he knocked his over when he turned around and caught his hand.

"Bloody hell! I've burnt myself!" he said holding his hand under the cold tap.

"Calm down, let me see," said Rachael. "You'll be fine, just a slight accident."

"Christ sake! Stuff the tea!" He threw the mug at the wall.

"James, it's okay, try to take it easy. I'll make you another one." She wanted to shout at him and tell him to stop being so childish, but she knew she herself had to stay in control and be patient.

"That was one of my good Denby mugs. It's broken now."

"I'll buy you another one, sorry, I just get so wound up!"

"There's no need to smash it just because you spilt your tea."

"I've burnt my bloody hand!" he yelled.

"Go up to bed now please before I lose my temper. I am trying to hold us together James."

"Okay, I am going, I am going now!" He grumbled heading for the stairs.

Half an hour later she went upstairs. His clothes were thrown on the floor and he was fast asleep under the duvet. She looked at her watch. It was 2:30 p.m. school would be out soon, and she would have to go out and get the kids. She hoped he was calmer when he got up later for tea.

Christmas was going to be here soon, she sighed to herself. Hopefully he would be able get through it without a meltdown. More than anything, she wanted them all to be able to have a nice Christmas. Just the other week he had pushed the tree over in a temper. She knew he didn't mean it, but she didn't know how much more she could take.

It was four p.m. and Rachael had just got home with the kids. She told them daddy was in bed asleep and to be quiet, but Cameron was so excited now. Christmas was getting a little nearer, so he was making rather a lot of noise and running around.

"Cam! Shush! Daddy's asleep."

"Mum, why's dad in bed. It is only four o'clock?" asked Scarlett.

"The tablets he is taking make him drowsy, and when he gets tired, he gets snappy."

"Can I go up and see him?" asked Cameron.

"Okay, you can go up quietly and see if he's awake. The amount of noise you make is enough to wake the dead."

"Daddy, Daddy, I'm coming," said Cameron, tip-toeing up the stairs.

Cameron looked around the door and saw that his Dad was still asleep.

'Oh, I need a wee,' he thought.

He went into the bathroom, but the door banged shut. He didn't mean to make a noise.

James woke up and sleepily padded across the landing. Cameron came out of the bathroom.

"Daddy!"

"Hello son, all right?"

"Yes, erm Daddy, where are your pants?"

"Oh sorry, I was half asleep, nothing you haven't seen before."

James walked into the bathroom.

Rachael came upstairs.

"Where's your dad?"

"Bathroom, he's in the nuddie!"

"Oh, he's just so tired Cam. Go downstairs, I'll see if your dad is okay and then we'll come down and make tea."

"Can I play rudey dudies?"

"Err no."

"Scarlett, daddy's playing rudey dudies!"

Giggling could be heard from downstairs.

"James? Yes, coming."

James came out of the bathroom and led her to the bedroom. He held her close. She tried to pull away but then let him hold her.

"So sorry love. I am going to try honest."

"James, we will get through this, but I am not sure how much more I can take."

"I know, I am sorry, look I will make tea."

"Has that sleep helped then?"

"Yes, you were right, I needed a rest. I am sorry you have to put up with this, I'll take my meds after tea. Think I will just put my pyjamas on if you don't mind?"

"Doesn't bother me; whatever you feel comfortable in, only don't come downstairs like that, with nothing on. We might have visitors."

"Don't worry, I won't."

"Yeah, you will give everyone a shock."

James went downstairs, dressed in pyjamas.

"Dad is it bedtime?" asked Cameron.

"No son, I just want to feel comfortable."

"Can I put my pyjamas on?"

"If you want to."

"Mum, what's for tea?" asked Scarlett.

"Ask your dad. He said he would cook it; I am having a night off."

"I thought I would do Burgers and chips; how does that sound?"

"Yay!" said Scarlett.

He high fived her and gave her a hug.

"Daddy, are you okay?"

"Yes, I am after having a kip, try not to worry sweetheart."

"I love you," she said wrapping her arms around him.

"I know you do, and I love me too." She dug him in the ribs and giggled. "Scarlett, I love you very much, and Cam and your Mam."

The other two joined in for a group hug.

"Right then," said James. "I had better get my chef's hat on."

"Well, it's more than you had on before Daddy!" shouted Cameron.

"Hey, you, you little …" he went to chase Cameron and tickled him. "Rachael, you go into the sitting room, and I will open a bottle of wine."

"I don't think you should have any alcohol James."

"No, it's for you, go and put your feet up and I will bring it in."

"Oh, thank you."

"And you two little monsters can help me. Cameron, lay the table please and put the sauces and vinegar out. Scarlett, you can be my sous chef. Can you get out the cheese, salad and bread buns."

"Can I make the salad to go in the buns?" she asked.

"Yes please."

James set about peeling and chopping potatoes into chips. He made everything from scratch when he cooked. He did not use frozen chips. The potatoes he was using had been grown on the farm. It felt good to be useful and be doing something he enjoyed doing. He knew he had a long way to go but he wanted to try to get back to normal. Christmas would soon be here, and he wanted to enjoy it with the family. Rachael's parents were coming up from Hebden and his parents were coming across for Christmas lunch, and spending the day with them.

The meal was soon ready, and they sat down together and had a nice meal.

Rachael stood up to clear up and James stood up and stopped her. "No, Rach."

"What?"

"You have done enough around here what with looking after me and the kids. Tonight was my first step to make it up to you. I know I have a long way to go but you three are very important to me." He put his arms around her and pulled her in for a kiss. "Go and sit down and watch the news, the kids will help me."

"Okay, I could get used to this."

"And later, when these munchkins have gone to bed, it is you and me time," he whispered, nuzzling into her ear.

"Err Dad, get a room!" said Scarlett.

Rachael walked away and he patted her on the bottom.

"Ha-ha," said Cameron giggling.

Later on, when the kids were tucked up asleep in bed. Rachael and James snuggled up together on the settee.

"I love you James," said Rachael.

"And I love you, very much."

"I meant what I said before. I can't take much more. I will support you all I can, but this is having an effect on our relationship."

"Rach, I don't want to lose you," he sniffed back the tears. "I want to make it right again, please give me a chance to prove to you that I love you and I want to make this work."

"James, I am not leaving you and I am glad we have had a nice evening. It's just, it's just ..." she started crying. "Oh, James, what is happening to you, to us?"

"I don't know, I don't know how many times I can say sorry or how to make it right. I do love you, very much and I want to show you that I do care about you and the kids and look after you all again. You've done enough looking after me recently"

"Only because you need me to, in sickness and in health remember. I hope you would look after me if I was ill?"

"Of course, I would."

"This is so hard," she cried.

"Come here." He drew her in for a cuddle and held her while she sobbed. "I hope things get better, it's nearly Christmas and our parents will be coming, and we should give the kids a good Christmas. They deserve it."

She sniffed. He stroked her back and sighed.

"Rachael, I think I should come off my tablets."

"No, you can't yet."

"But they only relieve my symptoms for a short time. After three or four hours, I feel tired and irritable, and I don't like taking it out on you. I wouldn't normally be like that."

"You used to be so happy, but James that was before you became ill before you took tablets. When you were becoming ill, looking back now, I realise that you were starting to become snappy and irritable then. You can't help being ill. You're not doing this on purpose. I know this isn't the real you."

"I am scared I can't get back to how I was."

"Oh, James. Look; we will see if Doctor Mansfield can prescribe you some different tablets, ones that agree with you better. I don't plan to go back to work until after Christmas, but we can see if we can get you an appointment this week. Do you feel you need to go for a therapy session before Christmas?"

"My next appointment is on 2nd January."

"Shall we see if we can get you one next week before the holidays?"

"We could try, but I may have to leave it till the new year anyway."

Rachael yawned and stretched. "I think I'll go to bed now. I am tired."

"Can I come and snuggle up warm with you?"

"Yes, come on," she said, pulling him up.

"Maybe we could do a bit more than snuggle?"

"James, will you just hold me, and we'll see what happens. We have both been stressed lately."

"Well, doctors' orders were – I had to do relaxation techniques. What better way is there to relax," he grinned.

"I don't think he meant what you mean," she smiled. "We are going to be all right, aren't we?"

"I hope so, we both love each other, and we can get through this like we have on other not so good times," he answered trying to be positive.

They climbed the stairs. It didn't take them long to get undressed, especially James who just had his pyjamas on.

James and Rachael snuggled under the covers after James had turned the light off. He stroked her skin and kissed her back.

"I don't ever want to let you go," he murmured into her neck.

"Well at least for the next eight hours," she answered. "Then we have to get up."

"It's Saturday tomorrow. We can stay in bed."

"We have two noisy children."

"They can watch cartoons, while we have some of us time." He tickled her.

She started to giggle and relax, glad to feel safe and secure in James' arms. James looked down at her and smiled. To him, she still looked as young and as beautiful as the night he first met her in town on a night out. She had just started Uni at Leeds and had come up on a weekend with her fellow student nursing friends. After they started seeing each other for a while and she completed her first year's training, she decided to transfer to Northumberland University, which meant they could see each other more often. And it wouldn't be as expensive as travelling on the train between Leeds and Newcastle.

"You look thoughtful?"

"I was thinking about when we first met and how you haven't changed. You still look as young and beautiful now as you did then."

"Why thank you kind sir. More grey hairs though."

She looked up at him and stroked his cheek. And then her lips found his and she slipped her tongue into his mouth and gave him a long and passionate kiss.

"Ooh, that was nice Nurse Macalister and what other treatment do you have for your patient?"

"Well, you are my patient, and I am going to give you a massage, relieve some of that tension that has been building up the last few months. Turn onto your tummy and I will do your back."

"I could get used to this, nurse."

"Shut up and do as I tell you."

"Why don't you put your uniform on, just your uniform?"

"Err, why?"

"Thought you were playing naughty nurses!"

She laughed. "My sisters' uniform is hardly sexy!" she said, smacking his bottom. She started massaging his shoulders which were very tight. "You have a lot of tension in your neck and shoulders," she said, trying to relieve the muscles.

"That's nice."

She worked her way down his back, her hand movements getting slower and more tender as she moved down his body, the massaging turned into kissing and before she knew it, she couldn't help herself, all of the tension that had built up over the months, suddenly needed to be released. She fell into James' arms and together they made love, like they hadn't done for what seemed like a long time.

James snuggled down the bed under the covers and found the curve in between her legs and entered her, where they were joined in harmony and became one. He gave a big sigh. He was happy to be in her arms and felt safe and secure. He didn't want the night to end, and he hoped that he had turned a corner on his road to recovery.

There was no one more important to him than Rachael, other than his children; and he felt guilty about the way he had behaved, but he knew that it was down to his condition, his illness. All he wanted now was for things to get back onto a normal footing. He knew he wasn't ready for work yet, but he was ready to start looking after his family. He suddenly felt stronger and revitalised. But this was what happened to him, he felt great again and then bang, it came back to hit him in the face with a vengeance. He hoped the doctor could give him some different tablets.

Rachael stretched in bed and yawned. She felt on James' side, but no James. She looked at the clock and it was nine thirty in the morning. Surely, she hadn't slept that long?

'God, where is he?' she thought. He was normally snoring by her side. Lately, he had been so tired, it was her that had to get up first and see to the breakfast.

She got out of bed and realised she had no pyjamas on and then she remembered last night and smiled to herself. She was anxious as to where he was though. She hoped he hadn't wandered off again. She was pulling on her pyjama top when James came through the door.

She stood up with just her top on.

"James, I was worried, I thought you had wandered off again."

James put the breakfast tray down on the bed. "Now you, back into bed, I have brought us bacon croissants, tea and orange juice, and this red rose is for you. I know it's plastic but needs must."

She climbed back into bed.

"This is lovely, thank you. You should have woken me, what about the kids' breakfast?"

"They've had theirs, don't worry. They're sitting downstairs watching telly. He closed the bedroom door, pulled his pyjamas off and climbed into bed. James couldn't stand wearing anything in bed. He got too hot.

"We'll get crumbs in the bed."

"Err, doesn't matter, we will clean up afterwards, or rather I will. You are not to do anything today. I am going to wait on you hand and foot," he said, lifting a croissant to her mouth.

"You don't have to try so hard, and I can feed myself!" she said grabbing the croissant. "Still the attention is nice though."

"I haven't been paying you enough attention," said James. "But that is going to change."

They finished their breakfasts and looked at the newspaper.

Cameron came charging in, wearing his favourite Simpson pyjamas.

"Yabba, dabba, doo!" he shouted, flinging himself on the bed and bouncing up and down.

"Dad."

"Yes Cameron?"

"Guess what we were watching?"

"Ooh, I don't know, the Flintstones?"

"How did you know?"

"Because, you said Yabba dabba doo!"

"I can't believe that's back on. That was on CBBC when your Dad and I were little," said Rachael.

"They had CBBC when you were little, and you watched the Flintstones?" he asked.

"Yes, don't sound so surprised!"

Scarlett came running into the bedroom and jumped on the bed.

"You're in bed late Mum, it's ten thirty!"

"I let your Mam have a lie in, Scarlett," said James. "She deserves it."

"Just teasing, when are you getting up?"

"In a while," said James. "Scram!"

"Mammy?"

"Yes, Cammy?"

"Will you play my Simpson's game with me on the PlayStation?"

"Yes, I don't see why not, but this afternoon we are being Santa's helpers and delivering some Christmas Cards and presents to friends."

"Where are we going?" asked Scarlett.

"Well, we need to deliver cards to the nearest neighbours and then we are going over to Emily and Tom's for tea."

"Will the twins be there?" asked Scarlett.

"Yes, I am sure the four of you can find something to do."

"They're big boys!" said Cameron. "Come on Mam, out of bed," said Cameron grabbing her hand and trying to pull back the duvet, which Rachael grabbed just in time before he saw she just had a pyjama bottoms on.

"Hey, Cam, we'll be down in half an hour son, all right?" said James.

"Okay, come on Scarlett."

"Race you to the controllers!" shouted Scarlett.

"Be careful on those stairs!" shouted Rachael.

James and Rachael looked at each other and laughed.

"They're a joy," she said.

"Wouldn't have it any other way," he said.

"Half an hour you said and then we'll get up?"

"Yes, gives me just about time to do this!" he said, diving under the covers and tickling her, making her shriek with laughter.

"Tell you what, we'll send the kids ter do the present deliveries and we'll stay in bed," she said jokingly.

"If only!"

"Mam! Dad!" bellowed Cameron.

"We'd better get up. I've lain here long enough."

"A few more minutes, he has to learn that you are not at his beck and call Rach."

"I know, okay a few more minutes and then showers and then we'll go down."

"Course, we could always save water and I will join you in the shower?" said James.

"Promises, promises."

"Come on," he said, grabbing her and running to the bathroom, locking the door behind them.

James let the water fall over Rachael and lovingly washed her body and she did the same to him.

They then went downstairs dressed and ready for the day, holding hands.

Chapter 23

It was now the last week of term and Rachael and James were standing in the queue, waiting to go in to watch the school play.

"Hope I stay awake," murmured James, trying not to yawn.

"You're doing much better," said Rachael. "We'll have to go and pick up your prescription after this."

"I know, it should be ready," replied James.

"Rachael, James!"

They both looked up and Rachael's parents were walking along the path, to join them at the end of the queue.

"Mum, Dad! Oh, it's so good to see you both," she said, giving them both a hug. They hadn't seen them since half term.

"Marian, George," said James, giving his mother-in-law a kiss and shaking George's hand.

"How are yer son?" asked George, squeezing James's hand gently.

"Not so bad; getting there. I have good days and not so good days."

"You're okay though?" asked Marian concerned.

"Yes, I am feeling more positive."

"Good, I am glad James," she said, patting him on the arm. "How about you love, how are you?" asked Marian.

"Okay, we're doing okay Mum."

She looked at her daughter and thought how tired she looked. She had dark shadows under her eyes. Still at least she and George would be able to help out while they were there.

"How was the traffic?" asked James.

"Bloody awful," said Marian.

"I needed ter pop into Halifax ont way and there was a crash, which delayed things," said George.

"Everyone okay?" asked Rachael.

"Heard on t'news that there was a head on crash, involving a lorry and a people carrier. Some were teken ter hospital, and we are not sure whether there were any fatalities at the moment," said George.

"It were a right old smash up, we saw it when we passed int car. I expect we'll hear more on the news later," said Marian.

They all piled into the school hall and all of the children were sitting on the floor and on benches. After all the audience had found their seats and everyone had settled down, the head teacher stood up. Cameron spotted his parents and grandparents and gave them a wave.

"Welcome, everyone; your children and grandchildren have worked ever so hard in producing this play and they have completed some very good work which you can see on their classroom walls afterwards, when tea and coffee will be served. The year two children have made some biscuits, so without further ado, I will hand you over to your lovely children."

Matthew stood up a little nervously and introduced the play, and the children from reception came out and performed the Christmas story. Mary nearly dropped baby Jesus. Good job it was a doll.

When it came to Bill and Cameron's lines. They stood up together holding hands.

"There is no room at the inn," said Cameron.

"There's a Premier Inn down the road, does a very nice full English," said Bill.

The audience laughed.

At the end Bethany stood up and sang the first verse of 'Away in a Manger' and all of the children joined in with the other verses.

Matthew stood up.

"We hope you enjoyed our Christmas story and now we would like to wish you a merry Christmas." The children and staff all joined in singing 'We wish you a merry Christmas'.

Then it was the head teacher's turn to stand up. "Thank you all for coming, the children are having their Christmas parties tomorrow and we may have a special visitor. You'll find refreshments at the back of the hall and the catering staff have made some mince pies."

The end of term passed quickly. Christmas Eve was on Saturday, the beginning of the Christmas period.

James woke up early and looked outside. Everywhere was covered with white frost. He checked his phone for a weather update, and it said that they were expecting heavy snow that day and the odds were high for a white Christmas. His mam and dad were coming tomorrow morning to spend Christmas Day with them. Neither of them was able to drive now due to their failing eyesight.

'I had better get them today,' he mused to himself. 'Chances are we'll be snowed in up here.'

They got quite a bit of snow up there when it did snow and the last thing he wanted was for them to be snowed in and his parents not being able to make it for Christmas.

He looked over at Rachael.

She was in a deep sleep, lightly snoring. He lay next to her and watched her sleeping. Some of her hair had fallen over her face. He gently pulled it back and kissed her lightly on the forehead. She didn't even stir. He smiled and put his arm around her, and gently drew her towards his body.

He was thinking how beautiful she looked, and he wanted to protect her, more than anything. He wanted to put his depression and mental health issues behind him and move on.

At least now he was accepting that he had problems and was trying to overcome them. He had been to the Hadrian last night for some drinks with Tom. He just had coke; he didn't want alcohol to affect his medication. They had had a nice evening. They went early at about seven o'clock and stayed a couple of hours. They had enjoyed each other's company and had a few laughs. A couple of hours out was enough for him just now and he knew he wouldn't be able to cope when the pub became busy and noisy. Plus, he didn't want to rock the boat at home after everything that had happened; but Rachael had said it would do him the world of good to get out and socialise. She herself had been out with Emily earlier in the week for a works do; only she felt she could only stay out a few hours herself as she still didn't like leaving James too long.

James turned onto his back and looked up at the ceiling. For the first time in months, he felt that he could look forward to the future and he hoped that 2020 would be a good year for him and the family. They had been through enough.

Rachael had made him promise that when he felt anxious and things were getting too much that he would talk to her and be open about it; and to attend all of his therapy sessions, which seemed to be finally working for him.

He was never one for talking about his feelings but after his recent experience, he had learned that it was good to talk.

Suddenly the bedroom door banged open, and Scarlett and Cameron came running in.

"Daddy, it's Christmas Eve!" shouted Cameron excitedly; jumping onto the bed and getting onto his knee for a cuddle. "Santa's coming tonight!"

"Shush! Look," he said, pointing at Rachael.

Rachael started to stir. "What's all the noise about?" she said sleepily.

"Come on lazy bones, get up!" said Cameron, gently prodding her.

"Daddy can we follow Santa's journey on Google, on the laptop," asked Scarlett.

"Yes, I don't see why not. Let's do it this afternoon.

"We have to erm, get carrots, for the reindeers, leave mince pies and biscuits out for Santa, he has to have his supper, he'll get cold and hungry, erm what else?"

"Are you going to come up for air and breathe Cam?" asked James smiling at his son.

"There is so much to do, come on," said Cameron.

"Who'll get cold and hungry?" said Rachael sleepily trying to pull herself together and sit up.

"Mum! SANTA!" shouted Scarlett. "He's coming tonight!"

"Oh, right, hang on what time is it?"

"Six thirty!" said Scarlett.

"Six thirty on a Saturday! God knows what time you'll be up tomorrow morning then," moaned Rachael, but she was smiling at them. They were only going to be little once, and she wanted to make the most of it.

James looked over at Rachael. "Rach have you seen outside? It's covered in white frost. My phone says we are in for heavy snow today and the odds are high for a white Christmas."

"They always say that," said Rachael, standing up and looking outside.

The children rushed to the window.

"Wow!" they both said in unison.

"Jack Frost has been!" shouted Scarlett excitedly.

"I am worried though. If it is going to be thick with snow how is Santa going to get here, with our presents," pondered Cameron, standing with his finger on his lip.

"Well," said Rachael picking up her little boy for a hug.

"What happens is Santa has a magic dust and his sleigh is so well built that it can get through all kinds of different weather, and the reindeers will have their special feed to make them fly in the air and pull the sleigh behind them."

"Whoa! They can't go too fast though; Santa and the presents might tip out!"

She put him down. "You are getting heavy," she said, ruffling his blond curly hair. He looked the image of James, with the same hair colouring. Scarlett was more like her with light brown hair. "Don't worry Cammy, I am sure Santa will get here in one piece.

"Can I go and wake my Grandma and Grandad up," he asked.

"No, let them sleep, but they'll probably be awake now, the amount of noise you two make," she answered.

"Rachael, I think I will go and get Mam and Dad in the car this morning, I don't want us snowed in tomorrow and we can't get to them," said James.

"James, I don't think you are ready for driving yet. I can go for them."

"I need to start sooner or later."

"Yes, but later, come with me and I will drive you over in the car."

"Okay."

"I don't know where we are going to put them though."

"They could have our bed and we could sleep downstairs on the settees.

"Right, okay then. This bed will have to be stripped."

"I'll phone them a bit later on; they'll still be asleep. It is only quarter to seven.

"Are Grandad Jack and Gran coming today?" asked Scarlett.

"Yes," said James.

"Wahey!" said Cameron.

"Get in!" said Scarlett grabbing Cameron's hand. "Come on let's watch some cartoons, I get first pick."

"Aah!" moaned Cameron. "Okay then."

James and Rachael looked at each other and laughed.

"James?"

"Yes?"

"Come here for a hug."

He got out of bed pulling on his boxer shorts and joining her at the window.

They held each other close.

"James, I love you."

"I know, irresistible me, how can you resist this muscular body of the gods!"

"Shut up!" she laughed, hitting him gently on the back.

"I love you too, my little lovey."

"Little lovey?"

"Yes, that is what you are, and I am going to look after you, now Madam."

He held out his arm.

"Shall we?"

"What?" she said, laughing.

"We are going downstairs, and I am going to make you a delicious breakfast."

"You had better put some clothes on. We don't want my mother having a heart attack."

"What with this body, never!" he said grabbing his dressing gown. "Maybe when the kids are at school, we could have a naked chef day," he whispered grinning.

"You have a one track mind," she grinned.

"I am just talking about cooking. I don't know what you have in mind," he mocked.

"Mind you, you would look good in a naughty French maid outfit!"

"Get down those stairs," she said, giving him a friendly push.

She was glad to get back to some sort of normality. Things seemed to be going well and hopefully they were going to have a nice Christmas. James still got upset and uptight about some things, but he was learning to control it now. He seemed to want to get better. She prayed every night to herself that nothing would tip him over the edge again after she had found him in the barn on that fateful night, when he was going to end his life.

Chapter 24

Jack Macalister got out of bed and looked out of the window across the fields. It was still quite dark and thick with snow. As a child he had seen many a bad winter on the farm when he was growing up. The farm had been in the family for generations. He still had some money invested in business.

As he looked outside, he didn't see the snow or that it was still dusk. In his mind's eye he was transported back in time. He imagined going out and taking the sheep over the fields with his Border Collie in tow and how his dad had taught him about sheep farming and lambing.

Even as a young lad he had often helped around the farm. It was expected of him. Everyone had to do their bit. It was wartime when he was small, and rations were in short supply. So, they grew a lot of vegetables, fruit and salad greens, which they sold to local families and shops. James had kept the tradition going.

He looked across at his wife. He had known Elsie since school days. They had grown old together and were happy in their twilight years.

He felt happy to be back in his childhood home and the same house where they had spent most of their married life, until James took over the running of the farm and had a family of his own.

Elsie sat up in bed and looked around.

"What time is it?"

"Time to get up, we have jobs to do."

"Oh, I forgot where I was there. It's nice to be back here isn't it Jack?"

"And we haven't spent a night here for a long time."

"I know, I was just thinking what it was like growing up here and our married life living here. The farm is more modern now, but in some ways it's much the same."

Now in their mid eighties they were enjoying life at a slower pace. They had some health problems, Jack was in the early stages of dementia and Elsie had experienced heart failure. She had had a few attacks and it was found that she had Mitral Heart Regurgitation, a leaky heart valve, which they repaired. She had also undergone a triple heart bypass; and had to try to keep herself healthy by eating well-nourished food and taking daily exercise. She used to love to go out for walks, but these days she didn't get very far. She used her four wheeled walking frame and liked to walk around to their local park. She had rheumatoid arthritis in her joints, which put pressure on her knees, if she walked any distance.

She lay in bed thinking about days gone by and life living on the farm. When she looked up, Jack was gone.

"Jack?"

He had a tendency to wander off and become disorientated with his surroundings. She looked at the clock. It was only seven a.m.

'Maybe he went to the bathroom.'

There was no one in the bathroom. She went downstairs and the back door was open.

'Oh, know, he must have gone outside.'

She went into the living room to wake James. She gently tried to jostle him awake.

"Cameron, I said we'd open the presents later, go to bed," he murmured.

"James, James wake up!"

"Huh, whassup?

"It's your Dad, he isn't here."

"What?"

He stood up and looked out of the kitchen window, he put the security light on and saw that it was still quite dark.

"I hope he's not walking towards the fields."

He went and pulled on his jeans, put a warm jumper on and grabbed his coat, boots and a torch.

'God! please, let him be okay,' he thought, setting out towards the fields.

Jack was quite sprightly for his age and could walk at a quick pace. He was walking across the fields wearing his dressing gown over his pyjamas, with his coat on top. He was carrying the crook that was used for herding the sheep.

James shouted as loud as he could. "Dad! Dad! Dad! Where are you going? Flaming Hell!" he said, panicking, looking around. A voice in his head said 'Keep calm James, count to ten.' He looked ahead and saw a solitary figure out in the next field. James tried to run after him but fell flat on his face in the snow. After fifteen minutes he managed to catch up with him.

"Dad! Dad! Where are you going?"

"Oh, hello son, you've come to help me, there's a good lad," he said, patting James on the shoulder.

"What are you doing? It is only quarter past seven in the morning."

"I was going to bring the sheep down to the lower field."

"You don't do that anymore. Paddy brought the sheep down before the heavy snow."

"Who's Paddy?"

"My farm manager."

"That's my job."

"No, Dad."

James looked down at his dad's feet. He was standing in his slippers. His feet would be cold and wet.

"Right Dad, let's get you back home."

"Oh, has your Mam got breakfast ready?"

"No, we'll have it soon. Let's get you in the warmth before you become hyper thermic. You must be freezing, it's minus 2 degrees."

James started to steer his dad back towards the farmhouse.

"Haven't you got school today?" asked Jack, confused.

"No, I left a long time ago and it is Christmas morning."

"Oh, we had better get back and you can open your presents. We got you a Thomas train set."

"Really Dad?"

They were halfway across the field now. James was concerned about his dad. The last thing he wanted was for his dad to get ill.

"James, would you like a ride on the tractor. You have always enjoyed that."

"Let's just get you back."

James looked up and could see his Mam and Rachael standing at the back door.

"Is he okay?" asked Rachael concerned.

"He's very cold and he only has his slippers on. Let's get him by the fire."

"Jack, what did you think you were doing walking out there in the cold and wet?" asked Elsie.

"I went to see to the sheep."

Rachael got the thermometer, the SATS probe and blood pressure machine out of the cupboard.

"Let me check you over Jack," said Rachael.

"Right, you have a low temperature of 34 and your blood pressure is low. James, get a blanket," she said, taking off Jack's slippers, "and a bowl of warm water and a towel."

She looked up and James was standing with his arms wrapped around his body, trying to control his breathing. He could feel a panic attack coming on.

"Oh, God!" said James. "He could have become hyperthermic and died!"

"James come and sit by the fire and try and slow your breathing down, remember in and out, in and out."

Marian walked into the kitchen.

"What has happened?" she asked, worriedly.

"Jack wandered off into the fields in his pyjamas and James went and got him, now they are both freezing," answered Rachael.

"Owt I can do?"

"Yes, can you get two blankets, a towel and a bowl of warm water please?"

"Of course."

Rachael carried out observations on James, which proved to be normal. He was quite cold though.

George joined them in the kitchen.

"Marian's just told me what happened, you two okay?" he asked.

James was sitting rocking, and Jack was shaking with the cold.

"Shall I make some hot tea?"

"Yes, please Dad. They are a bit shaken."

Scarlett and Cameron came charging into the kitchen. "He's been! He's been!" they shouted excitedly.

"Can we open our presents, can we?" asked Cameron. "Why has Grandad Jack got his feet in a bowl of water?" he asked.

"Grandad Jack decided to take a walk and was going to fetch the sheep," said Elsie. "Had us all worried."

"A lot of fuss about nowt", said Jack muttering to himself.

"Silly Grandad is he keeping warm?" asked Scarlett.

"Yes."

"Dad are you okay?" asked Scarlett, looking at her Dad.

He looked up at his daughter and painted on a smile, whilst silently counting to ten, to calm himself down. He hadn't taken his tablets yet.

"Yes sweetheart, just cold, come here, and Cam." He gave them both a hug.

"Dad, can I open my presents?"

"Soon," he answered.

Cameron had been up at 2 a.m. and then 4 a.m. to ask if Santa had been and was it time to open his presents. He was promptly sent back to bed.

"We are going to have breakfast and then open presents," said Rachael.

"Happy Christmas, everyone."

"Merry Christmas!" they chorused.

"Elsie, have we got that Thomas train set we promised our James?" asked Jack, again confused.

The children started to giggle.

"Jack, what year is it?" asked Rachael.

"1979."

"Oh, Dad," said James.

The rest of the day passed smoothly with no more disasters. The children loved their presents. The weather settled in the afternoon and the kids did some sledging. Scarlett was thrilled with her snow board. And she and Cameron took turns on it.

The grandparents gathered everyone around the television at three o'clock, to watch the queen's speech. They said that everyone should watch it.

❧

At the Seddon's they had just finished eating and were settling down to watch the afternoon film. They were watching 'Paddington 2'.

They were all curled up on the settees when Charlotte started to cry.

"Oh, can she not be quiet?" moaned David. "I'm trying to watch this."

"I'll go and see to her Sarah, you watch the film," said Sally, going to pick her up out of her baby chair.

"No, Mam, I'll do it."

"Okay, I was just going to give you a break."

"She's my baby, but thanks," said Sarah.

"I know that love, I wasn't trying to take over."

Rick looked up. "Your mam is only trying to help Sarah."

"All right, all right, you can see to her bottle while I change her nappy, please."

"Can we just watch the film?" said Max rewinding it.

Sally was enjoying being a grandparent but felt Sarah was becoming a little possessive and overprotective. She didn't like to leave Charlotte's side. Sally thought that this was only natural given what had happened to her, but she still got the impression that Sarah didn't like her picking her baby up.

Sally went through to the kitchen and boiled the kettle and set about preparing Charlotte's bottle. She didn't want to take over, but she thought Sarah could do with a break. She was starting to look worn out.

Sarah was still very young, and Sally and Rick wanted to support her and help out where they could. They thought Sarah could do with having a night out with people her own age, but she hadn't had a chance to make any friends in the village yet. They had only been there a couple of months. She was due to start at a sixth form college in the new year which supported teenage mothers.

Sarah still seemed traumatised from the assault and Sally was beginning to wonder if she needed professional help.

Sarah appeared in the kitchen doorway, holding onto Charlotte.

"Hello, love, I have her bottle ready."

"Sorry about before, I didn't mean to snap at you."

"It's okay Sarah, I just thought that you could do with a rest, you can't do it all yourself; you will burn yourself out," she said, handing Sarah the bottle.

"I know, I just want to be a good mam to her."

"And you will but you should try to accept help when it is offered. I do know that you want to do it all, but you are still quite young." Again, she held out the bottle.

"No Mam, you can feed her if you like, I am sorry."

"Really?"

"Yes, here Charlotte, go to 'Granny'."

"Granny? I'll Granny you!"

Sarah grinned. "Sorry, Gran."

"Come on gorgeous, let's give you your milk."

Charlotte stared up at her Gran with big round eyes. Sally thought that she looked the image of Sarah.

"She looks the image of you when you were little Sarah."

"I can see him," she muttered, referring to the baby's father and her rapist.

"Oh, love!"

They went through to the sitting room and joined the rest of the family. They had had a quiet family day, just the six of them. The rest of the family were going to visit from Manchester in the New year.

They wanted to have their first Christmas in their new house on their own.

Max piped up., "Mam, what's for tea?"

"You only finished your lunch an hour or so ago. Surely you can't be hungry?" enquired Sally.

"I am a growing boy you know."

"I was just going to put out some snacks in the kitchen. I am busy feeding Charlotte; you boys can go and sort tea out if you want something."

"Rick, do you want anything?"

"No, not with all that dinner, which was beautiful by the way, just like you," he said reaching over and giving his wife a kiss.

David stood up. "Come on Maxie, let's raid the cupboards. Sarah, you comin'?"

"No, I am not hungry."

Charlotte guzzled the rest of her bottle and fell asleep on Sally.

Rick looked down at his granddaughter.

"Ah, bless, look at her, she looks so peaceful." He turned to Sarah who was sitting on the opposite chair with her feet up, looking at her phone.

"Have you enjoyed your first Christmas with Charlotte in our new home Sarah?"

"Yes, it's been mint."

"Oh, so good then?"

"Yeah, it's been all right," she murmured, looking at her phone.

"So conversational the youth of today," he remarked.

Sally laughed.

The boys came through with bowls filled with Christmas pudding and ice cream.

"Dad, can I have a drink?" asked David.

"Of course, why didn't you get one when you were in the kitchen. There is plenty of coke."

"Nah, a proper drink, beer."

"That's mine and you are too young."

"Aah, but my new friends drink."

"I bet they don't."

The house was looking very festive. The house seemed much more homely now. Rick had lit the wood burner and it gave off a warm cosy glow in the inglenook fireplace.

They enjoyed their evening together and Rick was glad that they had moved here. Everyone seemed more settled. Although he was still worried about his kids and the issues they were having; overall, he felt that they had made the right decision leaving Manchester and moving to Northumberland.

"Hang on a moment, I have an idea," he said, getting up.

"Where is he going?" asked Sarah.

"Don't know," said Sally.

Rick returned ten minutes later with a bottle of prosecco and five champagne glasses.

"Right, David you wanted to have a drink?"

"Yeah, can I get drunk?"

"No, you can't."

"Right a little bit each for you three," he said handing them all a glass. He pulled the cork out of the bottle which made a loud pop. Charlotte hardly stirred in her sleep.

"Right, I have been saving this for a special occasion. To Sarah and our beautiful granddaughter, two fine young men and my gorgeous wife, cheers everyone."

"Cheers!" they chorused.

"And to our new house and a Merry Christmas!" said Sally

"Merry Christmas!" they cheered.

Rick walked towards Sally and gently pulled her into his arms.

"Merry Christmas darling, I love you."

"I love you too and thank you all for making this a lovely day," she answered, looking around the room at her children and grandchild.

∾

Over at the Hadrian, it was business as usual, and the pub was busy. Matthew and Caitlin were behind the bar serving and Adam and Simon were busy collecting glasses and serving up bar snacks. They had served Christmas dinner at lunchtime, but it was quieter then. They had had about twelve bookings. Matthew and Caitlin had their Christmas dinner that afternoon when they closed up for a few hours. Simon and Adam had just come in for the night-time rush, and other bar staff came in at lunchtime.

When things quietened down a little, Matthew finally had time to talk to Caitlin.

"So, how has your day been then?"

"Busy but nice."

"Think we'll close at ten tonight; I want you all to myself."

"Why, have you got me another present?"

"Well, you never know if you play your cards right," he whispered.

"Aye, aye," said Mike one of the regulars. "You on a promise Matt?"

"Mind your own business."

"Charmin' I wouldn't mind a pop at her when you're finished," he said drunkenly leering at Caitlin.

"Hands off, she's spoken for," said Matthew.

"Can I have a double whisky, Caitlin?"

"No, Mike, I think you have had enough," she answered curtly.

"Oh, go on – a Christmas kiss under the mistletoe."

"NO!"

"Right, come on Mike, time to go home," said Matthew, walking around the bar and showing him to the door.

"I'll see you in the mornin' Matty," he drawled.

"Go and sleep it off," said Matthew, giving him a little shove.

Over on the far side of the bar, Patrick and Philip were having drinks with their brothers Pete and Steve.

"He never changes that one," said Patrick.

"He looks like he has had a fair few," remarked Pete.

"So, bruv, how was your first Christmas as a married man?" asked Steve, looking at Philip.

"It has been a very nice day and I am glad we could all get together and have a big family Christmas."

"The parents all seemed to get on," said Patrick.

"Yeah, it's been really nice said Pete. "Hey, Patrick, remember that Christmas when we were kids, and we were going to look for presents and we looked in that walk-in cupboard and the door shut on us and we couldn't get out."

"Yes, and if I remember rightly, you opened one of them, you couldn't resist the temptation."

"Well, you know, I wanted to see what I was getting."

"But I got told off as well and I hadn't opened any."

"Well, you came into the cupboard."

"Yeah, you dragged me in."

"What are you two doing tomorrow?" asked Steve.

"Staying in bed and recovering," answered Patrick.

"Actually, I have four tickets for the Sleathwaite Warriors against Tynedale Tyrants tomorrow. I thought it would be a nice surprise," said Philip.

"Oh, nice one Phil," said Patrick. "Up for it, lads?"

"Yeah, great, count us in," said Steve.

"Well, we are staying tonight anyway. Why not? Be a good afternoon," said Pete.

"Have you ever thought of signing up Patrick, you used to be good at school."

"That was a long time ago Pete. I have tried to persuade Philip, but he doesn't seem keen."

"Well, you could though, couldn't you?"

"I'm not sure I have the time mate. Our nephew is learning at school, they taught him the 'Haka'," said Patrick.

"Yeah, he showed us. Come on Patrick, on your feet."

"Can you remember all of it?"

"Yeah, think so?"

They proceeded to perform the Haka and Philip and Steve joined in and then some more customers joined in, including some of the Sleathwaite Warriors.

"KA MATE! KA MATE!
We're going to die! We're going to die!
We were at war.
KA ORA, KA ORA!
We're going to live! We're going to live!
But now there is peace.
KA MATE! KA MATE!
We're going to die! We're going to die!
We thought we were all going to die.
KA ORA, KA ORA!
We're going to live! We're going to live!
But now we are safe.
TENEI TE TANGATA. PU'RU- HURU.
This is the man, so hairy.
Because of our leader, so strong and masculine.
NA'A NEI TIKE MAI WHAKA-WHITI TE.
Who fetched and made shine the.
Has united us and brought back the sunny days of
RA! UPANE! KA UPANE!
Sun Together! All together …
Peace. We are all working in harmony, side by side.
A UPANE! KA UPANE!
Together! All Together…!
Moving in unison like the hairs on our chief's legs.
WHITI TE RA!
To sun shines!
To prolong these sunny days of peace.
Hi!
Yeah!"

The staff and other customers who were sitting down stood up and gave them all a standing ovation; the cheers went all round the pub.

Over at the bar. "Getting lively in here," said Caitlin, smiling.

"Good to see people enjoying themselves," said Matthew.

The lads sat back down at the table out of breath.

"Fancy another round of drinks? Matthew said they were closing at ten and it's nine thirty already," asked Philip.

"Yeah, I could do with one, four pints?" asked Steve.

"Yes, let's make it shots this time," said Patrick.

"I'll get them, vodkas all round?"

"Yes, doubles, and pints," said Steve.

"I'll get them," said Philip, standing up and almost falling over. "Think I'm a bit pissed, good job that game isn't until the afternoon."

"Well hair of the dog will sort that out bro."

It was now nine forty-five."

"Last orders at the bar please!" shouted Matthew.

"After we have got rid of this lot, let's have a night cap and some supper," Matthew whispered to Caitlin.

"Yeah, why not."

Philip, Patrick, Steve and Pete were the last ones seated when they were trying to close up.

Matthew walked over to the table. "Come on lads, haven't you got homes to go to?"

"Yeah, we had better go," said Steve.

"One for the road?" said Philip, drunkenly.

"Err, I think you have had enough," said Matthew. "Come on guys."

They all stood up and staggered towards the door.

Patrick started singing. "Show me the way to go home, I am tired, and I want to go to bed!"

"That's exactly where you need to go," said Matthew.

"Want to join me?"

"No, he'll be on a promise," said Philip, laughing.

"Night, Matthew, Merry Christmas!" said Steve, shaking his hand.

Caitlin came over to see what all the commotion was.

"Merry Christmas fellas, see you again," she said.

"Don't we get a Christmas kiss Caitlin?" asked Pete.

"No, you don't and good night."

"Night!"

"Night, we aren't deaf," said Caitlin.

After they had got rid of the last few stragglers they cleared up and locked up for the night.

"Merry Christmas Caitlin," said Matthew, giving his wife a hug.

"And to you, Merry Christmas, it has been a good first Christmas hasn't it, quite a night."

"Yes, a lively one, but good and it isn't over yet."

"Let's get cosy on the settee and see if there are any films on."

"Yes, and our recordings," said Caitlin as they padded through to the sitting room.

"Do you think maybe next year, we could think about starting a family?" asked Matthew.

"Yes, I think the time could be right now, we are all settled here, why not?"

"We could get plenty of practice in," said Matthew giving her a tickle.

"Oh, so that's what you are after?" asked Caitlin, smiling at him.

"No harm in a bit of exercise," remarked Matthew.

"Oh, I like your sort of exercise. Good job it isn't a sport. Just imagine!" she said laughing.

"Rather not."

"I thought we were watching this?" she asked, as he proceeded to kiss and cuddle her.

"Okay, sorry got distracted, half an hour and then bedtime?"

"You are terrible."

Later on, in bed; they were settling down to sleep when they heard the sound of light footsteps, running above them.

"Ghosts are at it again," remarked Matthew.

"Shush, what's that, sounds like singing."

There was a very faint sound of: 'Silent night. holy night', a ghostly voice said.

"That's weird, how would ghosts know it's Christmas?" remarked Caitlin.

"God knows, let's go to sleep. This happens every so often anyway."

"Yes, still unsettling though, but I suppose we have to get used to it."

"I wonder what the new year will bring?" mused Caitlin.

"Well, maybe a new baby," he replied hopefully.

"That would be lovely. Let's go to sleep now, night."

"Okay, night sweetheart."

PART THREE

Chapter 25

Over at the farmhouse James sat on the edge of the bed nervously buttoning up his shirt. Rachael came into the bedroom having been doing her hair in the bathroom. They were getting ready to go out. They were meeting Tom and Emily for a quiet drink at the Hadrian before it got too busy.

She looked over at James, she thought he looked anxious.

"Are you okay about this?", she asked.

"Yes, I feel a bit nervous that's all".

"Well, we can cancel if you like?"

"No, I don't want to let you down, or Emily and Tom".

"They would understand".

"No, look you have gone to all of this effort now and you look gorgeous".

"Well, we are going early so hopefully it won't be too busy".

"Come on then let's go downstairs".

George and Marian were sat in the living room with the children watching television. They looked up when they entered the room.

"You both look smart", said Marian.

James gave half a smile and stood there with an anxious look on his face.

George looked over to James and noticed how nervous his son in law was".

"Are you alright lad".

"Err, yeah fine thanks".

"You'll be okay James, once you see you friends".

Cameron came up to James in his pyjamas.

"Daddy, we are going to watch films all night".

"Maybe watch one film Cameron", said Marian.

"Yeah, we're going to stay up until midnight and wait for the new year", said Scarlett.

"You have my mobile Mum and Tom's number is on the side", said Rachael.

"Go off and enjoy yourselves", said George.

"Thanks", said Rachael. "Come on then James, you'll be fine",
she said encouraginigly.

James bent down and hugged both children.

"You two be good, okay?"

"I love you Dad", said Charlotte wrapping her arms around him.

After hugs from both children who promised to be good, they set off
on their walk to the pub.

James turned on his torch as it was quite dark and there were dark
ice patches on the road.

When they arrived the pub looked almost magical in the moonlight, all lit up with the Christmas lights.

They entered the pub it was starting to fill up with people even though
it was still only early. He walked up to the bar where Matthew was serving.

"James, good to see you out again".

He knew James had been ill but didn't know what had been wrong.

"Thanks".

"What can I get you?"

"A pint of Black Sheep and Rach, what do you want Cider?".

"Yes please".

Tom and Emily came in and stood behind them.

"Hello everyone", said Tom.

"It's getting busy", said Emily.

James felt hot and dizzy. He gripped the side of the bar whilst
holding is wallet.

"Sorry, I feel dizzy".

Emily was behind him and quickly grabbed a chair and pushed
him into it.

"Sorry, I don't' know what's wrong", he said looking around at
the pub which was starting to fill up.

"You, okay?", asked Emily.

"I just need some where quieter, it's getting too busy for me in here".

"Oh, James", said Rachael.

She looked over at Matthew.

"Is conservatory open Matthew?"

"Caitlin has got that ready for tomorrow's lunches, hang on".

He signalled to Caitlin, and she came over to them".

"Hi guys, everything okay?" "It's good to see you James, you look a bit pale".

"I'm okay, just felt hot and dizzy that's all.

"Can you find them somewhere quiet in the conservatory, I don't think James is up to this", asked Matthew.

"Yes of course, come through to the conservatory, it's closed off but it is cooler in there and nice and quiet.

She took them over and got them settled.

"I'll bring your drinks over".

"Thanks, Caitlin", said Rachael.

"That's all right, it's no bother".

James started to relax. Tom was telling him the news about the Rugby.

"The lads would love to see you".

"Yeah, I was thinking of coming to some of the training sessons".

"Well, we'd all love to have our star player back".

"Oh, I'm not that good".

"Yes you are, you're to modest", said Tom.

"I was thinking about starting back at work in the new year as well, just part time".

"Oh, James I don't think your well enough for that yet", said Rachael worriedly.

"No, not farming, just in the office, there will be a ton of paperwork to do".

"Well, I suppose it will keep you more occupied".

"Yeah".

"It will be good for him Rach", said Emily.

"Yeah, I know, I just worry that's all".

"Are you both coming back to our house for a new year drink?", asked Emily.

"Yes, well we'll see how James is".

The evening was going well, and the four of them sat enjoying each other's company.

Tom went to the bar to get some more drinks. The bar was getting quite busy now and some of the players from the Rugby team were in. They had a bit too much to drink and were starting to get rowdy.

Alex, one of the players looked over at the bar and saw Tom.

"Hey, it's the Rev!", he shouted.

They all gathered around him.

"Hi Tom, good to see you", said Mike the coach.

"Who are you with?", he asked.

"Oh, just Ems, Rachael and James".

"How is he?", asked Mike.

"Oh, he's getting there slowly".

"Good, where are you sat? We'll come and say hello to them".

"In the conservatory, only go easy, he still isn't feeling well."

Alex, Who was one of the louder members of team started shouting.

"Jamesy!" "Jamesy!" "We want Jamesy".

They went over to where they were seated and stood around chatting.
James could feel himself go tense.

"So how are you", asked Paul.

"Oh okay, getting there".

Alex who gave him a playful push.

"Who James, how ya deing man?!"

"Fine thanks".

He gave him what was meant to be a playful pat on the back but
ended up being a bit more forceful. James tried to push him off.

"Alex go easy mate", said Mike.

"Sorry, I'll get yer a pint".

"No, I can't because of my tablets".

"Ah gan on".

He looked at Rachael, grabbed his jacket and made his way out
of the busy pub. He had to get as far from the rowdiness as possible.
He hadn't liked being jostled about.

He reached the wall by the entrance and stood taking in the fresh air.

'Must calm down, he didn't mean anything. Alex was always a bit
rough and tumble but had a heart of gold.

Rachael caught up with James.

"James?!" "Are you alreet?" "Sorry I didn't kna man",

"I'm just not in the mood".

"Howay James, I didn't mean owt yer kna".

"I know Alex, it's not you, it's just me", he said shaking his head.

"Are divent fret man", "You tek yer time son, there's ne rush, is there?"

Tom and Emily joined the little group concerned.

"Look I'm okay now, think I'll just go home".

"Oh, but we were going to Emily's".

"Well, you go if you want to".

"Come on James, it will be just the four of us". "You can stay as long or short a time you like". "Even stay over if you want", said Emily.

"Say yes James, please", Rachael.

"Okay, but just one drink and we'll see".

"Good lad!", said Tom. Midnight had soon come around and it was the start of 2020. There were going to be new beginnings for some and much the same for others, out with the old and in with the new.

After all the snow they had had over the Christmas period, New Year's Day was bright and sunny.

Some were waking up with hangovers. Others were waking up full of hope and looking forward to the New Year. Others felt a bit nervous and uncertain about the coming year. New Year's resolutions would be made, which some would stick to, and others wouldn't.

The Seddon's had lived in the village for a good few months now and were starting to find their feet there. They had wanted a small Christmas in their new house with just the six of them; but today they were having a New Year's Day/housewarming/baby shower party and were expecting relatives from Manchester.

They had got everything organised for the party the day before, so they just had last-minute jobs to do. They had all seen the New Year in, but all went to bed shortly after midnight.

It was about 11 a.m. and they were getting sorted out for the party.

Rick came into the kitchen, and opened the medicine cupboard, as he was nursing a hangover.

"Oh, my days! My head hurts," he moaned holding his head.

"Well, I did tell you to go easy on the whisky," remarked Sally reproachfully.

"Oh, look at you. You're a fine one to talk, you had a few glasses of wine!"

"I haven't got a hangover, though have I?"

"Well, we had a lot of toasting to get through. Have you heard from anyone?"

"Yeah, mum and dad were at Carlisle, when they phoned half an hour ago, so they shouldn't be too long. Your parents were coming through Durham, and I haven't heard from my sister or your brother and sister yet."

"They will all have the kids with them, so at least they can all go in the garden and play for a bit. It's a nice day isn't it?"

"Yeah, it is. Rick how do you feel about a conservatory?"

"How do I feel about a conservatory, conservatories in general or what?"

"For our house silly; we have a big garden, so it won't swamp the garden and it would give us extra space, now we're a bigger family."

"Good idea, but I was thinking of a loft conversion to give us more bedrooms. Err, well I am earning more in my new job, and we did make a profit on our old house. We will have to sit down and work out some figures, but I don't see why not."

"Great."

Sarah came down, carrying Charlotte in her arms.

"When is everyone coming?"

"Shouldn't be long; maybe an hour at most."

"Right," she murmured, looking at her phone while lounging on the settee with Charlotte cuddled into her.

"I do hope you're going to put that thing away when they come?" said Sally.

"Yeah, yeah, whatever."

The boys came running down the stairs, two at a time.

"When our cousins come can we play Fifa upstairs?" asked David.

"No, you can play footy outside, in the garden, it's a nice enough day," said Rick.

"Ah yes and Aadi, John and Jamie can join in!"

"No, you can play with your cousins. They are coming all of this way, the least you can do is to be sociable," said Sally.

"I can be sociable on my Xbox," said David.

"NO!" said Sally and David in unison.

"It will be cold outside!" protested David.

"You can wrap up warm," said Rick.

"You look smart Max, with your new shirt and trousers," remarked Sally.

"He could do with a haircut though, people might think you're a girl," said Rick.

"Oh, it suits him," said Sally.

"I like it long; boys can have long hair too Dad, don't be so sexist."

"Hey Maxie, what are you wearing, you smell like a flower shop," said David.

"Oh, erm it's that shower gel, there was only one there and it smells of Jasmine, it's nice Davy," said Sally.

"Really, if you say so."

"There was Lynx on the windowsill, no need to use that," said Rick. "People might get the wrong idea."

"Oh, leave him alone, no harm done," said Sally.

"Well, I didn't see it and I like this; I can put on what I want!" said Max, as he threw himself into an armchair with his arms folded.

"Rick say sorry," said Sally. "Everyone's different. It would be a boring world if we were all the same."

"All right, sorry son, whatever makes you feel comfortable."

"Right," said Max looking out of the window. "Ah great, grandma and grandpa are here!" He leaped up and ran to the front door.

"Grandma! Grandpa!" he shouted excitedly.

"That's our Max, what a fine smart young man you are," said his grandma.

"You've grown son. It's good to see you!"

"Mum! Dad! Hello," said Sally, pleased to see her parents.

"Hi Davy! My goodness you've grown as well, makin yer old Grandma feel small," she said, giving him a hug.

"That's because you are small."

"Hi Gran, this is Charlotte."

"Oh, Sarah, she's beautiful, just like you when you were little."

"Rick, all right there, fella?" asked Stan.

"Could be better Stan, nothing some Alka Selzer won't cure."

"Appen he had too much booze last night and he has a hangover," Sally told them.

"Have you had too much sauce son?" asked Joyce.

"Just a couple of whiskies."

"Huh, more like three quarters of a bottle," said Sally.

Ding Dong! Ding Dong!

Next to arrive were Rick's parents Bill and Maureen.

"Hi Mam, Dad, welcome to the madhouse!" said Rick, showing his parents into the living room. "You know Joyce and Stan, don't you?"

"Yes, hello, nice to see you all," said Maureen, "and who are these two handsome men? Girls will be after you two."

"Ah Davy has the hots for the girl next door," Max told them.

"Any luck?" asked Bill. "I have some good chat up lines, ask me later David," said Bill, winking at his grandson.

"No, you're all right Grandad."

"Oh, don't encourage him please," said Sally.

"Ah Sarah, you look a picture honey, and she's a right smasher," said Maureen. "Can I have a hold?"

"Oh well, I have just got her settled."

"Sarah, let them have a hold. Charlotte will be okay," said Sally soothingly.

"Okay, but not for long, you can each have a hold."

Next to arrive were Sally and Rick's brother and sisters with their families. Soon they had a house full. They all had party food and sat around talking and drinking.

After lunch, Rick made sure there was enough Prosecco for those who could drink it and that everyone had a drink.

"Right, everyone, first of all my lovely wife and I would like to thank you all for making this journey to come and see us in our new home."

"You didn't say it was out in t'sticks!" remarked Joyce.

"Yes, well, we love it, and I would like to make a toast; first of all to our new granddaughter Charlotte and to Sarah for doing a fantastic job of being her Mum."

"To Sarah and Charlotte!" he said.

"Sarah and Charlotte!" they responded, everyone raising their glasses.

"And also, I would like to remark on David and Max for being supportive brothers to Sarah. They both love Charlotte, but only if she isn't being noisy while they're watching a film or playing on the Xbox. Max said to me the other day, does she have Duracell batteries? then we can take them out!"

Laughter all round.

"But seriously though we wouldn't be without any of the kids. We wouldn't know what to do without them for a start. I would like thank Sally for helping me make this house a home. She chose the colour scheme and soft furnishings with my professional approval, of course. You've really made it cosy, and you are the anchor of this family; you keep us grounded and feeling safe and wanted. To the light of my life, Sally."

"To Sally!" they said.

"Now, you don't want to hear me waffling on, but this village has been the turning point for us. We were undecided on whether to leave

Manchester, but we are glad we made the right decision. Although we miss home, we have been welcomed and accepted here in Sleathwaite, though I don't know what they have let themselves in for. Finally, to Sleathwaite and Northumberland's beautiful countryside!"

"Sleathwaite!"

It was now sunny outside, and the cousins piled out into the garden, wrapped up in their coats to play and Sarah hung back.

"Go and be a kid while you have the chance. We'll keep an eye on Charlotte," said Rick.

"Oh, I don't know."

"She'll be fine."

"Err, okay, I won't be long," said Sarah anxiously.

She reluctantly walked out into the garden and joined the rest of them. She got talking to one of her cousins Jasmine and they were looking at their Twitter pages.

David was showing off his football skills and his cousins joined in on a game. Rick had set up goal posts in the back garden.

Max tried joining in but didn't feel comfortable. It wasn't really his thing. Two of the girls were talking about fashion and make-up. He really wanted to join in but wasn't sure if they would think he was weird. He kept hovering. They were looking at magazines and discussing clothes and what they thought they would look good in.

"Max, come and sit down, you can give us your opinion, you always are a good dresser," said Maddie, Jasmine's sister.

"Err, okay, why not," he said, relieved to be asked.

After about forty-five minutes, Sarah went back into the house, and watched from the French doors. Charlotte was being passed about and her Grandma Maureen started giving her a bottle.

"What are you doing? She, she is not a parcel to be played with, and I am the one who feeds her!"

"Sarah, they aren't doing any harm love," said Sally.

"No, she, she's mine, nobody's taking her away from me. I know what this is."

"What love?"

"I know what's goin on. You all think I'm an unfit mother, too young and unable to look after her!"

"Sarah, Sarah, no one thinks that love."

"Grandma, can I have my baby please."

"Of course, dear, I didn't mean to upset you."

"You haven't, Mam has," she said, grabbing Charlotte and the bottle. Charlotte protested profusely.

"What?" asked Sally.

"A word, you as well Dad."

They went out into the hallway, out of earshot.

"Sarah, that was uncalled for. They are only here for a short time. They just wanted to see the baby, that's all," said Rick.

"I didn't like her being passed about like a parcel. Why did you allow it Mam?"

"It was only a little while; she has been on your dad's knee most of the time and we didn't see the harm in your grandma feeding her."

"Isn't that my decision? I am her Mam!"

"We know that sorry love."

"I am taking her upstairs, not sure if I'll be back down," she said walking away.

"Oh, Sarah! look we didn't mean to upset you," Rick called after her.

"Well, you did, and I am tired, good night."

"Good night? It's only four o'clock."

"We're going to bed."

Rick and Sally looked at each other worriedly. They walked into the sitting room.

"Sorry about that everyone, sorry Mam," said Rick.

"It's all right son, is she okay?"

"Well, she's gone to bed with Charlotte, she's tired and stressed."

"She didn't mean anything. It isn't easy for her," said Sally. "I'll go and check on her later."

"Yeah, she just needs a rest," said Rick.

"It's quite understandable," said Joyce. "I am sure she will come down when she's hungry."

"That's another thing, getting her to eat, she either says she isn't hungry or she's too busy with Charlotte and will have something later. She's on the go all of the time, so we are frightened that she will burn herself out," said Sally.

"Oh, dear, should we all go and leave you to it?" asked Bill.

"No, no stay a while longer. Sorry about that, when you have driven all of this way."

"It's okay Sally, well we can't leave it too long, we have all booked into the local hotel and we need to check in before six," said Bill.

"Really, you didn't tell us that Dad."

"Oh, well we knew you didn't have the room and it's a bit of a hike back, plus we have had some alcohol. We don't want to be stopped, or worse, kill someone."

"No, course not," said Sally.

"Oh, well you have a bit of time yet then," said Sally.

"Well, we are staying at the Beaumont Hotel at Hexham and we have booked a table for us grandparents and you two and the kids tomorrow for lunch. Stan and I are paying for it."

"That's very kind," said Sally.

"Oh, we couldn't let you pay for it," said Rick.

"We haven't seen you lot in a good few months and it's our treat, no arguments," said Stan.

The kids came into the house, as it was now dark. The party continued until about six o'clock. Sally had checked on Sarah and Charlotte, but they were both flat out, snoring away. Charlotte was in her cot and Sarah who had changed into her pyjamas was snoring away peacefully in bed with the duvet wrapped around her.

She gently sat down next to her daughter and stroked her hair and gave her a kiss on the forehead. She kissed Charlotte and neither of them stirred. They were both worn out and looked so peaceful that she didn't want to disturb them.

She had gone downstairs and made her apologies. Sarah would see her grandparents tomorrow.

She and Rick were becoming more and more concerned about her. At first, they had thought of it as post-traumatic stress disorder from the rape. Then they just thought it was baby blues. It was still early days; Charlotte was only two and a half months old.

She had read recently about Post-Partum Psychosis and was worried that it could escalate into such a disorder. All she knew was that her young daughter had been through an awful lot and could become mentally ill if not carefully handled.

Chapter 26

It was the second day of January 2020; a busy day for some who were busy pulling down all of the Christmas decorations down and put away for the coming Christmas; and now it was out with the old and in with the new.

The village had looked beautiful over the Christmas Season with all of the Christmas lighting and decorations. The church and pub were lit up at night and people had decorated the outsides of their houses with lights and decorations.

It was a time to reflect on the previous year and look forward to the new. There would be some great opportunities for some and difficulties and sorrow for others. While some people would be optimistic about the coming year, others were not.

And for one girl, life was already tough, and she was struggling to cope. Sarah Seddon was lying on her bed, watching her baby daughter lying in her cot. She had bathed, dressed and fed her. Sally had offered to help but she said it was fine and she could manage, so Sally had gone back to bed. She could manage on her own, she didn't need or want help from anyone else. She was Charlotte's Mam, and it was her duty to look after her daughter and tend to her needs, no matter how well intended the offer of help was. She could do without interference from other folk.

She thought about the previous day. She hadn't liked people touching her baby, she knew that they were just excited to see Charlotte and welcome her into their lives, but she couldn't help it, Charlotte was hers.

Sometimes she would often look at her child and thought that she could see her rapist's face looking up at her. She had already had nightmares and hallucinations when she thought he was in her bedroom and was threatening to take Charlotte away from her. She needed to get protection for Charlotte.

Sarah looked at the clock, they still had a couple of hours before they left for the restaurant, just enough time for half an hour's nap, Charlotte seemed settled enough.

Charlotte lay in her cot happily and stretched her little toes. She was a happy baby and was starting to recognise faces belonging to people closest to her and would often smile, although this could have been wind. She lay gurgling away and trying to grab her feet. The gurgling grew louder.

Sarah leaned over and looked at her lying there.

"Shush, baby, shush."

She stroked Charlotte's head, face and eyes, trying to get her off to sleep. However, Charlotte was having none of it. The gurgling grew louder and turned into crying.

"Charlotte be quiet for two minutes! Please!"

Charlotte's crying turned into screaming and she started banging her feet and turning her little hands into fists. Sarah stood up, she had had enough of this screaming, all she wanted was to get some sleep.

She stood over the cot and yelled. "What is it you want? You have been, bathed, changed and fed! What more do you want? What do you want from me?"

Charlotte continued to scream, going red in the face.

Rick was standing on the landing listening to the commotion. He wanted to go in and check on them, but both he and Sally had promised they would give Sarah some space.

Sally came up the stairs. "Rick, what are you doing? Charlotte's crying."

"I know Sal."

"Well, we can't just leave her crying like that."

"Sally, we promised to give Sarah some space."

"I don't like hearing Charlotte crying like that."

"Neither do I!"

"Do you?"

"Of course, I don't like it any more than you do."

"I am worried about Sarah; she is going to make herself ill and it isn't good for Charlotte. She's getting distressed."

"Sally, can you remember when we first brought Sarah home from the hospital? It was hard in the early days, and we wanted to do it all ourselves and I seem to remember that you wouldn't accept help either."

"I know but, I just want to help, we had each other. Sarah is on her own and she is so young."

"She'll let us know when she needs help."

"Will she though, really."

"She knows we are here, if she needs us."

Rick walked over towards Sarah's bedroom. It had gone quiet in there. He opened the door and saw Sarah walking around the bedroom, holding Charlotte close. Sarah didn't see her parents watching her.

"Shush baby, hush, there, there, it's okay now. Mammy didn't mean to shout."

She walked over to the bed with Charlotte, laid her on the bed and started playing with her. She tickled her toes and Charlotte giggled.

"There, she seems fine now," said Rick, closing the door. "Let's leave her to it."

"Okay, let's go and get ready for the restaurant."

A while later, Rick and Sally were sitting downstairs in the living room, waiting for the kids to come down.

Sally looked out of the window. "Nice day today isn't it?"

"Yeah, not bad."

"I was thinking, it would be nice to go to the Sele for a walk after we've had our dinners."

"Yeah, It would be nice to do that. Our parents are going home this afternoon, so it'll be nice for them to stretch their legs."

Sarah came downstairs carrying Charlotte. She was smartly dressed for the restaurant and Charlotte was wearing a yellow dress, with white cardigan and white tights.

"Oh, don't you two look a picture," remarked Sally.

Rick got out his phone. "How about a photo - just you and Charlotte?"

"Why?"

"Because it would be nice."

"Oh, my days, if it will shut you up, fine!"

"Sarah, I was wondering, it would be nice to have a walk in the Sele after lunch," said Sally.

"What's the Sele?"

"It's what they call Hexham Park.

"Why?"

"Because it would be nice, and it would be good for you and Charlotte."

"What, No! Its cold out. Why are you always telling me what's good for me?"

"It's my job, I am your mother," said Sally, giving Sarah one of her looks, meaning she seriously wanted her to do it.

Sarah caught her mother's eye. "Oh God, yeah fine, I'll think about it."

"Good."

"I only said I'd think about it."

Max came downstairs impeccably dressed as always. He was dressed in his new shirt and jeans. He didn't have a hair out of place.

David came bounding down the stairs. He had been under strict instructions to put on smart clothes. He walked into the living room and threw himself into the armchair.

"David! You are not going out dressed like that!" said Sally reproachfully.

"What, whassup wi what am wearin," said David who was dressed in tatty Adidas tracksuit bottoms and a Man United football top.

"Son, we are going to a restaurant you were under strict instructions to wear smart clothes," said Rick.

"You look scruffy," said Sally.

"Go upstairs and change quickly, you can put on your new shirt and jeans we got you for Christmas," said Rick.

"Oh, but …"

"Now! Quickly before I lose my temper," said Rick. "Why can't you be more like your brother?"

"What, gay?"

"Enough!"

David thumped up the stairs.

"Why is he having a go at me for?" asked Max.

"Take no notice love, it's just because he didn't get his own way," said Sally.

David came down a few minutes later, he had done what he had been asked but he had thrown his shirt on, and it was half open exposing his chest.

"Fasten that up, you'll put everyone off their dinners," ordered Rick.

"Oh, my life," said David, who didn't want to go to a stupid restaurant and wanted to play footy with his mates.

They all filed out of the house and got into the car. It took only ten minutes to get to the restaurant by car.

The Beaumont Hotel was busy and was extremely popular with locals and holiday makers. They often had celebrities staying there when they were giving performances.

They walked through to the bar and found Joyce and Stan seated with Bill and Maureen.

"Ah, here they are," remarked Bill, looking up.

They walked across to their table and exchanged greetings. Sarah carried Charlotte in her car seat over to her grandparents.

"Oh, doesn't she look sweet," remarked Joyce, patting Charlotte's hand.

"I erm, I am sorry about yesterday. I was just tired, I guess."

"That's okay love," said Joyce.

"Are you okay today?" asked Maureen.

"Err, fine good yeah," said Sarah awkwardly.

"And who are these two handsome young men?" asked Joyce.

"That's never our David?" asked Maureen.

"You look smart son," said Stan, looking at his grandson.

"I look like him," said David, looking at his brother.

"And what is wrong with me?" asked Max.

"I wanted ter wear me tracky bottoms and footy top but Dad made me change."

"Ah well we all have to do things we don't want sometimes," said Bill.

"Right, I'd better get some drinks organised," said Rick.

"That's all taken care of son, this is on us," said Bill.

"Well, if you're sure Dad."

The waiter came across.

The Seddon party?"

"Yes, that's us," said Rick.

"If you'd like to follow me, I will show you to your table."

They all sat down at the table.

"We'll let you get settled and then we'll take your orders," the waiter said, handing out menus.

They were halfway through lunch when Charlotte started crying for her bottle.

"Oh, Charlotte every time," said Sarah, reaching into her bag for her bottle of milk.

"I'll feed Charlotte," offered Sally, who had just about finished her meal.

"No, it's all right."

"I am nearly finished, and you have hardly got started."

"Go on love, it'll be okay," said Rick, encouragingly.

"Well okay."

Joyce and stan were churchgoers and thought it was time to mention about the Christening.

"So, when's the Christening," asked Joyce.

"Oh, we're not religious," said Rick.

"Well, the kids were Christened; you have to have a Christening," said Bill.

"Yes, but we didn't really go to church. It wasn't right really," said Rick.

"There are those naming ceremonies these days," mused Maureen, attacking a roast potato.

"Well, it's something we'll have to discuss. It depends on what Sarah wants," said Sally.

"I want her Christened," said Sarah.

"Really love," said Sally.

"Yes, why are you all looking surprised?"

"Well, you went to Sunday school, when you were small, but as you grew older, you complained about going," said Sally.

"Well, we could talk to Tom the local vicar. He lives across the road," said Rick. "If it's what you really want?"

"It is for protection."

"For protection, what do you mean love?" asked Sally worriedly.

"Protection from God, Charlotte needs protection, and I am going to get it for her."

"We are going to start going to church regularly," she added.

"Well okay, good for you," said Sally. "Maybe we could all start going, show a united front. We are new to the village and what better way to get to know the local villagers."

"We could just go to the Hadrian for that Sal," said Rick.

"Trust you to think of your beer belly."

"I am not going to church Mam," said David, and Max nodded in agreement.

"No Mam, this is something just for me and Charlotte," said Sarah.

"Well, I can go if I want to."

"Sally leave it," said Rick, trying to avoid a row. "Let's change the subject. Davy, you going to try out for the footy team at school, aren't you?"

"I might do yeah, the twins were asking me if I was going to join the Sleathwaite Warriors junior league, that's where they go ".

"That'll be good for you," said Stan.

"Are you going to try out for football and rugby Max?" asked Bill.

"No Grandad, it isn't really my thing, I play for P.E and have the odd kick about with Davy but I don't want to join any teams."

"Ah kid likes his drama," said Rick.

"Ah yeah, course.

"Yeah, I was going to join the drama club. They are going to do Oliver for an Easter performance and I was going to sign up."

"He'll be performing at the west end before we know it," said Joyce, proudly.

Max had already performed some plays and workshops at the Theatre Royal in Manchester.

"You used to be a member of the young performers for the Theatre Royal do you not fancy signing up for Newcastle," asked Maureen.

"Yeah, I might give it a go."

"You should, you're really good."

"Thanks Grandma."

"You're quiet Sal?" said Rick.

"Just thinking," said Sally looking at her daughter as she fed a hungry Charlotte. She was still concerned about Sarah, especially when she mentioned protection but maybe it could be a turning point if she found faith in religion.

Chapter 27

It was the middle of the first week back of term and David was standing, waiting at the bus stop. He wasn't going anywhere; he was waiting for Shireen to get off the bus. As Shireen went to school in Hexham it took a little bit longer to get home. He liked Shireen and had been wanting to ask her out for ages but had only just got up the courage to ask her.

Max was walking past when he saw his brother standing at the bus stop. Max was with Aadi and the twins.

"Where's he goin'?" wondered Max.

"I dunno," said Aadi.

"Hey, David where are you going?" shouted Max.

"Nowhere."

"Well, you're standing at the Newcastle stop?"

"Just go home Max, I don't know what time I'll be back."

The Newcastle bus pulled up at the stop and Shireen and her friend Hannah got off the bus.

"Ah, that's why, woo!" whooped Max teasingly.

David went red in the face.

"Max, I am warning you!"

"David and Shireen sitting' in a tree, KISSING!" chanted the boys.

"Go home Max."

"Come on lads let's leave lover boy to it."

"See you tomorrow Shireen," said Hannah, grinning at David.

"Yes, see you tomorrow."

"Hi," said David awkwardly.

"Hey, David."

"Hi."

"Are we going to get past the word hi or?"

"I err, well I…"

"Yes, what can I do for you?"

"Oh, my days! I had this all planned of what I was going to say and now …"

"And now you are lost for words?"

"Something like that."

"Well?"

"You're not going to make this easy for me, are you?"

"No."

"Look I like you Shireen and well …"

"I will."

"I wasn't going to ask you to marry me."

"I should hope not, we're too young, but you were going to ask me to go out with you right?"

"Yes, will you go out with me?"

"Depends on where you are taking me?" said Shireen, smiling at him.

"Do you like pizza?"

"I love pizza."

"Do you want to come out with me on Saturday for pizza at Hexham?"

"I would love to David, that wasn't so hard was it?"

"No, I have liked you for ages, but I only just got up the nerve to ask you."

"I liked you the first time I saw you."

"Me too, what are you doing now?"

"Going home, I have a load of homework to do."

"Do you have time for a walk through the park?"

"Yes, okay, why not?"

They walked along to the park. It was always kept immaculate, but being only early January, a lot of the flowers and trees had died off. They sat down on a bench and got to know each other and found that they had a lot in common and similar interests.

David pulled an unopened bag of crisps out of his school bag, which he shared with Shireen.

"So, do you like living here David?"

"Yeah, it's nice and everyone is friendly."

"Don't you miss home and your friends."

"Yes, I do, but we all still keep in touch, and we will be going back for visits because we still have family down there. Anyway, I have made some new friends."

"Good."

"How long have you lived here?"

"All of my life, I was born here."

"What do your parents do?"

"They are doctors at the hospital. Dad's a Cardiologist and mam's a Neurologist."

"Wow! They must be very clever. Shireen, I hope you don't think I am speaking out of turn or being racist or anything, but will they mind you coming out wi' me?"

"I know they follow Asian traditions and all that. They may not approve of you goin' out wi' a white Manc."

"No, I don't think you are bein' racist or speakin' out of turn. Yes, they followed traditions when they were young, but this is the twenty-first century. I will do what I want to do and if they don't like it tough."

"Wow, feisty one."

"Yeah, no messin'," she said, laughing. "If things are awkward, I could just say that I am going out with friends."

"Right."

Shireen looked at her watch. "I think I had better start walking back, Mam and dad were finishing work early today and she has planned an early tea."

They cut up through the streets and made arrangements to meet in Hexham on Saturday lunch time. They reached Shireen's house first and she started to walk up her path. Aisha was standing looking out of the living room window.

"See you Saturday, David."

"Yeah, laters."

"Laters," she said, smiling.

Shireen put her key in the lock and put down her school bag and kicked her shoes off.

"Hi Shireen, good day at school?"

"Fine thanks," said Shireen, heading for the kitchen and helping herself to a glass of juice from the fridge.

"What did David want?"

"Nothing."

"You looked very pally."

"We were just talking; he does live next door."

"While we are on the subject of boys, I think it is time we arranged a suitable suitor for your marriage, and we can talk about courtship."

"What? Marriage, suitors, Mam I am only fourteen."

"I know but I was talking to your father, and we think it is time."

"And what about Aadi are you going to arrange a wedding for him?"

"That is different, he is a boy."

"Why is it different?"

"It just is."

Sanjay came into the kitchen, yawning, They had both been on an early shift following a night shift, and he was feeling tired. It had been busy at the hospital.

"So, what's happening?"

"Dad, what's this about you two arranging my wedding. I am too young for that."

"Well, I …"

"I choose my own friends and boyfriends. I don't want to be tied down,I am too young having babies, I want to go to Uni."

"Well, you still can after you are married," said Aisha. "Look we don't want you going off and ending up with someone unsuitable, who wouldn't treat you right," said Aisha.

"No, but you would rather I went off with some stranger?"

"It wouldn't be like that Shireen; you would have plenty of time to get to know him first."

"Dad, what do you think about this?"

"Well, I think that you should be allowed to make your own choices, but if you don't find anyone suitable, we can talk about the traditional marriage in the future."

"I will never talk about having an Asian traditional marriage Dad. This is you isn't it; you have talked Dad into this," said Shireen, turning on her mother.

"Look, I am just concerned about you, I don't want you to end up pregnant like Sarah at sixteen, sleeping around!"

"That won't happen and what happened to Sarah wasn't her fault Mam! and talking about boys, I am going out with David on Saturday, and you are not going to stop me! I was going to say I was meeting friends, but to hell with that! I will do what I want to do!"

"You are not young lady!"

"I am and I have homework to do!" Shireen angrily walked out of the kitchen, slamming the door behind her."

"Don't slam that door!" yelled Sanjay. "Well done! I thought we'd agreed not to talk about this until she was older?"

"Yes, but she was talking to David, and I guess I just panicked."

"Things are different now. She has to be able to make her own choices, just as much as Aadi does. You never know she may decide to have a traditional wedding, but it should be her choice."

"I know but …"

"Look, I think we should allow her to go out with David. He is a nice boy, and he won't harm her."

"I didn't say he would and yes he is nice, a bit shy at times, and I didn't mean what I said about Sarah, oh, she is going to think I don't like our neighbours and that's not true," she said standing up and heading for the door.

"Where are you going?"

"I need to talk to her."

"I would wait until she has calmed down."

"Okay."

They set about making tea. They were having chicken Bhuna with pilau rice, chapatis and bhajis. A while later, when it was ready, they called the kids down to a family meal.

Shireen was still annoyed and sat pushing her food around her plate with her fork.

"Aren't you going to eat that?" asked Aisha.

"Not hungry," she said, pushing her plate away.

"You have to eat Shireen."

"Aisha leave it love."

"She's probably lovesick," said Aadi. "She was all dreamy with David."

"Shut up Aadi!"

"Enough!" said Sanjay.

"Shireen, I am sorry about earlier," said Aisha.

"What for forcing me into an Asian marriage?"

"What, she's only fourteen!" said Aadi.

"I don't want to force you into anything Shireen, I just thought it would be best for you."

"Do I have to have an arranged marriage?" asked Aadi.

"The Asian way would be to follow the tradition of arranged marriage and if you are picked as a suitable suitor and you are both compatible, then yes, if you are agreed," said Aisha.

"I am going to pick my own girlfriends thank you," said Aadi.

"As you say it should be your choice, although we were brought up to follow our faith and traditions."

"Oh, so Aadi gets to choose, but I don't?"

"Neither of you is going to be forced into anything and we want both of you to be able to make your own choices," said Sanjay.

"Shireen, I want you to be able to have as many opportunities as Aadi and yes you are a clever girl and should go to University, if that is what you want. I want you to understand that we were introduced to each other, had a chaperone for a while, which I must admit was annoying, but that was the way then."

"I am not being chaperoned," said Shireen.

"When me and your dad met, we hit it off straight away. We were lucky."

"So, you two have successful careers and from what I can tell a successful marriage as well," said Aadi. "Did you get married before or after Uni?"

"Before, then we went to Uni, living in our first house, together, concentrated on our careers and then when the time was right, we moved here and had you two. That's what I was trying to tell you Shireen. There is no reason why you can't have both, and yes, as your dad keeps pointing out, things are different now and you have to be free to make your own choices, whether they be right or wrong. We only learn by our mistakes."

"But you made me feel as if I had no choice?"

"I know I am sorry. We were going to talk about this when you were a few years older, but when I saw you talking to David, I guess I just panicked. It's okay. I was just shocked that's all and who knows; if I do marry an Asian boy, we will probably have a traditional wedding, but that is way, way in the future."

And that brings me back to David. Look, I may have given you the wrong impression about him and his family. He is a nice boy, all of them are and yes you can go with him on Saturday as long as it is at lunch time. I don't want you into Hexham on a Saturday night."

"Really, oh Mam thanks."

"It's your dad you should be thanking. He made me see it from your point of view."

"Thanks dad."

"That's okay."

"It must be love, love, love," sang Aadi, teasing her.

"Aadi, shut up please," said Shireen.

"And I shouldn't have said what I did about Sarah. I don't know the details, it is her business. I can only imagine that it is very tough for her, and I think it would be nice if you made friends with her, I know she is a couple of years older than you, but then so is David, and he still plays with Aadi and the twins."

"Yes, I will. No doubt I will be round there at some point."

"And David should come for tea," said Aisha.

"He's round here a lot anyway, playing footy or on the Xbox," remarked Sanjay."

"Why? Are you going to check him out Mam?" asked Shireen.

"No, not at all, I just thought it would be nice."

"Can Max come as well?"

"Yes, if you like, Aadi."

"Great! hey Shireen, are you going to join in with playing footy and Fifa on the Xbox."

"I might, why are you scared about being beaten by a girl?"

"No, but …"

"Well bring it on then," she said, giving him a high five.

Next door, Sally was in the kitchen, getting tea ready for Rick coming home from work. He was finishing later tonight, and so they would be having their meals when he returned.

David was in a happy mood and came into the kitchen, bouncing his ball and singing.

"Glory, glory, Man United, Glory, glory Man United! Back of the net, get in!"

"You're in a good mood, don't bounce that thing in here please you'll break something."

"Sorry," he said, helping himself to a coke out of the fridge.

"You were back a bit later tonight; you haven't been given detention, have you?"

"No, why do you automatically assume that I have been in trouble? I haven't been in any trouble, I avoid trouble."

"All right, sorry."

David sat looking dreamily at his phone. Shireen had texted him a photo of herself and a text saying that her parents knew about Saturday and following a row, had ended up letting her go out with him. He sat looking at her photo with a faraway look in his eyes.

"Earth, calling David!"

"What?"

"I was asking you how you enjoyed your day, but you must have."

"Eh?"

Max came wandering into the kitchen.

"Mam, when's tea ready, I'm starving."

"In twenty minutes, your dad is on his way, shouldn't be long."

"We could have had ours earlier," he moaned.

"It's nice to sit down together."

"What you looking at David," said Max grabbing his phone.

"Hey! Nosey, get off!"

"Ah a photo of the lovely Shireen!" he teased.

"Give it back to him Max, now please," said Sally.

"Mam, can I have my hair cut tomorrow?" asked David.

"The amount of times I have tried to persuade you to get it cut, what's brought this on?"

"He's in lurrve!"

David went red in the face.

"Well, I can change my mind, can't I?"

"Yes, of course."

"Mam, can I ask you something?"

"Of course, anything."

"Don't mind me," said Max, grinning and sitting down.

"Max please," said David. "I want to talk to Mam."

"Stop teasing your brother, go and sit in the sitting room. I'll call you as soon as tea is ready," she said.

"Okay."

"So, what can I do for you?"

"Well, you know Shireen?"

"Yes, you fancy the pants off her!"

"Mam, is it that obs?"

"Yes, obviously is the word, why do you have to abbreviate everything, well?"

"Well, I felt too shy and nervous up until now. I know I act cocky, but that's just a cover up. I waited for her coming off the bus from school and I asked her to come for pizza on Saturday at lunchtime, at Hexham, can I go?"

"Oh, I don't know. I don't want any trouble, they have traditions that they follow."

"No, it's okay, they know all about it, she texted me before. Her Mam saw her talking to me and they had a row about Asian marriages and courtships, as they call them. Anyway, she has told them she will pick her own boyfriends. In the end they gave her their blessing to come out with me on Saturday."

"Well."

"Please Mam, I really like her."

"I know that, my boy has a girlfriend. She is pretty, isn't she?"

"Does that mean you don't mind?"

"Of course, I don't mind, why should I?"

"I dunno, I wasn't sure."

"I'll give you some money, for Saturday."

"No, Mam, I don't need it."

"Huh?"

"I am paying for it. I want to. I have been saving up my pocket money."

"My! you're full of surprises tonight, aren't you?"

"Yes, and can I wear the clothes, I wore last week for the restaurant, when they are clean?"

"What, the ones you complained about?"

"Yes, well I wanna look my best don't

"They are in the machine now."

David felt triumphant. He had just had the best day and couldn't believe his luck.

Chapter 28

Tom was at home working in his study. He had worked his way through a pile of paperwork which had been building up. He looked at his laptop screen and brought up his schedule of appointments to check what appointments and commitments he had for that week. It being Monday morning he liked to plan for the week ahead.

It was quiet at home; Emily was out at work and the boys were at school. There was only himself and his dog Charlie, who was still just a puppy. At least he was on hand to take him out for walks.

He enjoyed his work. Although it was rewarding to help people with their problems it also brought both joy and sadness, in life and in death. Being a vicar wasn't just about holding Sunday service, christenings, weddings and funerals, it was about helping people who came from all walks of life, whether they were religious or not. At times it could be quite stressful and emotional, which could affect a person psychologically if you didn't put work to one side and try and concentrate on other things; which sometimes was easier said than done.

Tom had done a lot of work with charities such as the Homeless Shelter, the Salvation Army and Age UK etc. He often took part in events such as fun runs and charity tea parties. The list was endless.

Although a lot of his work was behind the scenes, which brought some solitude, he never felt lonely because he always found he was busy and sometimes it was a relief to have some peace and quiet.

He got up and went into the kitchen to make himself a brew, Tom loved a cup of tea and a biscuit mid-morning. Charlie was asleep in his basket, so he probably would take him out just before lunch. He had a couple of parishioners to call on that afternoon and he had also been called up by the hospital to call in and see a patient from the village, who was receiving palliative care. He didn't have long left to live. Tom was also a chaplain at the local hospital, but this was mainly just to cover for sickness and holidays, when the other chaplains weren't available.

He went back to look at his appointments. He had an appointment to see the Seddon's that evening at six p.m. about arranging a christening for baby Charlotte.

He had made a point of calling in on them when they had first moved onto the street and always said "hello." He didn't know them very well, but they seemed to be a pleasant family. He thought about Sarah and how tough it must be for such a young girl bringing up a child on her own, although she did have the support of her family. He had met some teenage mothers at the homeless shelter, who didn't have any support at all and no friends or family to rely on. Sarah was still a child herself and had to grow up quickly. He didn't know the details behind Sarah's pregnancy, but he hoped he and the church could be of some help to her.

Sally was downstairs looking after Charlotte. She had finally persuaded Sarah to go up to bed and have a sleep. She had looked dead on her feet. She was still insisting on trying to do everything herself and didn't like anyone going near Charlotte, let alone pick her up for a cuddle. Every time a family member did so, she got anxious and was afraid something bad would happen to her baby, even though she really did know that Charlotte was perfectly safe with them, she still couldn't shake off the feeling.

Sally had Charlotte lying on the floor on her baby mat. She had an activity frame over her. Charlotte was grabbing the toys that hung from it as they made different noises. She loved the cuddly cow. When you pressed its nose, it made a mooing sound, which made Charlotte giggle. Sally was having a lovely time playing with her granddaughter.

She had suggested to Sarah that come September she could stay at home with Charlotte to look after her while she went back to school and took her GCSES's, she would be a year behind, but she had had a lot to cope with in the last year. Sarah had hoped to eventually go to university to study medicine. She had hoped to become a doctor, Sally was keen to support her in this, but at the moment she had her work cut out. Sarah had said that she couldn't think about school at that moment.

Sally wasn't going to give up. She was determined to help Sarah with Charlotte. She needed to get her GCSE's and A levels out of the way. She had explained to Sarah that there was no reason why she shouldn't go back to school and do the things she had first set out to do.

Sally felt that this would be a good way for Sarah to make some friends of her own age and be able to go out and enjoy herself.

Sally had found out about a local baby and toddler group in the village and was trying to persuade Sarah to take Charlotte there, but at the moment it was difficult even getting Sarah out of the house. Sally was becoming increasingly concerned about Sarah's state of mind.

Sally looked at the clock. It was a quarter to four, so the boys would be home from school soon. Rick was also coming home earlier. They were going to have an early tea, so they were ready for Tom to come round to discuss the christening.

Right on cue, she heard a key being turned at the front door. Both her sons came in, dumped their bags in the hall and kicked their shoes off.

"Mam, Mam, what's for tea?" asked Max.

"I am starving," said David.

"Hello boys, good day at school?"

"Yeah!" they said in unison.

"What are we having?" asked Max.

"Fish and chips, I wanted to have something quick and easy. The vicar is coming around at six."

"Ooh my favourite," said Max.

"We always have fish on Friday from the chippy and it isn't fish Friday," said David.

"Well, that's what we are having. Can you two keep an eye on Charlotte while I peel some potatoes?"

"Yeah, sure," said Max.

They both went and lay on the floor on either side of Charlotte and played with her.

"Hello Princess Charlotte, how's my little niece?" asked Max, tickling her feet.

David turned on a little plastic radio and it played 'Old Macdonald had a farm'.

He sang the song to Charlotte and she giggled when he made farmyard noises. She grabbed David's nose and held Max's finger.

"Ow! What are you doing you little tinker you," he asked, putting his tongue out at Charlotte and blowing a raspberry.

Max was turning the noises on, on her activity frame. He squeezed the cow's nose and it mooed; Charlotte giggled.

"You like that don't you, yes you do!" he cooed over her.

Both boys adored Charlotte and loved to play with her when they got the opportunity. She lay beaming at the boys and kicking her legs.

The sitting room door opened, and Sarah walked in.

"All right Sis?" asked David.

"What are you doing?" asked Sarah.

"We're only playing wi' our Charlotte," said Max.

"No, no, no, get away from her!"

"We weren't doing any harm," said David.

"What?" said Max, standing up and looking shocked.

"You still have your school uniforms on and you are dirty. Did you wash your hands before playing with her?"

"No, my hands are clean, and I am not dirty," said Max indignantly.

"You have got ink on your hands Davy."

"So, I can't get it off, I am clean otherwise."

"You, you could infect her!"

"What are you on about, infect her? with what?" asked David, perplexed.

"Where's Mam?"

"In the kitchen mekin' tea," said David.

"Mam, Mam!"

"What on earth is all of the shouting about?"

"Why did you leave Charlotte wi't'lads?"

"They are looking after her while I make our tea and hey, they aren't doing any harm."

"Charlotte was having fun," said Max.

"They, they shouldn't be near her!"

"Why not?" asked Sally, puzzled.

Sarah bent down and picked Charlotte up off the floor. Charlotte started to cry; she had loved having the attention from the boys.

"What's going on Sarah? What is this all about?" asked Sally.

"It's okay, darlin, no more smelly boys. She's my baby, not yours," she said to the three of them who stared open-mouthed. "Mam, I told you she needs protection," she said, turned, and walked out of the room.

"Sarah, wait, don't go!"

"I can look after her me sen!"

"What were all that about?" asked David.

"Mam, we weren't hurting Charlotte, she was loving it."

Sally could see that her boys were clearly hurt. She sat down heavily on the settee and put her head in her hands.

"Oh, boys, I don't know, I don't know what is happening here." She looked up, tears rolling down her cheeks.

"Ah, Mam," they both said in unison and sat on either side of her, putting their arms around her.

"I don't understand it, protection from who, us? We aren't going to harm her, we love her," said David anxiously.

"I'd better get on with the tea."

"No, Mam, leave it. I'll go and do it," said Max. "And Davy can help me," he said, grabbing his brother's hand and pulling him up.

"Am I hearing right?"

"Yes, you are," said Max. "It's about time we helped, you're tired."

"Mam, do you want a brew?" asked David.

"Do you even know how to even use the kettle and make a cuppa?" she asked, wiping her tears away.

"I am sure I can do it."

"I don't believe my ears."

Rick came through the door. "Hello everyone. Sally, you okay?"

Sally looked up tearfully. "I was starting to peel the potatoes and prep tea; I left the boys to look after Charlotte. I managed to persuade Sarah to go up to bed for a sleep. She looked dead on her feet, insisting she could do everything herself, while getting more and more stressed. Then she came down and tore a strip off us. She had a go at the boys and me. She said the boys would infect Charlotte."

"Eh, right that's it, I am going to have a word with that young lady."

"No, Rick, don't, leave it."

"She needs to apologise; I won't have it. Where are the boys, upstairs?"

"No, they are in the kitchen, making tea."

"What, what did you say. They are mekin' our tea? Did you bribe them?"

"No, they saw I was upset and offered to do it, David even made me a brew. It was Max's idea to do the tea."

"Blimey, I don't believe my ears, what good lads; makes a change that does."

"The boys were hurt by the way she spoke to them; they were only trying to help."

"Okay, well I won't say anything at the moment, let's get tea over with and she can help with the dishes. I will be tactful and ask her to apologise to you and the boys. I know she is under a lot of strain, but it is affecting all of us."

"I don't want any trouble, especially with Tom coming."

"There won't be."

Rick went and checked on the boys in the kitchen to see how they were getting on with tea and to ask if they were okay.

"Well, this is a nice surprise, you two working together without being asked and without fighting. Well, done to you both."

"It was my idea, we should be helping," said Max.

"It doesn't matter whose idea it was, but it's nice to see."

"Max finished peeling the spuds, while I made Mam a brew and I set the table."

"We did the cooking together, making sure everything was at the right temperature and the right timings," said David proudly.

"See, you can do these things."

"Is ah Sarah all right?" asked Max.

"I haven't been up to see her yet, I wanted to make sure your Mam and both of you are okay before I do."

"She said we were dirty smelly boys and shouldn't be near Charlotte, because we are still in our school uniforms and hadn't washed our hands," said David.

"She said to Mam that she shouldn't have left us looking after Charlotte, because she needs protection," said Max. "Protection from who for God's sake?"

"I don't know, but I will be speaking to your sister and I will make sure she apologises to you all. Are you both okay?"

"Yeah, all right I suppose," mumbled David, shrugging his shoulders.

"Fine, no bother," said Max.

The alarm on the timer for the oven went off and the boys finished off making the tea. Sarah came downstairs and they sat down quietly eating their meals.

"Right, we'd better get these dishes done," said Rick.

"I have homework," said Max.

"Me too," said David, standing up to leave the table.

They all stood up and Sally started clearing the table.

"Right, boys upstairs and do your homework, Sally leave that please."

Sarah started to walk out of the room.

"Sarah, you can help me."

"What, why can't the boys do it?"

"They made our teas."

"What? What do you mean they made our teas? You mean I ate what they cooked?"

"That's right."

David and Max hung back and listened to the conversation.

"Oh, my God! Oh, my God! They could have poisoned us!"

"Oh, thanks very much!" said Max storming off.

"He hardly washes his hands; it could infect Charlotte!" she said, pointing at David.

"Just calm down, there is no need for any of this. You are overreacting, they did a good job between them."

"What do you mean anyway? I gave my hands a good wash before I even cooked the food. What do you think I am?" said David, indignantly.

"Davy, go and do your homework. I'll handle this."

"No, I want to know!"

"Davy please!"

"Fine!" said David, also storming off after his brother.

"Sally, please, I want to talk to Sarah, we'll clear up love."

"Okay then," said Sally closing the kitchen door.

"Right Sarah, fill the sink with soapy water. We'll talk while we work."

Sarah quietly did what he asked. She suddenly felt guilty and realised that she had gone too far.

"Now, listen, I don't know what sparked off tonight's episode, but I have been at work since an early hour and came home so I could see the vicar with you about your daughter's christening. I did not expect to come home to World War three, understood?"

"Yes Dad, I am sorry."

"Oh no, it is not me you need to say sorry to. There is your mother for a start who is bending over backwards to help you and Charlotte."

"I didn't ask her to."

"I know that, but she said you were stressed and exhausted and were insisting on doing everything on your own. This is not good for Charlotte. You need to learn to let go love."

"All right, right well I'll apologise to her."

"And there are two boys up there who have been at school all day, have come in and looked after your little girl while your Mam started tea. They did not deserve to be spoken to like that. They are not dirty, poisonous, or going to put Charlotte in danger."

"All right, all right!"

"It is not all right; it is far from all right. You've upset your mam and the boys. The boys saw how upset she was after the way you spoke to them all and offered to make tea. I will not stand for this kind of behaviour Sarah."

"Do you want me to leave?"

"What? No! Of course not, where did that come from? You have nowhere to go for a start and we want you here so we can look after you both. and that's not just out of a sense of duty it's because we love you, we love both of you, okay."

"Right, okay," said Sarah quietly. "I'll apologise ter ah Davy and Maxie."

"Good girl. Right now, we have finished the dishes, there is just one more thing I want to ask you."

"Yeah, what is it Dad?"

"I am going to try to be as understanding and sensitive as possible, but me and your Mam are very concerned about you."

"Why?"

"Well, it's just that erm, you seem to think that everyone is out to harm Charlotte. We won't you know. Why do you think we would or anyone else for that matter?"

"Oh, Dad!" said Sarah tearfully.

"Oh, come on love, I didn't mean to upset you," he said, bringing her in for a hug.

"What is it love, tell me please."

"You can't nobody can, that's why she needs protection."

"Sarah, I am trying but I still don't understand."

"She needs protection from my rapist!"

"Oh, love, he's in Manchester. He can't get to you or Charlotte. You are safe here."

"I'm sorry, I can't help it."

"Oh, darling, you have been through a traumatic time. It was bound to take its toll on you. That's why we want to help you, do you understand?"

"Yeah, I think so, where's Mam?"

"I'll go and get her, wait here," he said closing the door behind him. He went into the sitting room and sat next to Sally. He put his head in his hands and sighed.

"Rick, what's happened? You okay?"

"No not really, but I hope we will be." He took hold of Sally's hands and explained everything to her. "I think we may need to get her professional help. She is still struggling after her rape ordeal."

"Well, Tom is coming, so maybe he could be of some help," said Sally.

"In the short term yes, but we need to keep a close eye on her. All this talk about protection, it's becoming an obsession."

"Oh, God! I hope she doesn't end up being sectioned."

"That's why she needs our help and right now she wants her Mam."

"Mam, I am very sorry," said Sarah appearing in the living room doorway.

"That's okay love, come and sit down." She sat in between her parents and Sally put her arms around her. "Sarah, your dad has told me what the two of you have discussed and well we think we might need to get you a little bit of help."

"You think I am crazy?"

"No, but you have had a very traumatic and stressful time and may need some more counselling."

"No, they'll take me away. They'll tek my baby. No one's takin' her."

"Sarah, love, no one is going to take her. You just need some help. You are so tired and your Mam wants to help, and she will, but I am afraid the time has come when we need to ask for some extra help, that's all. No one is taking you anywhere."

"Sarah, Tom is due to come in half an hour or so. I am going to have a word with him about what he can do to help, you never know … He may have some contacts."

"Well, I want help from God. He'll know what to do."

"Well, if you want to discover your faith, he can also help with that. You never know, it may be of some comfort to you."

"Okay then."

"Right, go and wash your face and get freshened up. He'll be here soon," said Rick. "And err, you have something else to do as well."

"Oh, yeah, thanks for … understanding."

"That's all right, but you need to apologise to your brothers."

"I know, I am going to ask them to be Godparents."

"Oh, that's a nice gesture. They'll like that," said Sally.

"Max! David! I want to talk to you both," shouted Sarah, climbing the stairs. They both came out of their room onto the landing.

"What'd ya want? I am busy," said David.

"Hurry up sis, I want to get my homework finished," said Max.

"I erm, well I owe you both an apology, for earlier."

"Too right you do," said David, still annoyed.

"Davy," said Max, holding his brother back. He thought he was about to have a go at their sister; not that she didn't deserve it.

"I am sorry about the way I spoke to you both and the things I said. I shouldn't have done it."

"No, you shouldn't. We weren't doing no harm," said Max.

"I know and I am sorry."

"Okay," they both said in unison.

"And … I have something else to ask. I'd like you both to be Godparents."

"Really?" asked Max. "Nice one."

"Are you sure we are up to the job; I mean you don't want two dirty low life boys doing it do you?"

"Look, David, I am sorry, please say yes."

"David?"

David looked at his brother, who obviously wanted some peace.

"Okay, no bother. I would love to."

"Great."

Half an hour later, the doorbell rang. Tom had arrived. They welcomed him and showed him into the living room.

"Would you like a cup of tea Reverend," asked Sally.

"Oh, Tom please, and yes, I would love a cup please."

"I'll go and make it," said Rick.

"So, you were thinking about a baptism for baby Charlotte?"

"Yes," said Sarah, cuddling her baby.

"She's grown quite big since the last time I saw her."

"She's over three months old now," said Sarah.

"She's lovely."

"Thanks."

Tom reached into his bag and took out his diary and notebook.

"Right, I'll go through the baptism service and you can tell me if you are in agreement Sarah, anything anyone isn't sure of, please feel free to ask me."

He handed them each a booklet on a typical baptism, and what would be said and when.

"Right, Sarah, can I take some details please?"

"Yeah, course."

"What is Charlotte's full name?"

"Charlotte Sally Seddon."

"Ah, that's nice after her grandma," he said, writing it down.

"Yes."

"Now can I ask have you thought about Godparents.

"Yes, I have asked my brothers and they said they would."

"Good, that's fine."

"What are their names?"

"David and Max."

"Oh yes, friends of my twin boys."

"That's right," said Rick.

"We haven't seen you in church yet. Is there any reason why not. We always welcome new parishioners to the church."

"We've just been so busy lately, since we moved to our new house and Charlotte came along, we haven't had time - sorry," said Sally.

"Oh, don't apologise. You would be very welcome, I realise you must have a lot on at the moment. Now Sarah, can I ask, when you lived in Manchester did you go to church then?"

"I did when I was younger. I went to Sunday School for a while."

"And were you baptised?"

"Yes, Methodist."

"We were all christened Methodist, but Rick is Church of England," said Sally.

"And you want Charlotte to follow this faith?"

"Yes, I would like to start coming to services with her."

"Well, that's good to hear. You will be welcomed by the other parishioners."

"Right; now we have a full calendar for the next three weeks, but I can book you in for the first Sunday in February at ten thirty? I assume it is okay to have it within our regular service. That's what we normally do."

"That's fine," said Rick.

"Can we finish with a prayer? Is that okay?"

"Err, yes, why not," said Sarah.

"Close your eyes and put your hands together."

Rick looked a bit unsure but joined in all the same.

"Dear Father, please guide this family through good times and bad, joy and sorrow. Help Sarah and Charlotte on their path of life, through sickness and in health. Give hope and opportunity to them both, let them all have rich and fulfilling lives with love and understanding through difficult times, and give them love as God's children. Bless them all, Amen."

"Amen."

"That was lovely," said Sally.

He stood up and went to take his leave. "Right, well we'll leave it there for now and I will see you all on the first at ten thirty, okay?"

"Yes, thanks Tom," said Sarah.

"Erm Tom, could I possibly have a word in private?" asked Sally.

"Yes of course."

She led him through to the dining room and they sat at the table, and she explained all that was happening with Sarah.

"So, I was wondering if you had any contacts or if you could suggest where we could get help?"

"Right, well I am sorry to hear she is going through such a tough time. Everything you have told me is highly confidential by the way.

It is hardly surprising, given what she has been through. Did she have counselling after her assault?"

"Yes, for a while, she stopped going because she felt she was doing fine. Oh I am worried about her and so is Rick."

"I understand that you are all under a great deal of pressure and that it must be a great strain on the whole family."

"She thinks the boy who raped her is going to take our Charlotte away. She has had nightmares and hallucinations. Tom, I am scared that it could reach the point where she is sectioned."

"She seemed calm when I just saw her, but I suppose she could have just been hiding it."

"That was after a meltdown."

"Well, to start with I can talk to her if you like. I can call this week and we can have a chat, just the two of us. I have had experience of talking to people in similar situations, and it is good that she wants to follow her faith. I hope that will be of some comfort to her."

"That's what I thought."

"We have a teenage group at the church for people who have been in these sorts of situations, which may be of help to Sarah. It is led by a qualified counsellor."

"Like a support group?"

"Yes, just talking about her problems and meeting people her own age, could be a good start."

"Thanks Tom, you've really helped us."

"It's my job and a pleasure; of course if you are really worried you could talk to the doctor. They have a good psych there who will be able to get Sarah the help she needs. If she ends up being sectioned it isn't like a normal psychiatric secure unit. The mothers go with their young babies and stay for a few weeks at a special post-natal unit, so they can get the right help and rest that is needed. I am no expert but given what you have told me she could be suffering from post-natal depression or something similar."

"I did wonder, I came across something the other week called Postpartum Psychosis, which is similar I suppose. I just hope she hasn't got that."

"Well maybe we shouldn't jump to conclusions. She could just be exhausted. I will call and see her this week, but if you are really worried, talk to the professionals. That is what they are there for and I will help all I can."

"When will you call?"

"I need to look at my appointments, hang on."

He pulled his diary out of his bag. "I am free on Friday at three thirty. Do you think she'll agree to see me?"

"I don't know, she might kick off before then."

"Well try and keep her here, and I will catch up with her then. It may be best not to tell her I am coming. We don't want her panicking, but I will leave that up to you."

"Well, thank you very much. You've been a great help and it has been good for me just talking to someone not directly involved in it."

"You are very welcome. I look forward to the christening and seeing you all in church and I will try and catch up with Sarah on Friday, okay?"

"Yeah, thanks, I'll see you out."

Chapter 29

Caitlin had been feeling a bit under the weather and out of sorts recently, which was very unlike her. Normally she would be all get up and go but she just didn't seem to have the energy or the inclination. Maybe she was just run down. She seemed to be having a lot of headaches, fatigue and vomiting.

She had plenty of work coming in from the BBC program which she was researching, as well as other work, which was near to completion, including her article on Roman history and their settlement in England.

She normally got her housework jobs out of the way in the mornings and did her research in the afternoons. She also helped out in the bar and restaurant when she could, but was finding that she was so busy at the moment that she was burning herself out.

A couple of times recently, Matthew had come up in an afternoon or early evening and found her fast asleep, sprawled over her work at the kitchen table. He was concerned that she was burning the candle at both ends.

She looked down at the pile of work she had to do and gave a sigh. She liked to be busy and enjoyed her work. She knew Matthew was beginning to worry about her and suggested that she made an appointment with the GP. She was feeling stressed at the time and snapped that she was fine. She wouldn't normally snap at him. She knew he was really trying to look after her.

She stretched, yawned and rubbed her eyes.

"Oh, my head aches," she said to herself, standing up and helping herself to a couple of Paracetamol out of the medicine cabinet. She thought she should really go for a walk and get some fresh air. She had been busy on her laptop for the past three hours. She hadn't realised the time. She just seemed to have got lost in her work, she was so engrossed.

She looked at the calendar on the wall and thought that she had missed something or forgotten to do something. She didn't like this feeling of uncertainty in case it was something important.

She checked her personal diary and her work planner and schedule, but everything seemed to be on track. She just had a few loose ends to tie up on her outstanding work. It just needed tweaking a bit before submission.

She sat down at the kitchen table with her glass of water, having taken her headache tablets.

'I wonder what I have forgotten. It's not our anniversary or anyone's birthday,' she thought, running her hand through her hair. She finished her water, closed down her laptop and put her work to one side. She needed a break and some fresh air. She went to the bathroom and freshened up, getting ready to go out.

She wrapped up warmly. It was still only January and was really quite cold. She went downstairs and looked for Matthew. He was coming out of the kitchen. He had his chef's whites on, and was carrying two plates of food. A couple of staff members had called in sick and they were shorthanded.

"Oh, hey Caitlin, all right? You off out?"

"Yes, I need a break and some fresh air. Why? Do you need me to help out?"

"Well, we are okay for now. The evening staff are due in at five, so hopefully we should manage for a couple of hours."

"If, you're sure?"

"You have enough to do, but thanks, only if it becomes so busy and we need your help. I'll let you know."

"Do that, do you want anything from the shops?"

"Can you get me my prescription please? I ordered some new inhalers and Montelukast."

"Yeah, sure."

"See you later."

"Yes, of course."

Caitlin walked along the road to the village. It was nice to be out of the pub and getting some fresh air. She couldn't wait for Spring. She and Matthew often went for walks along the Roman Wall, and she had some digs planned, weather permitting.

There were snowdrops growing on the grass verges. Come the Spring the village would have new plants in the flowerbeds, it was normally awash with tranquil colours. She decided to walk through the park before going to the chemist. There weren't a lot of people outside today. She came across a few dog walkers and they exchanged greetings, a smile, a nod or hello.

She reached the top of the park and walked down towards the market square, which was closed today. She found the chemist and went in.

She asked for Matthew's prescription and had to wait. She looked around the shelves. She still had this nagging feeling at the back of her mind, did she need something from here?

She came to the sanitary towels and tampons, was that it, no she had plenty at home. She scanned the shelves, pain killers, analgesics, muscle wraps, creams, pregnancy kits, condoms. No, she couldn't think of anything.

"Prescription for Matthew Turner?"

"Yes, please," said Caitlin, heading towards the counter.

"Can you confirm the post code please?"

"Yes, NE45 4JS."

"Are you paying cash?" asked the pharmacist.

"Yes," said Caitlin, getting out her wallet.

"Thank you. Is there anything else, I can help you with?" she asked handing Caitlin her change.

"Err no, thanks, bye."

"Thank you, bye."

Caitlin walked along the road and her mind started to wander. 'A baby would be nice in the new year.'

There was a screech of tyres and someone beeping their car horn.

"Oops, sorry, I got a fright." Caitlin had wandered into the road and had not seen the oncoming car.

"Are you okay," asked the driver, having wound down his window.

"Yes, thanks, I just got a fright. I was miles away."

"Keep your eyes wide open, good job I wasn't going any faster."

"Yes, I will."

"You haven't hurt yourself?"

"No, I am fine. Thank you for stopping."

"Okay, who wouldn't for a pretty girl like you."

'BEEP! BEEP!'

"All right, all right, I am going!"

Caitlin sat down on a bench next to the entrance to the park, feeling a little shaken. She thought back to Christmas and looked at her phone calendar.

"Oh, God," she breathed. She counted back the weeks and realised that she hadn't had a period since the end of November. It was now nearly the end of January.

'Can't be,' she thought.

They had always planned to have children but since talking about it at Christmas, she hadn't expected it to be so quick.

'Must be a mistake,' she mused. She was nearly two months late. She headed back to the chemist and walked through the door.

"Oh, hello, did you forget something?" asked the pharmacist looking up.

"Yes, I did."

"Can I help you?"

"Erm, it's a bit embarrassing."

"You can't shock me; we get asked for all sorts in here."

"I have just realised that I haven't had a period since the end of November. I have been feeling a bit run down recently but just thought I was overworked and stressed," she said quietly.

"We do have some tests over here. They are ninety-five percent accurate, but if you have been feeling run down, I would suggest you make an appointment to see your GP. If you are pregnant, they will want to see you anyway."

"Yes, I'll take two of those clear blue tests please."

"Do you need two?"

"Oh, I just want to be sure."

"Okay then," she said carrying the pregnancy kits towards the counter.

Caitlin took out her credit card and paid for them.

"I hope you get the result you want," said the pharmacist, smiling reassuringly.

"Thanks, so do I."

She left the chemist and walked back home. She felt half excited and half anxious to find out the result. She hurried along the road. It was cold and there was dampness in the air. She looked up at the sky and the clouds looked full of rain.

'We're going to have a right downpour,' she thought, walking fast clutching paper bags she got from the Chemist. She walked through their front door which was at the side of the pub and up the stairs that led up to their flat. Matthew was in their kitchen making a cup of tea.

"Oh hi, you remembered then."

"Of course, I remembered. I am not doolally."

"Okay, okay, thanks; it's just that your head has been all over the place recently, are you all right."

"Yes thanks," she said, handing him his prescription.

"Oh, did you have one to collect as well."

"No, I …"

"Oh, don't tell me it was women's things."

"Something like that," she said, putting the package on the shelf. "Can I have a brew?"

"Yes, coming up."

"Matt."

"Hmm."

"I think we need to talk."

"Nothing wrong is there?" He turned around and gave her the cup.

"No, I don't think so."

"I haven't done anything I shouldn't have, have I?"

"No, it's about this package," she said, grabbing it off the shelf.

"Yeah, period stuff."

"No, but you're close."

"Matthew I had this nagging feeling that I had forgotten to do something all day and when I went into the chemist, I scanned the shelves to see if I needed anything and I couldn't think of anything, so I left. I hadn't forgotten anyone's birthday or anniversary or anything important. I was walking along the road thinking about you, and I just missed being hit by a car."

"My God! Are you okay? Was he going fast?"

"No, I am all right."

"You need to be more careful, have you had your eyes tested lately?"

"My eyesight is fine. I had your voice in my head from Christmas saying, 'A baby would be nice,' so I was distracted. The driver stopped and asked if I was okay."

"Well, I should think so."

"I was a bit shaken, so I sat down on a bench. I pulled my phone out and checked my calendar?"

"You're not …?"

"I checked the dates, and I haven't had a period since the end of November."

"You are pregnant?"

"I don't know, possibly. That's what these are, pregnancy kits. I just about ran home; I was half excited and half anxious to know."

"Well, you know what this means?"

"What?"

"Come on, get in the bathroom and do what you have to?"

"I am scared."

"Caitlin, whatever the outcome, if it's meant to be, it's meant to be."

"Okay."

"Look, I am excited to have our babies and I can't wait for us to be parents and if you are not pregnant, there will be other times."

"Yeah."

"Go on then, don't keep me in suspense."

She walked into the bathroom and shut the door. After a few minutes, she asked him to come into the bathroom.

"So, what's the verdict, is it good news."

"We have to wait."

"This is the longest time ever."

"Well, I am shaking, look, I'm a nervous wreck."

After what seemed the longest two minutes ever, they looked down at both tests. The screen of each test had the word 'pregnant' displayed on it.

"Oh, you little beauty!" said Caitlin.

"Back of the net! Get in!"

"Come here Daddy!"

"Come here Mammy!"

They hugged each other and Matthew carried her around the landing, whooping for joy.

"Put me down you nutter!" shouted Caitlin, but she was laughing.

"Right, you, I am putting my foot down, you my little Queen aren't to do anything. I will wait on you hand and foot, like a Prince should and when Princess bump comes along, I will give you a life like a royal."

"Well, I'll expect to be treated in the manner in which I will have become accustomed, when are the butler, the maid and the servants starting work?"

"Tomorrow my lady," he said, with a bow and a flourish.

"How do you know it's a girl?"

"I don't know, just a feeling."

"Are you pleased?"

"Well, what do you think? Wally! Of course, I am pleased, but you have to make an appointment at the doctors now. No excuses, I have been worried about you, I knew something was up."

"I had no idea; I hadn't even thought about my missing period in December."

"Well, it's lovely news, just get it confirmed. We had better tell our parents."

"No, Matt please. Not yet; it is still early days, and I haven't been to the doctors yet. Let's just keep it between us for now and enjoy it."

"Okay, I am just excited that's all."

"I know, so am I."

"I love you Mrs Turner."

"And I love you Mr Turner."

Chapter 30

Max sat in his bedroom. He sighed to himself. He was still feeling anxious about his gender and confused about his sexuality. He grabbed his laptop and sat for what felt like the thousandth time, looking for answers online.

He had joined an online forum with other teenagers who felt the same way and it did help a little and gave him some comfort to know that other teenagers were feeling the same way.

In his head he felt female, but when he looked in the mirror there was this reminder that he was in fact a boy. When people referred to him as him or he, he wanted to correct them.

'I feel so confused. I still like doing boy things, but I also like girls' things like fashion and make-up and hairstyles. Am I wanting to be a girl or am I just a male version of a tomboy?'

He opened another tab and looked up what was available on the NHS for Gender Reassignment and the emotional and physical effects of becoming transgender. He didn't like the idea of having parts of his body removed, but he still didn't feel right about the way he was.

He made sure the bedroom door was shut and put a chair against it. He looked in the mirror and felt down below in his pants. He pulled them down and stood looking at his penis.

'I really don't like having it and I will start getting hair down there soon. It gets in the way, and I don't want it to grow.'

"Max! Max!" The door handle started moving and Rick was trying to push it open.

"Hey! Don't come in! Just a minute, right okay," said Max moving the chair.

"What are you doing in there, the door was stuck. I'll have to get that seen to. We have been calling you for the last ten minutes."

Max quickly fastened his trousers, standing in front of the laptop screen, so his Dad didn't see what he was looking at.

"Sorry, mate, were you in the middle of changing?" asked Rick.

"Something like that," he said red in the face.

'Oh!, he thought he had disturbed him in the middle of masturbating.'

"What did you want?"

"Your tea is ready. Are you okay?"

"Yes, why?"

"You've been very quiet lately."

"I am always quiet."

"More so than usual, anything troubling you?"

"Err no, I'll be down in a minute."

"Doing your homework were you?"

"Of course."

"A likely story, been looking at girls online?"

"Dad!"

"I was young once you know."

"Yeah, like a hundred years ago."

"Cheeky little sod."

"I wasn't doing anything."

"Hurry up and come down pronto, your dinner is going to get cold, Ha-ha, I know what goes through young lads' minds."

"It's not what you are thinking."

Rick closed the door and walked away.

Sally called up the stairs.

"Rick! Max! What are you doing up there?"

"We're just coming," said Rick smirking to himself.

All the way through dinner, Max felt pre-occupied and pushed his dinner around his plate.

"Come on Maxie, I have cooked that specially for you, it is your favourite, what you asked for," said Sally.

"I know, but I'm not hungry now."

"Are you not feeling well?"

"Just a bit tired, can I go and have a bath and get into bed. I want to go to sleep."

"Son, it's only five thirty," said Rick.

"Go on then," said Sally.

Max got up from the table and headed upstairs. He ran the bath, went into his bedroom, and took all of his clothes off. Again, he looked in the mirror at his body. 'Could he really go through puberty feeling like this or was it all part of growing up these days,' he asked himself.

He went into the bathroom and got into the bath. It was warm and inviting. He liked lots of bubbles in his bath. His Mam always had a go at him for using too much bubble bath.

He lay back in the bath and closed his eyes. He did suddenly feel sleepy, he hadn't been sleeping very well the last few nights. His mind started to wander. He was suddenly on a white sandy beach with palm trees and brilliant blue sea and sky with beautiful mountains in the background. He shaded his eyes against the brightness of it. He looked down at his feet and felt the soft sand in between his toes, he walked towards the sea and decided to go for a swim. The sea felt luxurious against his body. He could stay here forever. This was his paradise. He lay on his back and stretched his legs out in the lovely warm sea.

"Max, I need the loo."

"What?" he sat up in the bath and saw his brother on the toilet.

"Sorry, I couldn't wait."

"God, all right, hurry up."

David washed his hands in the sink.

"Did you have P.E today?"

"Yeah why?"

"I just heard these lads saying that you got changed in the cubicles and wouldn't shower wi' the rest of them."

"So, what, mind your own business, Davy I'm in the bath."

"What, you scared it isn't big enough?"

"Get out!"

"All right, going."

Max sighed to himself, it was true. He didn't like changing with the rest of them or showering with them or using the urinals in front of them. He liked things private. He used the showers in the cubicles and got changed in there. He didn't have to do what everyone else did. He was still in the boys changing rooms at times though he wished he was in the girls. Whenever he walked past, it always smelt much more pleasant and was probably cleaner.

He lay back and closed his eyes again. He relaxed for a while and started to wash himself, lathering himself in shower gel. He used the sponge down below and gave himself a good wash.

'Can I chop it off?'

Don't be ridiculous,' said a voice in his head. He sat looking down at himself and shook his head.

'I am sick of feeling like this.' He felt the tears sting his eyes.

Rick for the second time that night, burst into the bathroom and disturbed him.

"Sorry, son, I was desperate, only one bathroom."

Max was again red in the face.

"Hey, what's the matter? Has David been teasing you?"

"No more than usual, it's not him."

"You're crying."

Max wiped his eyes, sat up in the bath and looked at his Dad.

"Are you in pain?"

"Yes, I…"

"Where?"

"Well, I am not in pain as such, but I feel uncomfortable."

"Oh, that's just growing pains son. Your body is going to start changing."

"I don't like it."

"What?"

"You know."

"Ah, your…"

"Yes, it gets in the way. Can I take something to stop it getting bigger."

"No, Max, it's natural. It will just get bigger like Daddy's. You can't stay a little boy forever."

"I feel so confused," he started to cry again.

"Oh, son, come on. Let's get you out and dried."

"I am not a baby," he moaned.

"I know, but you are upset. Let me," he said, grabbing Max's towel. "Come on, let's get you dried."

Max shyly stood up and his dad put the towel around his boy and held him close.

Max sobbed in his dad's arms.

"Come on, let's get your pyjamas on."

He opened the bathroom door and led Max out to his bedroom. David was lying on his bed with his headphones on, oblivious to what was going on. Rick gave him a little push.

"What!"

"Davy go downstairs please."

"Why?"

"I want to talk to your brother please?"

"Can't he get himself dried?"

"You know he can, go downstairs now."

"God all right, can't even lie on my own bed," he moaned, walking out and slamming the door.

"Hey, David stop slamming doors," said Sally, coming upstairs with the ironing.

"Where's your dad?"

"Seeing to the baby in there. When is his nappy delivery coming?"

"Oh, leave him alone, I don't think he is feeling very well."

Sarah had followed Sally upstairs carrying Charlotte. "Is ah Max okay Mam?"

"I am sure he'll be fine after a sleep."

In the bedroom, Max got into bed and pulled his pyjamas on under the duvet. His face was still damp with tears, he hadn't meant to let his guard down.

Rick put the damp towel on the radiator and sat down next to Max on the bed.

"Do you want to have a chat?"

"I don't know, it's embarrassing. You might think I am a freak."

"Oh, Max, I could never think that, are you being bullied?"

"No, but Davy heard these lads commenting that I didn't use the main showers and how I always use the cubicles, to change and for the toilet. I just like things private that's all."

"Nothing wrong with that. Not everybody likes to strip off in front of others," said Rick. "Take no notice. Is that what's upsetting you?"

"No."

"Well, what then? I can't help you if you don't tell me what's wrong."

"It's just, can you get Mam?"

"Yes, do you not want to tell me, you don't have to."

"No, I do. I need both of you," said Max, fighting back the tears.

"All right son."

Sally was in her and Rick's bedroom putting away the ironing.

"Rick, is he okay?"

"No, he's not, can you come?"

"Yes, okay."

Rick and Sally walked into the boys' bedroom. Max was sitting up in bed, wiping his eyes.

"Max, sweetheart, are you poorly? Do you want me to get the doctor? You are very hot. I think you might have a temperature," she said, feeling his forehead and sitting on the bed where Rick had been sitting.

"Mam!" said Max sobbing.

"Ah darling what's wrong?"

Rick sat down opposite on David's bed.

"He's not poorly Sal."

"Can I talk to you both?"

"Of course, sweetheart," said Sally, concerned. "Something has obviously upset you."

"I erm, oh it's embarrassing. Well, you know that I am eleven nearly twelve, and well I should be starting puberty by now."

"Max, everyone develops at different speeds. It's nothing to worry about," said Sally.

"It's not that."

"Just listen to him, Sally."

"I don't want my body to change, not in that way anyway."

"What do you mean love, it's part of growing into an adult."

"Mam, Dad, I don't want you to think of me as a freak."

"Oh, darling, never."

"I haven't finished yet; you may change your mind when I tell you."

"Are you trying to tell us you are gay, when you said you were confused?" asked Rick puzzled.

"Just tell us Max. We won't be shocked or anything," said Sally.

Max rubbed his face and put his hands through his damp hair.

"Right, here it goes. When I look at my body and down below, it looks all wrong. I don't feel comfortable about myself, and my privates just get in the way. I don't like it."

"Max we all have complexes about our bodies at some stages of our lives, especially at your age," said Rick. "It's part of going through adolescence."

"Really?"

"Yes, you just don't like the idea of your body changing. We get it, we all go through it," said Rick.

"But what I mean is that I have these different feelings going around in my head. You know how I don't like football and I am not your average sort of lad?"

They both looked at each other but didn't say anything.

"A lot of times in my head, I am female and want to correct people when they refer to me as him. I like girl's things; fashion, hairstyles, make-up. I have even thought about changing to a girl but don't like the idea of having parts chopped off me. I also like boy's things and that is why I am confused. I feel shocked at myself for thinking such thoughts but then I can't help it. I am confused by my gender and I am also confused about my sexuality, because I want to be a girl, but then I think well should I like boys or girls? There I have said how I feel. Now you know, I have been torturing myself for months with these thoughts and I don't know what to do."

"Max, we always knew you weren't like other boys, but you always, tried to join in. When you were little you liked to dress up in Sarah's fairy costumes and play with her dolls. You and David used to play action man with barbie. There is nothing wrong with liking girl's things as well. There are plenty of girls that like to do boy's things," said Sally. "That doesn't make you a freak."

"I don't want David or Sarah knowing about this, not yet, not until I know what to do," said Max.

"Max, do you want to be a girl, is that what you are saying?" asked Rick.

"I think so, but I don't know how to cope with it, oh, I don't know …"

"But you are my beautiful boy," said Sally.

"Mam, I don't feel right, I feel like a failed attempt at both. I must be a freak." He started crying again. "You're both shocked, aren't you?"

"In some ways I am not surprised, I have noticed my cosmetics and perfume being moved about my dressing table and a blouse hanging out of my wardrobe and I knew it wasn't Sarah. She has her own things."

"I didn't try it on. I was just curious, I am not saying I want to start wearing dresses, I don't like them anyway."

"Max, I have noticed and a while ago I found fashion and cosmetic magazines under your mattress. I wasn't prying. It was when I was changing your bedding."

"Dad, you've gone very quiet."

"I am just listening to you, I want you to know that I don't think you are a freak and yes I am a little surprised. I just thought you were taking a pride in your appearance. You are always very smart, but I can see why you would be confused. I think I would be if I were you. What I don't understand is how you can even consider changing your gender, it's hard for anyone to get their head around, especially someone your age."

"I can't help feeling like this, I wish I didn't, but I do."

"All right son, I can see how upset you are about it; it can be a very traumatic thing to go through. You should have come to us sooner."

"Max, why didn't you tell us how you were feeling earlier instead of bottling it all up?" asked Sally.

"I was scared to, scared you'd disown me. You hear of such stories on the internet."

"The internet has a lot to answer for. Hang on, you weren't looking at girls online or doing what I thought you were doing."

"No Dad."

"Rick, one tracked mind!"

"You were looking up about Gender reassignment, weren't you?"

"Err, yeah, only because I don't know what to do."

Rick and Sally stared at each other they seemed to have this knack of communicating telepathically.

"Max, if you're not sure about this, you shouldn't go through with it and you need our consent," said Rick.

"And you won't give it, will you?"

"I never said that. I just think you need to be sure that's all. You can't chop and change, and there could be age restrictions."

"Your Dad's right Max. I think we need to get in touch with the youth sexual health team. They can help discuss how you are feeling about all this," said Sally.

"I'd be embarrassed. It was hard enough talking to you two."

"Max, they are trained to listen to youngsters like you. You aren't the first and you're not the last. They will put you at ease."

"Well, if you think it would help."

"Darling, you are going to drive yourself mad, if you don't get some help. We aren't professionals. We can't offer you this sort of advice, but we can support you."

"Dad, what do you think? Oh I've shocked you haven't I?"

"Max, I have always encouraged you to be like Davy, but I realise you are both different and like different things. I can't make you into something you're not. We are all different. Your grandad brought me up to believe that things were black and white, as in 'a spade's a spade'. He had old fashioned ideas and that goes back to his upbringing. In those days there was a lot more prejudice around. People were judgemental and if you weren't one of the lads, you got picked on and called a poof, especially if you didn't take part in masculine activities like rugby or football. I am not saying that because you don't like those things, it doesn't make you any less of a man. Things have changed these days; and yes, anyone who was different was called a freak."

"That's what I am worried about. What people will think about me; especially err Davy and Sarah."

"I don't think Sarah would be surprised and Davy; well, he is still growing up himself and you might find he will be more understanding than you think," said Sally. "I know he teases you but what siblings don't tease each other. You tease him too."

"Max, we don't have to rush into anything. You take your time and think about it and we are here if you need us," said Rick.

"Well, you both took it better than I thought you would."

"I love you my little buddy," said Rick, giving him a hug and ruffling his hair.

Max started yawning.

"I think you need a good night's sleep. Things will be clearer in the morning. Are you glad you told us?" asked Sally.

"Yeah, I think so. Thanks for being so understanding," said Max, yawning again. "Sorry I know it's quite early, but I feel really tired."

"Good night darling. Come here, everything will be okay," said Sally, hugging him and giving him a kiss on the cheek.

"Night Mam, night Dad," said Max, drowsily.

"Good night son. You'll be fine I am sure."

David came upstairs. "Can I go into my room now and play on the Xbox?"

"No, Davy, let your brother have some peace," said Sally.

"Is he not well?"

"He just needs some sleep and he'll be fine."

"But I wanted to play my new game."

"Another time pal," said Rick.

"You two took your time with him, is everything okay?"

"He's not feeling a hundred percent Davy, let him be," said Sally.

"All right, can I go and choose a film."

"Yes, okay, not too loud."

David headed downstairs.

"We need to have a chat," said Rick quietly when David was out of earshot, leading her into their bedroom. As to where we go from here, I want to support him, and I will, but he is still our boy and I think we need to tread carefully."

"Of course, later on, in bed."

"Right."

"Rick, I was proud of you for what you said to him."

"Well what else could I do? I saw how upset he was. I didn't see the point in having a go at him. He has enough going on. I can't say I understand it, maybe he is just like a male version of a tomboy."

"Nothing more than what we're doing I suppose, but this is going to be difficult, and I am glad he has finally told us. He must have been going through turmoil," said Sally; "and from what he said it is more than just being interested in girls' things, but you never know he may decide that is all it is. He is reaching an age when you go through so many changes."

"I never thought he would think about changing into a girl, but I am just going to have to accept that times have changed. We'll muddle through, but we must have a chat later, when they are all in bed as to how we are going to handle this one. It won't be easy."

Chapter 31

It was a rainy Saturday afternoon and Rachael was sitting at the kitchen table with her two children. They were trying to get their homework done. They each had their reading books. They had to write a book report and do some maths and spelling. They had read their books and done their reports. Cameron struggled with his writing but managed to write a few lines. His writing was still quite shaky and difficult to read, but he did try. The trouble was he had a very short concentration span.

Scarlett was trying to do some fractions, where she had to find a common denominator and break the fractions down. She was above the target for her age on most subjects, but struggled a little with maths. She got there in the end, but it took her a bit longer.

Cameron had number ordering and sequencing to do, which he found difficult. His dyspraxia was affecting his schoolwork, but the school had set him small tasks adapted to his needs.

"Mum, can you help me with this I'm stuck," said Scarlett.

"Of course, love," said Rachael, standing up and moving around to the other side of the table.

"I can't do this!" said Cameron, growing restless.

"Just have a try, I'll be there in a minute."

"Right, Scarlett, this is what you have to do," said Rachael, sitting down next to her.

"But it's too hard!" said Cameron.

"Cameron, I have been through it with you four times. Just try and I'll be there in a few minutes."

"I was working in a cocktail bar, when I was young!" sang Cameron.

"Cam, shush, look at your sums," said Rachael.

"Oh, don't you want me!"

"Mum, can you shut him up?"

"Cam, quiet, I am trying to help Scarlett. I'll be there in a minute."

Cameron grew restless and decided he was finished with his homework. He chucked his books, pen and folder onto the floor and grabbed his beloved headphones.

"Err, Cameron, pick that up and I said no headphones while we are doing homework. No music! Give me those headphones!"

"No!" said Cameron, trying to put them on.

Rachael grabbed them and put them up on the shelf where he couldn't reach.

"Mum, remember I need money for my trip," said Scarlett.

Cameron walked over to the stereo, turned it up full blast and started dancing.

"Right, Cameron, enough."

"Mum! Oh, why do I bother it is always about Cameron isn't it?"

"What's that supposed to mean?"

"I don't get any time with you, because you are always focusing on Cameron's needs."

"Look, I am sorry, but he just needs a lot of help."

"I know that, but for once I needed your help! Just forget it, I'll ask dad when he comes in."

"Cam – turn that off!"

"Oh, I am going upstairs to do this," said Scarlett gathering up her books.

"Oh, Scarlett, I was going to help you, I will."

"Forget it."

"That is going off young man."

"Ahh!"

"We'll finish your homework in half an hour. You can have a break, but no music. Your sister is trying to do her homework."

"Can I play my new game?"

"No."

"I can't have music, I can't have my game, what can I have?"

"I am not rewarding bad behaviour with treats."

"I wasn't bad."

"Well, you threw your things on the floor and grabbed your headphones to put on even though you knew you weren't allowed them when you are doing your homework, and then you put the stereo on full blast and didn't turn it off when I asked you to."

"But …!" said Cameron, the trembling lip coming on.

"You can go and read your comic and have some quiet time. I am just going to check on your sister."

Cameron wandered through to the sitting room and flung himself down on the settee. He looked at his Bart Simpson comic, but he really wanted to play his new game. It was a Toy Story game. He looked at the lamp standing next to the settee, pushed it over and then flung all the cushions off the settee onto the floor.

"He turned on his PlayStation, put his game into the console and sat down on the pile of cushions to play his game.

Rachael came down a little while later and found the mess Cameron had made while playing his game.

"Turn that off and tidy this mess up now!"

"Sorry, I just wanted my music and my game," said Cameron, doing as she asked.

James came through the back door, taking off his welly boots and waterproof jacket.

"God, it's pouring out there."

James was feeling a lot more like himself these days. He had started working part-time on the farm doing admin and odd jobs. He kept himself busy and still had to take his medication. He had cut down on his counselling sessions and was finding that working out in the open air and working with the animals was proving good for his mental health. Paddy was still mainly running the farm and taking the pressure off him. He had spent the afternoon doing some repairs to the tractor, which he had stored in one of the big sheds they kept for machinery. He filled the kettle and looked at the mess on the floor, where Cameron had emptied the contents of his folder.

"Rach, do you want a cuppa, I am making one!"

"Oh, yes please," she said, coming into the kitchen and sitting down by the fire.

"You look stressed."

"You could say that. I was trying to get t kids to do their homework, only halfway through, Cameron decided he had other ideas."

And, the mess ont floor are from his homework folder which he flung onto floor, while I was trying to help Scarlett with her fractions. He wanted his headphones, and I wouldn't let him, so he put the stereo on full blast, makin' a right racket it was".I got him to turn it off and I said he could read his comic only and not put his game or music on. I went upstairs to check on Scarlett and he decided to have a melt down by chucking t light on ter floor, along with the cushions from the settee and then proceeded to play his Toy Story game."

"Oh, no! I thought he was doing much better these days."

"He couldn't understand his maths. You know how he struggles with his schoolwork, and getting him to concentrate, well it didn't last long. He started off so well, but as soon as I turned my attention to Scarlett, he decided to have a meltdown. She wants you to help her. She wouldn't let me when I went up there."

"Oh, the joys of parenting. I'll go up when I have finished this."

"I have dealt with Cameron. He tidied up and apologised as you were coming through t door. I don't know what to do. As soon as he has to do something, he doesn't understand, he grabs his headphones."

"He's trying to block it out, that's why, but he does love his music."

"Well, we know where he gets that from."

Cameron came into the kitchen with his headphones back on and sat at the table.

James went and sat opposite him and sat down. He signalled for him to take his headphones off which he did straight away. He adored his dad.

Cameron looked at his dad and sang. "You're my wonder wall."

James answered and sang, "I said maybe …"

"You're going to be the one who saves me." Sang Cameron back to him.

"You're my wonder wall." Sang James, pretending to strum a guitar.

"Oasis, that is," said Cameron.

"That's right. Now, why have you been misbehaving with your mam?"

"I was bored!" said Cameron with emphasis on the bored. "Sorry Mammy!"

"You already said that" said Rachael, still annoyed with him.

"How about the three of us tackle this homework together. Then Daddy will go and help Scarlett, while you and Mammy play Toy Story? Deal?" asked James.

"Okay."

"Oh, so he gets rewarded for bad behaviour. We can't just give in ter him."

"No, he has to finish his homework."

"I don't know why I bother … Okay, I give up, but only when he is finished."

"How about it, Cam, for Mammy?" asked James.

"Yes, well let's get cracking then," said Cameron, picking his things up from the floor. "Come on crack on," said Cameron.

James and Rachael couldn't help but smile.

"I think, you must have the special touch James," said Rachael, who could never stay angry with her little boy for long. However, she let him know when he had done something wrong.

"Well, you know I have the gift."

"Get over yourself."

"Daddy, will you help me?"

"How about you let Mammy help you."

"No, you."

"Okay, is that all right love?" he said, looking at Rachael.

"Yes, okay."

"Mam, you can check the answers. Daddy might not be able to do it. It's tricky."

"Okay Cammy."

"I will help you on one condition."

"What's that dad?"

"That you promise to be a good boy and behave in a sensible manner when we do this."

"Okay!"

"Well let's work it out together."

After James had finished helping both Cameron and then Scarlett, he and Scarlett joined the other two for a game of Toy Story.

"Mum, can I please have my money for my trip?"

"Yes, sweetheart, but it's only Saturday night. I'll do it tomorrow after packed lunches are made, all right?"

"Yeah."

"Where are you going? I don't know about this," asked James.

"Oh, she's very excited," answered Rachael. "We are going to the Life Centre; they have an exhibition on about the anatomy and physiology of the body. They have this cool simulator ride where it takes you inside the body and you get to see all of the organs."

"Sounds gruesome."

"No, it'll be awesome!"

"Well, it sounds like your sort of thing. When you were younger you were always dressing up as medics," said James.

"Do you remember when she had chicken pox and we took her to the doctors. She brought her plastic stethoscope just in case they didn't have one," said Rachael.

"Did I?"

"Yes, you used to put bandages on your dolls," said James.

"We had better get tea cooked soon," said Rachael.

"Can we order Chinese?" asked Scarlett.

"Well, I was going to cook."

"Oh, have a night off love."

"I want McDonald's," said Cameron.

"They don't deliver it up here Cam," said Rachael.

"Ahh!"

"We could order them altogether on Deliveroo," said James.

"We shouldn't give into him all the time."

"Well, he won't eat Chinese, will he?"

"Oh, all right, I'm too tired to argue."

"Can I have a happy meal?"

"How about a please," said James.

"Please!"

"Okay."

"But Cam, it's only because you won't eat Chinese. It doesn't excuse how you behaved earlier," said Rachael.

"I said sorry."

"Rachael, leave it," said James.

After they finished the game and tidied up, James ordered the takeaway food and put a bottle of wine in the fridge. Rachael laid the table.

"When are you starting rugby training again?"

"Next Wednesday night. They are playing a friendly tomorrow against a Durham team. Tom is playing."

"What in the afternoon?"

"Yeah, I thought we might take a walk along tomorrow before taking the kids to the park and cheer them on."

"Yes, why not. I am glad you are more relaxed and starting to cope a lot better. It's good you are ready to start socialising again."

"Well, it's a start, I am still not ready for busy places or lads' nights out."

"It'll come, one step at a time."

"I still get a little nervous and anxious outside our home and the farm, but I am a lot better than I was."

"Good."

"Are you okay, working full time again on the district. I'd understand if you felt it was too many hours. You've already been very supportive of me."

"That's what I am here for. I love it anyway and the money always comes in handy. I thought we could save for a family holiday abroad this year."

"What about the farm?"

"Paddy is already doing a great job."

"I know but I don't want to take advantage."

"You wouldn't be, we need a break, especially after all of the stress we have been through."

"Because of me?"

"Not just you, t kids will love it; just the four of us, somewhere family orientated."

"I am not ready for busy places Rach, but I won't stop you taking the kids."

"No, this is for all of us. James you need this. We'll book somewhere quiet and go early in the year like May, when it isn't so busy."

"Kids only get a week off."

"Well, a week to ten days won't do any harm, if we can get the two weekends in."

"Go on James, say yes please."

"Okay then, I am being selfish, aren't I?"

"No, you could never be selfish, anxious maybe."

"Why not? I would love to. Shall we tell the kids?"

"No, let it be a surprise."

"We'll look later on, on the internet. We may get some cheap deals."

"They have never been abroad before," said Rachael.

"Well, we haven't had a proper holiday in years. Erm yeah, I think we probably do deserve it."

"That's the spirit."

Chapter 32

It was Sunday morning, and the day of the christening for baby Charlotte. It was a cold sunny day after the heavy rain the day before. The ground was really quite sodden.

Tom came downstairs dressed smartly in his black suit and dog collared shirt. Charlie came running towards him excitedly and trailing his lead behind him, carrying it in his mouth. He dropped it at Tom's feet and whined softly.

"Hello Charlie, sorry boy, I can't take you out right now," he said, stroking the dog's head.

He walked towards the boot room which was attached to the porch where they kept all of their coats and shoes. He grabbed a pair of his smart black ones and quickly buffed them up.

Charlie came running after him, this time with his ball in his mouth. He dropped it on the floor and rolled it towards Tom, where he was sitting, putting his shoes on.

"Sorry, boy I have to get to church."

The boys came downstairs and turned on the television. Emily was in the kitchen cooking breakfast. Tom had already eaten a quick bowl of cereal. He looked in the sitting room. The boys were sprawled on the settee, watching Family Guy.

"Jamie, John, take Charlie for a walk, won't you?"

"Mam's making breakfast."

"Well afterwards then, I have a busy day."

"Okay."

He walked into the kitchen where Emily was boiling eggs and making toasted soldiers.

"All right love?"

"Yes."

"I have asked the boys to take Charlie out after breakfast. Can you make sure they do."

"Yes, all right."

"He has been following me around with his lead in his mouth, and he just brought me his ball to play with."

"Ahh, how sweet."

"You're bringing the boys up to watch the match later?"

"Yes, we wouldn't miss it for the world. I'll make our Sunday dinner for tonight."

"Oh, let's go to the Hadrian for once, we can have the meat during the week."

"All right, I could do with having someone else make it for me for a change."

"Well, I would if I could, you know that."

"Are you off to church now."

"Yeah, bye love," he said, giving her a kiss.

"See you later boys," he called, as he headed out the door.

"Bye Dad!" they shouted in unison.

He walked around the corner to the church and went and unlocked the door. It was quite cool inside and eerily quiet, but that's how he liked it, when it was quiet, and he could sit down and take a few minutes to think and take stock.

Tom walked into the vestry and put on the white smock and sash he wore around his shoulders. He stood at his desk and pulled out his notes for the service. He had chosen hymns that fitted in with the christening and the rest of the service.

He walked back out into the main area of the church and put the numbers of the hymns up on the board, displayed in front of the large organ.

The Sunday school children came in and two of them had the job of handing out the hymn books to the parishioners; two others had been given the job of collecting the money for the upkeep of the church. He put two gold coloured plates out for the collection.

The church started filling up and he welcomed his parishioners. He spotted the Seddon's coming through the door and welcomed them to the church.

"Hello, welcome, welcome," he said, shaking their hands. "I have reserved some seats for you at the front."

"Thanks Tom," said Rick.

"Oh, doesn't she look lovely," said Tom looking at Charlotte in her christening robe.

"Thanks, it belonged to my Mum," said Sarah.

"Well, if you would like to take your seats in the front pews, please, we are nearly ready."

They walked up to the front of the church. The church was busy today as the Seddon family had invited their relations from Manchester.

Tom waited for everybody to settle down, when all was quiet, he walked up to the lectern and laid out his books and started the service.

"Good morning, everybody and welcome. We will open up the service with the usual notices and messages but first I would like to welcome the Seddon family who moved from Manchester to the village about six months ago. Today, we are going to have the baptism of baby Charlotte Sally Seddon."

Charlotte made a gurgling noise.

"Well, I am glad Charlotte is up for it," he laughed. "Now Norma is going to come up and read out the notices, Norma?"

After the notices were read and the first hymn sung, there was a Bible reading and then Tom asked the Seddon family to join him at the font.

"Right can I have the Godparents next to Sarah please?"

David and Max went and stood next to their sister who was holding Charlotte.

Tom handed the Godparents a lit candle each. He looked at Sarah and smiled at her reassuringly.

"May I?" he asked, holding out his arms to hold baby Charlotte.

"Err, yes," said Sarah, handing her over.

"I'll be careful, okay?" he whispered.

Charlotte looked up at Tom with wide eyes. She was just starting to grab things, she felt his silky sash and put her small hands around it and tried to pull it, she liked the feel of it and tried to lift it towards her face.

Tom looked down at her and smiled. "Hello, Charlotte," he said. "Right, we'll read it and boys you say that you agree to your promises to look after Charlotte when prompted, okay?" he said quietly.

"Yeah," they both said together.

After the reading of the baptism and promises and declarations were made, Tom held Charlotte over the font. "I name this child Charlotte Sally Seddon." He put his hand in the holy water and lifted it towards Charlotte's forehead. "With this holy water I now make the sign of the cross." Charlotte looked up at him and giggled, then continued to suck happily on his sash. "Heads bowed, let us pray, I welcome Charlotte into God's house, let him guide her, protect her and keep her safe and well. May she be guided through troubled times, protected in sickness and rejoiced in joy, Amen."

"Amen," said the congregation.

Tom handed Charlotte back to Sarah. She started to cry; she was enjoying being where she was.

"Shush, Charlotte, all safe now," whispered Sarah, stroking her head. Charlotte looked up at Sarah and grabbed her hair.

"Please go back to your seats," he said to the Seddon's. He waited for everyone to settle down. "Now please turn to number 365 in your hymn books, 'he's got the whole world,' this is for Charlotte, please stand."

The congregation stood and started to sing.

"He's got the whole world,

In his hands, he's got the whole wide world,

In his hands he's got Charlotte Sally,

In his hands he's got the whole wide world,

He's got the whole world in his hands."

The service came to a close and Sarah went over to Tom and thanked him for the service.

"Thank you Tom, that was lovely," said Sarah.

"Yes, the service was lovely, and these flowers are gorgeous," said Sally.

"Yeah, thanks vicar," said Rick.

"It was a pleasure really, you are all welcome here, it will be nice to see you in church again when you have the chance. We have a good Sunday school, which has many activities. It might be good for the boys and we have a messy play and toddler group for when Charlotte gets bigger," he said, holding Charlotte's hand.

"Is there footy?" asked David.

"Yes, we have all sorts of outdoor activities. They go off to camp, go bowling, abseiling, all sorts of things."

"You and your football," said Sally, smiling at him.

"Is there drama?" asked Max.

"They do have trips to the theatre, but I am not sure about actually doing drama," Tom replied.

"Can I come around and play footy wi'John and Jamie?" asked David.

"Well, we do have plans today, David. They are watching me play rugby and then we are going to the Hadrian for tea."

"David, let them have one day together," said Sally. "Sorry, Tom."

"It's all right. If you'd excuse me, I must say goodbye to the other parishioners."

"Are we going home now," asked Max.

"No, we are also going to the Hadrian for lunch. Remember, it's Charlotte's christening party," said Rick.

"Oh, yeah, sorry," said Max.

The extended family came up and said their 'hellos.'

"That was a lovely service and wasn't our Charlotte a good girl," said Joyce, patting her head. "She looks lovely in that robe, is it new?"

"No Gran, it was Mam's," said Sarah. "It's been washed and ironed, that's all."

"You were christened in that," Joyce said to Sally.

"I know Mum," said Sally.

"Shall we take a few photos," asked Rick, with his phone in his hand.

"Yes, okay then," said Sarah.

"One with you and Charlotte first Sarah," asked Rick, "and one with the boys and Charlotte and one with me and your Mam."

"Okay," said Sarah, sitting down on a pew with Charlotte.

When it came to handing Charlotte over for her photo, she still felt a bit reserved, but knew she was safe here in God's house.

After the photos were taken, they went outside, saying bye to Tom on the way out, and made their way up to the Hadrian. They had only been in the pub a couple of times since moving to Northumberland.

They soon arrived at the pub where they had booked a table in the restaurant.

Matthew showed them through to their table and let them get settled. He had some extra waiting staff on today and got them to take their orders. They had a lovely meal and a few drinks in the pub's conservatory, overlooking the garden, it was a bit too cold to sit outside.

Afterwards, at Sally's house, everyone settled down in the sitting room and Rick opened a bottle of sparkling wine and started filling up glasses and soft drinks for those who couldn't have alcohol. Sally had put a christening cake and some snacks on the table.

Charlotte was fast asleep in her pram and was missing her own party. They all stood with their drinks.

"Right, a speech I think," said Rick.

"No, not one of your speeches Dad," said Max.

"Just a short one Maxie," said Rick, winking at him.

"Oh, yeah right," said David smirking.

"I would like to start by saying thank you to everyone who came up from Manchester and thanks to Sarah for giving us a beautiful grandchild and …"

"Thought, it was going to be short," said Max.

"Nearly there, thanks to the boys, for being Godparents and also to Sally for organising everything."

"Haven't you forgotten someone?" asked Sally.

"Who?"

"Well, who is today about?"

"Ah and to Charlotte!" he said, raising his glass.

"To Charlotte!" they all agreed.

At the mention of her name Charlotte started to cry. Sarah got her out of her pram and carried her into the sitting room.

"I think you'll all agree, Charlotte is the star of the show. Sorry love, didn't mean to forget. To our Charlotte," he said, again raising his glass.

After the christening presents were opened, cake all eaten, and snacks demolished people started to say their goodbyes. The older members of the family had booked into the Beaumont, but some had to get back to Manchester for work and school the next day.

Rick's brother was putting on his coat.

"So, bruv, when are you coming back?"

"Back, we live here now."

"No, I mean when are you all coming down to Salford for a weekend?"

Sarah overheard this and shuddered. "I am not taking Charlotte there. Tell him Dad! Tell him, I just can't, I can't!"

"Erm, it may not be for a while bro; possibly in the summer if we're down that way."

"Okay, no worries. Just thought we could have a boys' night out."

"And girls," said Sally. "Sorry, what's this."

"Oh, he's just wondering when we are going back down to Manchester."

"Ah, that would be nice, be good to catch up."

"Sal, we will have to see, we'll let you know okay?" he said turning to his brother.

"Sure, yeah, err no problem."

"I won't be going," said Sarah, who went upstairs and slammed her door.

"Sorry about that, she's just tired," said Sally. "She is still struggling a bit since, well you know."

"Yeah, I understand, no problem really. We'll see you soon, hopefully."

"Yeah, we'll be in touch," said Rick.

After everyone had gone and the boys and Sarah and Charlotte were upstairs, Sally and Rick were sitting on the settee, watching television.

"Well, that was embarrassing, wasn't it with our Sarah I mean," said Rick.

"Yes, it was, but he seemed to understand. It would have been nice to go down for a weekend, but Sarah is still very fragile," said Sally.

"But we have family and friends down there, we can't always expect them to come up here and the boys would like it. Our David is still regularly in touch with his old mates."

"We just have to give it time, Rick."

"Yeah, I know. Hopefully, now we have had the christening, things will settle down."

"Yes, and we are still wating for her appointment with the Mental Health team."

"Yeah, well they will have just received the referral. It hasn't been long," said Rick.

"I don't know, what with Sarah and her problems, Max with his troubles and David mooning around like a lovesick puppy, where is it all going to end?"

"They're just going through tricky ages. It's not easy being a teenager in today's society. God it was hard enough back in the eighties."

"Yes, I know that. I suppose we all have our moments."

"What were you like as a teenager, Sally?"

"Me, well not much different, full of hopes and dreams. I think I thought I was going to conquer the world."

"You know, I believe that of you."

"Yeah, well I haven't changed much. Dad always said that I did too much dreaming."

"You care, nowt wrong wi' that."

Chapter 33

Emily drove along the road after seeing one of her patients. She was finished for the day. On her way home, she saw James sitting on the bench outside the park. He looked as if he were in a world of his own. He seemed upset about something.

She parked the car and went up to him.

"Hi James."

"Oh, hi Emily," he said, with his head down, barely even glancing at her.

"Are you okay? I was driving past, and you looked miles away. Has something upset you?"

"Ah, well I just had to come out for a walk. Things were getting a bit heated at home."

"Who with, you and Rachael, the kids?"

"Both, Cameron has been playing up recently, Scarlett has been demanding attention, saying that Cameron is always the centre of everything. We treat both of them the same."

"Well, kids will be kids."

"And Rachael keeps going on about this holiday abroad. I know it is what we all need, but I am scared in case I have a relapse when we are in a strange place."

"You could both do with a break. You know you have both been through a stressful time. Things are bound to take their toll. Have you been arguing?"

"A little bit, just about the holiday and the kids."

"Have you told her that you're scared of having a relapse."

"Yes, she's confident that I'll be okay and says that I have been doing much better, which I have, but I still get anxious at times."

"That's understandable."

"I love her, and the kids and we still get on like a house on fire. It's just that when things get stressful, I have to take a deep breath and take myself off for a walk."

"She understands that you always seem to have a good relationship and you both make great parents."

"Yeah, she knows it's part of my recovery process."

"Well, there you go then."

A couple came and joined them on the park bench.

Emily stood up and said, "Do you want to take a walk?"

"Yes okay."

They walked into the park together. James looked across at his old friend and smiled, they had known each other since early school days, Emily had always been a good friend. At one time, way before Rachael came along, they had gone out together for a while. They were teenagers at the time, just kids really. Tom was seeing another girl at the time, but Tom and Emily had been friends since they were small. They soon discovered that they were meant to be together.

"You're looking distant again," said Emily. "What were you thinking about?"

"I was thinking what a good friend you have been since I first saw you in Primary School with your hair in bunches."

Emily laughed. "Oh, God! Yes, don't remind me."

"You've always been good to me Ems and Tom; I am glad that we have all stayed friends after all this time."

"Well, that's what friendship is all about isn't it?"

"Yeah, you and Tom are meant to be together, I was thinking when we started going out at the age of fourteen that we thought we were it; you as a Brosette, and me thinking that I was going to be some kind of rock star."

"Yes, Bros, my God, I loved them, and you loved Iron Maiden, that time you dyed your hair pink, and your parents went mad with you. All of your blond curls were suddenly pink and spiky."

"It took months to grow out. It was permanent dye. I got detention for a week at school and was told to get a proper haircut and not all spiky like I had it."

They reached a park bench secluded by trees and sat down. It was a little bit cold, but they were both dressed warmly.

"So, are you feeling better now?"

"Yes, of course, I just get over-wrought sometimes."

"I know but Rach is right, you have been doing much better, so well done you!"

"You know Emily, I love Tom to bits."

Emily sat smirking. "Oh, something I should know about."

"Not in that way! It's been really nice just chatting as friends, without anyone else getting in the way. Do you know I can't remember the last time we sat down and had a good old chat like this, just the two of us."

"Yeah, it's nice," she said reaching over and patting his hand. She let it linger a little longer than she should have and then quickly pulled it away.

"Sorry."

"No, don't say sorry. It's all right, you weren't doing anything really."

"I love Tom," she said.

"Course you do, don't feel guilty."

"I always have, even when I was going out with you."

"I know that."

"I was just taken back to our youth for a moment and saw you in your school uniform, with your mop of blond curly hair."

"Ah, right."

They were sitting quite close together and couldn't keep their eyes off each other. James put his hand on her arm and leaned over and before he knew what he was doing, he was leaning over to kiss her. Emily responded and kissed him passionately, his hands went inside her coat and up towards her breasts. Her hand lingered at the top of his leg near his groin. She suddenly realised what she was doing, and then pulled away.

"What are you doing?" she asked, going red in the face.

"Sorry, I couldn't help myself. I got carried away I guess."

"I think perhaps we had better get home now before we both end up doing something we regret," said Emily.

"Yes, erm perhaps that is best, but you responded, you were tempted. Sorry, I am not thinking and letting my imagination run into overdrive. I am with Rachael, and I love her."

"Oh, look James, it has been nice just the two of us, but we are both married with kids. We can't do this to Tom and Rachael."

"I wasn't intending to."

"So, what was that then?"

"You just look so pretty sitting there in the sunlight, I didn't mean to get carried away, I am sorry."

"I guess I am partly to blame, I put my hand where I shouldn't have."

"Shall we just forget it happened and not mention it again?" asked James worriedly.

"I think that would be best."

"You're not annoyed, are you?"

"No, I was just taken by surprise that's all. More flattered than anything, you stirred up some old feelings. You always were a good kisser. God, what am I saying? You are my one of my oldest friends and we got carried away that's all."

"Come on mate, let's walk back," said James, grinning at her.

"You're not going to start calling me that are you?"

"No, but you always were one of the lads, a bit of a tomboy, you used to want to join in our games of football."

"Well, I did join in, and I did better than some of you boys."

"Are you going to tell Tom, that you saw me?"

"Why are you going to tell Rachael?"

"Well, we haven't really done anything have we, not much to tell. It's not as if I laid you down in the grass and had mad passionate sex with you."

"Well, I think we would have some shocked people and probably would have been arrested. No, you're right, it wasn't really anything, just two old friends spending time together, what's wrong with that?"

"Absolutely nothing at all. You know we have known each other for decades and you are very special to me, just the way Tom is, but as friends agreed?"

"Agreed; then why do I feel so guilty?"

"God, me too," said James. "I don't know what I was thinking of, sorry."

They had reached the entrance of the park and said their goodbyes.

"See you soon James, take care and try not to worry about things. We are okay, right?"

"I am worried now, what if someone saw us kiss?" he whispered.

"There was no one around and we were hidden by the trees, just forget about it, okay. Otherwise, it will cause trouble if Tom and Rachael find out?"

"Yes, you're right, well thanks for the chat pal, and I will see you soon."

She slapped him playfully on the arm. "That's more like it," she said.

Emily walked away and waved at him as she got into her car. To her he was her oldest school friend apart from Tom, and she adored him. They had both let their feelings get the better of them. She loved him more like a brother really, but just got caught up in the moment.

'What was I thinking, I love Tom with all of my heart and Rachael is my best friend.'

She knew that it wouldn't go any further, but after what she had said to James, she did have a pang of guilt. She had just been for a walk with another man and tried to hold his hand and then kissed him. It didn't make any difference if it was just James. She had still allowed herself to do it.

'I think I had better forget about this, like we agreed. It won't happen again. Oh, how could I have done it?' she thought, racked with guilt.

James was also having similar thoughts on the way home; he had just felt so relaxed in her company and was enjoying reminiscing about the past that he got carried away.

'I love Rachael. Why did I do it,' he wondered. 'I adore Tom and wouldn't want to hurt him and then there are his kids and ours.' He shouldn't have kissed her; he knew that. 'Best put it to the back of my mind and forget about it.'

Emily arrived home. The boys were arguing. Tom was trying to get tea organised and Charlie was barking his head off.

"Why were you playing on it? It's my new game. I paid for it, I saved up, I haven't even played it myself yet!" yelled John at his brother.

"Oh, get over yourself, I was only borrowing it!" shouted Jamie, throwing the disc in its box at his brother, which hit him on the shin.

"Ow! What did you do that for," said John pushing his brother over?

Tom walked into the sitting room.

"What's going on here, I am trying to cook tea?"

"Jamie nicked my game and then threw it at me when he was finished with it. It hit me on my shin."

"Jamie, you should have asked if you could borrow it."

"I'm sorry. I didn't know I was doing any harm. We always share games."

"Yes, but I hadn't even played it you nob head!"

"John! enough; right, I am turning this television off! Jamie, you can help me in the kitchen. John you take Charlie out, he has been barking for ages."

"Have I arrived home to World War Three?" asked Emily walking into the sitting room. "Stop arguing all of you!"

"Hello Ems. The boys were arguing over their Xbox game."

"My Xbox game!"

"All right John, your Xbox game."

"Good day at work Emily?"

"Yes, I have had a busy day, you?"

"Yeah, me too, didn't expect to be playing referee though."

"Oh, come on Charlie boy," said John. "Walkies!" He clipped the lead onto the dog's collar and put his favourite ball in his pocket.

"I'll come," said Jamie. "Sorry John, about taking your game and hitting you with it."

"Jamie, you know better than to treat things like that. It could have got broken, and they are expensive! John saved his pocket money up for that," said Emily.

"Yeah well, I have said sorry."

"All right, bro, come on," said John. He never stayed angry with his brother for very long. They were inseparable. "Only, ask first, right?"

"Yeah, I'll just get my coat."

"Err, Jamie, kitchen, now you are going to help with tea, call it your penance."

"Ah! My what!"

"He means your punishment," said Emily.

"But! how come John gets away with no punishment? He pushed me over."

"Go on, kitchen," said Emily. "What are we having?"

"Toad in the hole."

"Err, yuck," said John.

"It's sausages in Yorkshire pudding, you doughnut!"

"Will you two stop it."

Charlie looked up at John and whined.

"Okay, come on boy."

Emily went upstairs to the bathroom and found that she had a text from James.

It just said, 'Sorry.'

She sent one back saying, 'Okay, let's forget it, delete this message please. We are just good friends.'

She quickly deleted the message and went downstairs. Jamie was helping Tom in the kitchen with tea. He looked up when she entered the room.

"You okay love. You look miles away," asked Tom.

Emily didn't seem to hear him and sat down at the kitchen table.

"Earth calling Emily?"

"Huh?"

"You all right? Do you want some stuffing made?"

"What, yes okay, I'll do it!" she said, feeling irritable.

"No, Jamie will do it."

"How?" asked Jamie.

"Follow the instructions on the packet. You'll need to boil the kettle."

"Can I get you a glass of wine Ems?"

"No, erm, oh, I don't know," she said, standing up and going into the sitting room.

Tom followed her in. "Okay, what's the matter?"

"Nothing."

"Well, something is. You seem away with the fairies. What's troubling you?"

"Oh, nothing really, just had a stressful day. I think I'll have a bath."

"Well can it wait until after tea, it's nearly ready. I'll get the boys to help clear up."

"Okay."

"I could always come up and scrub your back or even get in it with you?"

"Not likely, with the boys up."

"Well, later on, when they have gone to bed."

"No, I want a bath and have an early night," she said, starting to yawn.

She was feeling mentally and physically drained. It had been a long busy day with some complex patients. It had been good to have a walk through the park. She just felt guilty about what had happened with James. She had better pull herself together, she had Tom and the boys to think about.

"That's a good idea, it has been a while, since we last you know…"

"You've got a short memory Tom; do you not remember Saturday night?"

"Yeah, like I said a long time."

"Get away, you are terrible!"

"Adorable though, you can't resist me!" he said, giving her a kiss.

"Oh, you two, give it a rest," said John, returning from his walk with Charlie.

"Am I doing this tea myself? I am not a slave!" said Jamie.

"Makes a change, you helping, come on," said Tom, going back to the kitchen.

"John hasn't done owt. How come I am doing everything!" he moaned.

"Anything," corrected Emily.

"Oh, sorry. Mother would you prefer me to speak the queen's English? Shall I talk like this?" he said, putting on a posh voice. "I am only the servant, don't need ter speak proper!"

"Jamie! John can help you clear up after tea."

"No, he can do it. I've done enough! Call me when it is on the table," he said, angrily stomping upstairs.

"Jamie, hey come back here!" shouted Tom. "Don't speak to your mother like that. What's got into that boy, he isn't normally like that."

"Oh, leave him," said Emily, sighing.

"John you can make the gravy please," said Tom. "Let's get this tea over with. I don't know what's wrong with you all."

"There's nothing wrong with me and Mam. Jamie is just in a bad mood because I stopped him from playing my game. I would have let him play it you know, it's just I wanted to first, it being my game."

"Okay, let's not get into that now," said Emily, feeling tired. The last thing she wanted was to come home to everyone arguing.

After they had had their tea, Emily stood up and scraped her dinner into the bin. She really hadn't been hungry. She had been off her food all day. She hoped she wasn't coming down with something or was it just because she felt stressed?

"You've hardly touched that!" remarked Tom.

"I am not hungry, sorry."

"Is there something worrying you Ems? Are you feeling poorly?"

"No, I am just really tired. I've been up since five o'clock this morning and it's been a busy stressful day. Don't worry I am fine. I think I'll have a bath and go straight to bed, to sleep," she said, empathising the word 'sleep.'

"Okay love, we'll clear up," said Tom, clearly worried. He knew she had a stressful job. He had an understanding of what it was like to deal with complex people.

"Will we?" asked Jamie. "I have done my share; John can help you."

"Okay Jamie enough. Go and do your homework."

"I don't have any."

"Yes, we do, we have Biology," said John.

"Go and get on with it then, John you can help with the dishes and then you can do yours."

"Okay Dad," said John.

"You are such a big mouth John and a crawler."

"No, I am not. What's wrong with you man?"

"Nothing, nothing at all, everything's got to be about you, hasn't it?"

"Right, that's it, enough! Your Mam has had a very stressful day as have I, now whatever is going on between you sort it out please!" shouted Tom, finally losing his temper. He was normally so good tempered. "Jamie, come here."

"What?"

"Come on son," he said opening his arms to hug his boy and comfort him. "You know you shouldn't have done what you did, and John shouldn't have pushed you over, right John?"

"But he had my game."

"Shake hands and apologise and let that be the end of it, you two are normally best pals, now come on."

"Sorry John, I shouldn't have taken your game."

"And I shouldn't have pushed you, sorry," said John, shaking his brother's hand and giving him a hug. The three of them stood and hugged.

"It was a wicked game though!"

"I wouldn't know, would I?" grinned John. "How about a tournament?"

"After dishes and homework!"

"I'll clean up and get rid of the rubbish," said Jamie. "Sorry if I was a pain."

"Well thank you Jamie and John. it was much better working together," said Tom when they had finished.

He was glad his boys had made up, it didn't take them long to forgive each other. They had been inseparable right from the womb to the birth, to growing up together. He was concerned about Emily. She seemed distracted.

'Probably just overworked,' he thought.

Over at the farmhouse. Rachael had finished work at mid-day and had spent the afternoon at home, she had brought home paperwork to do. James had gone and picked the kids up from school in the car. The children had been given spelling and a math exercise to do. Cameron had found it difficult and got frustrated. She was trying to be patient with him. He was okay with the spelling. He had to learn the three times table. Being dyspraxia he found ordering and sequencing of numbers difficult and was struggling to remember the order of the multiplication. She tried putting groups of objects together and getting him to count them. The school had said to work with him little and often, as in keeping the sessions short. In the end he threw his books on the floor yet again and screamed.

James couldn't cope after he had tried to help Cameron and he needed to get out of the house. Normally Cameron would do anything for his dad, but lately he had been difficult. Scarlett had been no bother and got on with her homework but still felt distracted by Cameron.

"So, did you enjoy your walk?"

"What, I haven't been to work."

"James, you are miles away. Did you enjoy your walk?"

"Yes, thank you, I did."

"What's wrong with you, that sounded sarcastic, I was only asking."

"Sorry, yes I did. It was good to get away from the farm for a walk, I went through the park."

"Meet anyone on t'way?"

"Like who, why, there were lots of people out."

"Okay, don't get shirty bertie with me! Have you taken your medication?"

"Yes, stop fussing I am fine."

"Sorry, I'm only concerned about yer"."

"Rachael, I am all right."

"You seem distracted that's all."

"Sorry, are you okay, got your paperwork done?"

"Some of it, they started running around after their homework was done, which doesn't make things easy. Oh, I know they are only playing but sometimes it would be nice to have some peace and quiet."

"Did Cameron settle down?"

"Yes, he's upstairs playing in his bedroom. He is just trying to push my buttons at the moment, see how much he can get away with. He does try with his homework, but it doesn't take long for him to lose concentration and that's when he starts being naughty. I wish he wouldn't throw his books on the floor. The school will be wondering what we're doing with him."

"And Scarlett?"

"She's upstairs, reading. They have both had an early tea. I thought we could have a nice meal together."

"Why?"

"To have some adult conversation, just the two of us."

"Oh, sorry, erm what are we having?"

"Oh, got it; cooking. We are having marinated lamb with dauphine potatoes, Chanternay carrots and parsnips."

"Ooh, lovely."

"And sticky toffee pudding."

"Delicious, what have I done to deserve this."

"I just thought it would be nice."

"Sorry for being a bit off with you, I didn't mean to be."

"That's all right," she said, giving him a kiss. "What's that smell? Smells like flowers, almost smells familiar."

"Ah, that's from when I sat down on the park bench near the rose bed, you know by the park entrance, they had quite a strong fragrance."

"Oh, right, well it smells lovely."

"What, I don't want to smell girly. I'd better go and change it."

"Don't be daft, it smells like the roses in our garden. It's quite a turn on."

James sat back on the settee, feeling guilty about earlier. God, he hoped he didn't smell of Emily's perfume. He would be in trouble if Rachael made the connection. What was he thinking of, he had a lovely wife and kids, last thing he needed was more trouble?

'Time to put a lid on that episode,' he thought feeling grateful for what he had.

But what neither James or Emily realised was that Rachael and Tom had shared an occasion where they had almost ended up kissing. Rachael had been upset about James's breakdown and attempted suicide and had ended up in Tom's arms.

Chapter 34

Shireen was sitting on the stairs pulling on her boots and her coat and scarf. They had had some more snow last week. Most of it had gone but it was still quite cold. It was Saturday morning, and she was going to persuade Sarah to go out with her and have a walk around the market and maybe pop into Costa. She had promised her mam that she would try and make friends with her. Now she had some spare time, she thought she would do just that. Not only had she promised her mam, but she wanted to get to know her better. Every time she had gone around to see David, she was engrossed with the baby.

Aisha came down the stairs.

"Oh, you off out love?"

"Yeah."

"Where? To see David, such a nice boy."

"Huh, that's not what you said when we first went out."

"Well, even adults make mistakes, so, are you going somewhere nice?"

"I am going to see David, next door, but I haven't arranged anything with him. I am going to try and persuade Sarah to come out, have a look around the market and go to Costa for a coffee."

"Oh, that's a nice idea."

"Yeah well, if I can coax her out, she is always busy with Charlotte and never goes out. Davy says that they all try to do their bit of looking after her, but she hardly lets them near her."

"Sally was saying that she needs to spend some time with people of her own age. She is lucky to have such supportive parents. A lot of young mothers don't have that."

"Yes, well, I'll see you later Mam."

"Have a nice time."

Shireen shut the front door and walked down her path. Once on the street, she turned to her left and walked up next door's path and rang the bell. David answered the door in his boxer shorts and t-shirt.

"Oh, hi babes. I didn't know we'd arranged owt ?"

"We haven't."

"Come to snuggle up with me in bed then?"

"Were you still in bed. It's ten thirty."

"Well, yeah; a boy needs his beauty sleep you know. You woke me up."

"Sorry, David are you going to let me in or am I to stay on the doorstep?"

David opened the door and let her in. He leaned down and kissed her on the mouth.

"Well, it's a nice surprise, I was dreaming about you."

"A nice dream, I hope?"

"Oh, yes, all of my dreams about you are nice. Well now I'm up I may as well make myself some breakfast, Cheerios and juice. Would you like some?"

"No thanks, where is everyone?"

"My mam, dad and our Max have gone down to the Metro Shopping Centre. He needed new shoes."

"And Sarah and Charlotte?"

"Err upstairs I think, why?"

"Just thought she might like to go out to the market and to Costa."

"And there's me thinking you'd called for me, give me twenty minutes and I'll come with yer."

"No, I thought just me and her."

"Oh," he said putting on a pep lip.

"Well, I would like to get to know her better. She is always so occupied with Charlotte. Has she made any friends here yet?"

"No, she never goes far and she's here with Charlotte most of the time, unless our mam can get her to go out with her and the rest of us."

"Can you see if she's ready please?"

"All right," "SARAH!" he bellowed. "SARAH! You're wanted," he said, shouting up the stairs.

"I meant go and see her, not shout," said Shireen, smiling at him and shaking her head.

"Davy! Stop shouting!" said Sarah, coming down the stairs. "What?" She hadn't noticed Shireen. "Oh, hi Shireen. You and David going out?"

"No, you and me are."

"Eh?"

"How would you like to have a look around the market and pop into Costa for a coffee?"

"Oh, well thanks for asking, but I have Charlotte."

"Well Uncle David could look after her."

They both looked at her and said, "What," in unison.

"Well, I suppose I could as long as you aren't too long," said David.

"No, you're all right bro. I could take her with me."

Just then Rick, reversed the car up the drive. And he, Sally and Max got out of the car. They had left really early and managed to miss the rush. They got the shopping out of the boot. They had been to Asda and Next for Max's shoes for school.

Sally put her key in the lock and let them in.

"Oh, hi Shireen, you okay?"

"Yes, thank you."

"David why aren't you ready yet?" asked Sally. "You could have at least been ready for Shireen calling round."

"I didn't know she was coming."

"I woke him up Mrs Seddon."

"Oh, Sally, please."

"Sally."

"Makes me feel a hundred and three."

"You are a hundred and three," said David.

"Well thank you Davy."

"Come on lad get a move on. You can't be standing around in yer boxer shorts and keep your lady waiting," said Rick.

"She hasn't come for me; she came to ask Sarah out – Shireen being thoughtful."

"Yeah, well I said I had Charlotte; Davy offered, but I don't like leaving her long."

"Sarah, we are here to look after Charlotte. Go and have some fun," said Sally.

Sarah looked at her dad for reassurance. She adored her mam, but she had always been a daddy's girl."

"Go on love."

"Yeah all right, I'd love to thanks," she said turning to Shireen and smiling. "I'll be five minutes."

She came downstairs, all wrapped up.

"Now Mam, she'll be due her next bottle soon at twelve o'clock and give her some potato and parsnip please. Don't give her too much and …"

"Sarah, we'll be fine," said Sally. "Where are you going?"

"Oh, just along to Hexham, to the market and to Costa," said Shireen.

"Bye babes miss you already," said David giving her a sloppy kiss.

"Put her down boy and go and put some clothes on," said Rick.

"Ah, but she likes seeing my muscly legs in shorts."

"What muscle?" said Max. "You're like Mr Bean."

"Well, you're like Ken off Ken and Barbie."

"Boys!" said Sally. "Have a nice time," seeing them out the front door.

She watched them walk down the path and turned to the others. "Well I think she might have found a friend," she said smiling.

"Yeah, my girlfriend," said Davy.

"It's a start," said Sally.

The two girls got off the bus at Hexham and headed for the market. It was bigger than the Sleathwaite one, had more craft stalls, booksellers, clothes, bags, jewellery Everything you could think of. They started looking at the craft stalls where local artists had displayed prints, landscapes and portraits. A girl was sitting under a canvas, having her portrait drawn. There were children walking around with their faces painted in different characters.

The market was busy and crowded. At the other end of the market there were food stalls selling local delicacies, and various artisans. There was fruit and veg, a butcher was located in a trailer and there was a stall selling craft beers.

The girls stopped at the jewellery stall. Everything was handmade. Shireen looked at some Indian jewellery. There were beaded necklaces and bangles.

"Aren't these lovely?" she remarked, showing Sarah the bangles.

"Yeah, they are lovely colours."

"Think I might buy myself this one. They have men's leather bands; do you think David would like one?"

"Well, he doesn't normally wear things like that, but you never know, he might like it, especially if it's from you."

"Ah!"

"You should see him when you're not there. He has this dreamy look in his eyes and is always checking his phone for texts or looking at your photo. He's got it bad."

"What like a stalker?" asked Shireen, worried.

"No, no not at all. Sorry didn't mean it like that. He's sweet on you that's all. God, listen to me. He'd kill me if he knew I said that. He likes to act tough and macho."

"Only he's not, at least not with me. I really like him," she smiled. "I think I'll get this brown leather one for him and a red bangle for me. Are you getting anything?"

"No, I want to look at the T-shirts along the way and I want to get Charlotte a toy from the baby stall."

"Okay," Shireen paid the man for the bangles and put her arm through Sarah's.

"Come on then."

"What are you doing?"

"Nothing, I just …"

"Sorry it's me, I am a bit, well since what happened to me, you just took me by surprise that's all."

"I understand, you're bound to be a bit jumpy."

Sarah patted Shireen on the arm and smiled at her, then linked arms with her and tried to relax. She felt more at ease than she had in months. They went to the T-shirt stall, and she bought a white one with a logo on it.

At the baby stall, she bought Charlotte a cuddly monkey which made a sound when you touched its tummy.

"Phew, I'm about ready for a drink and a sit down," said Sarah. "I've been up with the little un since 6 o'clock."

"Yes, let's go to Costa, I'll buy you a coffee."

"Oh, let me."

"No, this is my treat, please."

"Okay, thanks, can I have a deluxe hot chocolate with cream, marshmallows and chocolate sprinkles?"

"You can have whatever you want."

They started walking back through the market, making their way to Costa. There were a group of teenage boys being silly and throwing chips at each other and generally making a nuisance of themselves.

"Silly boys," said Shireen. "Come on."

They reached the point where the boys were.

"Woo, hello darlin, wanna chip?"

"No thanks," said Shireen trying to get past.

"Ah, you can have a lick of my sausage if you like," said another who was eating smoked sausage and chips.

"Your mate looks like she's gaggin' for it," said the third member of the gang, holding his groin.

"Can we pass please? Come on Sarah."

"Ooh, Sarah, I like that name. Do you fancy my sausage. You can have a feel if you like, he's called Dick."

"Let us pass. Come on Shireen, they are just idiots."

"Sarah and Shireen, must be Lesbos if they don't fancy us four studs."

The fourth member of the gang had been quiet up until now. They hadn't seen him as he had been standing behind the other three boys.

"Hello girls, so which one of you beauties is coming with me. I'm not fussy, both of you could come, we could go down that alley, where it's a bit dark and you can both have your wicked way with me."

"You are disgusting, the lot of you," said Shireen.

Sarah looked at the young lad who approached them. He looked familiar, he had dark short hair and wore a red hoody with a waterproof Adidas jacket. She did a double take.

"Huh! No, no, no, you stay away from me. I… I know who you are, you dirty Manc, get away from me. I'll get the police," said Sarah starting to panic and back away. In her mind's eye she had seen the boy who had raped her from Manchester. "How did you know I was here, you. You've followed me from Manchester"

"You're crazy! I am not even from Manchester!"

"Tell you what you can all come round to my place and we'll have an orgy!" said the boy who appeared to be the ringleader.

The other boys cheered and did fisties and high-fives with each other. The boy who Sarah thought was her rapist stood very close to her blocking her way. She could feel his breath on her.

"I can be whoever you want me to be sweetheart and if I want you, I will have you! I could easily shag you; you look as if you could use a ride."

"Huh, nice one Harry! yeah, a bike, they are both village bikes! Ha, ha!" they jeered.

Sarah, looked at the boy and said, "Harry?" Harry was the name of the boy who sexually assaulted her.

"Yeah, that's my name, don't wear it out."

One of the stall holders approached them. "Right, lads, on your way, or I am going to go and get those two police officers from down the street. Now move!" People were starting to gather round.

One of the boys had a bottle of Coke and he started pouring it all over the man's stall who had threatened them with the police. "Like some Coke?"

The stall holder couldn't believe what was happening. "Hey! Stop that now!"

Sarah tried to run but people were blocking her way. She turned around and shouted, "You stay away from me you rapist!"

The policeman saw what was going on and approached the boys.

"You lot! Stay where you are, I have just seen what is going on, harassing, these girls. I want all your names, addresses and parents' contact numbers." He spoke into his radio and his female colleague arrived.

"I forgot mine."

"So, have I, I have dementia." The other boys broke into raucous laughter.

"All right, less of the back-chat lads, names?"

"Ah well, my name is Joe Bloggs, he's Mr Tumble, Mr Blobby and him with the shaved head that's Fester."

The other boys started laughing again.

"Ah, so we have a comedian in our midst, perhaps you four would like to continue this down the police station?"

The female officer approached the girls. Sarah was standing shaking, deathly white and staring intensely at the boy who she thought had raped her.

"Are you girls okay, have they been harassing you?"

"Yes," said Shireen. "We were only trying to get past and they started talking to us in an obscene manner, they are disgusting! I am okay, but I am worried about my friend here."

"Can I have your name?" asked the police officer, talking to Shireen.

"Shireen, Shireen Patel."

"And you love, hey it's okay."

Sarah started to feel faint and unsteady on her feet. She suddenly felt very dizzy and sleepy. She needed to lie down. The next minute she was on the ground.

"Are you okay love, can you hear me?"

"What's her name?"

"Sarah Seddon."

"Sarah, can you hear me?" She felt her carotid pulse, which was racing. "Sarah, squeeze my hand if you can hear me? She's unconscious, but she's breathing."

"Is she going to be okay?" asked Shireen concerned.

"Well, I think she's collapsed from shock, could just be a faint." She put Sarah into the recovery position, took off her jacket and placed it under her head. She then proceeded to speak into her radio, requesting an ambulance.

"Could we have some space please, move away everyone! I'll need to take yours and Sarah's contact details just for follow up if that's okay?"

"Yes, okay," said Shireen clearly worried and agitated as she got out her mobile phone for emergency contact numbers which she gave to the police lady.

"Thanks, we will need to speak to both your parents, given that you are underage. It's nothing to worry about."

The boys were continuing to make unnecessary trouble and back up was called where they were put in a police van and taken to the station.

Sarah started to move. "Huh, where am I?" she asked sleepily. She put her hand out and felt the ground. "Oh, my word, what am I doing on the ground?"

"Don't try and get up. You have fainted. Paramedics are on their way, won't be long. My name is PC Chapman, but you can call me Jac. You're safe."

Sarah opened her eyes and looked around. everyone was staring.

"Could I have some space please, I won't tell you again. Has anyone got any water?"

"Here, she can have this," said Shireen going into her bag and bringing out a bottle. It hasn't been opened. "Sarah, it's Shireen, take this, small sips." She helped Sarah sit up.

Sarah looked around wide eyed. "Where, where am I?"

"You're in Hexham Sarah, remember we went to the market," said Shireen.

"Where is he?" asked Sarah.

"Who love?" asked the police officer.

"The, boy, he … he raped me, in Manchester and he has followed me here."

"I think you're confused sweetheart; I am sure they were local lads. They've gone to the police station. Did you bang your head?"

"No, I don't know." She felt her head and there was some blood seeping through her hair. "Oh God," she said, when she looked at the blood on her hand.

"Paramedics, coming through."

"Right, what happened here?"

"She fainted, she was being harassed by some boys. I think she's confused; she's saying one raped her and followed her here from Manchester."

"She could have concussion. Hello pet, what's your name?"

"Sarah, Sarah Seddon."

"Right, Sarah I am Bob, and this is Lynne, we are just going to check you over and do your obs, is that okay."

"Have you eaten today, Sarah?"

"Cereal, but that was early. I am going to be sick." She then vomited over the pavement.

"Your blood sugar is quite low, are you diabetic?"

"No, oh, I don't feel well."

"Your blood pressure is also low. We are concerned about your confusion. You may need a CT scan. We are taking you along to the hospital to get checked out."

"No, no what about Charlotte."

"Charlotte?"

"Charlotte's her baby girl, her mam and dad are looking after her."

"Charlotte's safe. She's being looked after. We need to take you in just to be on the safe side, especially with a head injury. You could have concussion which causes confusion. You may need stitches."

"I am not confused; I saw my rapist."

"Were you raped Sarah, when was that?" asked Jac.

"Last year in Salford, I moved here to get away from him and he's followed me."

"Right, we'll look into it, the boys are going to be questioned."
She got out her mobile phone and phoned her Sergeant to inform
him of this.

"Will you come with us to the hospital?" asked Bob looking at
Shireen.

"Yes, shall I phone her parents?"

"Yes, please tell them we are taking her to Hexham Hospital and
A&E will follow up with any developments. They will need to come
in, she is under-age."

"Right." Shireen got out her phone and rang the Seddon's home
phone number.

"Right Sarah, can you get on this trolley please, easy does it, there
we go."

"I… I can't go what about my baby, he'll take her away."

"Who love?"

"The boy, my rapist, he's come for me."

"Sarah hush, she's safe, at home, we are miles away from Salford,"
soothed Shireen.

David was sitting in the living room, still not having got ready,
playing on the Xbox. The phone rang next to him.

"Hallo? Madhouse."

"Davy, it's Shireen."

"Hello babes. Missing me already, ah you made me miss my shot.
You could have just phoned my mobile?"

"This is important, listen is your mam or dad there?"

"Yeah, Mam! he bellowed what's happened?"

"It's your Sarah, she's had an accident."

"Oh, no!"

"She's okay, she collapsed. She's cut her head open; we are going to
the hospital. I need to get on the ambulance, I haven't got much time."

"Mam!"

"Look, tell her we are going to Hexham Hospital, A&E, I'll call
later," she said, hanging up.

"Right, we will come to A&E to get some information from you,"
said the policeman. "We will follow the ambulance," he said to Shireen.

"Okay, I don't know what we can tell you, we don't know them."

Sarah was sitting up on a trolley when Sally arrived with Sanjay, Shireen's dad. He had taken her to the hospital and Rick had stayed behind to look after Charlotte and the boys. Sarah was attached to an IV drip.

The two girls looked up when they saw them coming along the corridor.

"Mum! Oh Mam, I saw him. I saw him, he's here in Northumberland!" Sarah was clearly very distressed.

"Are you sure love, I mean it seems unlikely."

"It was, he wanted to take me down a dark alley!" she said, sobbing.

"Hush, sweetheart, hush! you're safe here," she said, giving her daughter a hug.

"How do you know? Where is she, where's my Charlotte?"

"She's with your dad and the boys. He'll come later. Aisha is going to keep an eye on them all, while your dad comes up here and I'll go back."

"The lads, they, they need to keep a close eye on her, when he comes up, they're not to let her out of their sight. The boy might know where we live, Charlotte's biological father, my rapist, I saw him! I saw him," she said, becoming hysterical.

Sanjay walked towards his daughter and opened his arms, and she went in for a hug. The police had contacted both sets of parents about what had happened.

"Dad, they were horrible, so disgusting."

"Did they hurt you?"

"No, they were just out to cause trouble. It was Sarah they were mainly focusing their attentions on, well me as well I suppose. She thinks one of the boys was from Manchester, the one who assaulted her," she said quietly, so Sarah couldn't hear.

"It doesn't seem very likely, does it?"

"No, but I am concerned about her."

The police came to ask questions and Shireen told them all she could, but the doctors insisted that Sarah was not up to questioning yet. So, Sanjay took Shireen home.

A doctor appeared at Sarah's bedside. "So, Sarah, you have been through an ordeal, I see the nurses have looked after you and dressed your head wound. They have also administered some anti-sickness medication that should start to kick in soon? Do you have a headache?"

"Yes, across my head, where I bumped it."

"Right, I'll organise some pain relief. Are you allergic to paracetamol?"

"No."

"Sorry, are you a relative of Sarah's?" he asked, turning to Sally.

"Yes, I am her Mum."

"Right, well she is going to need to go for a CT scan and she'll need you to stay."

"Oh, I am not going anywhere for a while."

"Good, and is Sarah's dad around?"

"Yes, well he isn't here. He's at home looking after Sarah's brothers and little girl."

"We may need him to come in."

"He's coming to relieve me in a while."

"Well, we may need both of you together."

"Why?"

"Well, let's get the scan done first, erm can I have a quiet word with you?"

"Yes."

They went to the far side of the corridor to talk.

"Erm, when Sarah came in, she was very distressed, seemed to be rambling about being raped and coming into contact with the boy who assaulted her in Hexham, but she said it happened in Manchester. Can you throw any light on that, we thought she was confused?"

"Yes, we used to live in Manchester, until last Autumn. She was raped early last year and as a consequence became pregnant with her little girl. We moved here last November. We haven't been here very long. Today was the first time she felt confident enough to leave her daughter with us and go out with someone nearer her own age. She has been through quite an ordeal; we have been very worried about her state of mind."

"I am sorry to hear that. Tell me did she receive any counselling after the assault?"

"Yes, but she stopped going after a while because she thought she was doing better, but she isn't. She has had nightmares and hallucinations where she thinks he has been in her bedroom threatening to take Charlotte away."

"Charlotte?"

"Yes, my granddaughter, her little girl. She is waiting for a psych assessment, we've been on the list for three weeks, apparently it can take a while."

"Well, I could put in a recommendation if you like and see if we can get her seen sooner, get her fast tracked."

"You can do that?"

"Yes, we don't just patch them up and send them on their way. We look at the whole person and take a holistic view of it."

"Well yeah, if you can."

"Well, I'll get that organised. Is there anything else I can help you with?"

"When can she come home, I know she'll get distressed if she can't see Charlotte for a while."

"Let's get the scan done, see what the results are, but she is quite dehydrated, and her salt levels are low, so we will want to admit her for at least 24-hours for observation, given that she has had a head injury. She needs to be fit to be discharged to look after her little girl. Has Charlotte had all of her injections?"

"No, not yet she needs her MMR."

"Well, she shouldn't be exposed to infection in the hospital. Hopefully it shouldn't be too long."

"Okay, thank you doctor."

"The nurse is arranging for a porter to take her for her scan, you can accompany her, and we'll talk a bit later on okay?"

"Yes thanks, I had better phone my husband to let him know what is happening."

"Right."

She walked back over to Sarah.

"Mam, what was that all about?"

"Oh, he was asking general questions about past history. He says that your salt levels are low, and they want to keep you in for observation, especially after a head injury."

"I can't, I have to get back to Charlotte. I had better go, I can't stay here lying in bed. She needs looking after, she needs watching."

"Sarah, she's fine, she's safe at home."

"I need to see her though; can you bring her in?"

"No, because she hasn't had all of her injections yet. You don't want her to be ill, do you?"

"No, of course not."

The porter arrived.

"Sarah, hello, I have come to take you for your scan, your carriage awaits."

"What?"

He looked down at the wheelchair.

"Can't I walk?"

"Err."

"Sarah, you collapsed today. Get in the wheelchair please," said Sally.

"Oh, all right, thanks," she said looking at the porter.

"It's faster this way, sit back and enjoy the ride."

"I am going for a scan, not a ride out in the countryside."

"Well, you can imagine can't you. We have lovely landscape pictures on the walls."

After the scan, Sarah returned to the ED and Sally got them a sandwich each and phoned Rick. He came in later to see Sarah and Sally went home. As it turned out, the scan was normal. They took her up to an assessment suite, where she spent the night and was allowed home the next day on the understanding that she would take it easy and rest up a bit. Her psych assessment was fast tracked, and they would receive details in the post for her to go for an appointment at the hospital in a couple of weeks' time.

Chapter 35

Max was now attending a gender clinic set up for pre-teens and teenagers to talk about their feelings, what their options would be, which were limited. He could meet with counsellors, other children and teenagers in his situation.

His parents were supportive as always, but privately, Rick was struggling with the idea that Max may want to change genders. He saw how distressed he was getting, and he put his own feelings aside and focused on Max. The other two children were unaware that he was attending this clinic, which had been Max's decision, as he didn't know what he wanted to do next.

His parents accepted that he was different from their other two children and let him dress androgynously, wear face creams and use scents and body sprays to his tastes and basically let him be who he felt comfortable being, and being interested in what he wanted to be interested in. He didn't like sport, so it wasn't forced upon him.

Although Rick at first found it hard that he wasn't your average lad, he also felt a sense of pride instead of loss because Max had been brave enough to come forward and tell them the problems he was facing, and he respected his honesty and how grown up he was being about it.

Sally had always known he was different. When the children were growing up, they never tried to stop them playing something together just because it wasn't seen to be a boy thing or a girl thing. David used to have a plastic Dyson vacuum cleaner when he was little, and he helped with the cleaning. Sarah played with the boys' action men and brought her Barbie dolls into the game. At the end of the day, it didn't matter if roles were reversed. It was deemed to be how the world today worked. However, Rick had gone mad when Sarah had dressed Max in her fairy costume when they were little. He felt that there should be limits.

Max had just been to the clinic and had met with his counsellor, who had told him that pre-teens and teenagers didn't start transitioning at an early age in the UK. He now realised that it could take some time.

He still wasn't sure and enjoyed being his gender fluid self, but then he looked at his body when he had no clothes on and he still didn't think he looked right. He had changed from wearing boxer shorts to underpants because he felt more comfortable. David was out playing football and he was looking down at himself.

'It still looks wrong,' he thought. 'What am I going to do?'

He went downstairs and into the kitchen and took a small knife out of the knife block and stared at it.

'I could do it myself,' he thought, having a mad thought.

Sally walked into the kitchen.

"Oh, are you making a sandwich, will you make me one please?"

"What?"

"Cheese and pickle."

"What are you talking about?"

"My sandwich, you were going to make some, having got the knife out?"

"No, I erm," he started to push past her.

"Max, you weren't going to do something stupid were you?"

"Who me, mister sensible me."

"Max, I am not stupid. If you were having a moment's madness, I'd rather know about it."

"Is nothing private around here. Sorry, yes I was just having a mad moment, but it won't happen again, I promise. I don't know what I was thinking of."

"It had better not. I am here to support you, but if it is leading you to take risks, well, maybe you should stop going to the clinic."

"What? No, it is helping me, honest. I may not even go ahead with being trans, I may just stay gender fluid, I am still not sure."

"Gender what?"

"Fluid, apparently that's what they call kids like me who don't define everything by gender, I am just me."

"Well, I like you as you," she said, smiling, taking his head in her hands and giving him a kiss. "Only, no DIY surgery understood? Okay?"

"Yes, sorry to worry you. I don't really want to hurt myself."

"I should think not, imagine all the blood! Make a helluva mess wouldn't it?"

"You won't tell dad or anyone?"

"I think I should, we always promised to be honest with each other, no secrets."

"Ah, but you know what he's like, I'll get a lecture."

"Max, he's been very supportive of you but if this is a cause for concern?"

"Well?"

"Look, he won't lecture you. He will maybe be too embarrassed to say anything to you, but I'd rather he knew."

"Okay."

The next day, Max was in school. He was well liked in school and got on well with both boys and girls and the teachers liked him a lot as well. He was very popular with the girls. They all got on well with each other. Their genders were irrelevant, or so he thought. It was a good class on the whole, but like every class, there was always one group of students who tried to spoil it. He had only been at the school since November and had settled in well.

It was the beginning of art class, his favourite subject. He loved drawing and was really good at it. He took out his pencil case, his art book and his project. They had all been given projects to do, based on their hobbies and interests.

He sat down at the table along with the twins, Rhianna and Shannon, who he was good friends with.

Rhianna looked down at his project. "Wow, those drawings are excellent, look Shannon."

Shannon looked at Max's drawings. "They are really good, the attention to detail is amazing," she remarked.

"Oh, they're not that good, just some sketches," said Max modestly, "but thanks anyway."

John looked across at the drawings. "You're a really good drawer Max, you know our rugby club are looking to have new kits designed. You could be just the person."

"Oh, I don't know about that, I am not that good," he said.

"You are Max. Don't be so modest," said Jamie.

The teacher looked around and said, "Right, settle down now please. There seems to be a lot of chattering and excitement this morning. I hope you are all bright eyed and bushy-tailed and ready to put some of that energy into some hard work."

There were a few groans, but the majority of the class enjoyed art. The teacher always made it enjoyable.

Jack one of the boys who sat at the back of the class with his boisterous friends piped up.

"Well, I am certainly bushy-tailed miss you got that right," he smirked, feeling his groin under the table.

"That's quite enough Jack thank you. Right, as you will remember I set you the task of planning and making a start on your projects, remember you can either work in groups of two or on your own, whichever you prefer; just to recap, this is based on your hobbies and interests, so if you are working with others, you need to have similar interests. I thought we could start table by table to discuss ideas and to share what you have started. You will be graded on the quality of the work and the effort which you apply to it. You are also going to present your work and tell the class what inspired you to do your particular projects. It is not a race as to who gets finished first. I am giving you four weeks to complete it. You will only get out of it how much you put into it. Now can we start with John's table please? John?"

"Well, my brother and I decided to do it on Sleathwaite Warriors. We play in the junior league, every Saturday. We were going to base it on the history of the club miss. We've already started planning it."

"Good idea! and how are you going to present that in art form?"

Jamie looked up. "Well miss, we thought we would present it in a timeline but in picture format, drawing iconic rugby players and showing victories and cups and awards won, as they have moved up the league table."

"Well done. Max how have you got on?"

"I erm, well I made a plan and have done some sketches, I thought I would do a fashion portfolio, I love fashion miss. They are my own designs based on clothing suitable for both genders, you know unisex clothes. I enjoy designing different looks."

"Good work Max."

"Right now, girls are you two working in a pair or separately. You both seem to be looking at the same work."

"Together miss," said Shannon. "We both love animals and thought we would draw a booklet for wildlife sanctuaries and zoos."

"I love big cats miss and I was going to do a feature on them. I have been to the cat sanctuary in Kent and loved it. We want to show the importance of conservation. You should see Max's project miss. The drawings are excellent," added Rhianna.

"Good work girls. I am sure you are all going to produce some excellent work. I will be coming around to see how you are all progressing."

There was noise at the back of the class on Jack's table. They were all sniggering and being silly. The teacher had been walking around the class as she interacted with the children. These boys were all twelve and the oldest in the class and so they thought that they were top dog, the teacher walked towards their table. Jack seemed to be the ring-leader of this little gang and his cronies followed suit.

"Right, what is all this noise about?" asked the teacher. The boys started to laugh outrageously. "Well? have you made a start on your projects. Jack, you seem to have a lot to say for yourself, how about you start by telling the class what the joke is and then maybe you can get around to telling us what you are doing for your project?"

"Well miss, where do I start? I thought that I would base it on LGBT+, I was going to draw a leaflet about different orientations. You see I am thinking about becoming a woman, he's gay and he likes a bit of both." The other two boys started to laugh raucously. Jack was holding a leaflet. "Thought I'd use this for some ideas."

"Enough!"

"Yeah miss, we were going to ask Max, he's such a girl," said George who was sitting next to Jack.

"Where did you get this, well?"

"On the floor Miss. It fell out of Max's bag. We was going to ask him about how to change into a girl," said Daniel. "I fancy big tits!" he said, laughing along with his friends.

Jack turned to his teacher and said, "What's it like to have big tits like yours Miss? They would suit Max just fine!"

The teacher went bright red.

Max also felt his face colour and tears spring into his eyes. He was only just starting to cope with the way he was feeling. 'Oh, no it must have fallen out of my bag when I was getting my things out,' he thought.

"Right, you three on your feet. get your bags. Cooler now! I will not tolerate bullying in my class of any kind! Give me that leaflet."

Jack threw it in Max's direction. Max went to retrieve it, but the teacher beat him to it. She saw the upset look on Max's face.

"Forget the cooler, we are going straight to see the head. Class, I'll get someone to come and sit with you. Max, wait there." Max had stood up to make a run for it.

The class were really shocked, and hushed talking started around the class. Shannon turned to Max and put her hand on his arm. "Max, you have nothing to be ashamed of, it is accepted these days."

"They were really cruel, are you okay?" asked Rhianna.

Max started putting his things away in his bag quickly. He had to get out of there, no matter how much support his friends gave him.

John looked up and said, "Max where are you going?"

"Don't let them get to you. We're all on your side. Right class?" Jamie added, looking around.

"Yeah! Yes of course!" They all shouted words of encouragement.

Max put on his blazer, grabbed his bag and things, and then made a run for it, out of the classroom, down the corridor and outside. He ran over to the school railings and sat down and put his head in his hands and sobbed his heart out.

Meanwhile, in the classroom another teacher had arrived.

"Right class, a bit of hush please. Right, I heard what happened. Where is Max?"

A lady from Pastoral care had followed him in.

"He has gone sir," said Jamie.

"Gone?"

"Yeah, packed his things up and went," added John.

Joanne the lady from Pastoral care said, "He can't have got very far. I'll go and look for him."

She left the classroom and told some colleagues standing in the corridor what was happening. They started to look for Max. After twenty minutes she saw him outside sitting by the railings.

Max looked up, grabbed his bag and started to run.

"Max! Max, stop! Stop please!" she shouted and started to run after him.

Max turned around. "I just want to get out of here please. I am going home; I can't stay here!" Tears were running down his cheeks.

"Come back into school please and we will sort this out. We take this level of bullying very seriously; any kind of bullying in fact."

"I… I don't know," he said. He dropped his bag and put his head in his hands.

"Come on," she said, picking up his bag and holding it. "You know, we offer a lot of support for students who have difficulties with identification and sexual orientation."

"I want to go home."

"We'll phone your parents, and they can get you. Those boys will be dealt with."

"I can't stay here; I am having difficulties with my gender and have been going to a clinic for counselling, now it is going to be all around the school. I am going to be laughed at."

"I think you will be surprised; the majority of the kids accept these differences these days. We have lessons on this very subject."

"I am not a subject."

"No, of course not."

They were still standing outside. A bus pulled up outside the school, it was going to Newcastle. Max suddenly decided he wanted to get as far away as possible. He grabbed his bag and started to walk towards the bus. Joanne followed him. He pulled out his wallet and got on the bus.

Joanne shouted. "Come back now, please." She got onto the bus behind him.

"Central station please?" He paid his one pound and went and sat down at the back of the bus. Joanne felt in her pocket and found a ten-pound note.

"Newcastle return please," she said, got her ticket and went and sat next to Max.

"Where are you going?"

"I told you, I have to get home. Why are you following me?"

"I thought you lived here in Sleathwaite?"

"I do, but my home is Manchester. I want to see my grandparents now; I can be there by train in a few hours."

"Oh, no, Max, I can't let you go off on your own."

"Why not? I am responsible, I am nearly twelve, and 'appen Im not a baby."

"You are still a minor and during school hours you are our responsibility. I can't let you travel to Manchester on your own. Let's get off at the next stop and walk back, we are only a few stops along, otherwise, I will have to call the police," she added, to frighten him into agreeing.

Max felt he didn't have much choice. "Okay, you can call my parents, but I am not coming back to this school for lessons after this. I will be a laughingstock."

"No, you won't, come on." They both stood up and got off the bus.

"Max, how much money have you got on you?"

"Five pounds."

"Well, that wouldn't have got you very far would it?"

"I suppose not, I just suddenly wanted to go back to Salford. I do like it up here, but I wanted my gran."

"Grandmas always make things, better, don't they?"

"Yeah."

She pulled out her mobile phone and called the school to let them know that she had found him, and they were headed back. After another twenty minutes, they reached the school. She then took him to the headteacher's office. The headteacher was sitting at his desk. He looked up when they entered the office.

"Ah, Max, the wanderer returns, sit down please. We have had a team of people looking for you."

"Sorry sir."

"Don't be," he smiled at him. "We have a zero tolerance regarding bullying and don't stand for it. You will receive full support. Your classmates are all upset about the way you were treated."

"Really?"

"Yes, they are on your side, and those boys have been dealt with. They have got detention for the next two weeks and are having lessons in the cooler. If they bother you again they could be looking at suspension. They will have their breaks at a different time to everyone else."

He looked across at Joanne, and said, "You were gone a while?"

"Yes, this one took some persuading to come back. We have been on a bus headed for Newcastle."

"Newcastle?"

"Yes, he was going to get off at Central station to catch a train back to Manchester, with only five pounds in his pocket."

"I was going back home."

"I thought you seemed to have settled in well here?"

"I like Sleathwaite, and I thought I would go on liking it here until today. I just had to get away. I felt dead embarrassed, I can't stay here; I'll be laughed at."

"You won't be, I'll make sure of it. Kids are a lot more accepting these days, those three were a minority. We give support to students like yourself."

"Sorry if I have caused trouble sir."

"You haven't, only no more running off understand. What if Joanne here hadn't found you, you would be halfway to town by now. While you are at this school you are our responsibility. You can't just go off travelling to a different region on your own. You're still a minor, understand?"

"Yes sir."

Max's parents were called, and they had a meeting with the head-teacher, the head of year and the class teacher. Max would be given support from the school on how to deal with this situation regarding his wellbeing and education.

Max went home for the rest of the day, but he was encouraged to attend school as normal.

David was sitting having his lunch when he heard gossiping going on about Max. Rumours were starting to spread. There was a group of year eight boys at the next table. He listened intently.

"Did you hear about Max in year seven, you know the Manc lad?"

"What about him?"

"Some lads in his class showed him right up, because he is trans."

"What, he's turning into a girl?"

"So, I heard, straight up; goes to a gender clinic."

"Really? You know I think you can take tablets and that helps you grow the opposite gender parts, and you just turn into the opposite sex. If you are male, your willy shrinks and if you're female you grow one."

"No man, you take hormone tablets, but you have to have surgery. You've got to be a right queer to have that done."

Another lad sitting at the table looked up. "That's his business isn't it, you shouldn't be talking about it."

"A bit strange though isn't it? I mean I'm not saying anything is wrong with it, but why would you want to put yourself through that, Urrgh!"

"A lot of kids feel like that these days, confused about their gender. Anyway, that's up to him, let's not spread rumours."

"Yeah, okay."

"I still wouldn't get my dick cut off though, weird."

"So that's arranged then, we'll meet up at the weekend to go to the cinema?"

David continued to stare at the table next to them.

"Davy! You haven't heard a word I've said, have you?"

David was sitting with two of his classmates.

"No, he's not with us," said one of them, moving his hand in front of David's face, trying to get a reaction.

"Sorry lads, hang on a minute."

David was never one to cause fights or get into trouble of any kind. He didn't like confrontations, but he couldn't just sit there and listen to them talk about Max like that. He knew Max was different and liked things from both genders, but he accepted that, apart from when they were teasing each other; but that was just sibling rivalry. What he didn't know was that Max had been attending a gender clinic. 'Surely he doesn't want to change his sex though,' he thought, standing up and walking over to their table.

"Excuse me, what were you all saying about Max?"

"What's it to you?"

"You his boyfriend or summat ooh err."

"He's my brother, and I don't like you lot discussing him."

"We were only saying …"

"Well don't!" said David his hands clenching and unclenching.

"Ah, thought I recognised the Manc accent, so are you trans as well?"

"I am not trans and neither is my brother. I think he is very brave to live his life the way he wants to, and I don't want idiots like you lot making fun of him."

"We weren't."

"He was. You were all being transphobic whether you meant to be or not."

"Sorry pal."

"Yeah, well leave him alone, bloody nobheads."

He walked back to his lunch and sat down. His friends were staring at him.

"All right Davy?"

"Yeah, I am going outside, there's a bad smell in here," he said, looking at the lads.

On his way home from school, David decided to ask his mam about whether it was true, about Max attending a gender clinic. He cared about his brother and didn't like people being horrible to him.

The next day, when Max returned to school there was a big banner tied to the railings saying, 'Join us for our community pride day.' Supporting LGBT Equality and Diversity, Saturday 15 March two p.m. to ten p.m. Activities throughout the day; stalls, games, barbecue, comedians, bands and disco. No alcohol or recreational drugs permitted. Everyone is welcome.'

Max walked into the school yard and all of his classmates cheered and patted him on the back.

"Welcome back Maxie!" they shouted.

A girl from his year came up to him. He thought she was a girl. She dressed like a boy and had her blonde hair cut short.

"Can I just say that I heard about those idiots yesterday and it was total bigotry and small mindedness, I am going to transition when I am old enough and the school has been really supportive."

"Really?"

"Yes, I always knew I was mainly boy. My mam says I will change my mind, but I don't think I will."

"Well, I don't know whether I will yet, I am happy being gender fluid at the moment. I am still a bit confused about it. Still feel a bit awks. I am going to a clinic for counselling though."

"Me too, perhaps we can get together and compare notes, I am Mae by the way."

"Oh, Max."

"You going to the pride day?"

"I don't know, I've only just seen the poster. I might do, yeah, should be good."

"I like your accent you sound kind of Northern but not quite Geordie."

"I am Northern but no I am not a Geordie. I come from Manchester"."

"Oh, how long have you lived here then?"

"Just since November, my brother goes to this school as well. He's in year nine."

"Right, do you like it here then?"

"Yes, I do. I was all for going back home to Manchester after what happened yesterday. I got on the Newcastle bus and got a ticket to Central station. I only had five pounds. Joanne from Pastoral care got on the bus and persuaded me to go back to school."

"Huh, you wouldn't have got a train ticket for five pounds."

"I realise that now. I just felt so embarrassed that I needed to get away. I wanted to see my gran."

"You must miss her."

"Yes, I do. The rest of our family live there. They still come up quite a bit to see us."

"So, how come you moved here."

"My parents wanted a fresh start for all of us. My sister has had her fair share of troubles."

The bell rang and they all headed into school.

"Well perhaps I'll see you at break?" asked Mae.

"Yes, I'd like that," said Max smiling. "Laters."

He had a feeling everything was going to work out fine and he hoped he had made a new friend. He felt enamoured that everyone seemed to welcome him back and had not made him feel like a social outcast.

Chapter 36

It was now well into spring and getting noticeably warmer. The trees and plants were starting to come into bud. The village always looked pretty with its well- kept flowerbeds and hanging baskets. At about this time the village started to get many visitors coming there for days out, holidaying in bed and breakfasts, camping and caravan sites. The village also received a lot of hikers and cyclists.

It was the day of the Pride event at the school, and it was well attended by the community. A lot of age groups had come to show their support, including teachers, students and parents aged up to around the late fifties. Everyone seemed to be having a good time.

The school had arranged for a hot air balloon, which was rainbow coloured with pride emblazoned across it, to give rides for up to four people. It flew high above the school playing fields and school yard. It had four six form students in it, along with the person operating the hot air balloon. He was pointing out different areas to them.

"You should be able to see right across to the cheviots if you look in that direction," he said pointing with his finger, "and the lake district over to the right."

"This is so awesome," said one of lads called Will.

"Yeah it's brill isn't it," said his mate Owen.

The two girls they were with had grown quiet.

"I don't feel so good," said a girl called Stacey.

"I can't breathe," said her friend April, frantically searching for her inhaler and gasping for breath. She took the inhaler, but it didn't make any difference.

All four of them were soon gasping for breath. The man who was operating the balloon was struggling to control it, he was also starting to feel very sleepy and lose consciousness. The balloon had caught fire at the top and gases were starting to escape.

"Oh, my God, it's on fire!" said Owen looking up, coughing, and spluttering.

The operator collapsed on to the bottom of the basket and the balloon started to plummet towards the school. It eventually crashed into the school yard next to some classrooms. where a lot of people were milling around.

The balloon continued to leak gases and the flames were beginning to get heavy. It had burst at the top and a smoke cloud was starting to spread. The people in the basket were trapped. The lads were screaming, the girls and the man were unconscious. The lads continued to cough and gasp for breath. The two lads found some blankets in the basket and placed them over the four of them, to try and protect themselves.

It was a horrendous sight. People were running around screaming and quite a few people were injured and collapsing from the fumes.

Emergency services had been called; fire and rescue, ambulance and police. Several ambulances, two fire engines and four police units came. There were quite a lot of casualties. The people in the basket were rescued and taken to hospital. The younger ones were relatively okay and were put on oxygen and had some burns which needed treating. They would probably have to be admitted and put on a ventilator. The older man unfortunately didn't make it, and died on the way to the hospital.

It took a long time to get the fire under control.

Sometime later, the balloon was cordoned off and the area cleared of people and obstructions. The area was made safe. It had caused a lot of damage and multiple deaths. That night it was reported on national and local news.

The next day, the headteacher walked onto the school grounds and looked around at the debris that was left. Part of the building had caught fire and so there was damage to the front façade where part of it had collapsed. There was crumbled brickwork underfoot and a strong smell of smoke and gas fumes. He would have to organise a maintenance team and hire some contractors to make the building safe. The school would need a thorough deep clean. It could be a while before this part of the school could be reopened.

He started coughing; he had developed this terrible coughing since yesterday when it happened and couldn't get rid of it. He thought it was just smoke inhalation, which is what the doctors told him when he went to get checked over at a field hospital they had set up on the other side of school where it was safe.

'Oh, I really don't feel well,' he thought, wheezing.

He had felt exhausted since it had happened. He wondered if it was just stress, but he wasn't sure. His family hadn't been to the event, and they were feeling unwell too. He hoped he hadn't infected them.

His deputy head turned up. He had also attended the event and was struggling with his symptoms.

"All right Steve?" he said coughing. "What a mess!"

"I know Mike," said Steve, wheezing and holding his throat. "Do you feel okay after yesterday?"

"Not really no, I feel quite ill."

"I thought it was just the smoke inhalation but what if they were poisonous gases? The whole community might be infected."

"I know, I have this pounding headache and I feel really sick, but I thought I'd better come down to see what was needed."

As they were standing talking, the fire investigation officer turned up and introduced himself, along with three other colleagues. They were all dressed in full personal protective clothing, along with masks and shields.

"Hi, I am Steve the headteacher and this is Mike my deputy."

"Hi, I am Martin, the chief investigating fire office. We will make our checks and write up a report. A full investigation is to be carried out. You won't be able to open the school until everything is made safe, as everything will be contaminated. The gases may have been poisonous."

"Do you think this has been done deliberately?" Mike asked. "Balloons normally have helium in them don't they?"

"Modern day balloons have a gas called propane which can cause severe asphyxiation. This mixed with the smoke can cause people to feel quite ill. We have contacted some scientists to come and have a look. They are expected to come this afternoon and carry out investigations. They may be performing some tests to check the gas canisters in the balloon. Once we know more about it, we might have to get advice from Public Health England. Have either of you been symptomatic; you both look pale and clammy?"

"Yes, I have," said Steve, "and my family who didn't even come to the event have symptoms. Could I have infected them?"

"My family and I are symptomatic as well," said Mike.

"I suggest you both go straight home and self-isolate, along with your families and don't have any contact with anyone else. I am not a medical professional, but it seems strange how your families are feeling this way as well. All I can say is that your clothes and skin have become contaminated, and you have taken it into your houses. I suggest you dispose of the clothes you had on yesterday and today."

Steve and Mike looked at each other in horror.

"Almost our whole community could have been poisoned, we could end up with an epidemic on our hands," said Steve.

"You both need to seek medical advice. Are you keyholders to the school as we will need access to the building?"

"Yes, I'll have to turn the security alarm off, if it still works," said Steve.

"Okay, but put on some PPE before entering the building. I'll get one of the lads to get you something to put on, and then I will need both your contact details."

"What about the security of the school, if it is unlocked?"

"Well, the police are manning the area and it will only be unlocked when work is being done."

"Right, okay."

Steve went and unlocked the school and gave a spare set of keys to the fire officer. Inside the school there was a strong smell of gas.

He was glad to get outside again but it wasn't much better. He found himself gasping for air. He really needed to get checked out at the hospital but didn't want to infect anyone else if it was contagious. Maybe the fire officer was right, and his family were feeling like that because his clothes stank of fumes.

Mike came up to him, saying, "You all right mate?"

"No, but I will be, hopefully."

"How are you doing?"

"My head is pounding, and my eyes feel sore."

"You look glassy eyed."

"Let's get out of here."

"Yes, we'll have to contact everyone. I only have a few numbers on my phone," said Steve. "We'll have to put an announcement out on twitter, local radio and the news."

"Yeah, well why don't we get into my car and do it before we go home?"

"Yes, come on."

They walked out of the school grounds to where their cars were parked and sorted out what needed to be done before going home. They contacted local radio and television stations, put announcements on social media and on the school websites. Parents and students should receive notifications.

That night Matthew and Caitlin sat in the bar waiting for customers, but nobody arrived. Matthew turned the television on and the horrific event from yesterday was featured again on both National and Local news.

"Turn it up Matt," said Caitlin. 'In the aftermath of yesterday's pride event at a local north east school in Northumberland, chief fire investigators and scientists have been looking into the incident to determine what caused a hot air balloon to catch fire. They say that it could be due to poisonous gases. Hot air balloons these days are filled with a gas called propane, which can cause asphyxia and in severe cases, death. Multiple deaths have been reported, one of which was the fifty two year old man who was operating the balloon. The other four people were sixth form students who attend the school, who were in the balloon and are responding well to treatment. We have some footage from the scene.'

"God this is shocking and on our doorstep too," said Matt.

They watched the footage and the rest of the news. Then the local news came on. There was a local health professional warning villagers that they believed the gases were poisonous and that those who had attended the event and members of their households were to stay in isolation until the problem could be resolved, which could take at least two weeks. Anyone who had severe symptoms should seek medical advice. Anyone entering the village would be turned away.

"I hope nobody came in here yesterday after being at the event," said Caitlin worriedly.

"I doubt it," said Matthew. "If you remember, we were busy at lunch time before it started but then it went quiet, and we had mainly older people after that who wouldn't have gone to the Pride event."

"Even so, I am not taking any chances. I think we should close up now and get the place deep cleaned."

"Yeah, you're right."

Over at the Seddon's, the boys who had attended the event were both sick in bed. They were both struggling with their breathing and had flu like symptoms. Until now, it hadn't affected the rest of the family although they did feel like they were coming down with colds.

Sarah started to panic when she saw the boys and the news. She had been very frightened that they would contaminate her baby.

She was sitting in the living room, having watched the news. "The lads need to get out of this house. They'll poison Charlotte!" she exclaimed.

"We'll make sure Charlotte doesn't go near them," said Sally, who couldn't stop her nose from running.

"What? but it could be airborne. We are already starting to get colds. how long will it be before we end up like David and Max? I need to get out of here, out of this house, and take her to a safe place."

"No, you can't Sarah, we are under a local lockdown," said Rick.

"She could get really sick Dad."

"We'll keep an eye on her and if we need to get medical help we will get it. If the boys don't improve over the next day or so we'll have to call the doctor Sally," he said, looking at his wife.

"Yes, I am worried about them."

"Are you okay Sal?"

"Yes, just a bit run down. I am coming down with summat How about you?"

"Just a sore throat; feels like sandpaper."

They sat talking and Sarah went upstairs to check on Charlotte. 'I need to get her to safety; this is a dangerous place,' she thought.

That night she couldn't get to sleep she tossed and turned. She kept seeing Harry's face over and over, saying he was going to take Charlotte away. She woke up in a cold clammy sweat. She looked towards the window, and he was standing there, or so she thought. He was standing there, just staring at her and then came towards her taking a scarf out of his pocket and gagged her. Was she awake or was this a dream?

He walked over to her bed. 'I was just pretending to be someone else, that day in Hexham I bet you were really up for it. You're not really frigid are you? Perhaps I can loosen some of that tension. I'll let you suck me off if you like.'

'Get out of here!'

'Oh, come on, you know you want to.' He pulled his trousers down and leaned towards her, pushing himself on top of her.

'Go away, go away!' she tried to push him away.

She could feel his breath on her neck. He tried to enter her, but she pulled her knees up and managed to push him away.

He staggered back. 'Come on frigid!' He started to pull off his shirt.

'Get out you pervert! You rapist!'

'Okay, I am going,' he said, pulling up his trousers and putting his shirt back on. He walked over to Charlotte's cot and picked her up.

'She's coming with me.'

'No! Give her to me.' Charlotte started to cry. 'Put her down!'

He practically dropped her back in her cot.

'Didn't wanna have her anyway, but maybe if you are up to me shagging you all over again, I'll come back and try again tomorrow. You're just a slag. You came on to me back in Salford!'

'Get out! Go, Harry, you are disgusting!'

The bedroom light came on and Rick came in.

"Sarah, Sarah?! Wake up! you were shouting out in your sleep. Are you okay honey?"

"Huh? He's gone. It was that rapist Harry trying to make me have sex with him and he was gonna tek ah Charlotte away to Salford!"

"It's okay it was just a bad dream love, Charlotte's fine, look."

"He, he was here, he threw Charlotte into her cot!"

"Sarah, settle down! I thought you'd got over these dreams!"

"No, I only said that so you wouldn't go on about it."

"Try and keep the noise down, the others are asleep. Your mam isn't very well now either."

There was the sound of footsteps on the landing. Someone was coughing and then they heard retching.

David walked back and saw the light on in Sarah's room. He opened the door standing there in just his boxer shorts, wet with sweat. He looked really pale.

"What's all the noise about? You woke me up!" he moaned, feeling his stomach.

"Ah, your sister has had another bad dream."

David stepped into the room looking terrible. "You okay?" he asked.

"Get him out! Get him out! He's going to infect us."

"Sarah, settle down and go to sleep please. You are safe now."

David was a bit unsteady on his feet and Rick put his arm around him and guided him back to bed.

"How are you doing son?"

"Dad, I've been sick."

"It's probably your body's way of getting rid of the toxins in your body." He helped David back into bed and felt his forehead. "You're really burning up." He picked up the thermometer and placed it towards David's forehead. "David, you've got a temperature of 38.5."

"Is that bad?"

"Well, it's very high. We need to bring that temperature down. It's hot in here, let's open the window. I think I should phone for someone to look at you, phone an ambulance."

"No Dad! No, I'll be okay," he gasped. "I don't wanna go to the hospital," he wailed.

Max woke up.

"What, what's goin on?" he murmured. He opened his eyes and swung his legs over the side of the bed. "I need a wee," he tried to stand up and swayed backwards. "I feel dizzy Dad!"

"I am going to call for a doctor to come."

Both boys started to protest but didn't have the energy to argue. The paramedics came and checked them over and carried out observations.

Rick explained what had happened with the pride event, of which they were already aware.

"I think it is their body's ways of trying to get rid of the poison," said the paramedic. "Most of the village is down with it. How are the rest of you?"

"My wife has just become unwell tonight with it. I have a sore throat and a headache. My daughter has a heavy cold and my baby granddaughter seems fine."

"I think we should look over the rest of you just to be on the safe side. Were you all at the event?"

"No, just the boys."

"Their clothes could have been contaminated. Where are they?"

"I think my wife washed them."

"You should bin them, everything they were wearing, including jackets and shoes."

"Not my new trainers," moaned David quietly.

They woke Sally up and checked her over, as well as Sarah and Charlotte, and then they checked the boys again. Their temperatures had come down and their breathing wasn't as laboured. The paramedic had given them some oxygen.

They were satisfied that they didn't need to go to hospital and advised them on what to do.

After the paramedics had left, they all went back to sleep.

A couple of weeks after the event, things were slowly beginning to return to normal. Work was being carried out at the school and it would soon be ready to reopen.

Sarah was the first to wake up. She fed Charlotte, got her ready and helped herself to some cereal. She then put her in her push chair and slipped out of the front door. It was a cold bright sunny spring morning.

She walked across the road and down to the church, pushing Charlotte along.

"I am going to leave you somewhere safe," she whispered. They approached the church entrance. Sarah tried to turn the handle, but it was locked.

"Oh, I need to find somewhere safe for us, where no one can harm you Charlotte. I won't ever let anything happen to you. I love you."

Charlotte looked up and beamed at her. Sarah looked to the right past the church entrance and saw a bright light coming towards her. She thought she saw a man with longish dark hair, wearing a long white smock and sandals.

'Oh, my God! It can't be,' she thought, taking a few steps towards the man.

"Can you help me, please?" she said quietly.

The man looked at her and put out his hand towards, signalling her to go to him.

'He wants us to go with him,' she thought.

The man was smiling at her.

"Can you help me my find a safe place for my baby, please?"

'Am I going over to the other side,' she thought. 'Have I died and am I about to enter heaven?'

"Help me! Help me!" she shouted, lifting Charlotte out of her push chair. Charlotte giggled and gurgled at her mother.

Sarah held her out towards the man. "Take her please! Just take her some place safe," she said loudly. Charlotte started to cry. She obviously felt the panic and tension in Sarah's voice.

The light was very bright and moving towards her.

"Are you okay love?"

She heard a voice, but it was very faint.

"Sarah, it's Tom, are you all right? Do you need help?"

"Huh? Tom? Err, can't you see him?"

"See who sweetheart?"

"You know up there," she said, pointing up to the sky.

Tom walked towards her. He was wearing his white robe. He had been getting ready for the early morning service.

"But you're not him, I saw him, you know, your boss. He wanted me to go with him."

"Sarah, there isn't anybody there," he said gently. "You look cold, and Charlotte is upset. Come inside and I'll make you a nice cup of tea," he offered.

"No, no, no, you don't understand, he wanted me to go with him."

Just then they heard barking. Tom turned around and saw Emily standing with Charlie.

"Hi Tom."

"Hello love, you've met Sarah haven't you?"

"Yes, at the surgery." She stepped towards Sarah and Charlotte. "How is the little one?" she asked. Charlotte buried her head in Sarah's shoulder and sniffled, still upset.

"Get away! Get away! I don't know who you are."

"I am Emily, we've met remember at the surgery."

"You're after my Charlotte, you can't have her," said Sarah shakily.

Emily took a step towards her. "Come on love, it's okay. Let's get you inside in the warmth. Can we get her some tea Tom?"

"Yeah, I was just going to," he said walking towards the back entrance.

Emily started to steer Sarah and Charlotte towards the door.

"No, no, no! You don't understand, he was going to take us somewhere safe."

"Who sweetheart?" asked Emily.

"He was right here asking me to go with him, it were God taking us to a safe place. It's very dangerous here yer know," Sarah continued almost whispering and looking around her wide eyed.

"Look, I will take you somewhere safe, you and Charlotte," said Emily reassuringly.

"You will? This ain't a trick is it?"

"No, love, let's get in the warmth, that's a cold sun."

Sarah let her take her into the church and Emily took her through to the vestry for a sit down and some tea.

"Sarah, love I'm a nurse remember, can I just feel your pulse?"

"Why?" she asked holding out her wrist.

"Your pulse is racing."

"I need ter get her somewhere safe, somewhere safe. Where he can't find us."

"Who love."

"Harry, he's Charlotte's dad, my rapist, he's here, I saw him last night in my bedroom. He wanted to try it on and then threatened to take Charlotte."

"Sure, you weren't dreaming?"

"No, I could see him as clearly as I can see you."

"Why don't you let me hold Charlotte, while you drink your tea?"

"You won't take her to this safe place without me?"

"No, she won't go anywhere without you."

She handed her over and sat drinking the tea.

"Where's Tom."

"Oh, he's gone to make a phone call."

Ten minutes later Tom appeared.

"All done," he said quietly to Emily.

"Are we going now then, where is it?" asked Sarah.

"Not yet, your mam's coming?" said Tom.

"You called my Mum? What for? I only live over the road."

"Well, your mam and your dad are coming."

"To the safehouse?"

"Yes, if that's what you want to call it."

"How long till the service Tom?"

"Oh, I've got forty-five minutes yet, plenty of time," he said look-ing at Emily.

"I'll not be a moment Sarah," said Emily.

She walked out of the room and into the main area of the church and saw Rick and Sally enter the church.

"She's in the vestry with Tom, can I have a talk with you first?"

"Yes, of course," said Sally.

"We didn't even know she had gone," said Rick.

"Well, she thought Tom was God, come to take her and Charlotte to a safe house. She was very distressed."

"We have been concerned about her for some time," said Sally.

"We received a letter yesterday from the Mental Health Team at the hospital about getting her assessed and information about their teenage mother and baby unit," said Rick.

"Well, I am not an expert on mental health, but I have dealt with young teenage mums like Sarah who are experiencing problems and it has been a great help to them. If you have been sent the informa-tion and with your permission, I can phone them now and see if they have a room available today for her and Sarah?"

Sally and Rick looked at each other and nodded.

"Yes please, I think she could do with the break and support," sighed Rick.

"I have to tell you that I am duty bound to phone emergency ser-vices in cases like this."

"Oh, My God! Is she being sectioned?" asked Sally.

"No, not at the moment but the paramedics need to take them, just in case she becomes unmanageable. It is protocol, I am afraid."

"Well do what you need to do love, and thanks," said Rick.

"It's what I do, it is part of being a nurse. I'll just go and phone them."

"Okay, thanks," said Sally, holding back the tears.

Rick looked at her and said, "It's for the best love, you know that don't you?" he said, patting her hand.

"Yes, I just wish it hadn't come to this, but at least she can finally get some help."

"Yes."

Ten minutes later Emily returned. "It's all sorted. They are coming for her shortly."

The parishioners started to arrive.

"Shall we see Sarah in the vestry? I've asked the paramedics to come to the side entrance so the congregation don't see what is going on."

"Okay, yes."

They walked into the vestry. Tom was doing his best to calm her down.

"What is taking so long?" said Sarah. "I need to get us away from Sleathwaite. It is a dangerous place. God, will show us the way." She looked up and saw her parents standing in the doorway.

"Mam, Dad, are you coming? We're getting outta here, Emily has arranged for us to go somewhere safe."

Rick and Sally looked at each other worriedly.

"Err, that's right love, we're comin' as well."

"We have to wait a little while Sarah, for transport," said Emily.

"Can't I go in our car?"

"Err...," said Rick.

The paramedics arrived.

"Why are they here?"

"Are you Sarah Seddon?"

"Yes."

"I am Dan, and this is Jake. We have come to take you to hospital."

"Why, I am not poorly."

"No, to the safehouse, remember?" said Emily.

"Well come on then let's go."

Sally got in the ambulance with Sarah and Charlotte.

"Dad, come on."

"Dad's goin' to follow in the car," said Sally.

"But I don't understand why I am going in an ambulance?"

"We are taking you in style," said Jake. "Buckle up," he added.

They all got strapped in and the ambulance headed towards Hexham.

"We're going away Charlotte, somewhere safe," she whispered, kissing her on the head.

Fifteen minutes later they entered the hospital.

Sarah looked around. "But this … this is the hospital. I'm not poorly, I did tell you that."

The ambulance pulled outside a pretty looking cottage like building at the back of the hospital. There was a sign saying, 'Jubilee Wing, teenage mother and baby unit'. It looked out over the fields.

"Why am I here, Mam?"

"You are coming here for a break love."

"Why, I'm all right. What about Charlotte? Are they taking her away from me? Is this a nut house?"

"No darling," said Sally. They were standing outside the entrance to the young mothers unit. "Charlotte is going to stay here with you," said Sally gently.

"Teenage mother and baby unit," she said, reading the sign. "Is that just to lure me in? Do they have padded cells?"

"It's not like that sweetheart. It isn't a secure unit, although it is somewhere where you can get some support."

"This is the safe house? We'll be safe here?"

"Yes, both of you will be safe here."

"Are you and Dad staying?"

"No love, but we'll come and visit."

Rick pulled up in the car, and they entered the building. It was a brightly decorated place with flowers outside and lovely pictures on the walls. It had a welcoming feel to it.

The nursing staff were in uniform, but the support staff wore ordinary civilian clothes, to make their patients feel comfortable. They were trying to create a less clinical environment.

They waited in the hall and were welcomed by the sister in charge.

"Hello, hello, welcome. I am the charge nurse; my name is Maureen."

"Hi," they answered in unison.

"And this must be Sarah and baby Charlotte?"

"Yes, why am I here sister?"

"Oh, Maureen please. Well, your family feels that you need a little break. We'll go through a few things soon, but how about a tour?"

"Yeah, that would be helpful wouldn't it love?" asked Sally.

Sarah hung back warily. "Erm, is this an asylum?"

"We don't use that word anymore. We provide support to young mothers like yourself who may be struggling a little."

"Are you saying I can't look after my own baby?" asked Sarah.

"No, no of course not."

"Sarah, look at me you have been through a lot, and you need some proper rest. Charlotte is going to be right here with you," said Rick. "You are doing a brilliant job with Charlotte, and we will continue to help you, but we feel that it is wearing you out."

"Okay then, I'll look around," said Sarah.

They were shown the sitting room which looked very welcoming with comfy sofas and a lovely fireplace and pictures on the wall. It had a wide screen television and a music system.

Next, they were shown the creche and nursery and kitchen facilities.

Maureen turned to Sarah. "All the young mothers here still have their own independence, you can have full use of all the facilities. There is a lovely garden out at the back, through the conservatory. We'll have a look at that, later on. We have a gardener here who runs classes once a week about planting. I'll show you your room first."

"Is there bars on the windows?"

"Sarah?" said Sally.

"No, nothing like that. I can understand you feeling a little nervous and worried but really let me assure you that we are just here to help you. You won't be forced into doing anything you don't want to do."

"Okay, I must admit it does have a relaxed feel to it."

"We also have health and fitness, along with wellbeing and lifestyle classes."

"That's a good idea love," said Sally.

"How long will I be here?"

"Well, we'll see how it goes, a few weeks maybe to start with. When you start to feel a bit better about things you can come back for day visits and drop ins but that could be a little while yet."

They reached the bedrooms.

"This is going to be your room, there is a cot for Charlotte," she said, opening the door to a brightly coloured room. It had been decorated in a terracotta colour.

"Oh, it's very nice," said Sally. "What do you think love?"

"Yeah it's nice, I just hope Charlotte will settle."

"She'll be fine love, kids adapt," said Rick.

"You have your own bathroom and a balcony looking out on the fields. It will be nice to sit out there with Charlotte. We have even sometimes seen fallow deer out there."

"Can I see the gardens?" asked Sarah.

"Yes, we'll go there now," said Maureen, leading the way. "I'll introduce you to some of the young mums."

They walked through the conservatory onto a patio and out into the gardens. There were girls Sarah's age there. Maureen introduced them to Sarah.

"If you want to sit out here for a bit, I'll go and have a word with your parents."

"Right, if you come to my office, Sarah's notes should have arrived by now," said Maureen.

"Oh, we're from Manchester. We haven't been here that long, most of her notes will be at the General in Manchester."

"Well, we have some notes from when she was admitted by A&E after her collapse, but certainly we can get in touch with the hospital in Salford and get her other notes sent here."

"Now, how long has Sarah been struggling? Do you want to tell me what happened before the pregnancy and everything else since."

They told her about the rape and how Sarah had been having hallucinations; how she was being very protective over Charlotte and didn't like accepting help; about the incident that morning when their local vicar found her at the church when she was looking for God to take her somewhere safe, and how she had thought that Tom was God because he was wearing his robe.

"It sounds like she has been through a lot. We get a lot of young mothers with similar stories. I will pass this information onto the doctor, and she will want to examine her."

"Is it an illness?" asked Rick.

"Well, mental health is yes, but I can't diagnose her; the doctor will have to assess her and make that decision."

"I was reading about Post-Partum Psychosis. Is it that?" asked Sally.

"Well, I can't say, but off the record, it certainly sounds that way, but you didn't hear that from me."

She told them about visiting times and Rick went off to get some things for Sarah. She showed Sally the way back to the garden and found Sarah talking to a girl called Cassie about the same age. They were sitting on a mat on the grass and had their babies in front of them. They seemed to be achieving some rapport with each other.

"I will leave you with Sarah. Any problems you can get me on this number," she said, handing her a card with contact details on it.

"Thank you for all of your help," said Sally.

"That's okay. It's a pleasure and try not to worry too much. We'll get her some help."

"Maureen?"

"Yes?"

"She won't be sectioned will she?"

"Well, it doesn't sound like she's a danger to herself or her baby, so no, it is unlikely. She has been through a traumatic time at such a young age, but we will get her specialist help and she should start to improve."

"Thanks again."

"Don't worry too much, she'll be fine," she, said patting Sally on the arm and walked back towards the conservatory.

Sally looked towards her daughter and sighed with relief. She had a feeling that things were going to improve and that her daughter would finally get the help she needed.

Chapter 37

The year was passing by quickly and it was already approaching Summer. The village was looking very pretty, and the flowers were starting to come out in full bloom. The volunteers had been planting floral displays around the village and in the park, which looked very eye catching with their vibrant colours and the artistry which had gone into designing the displays.

The front façade of Sleathwaite Academy had a modern new look to it where the hot air balloon had crashed into the windows of the school, causing some damage to the building. The school had received funding from central government and was being given a whole new reconstruction. Old buildings were being torn down and new ones put up in their place. So, the students didn't miss any more important education, after being partially closed for four weeks after the balloon disaster. Most of the work was being done on holidays and weekends. The primary school was also due to have a new refurbishment, following the completion of the academy.

Once again, the village was starting to get busy with visitors and it was planned that the BBC were coming to the village, to film a new drama called 'The Hamilton's' and Sleathwaite Hall was to be used as the main film location as well as Brookfield Farm, the church and vicarage, the pub and other areas surrounding the village.

The plot of this film was about the lives of the Hamilton family in the early twentieth century and portrayed how the villagers played an important part in the upkeep of the house and grounds. The main part of the film was the dynasty of the family empire which was in the woollen and cotton trade. They produced excellent first class clothing products for all genders. The film was also about intrigue, embezzlement, murder, romance and affairs between gentry and servants, causing scandals and mayhem; and the shock of a Lesbian relationship which would bring shame to the family.

There was excitement about this forthcoming drama, as some of the villagers had been asked to be extras in the cast, alongside some well-known Northern actors from the North East, North West and

Yorkshire. Robson Dean and Sarah Lancaster were the starring roles playing Lord and Lady Hamilton.

Some members of the local primary school had also been asked to be extras to make up a small community school filmed in the community centre, alongside well known up and coming young actors.

The production company was starting to set up around the village, designing the sets and altering buildings to mimic those of the early nineteen hundreds. The BBC was paying residents and business owners a fee for the use of their buildings. The filming was due to start in September.

The film was good news for the village and would bring in new visitors to the area. It was going to be aired on national television for the whole country to watch, bringing in financial growth and recognition.

Max was especially excited, as he was one of the extras. His role was to help load fleeces from the sheep into a delivery van at Brookfield farm. He didn't have a speaking part; he just nodded and smiled. He was just glad that he was going to be in a major BBC production. It was another small part he could put on his CV. This was a definite boost to his confidence, given what he was going through with his gender confusion.

He was sitting at the kitchen table, drawing and talking excitedly to Sally and Rick about his Part: "So 'appen I've got this part, who knows what next, today Sleathwaite, tomorrow the world!"

"It's great to see you so enthusiastic son," said Rick.

"Yeah, well just you wait. I'm gonna have my name in lights, outside the theatre Royal and on billboards, 'Max Seddon, actor extraordinaire'!"

"Ah Max, it's great news. Well done, but let's keep your feet firmly on the ground; don't get too flighty," said Sally.

David burst into the kitchen.

"He's talking about that part again. He never shuts up about it."

"Well, why don't you put your name forward Davey?" asked Sally.

"Nah, not for me. I am gonna go pro with the footy, Man United here I come," he said, opening up the fridge and drinking from the milk carton.

"Hey, get a glass. We all have to share that," said Sally.

"Sorry, when's our Sarah and Charlotte getting home?"

"I am going to fetch them in a bit, you want to come?" asked Rick.

"No, just wondered, I'll have the welcome home scoff though."

"Thought you might," said Sally, smiling.

"Well, I'm not goin' to turn down a nice bit of scran am I?"

Sarah had been at the mother and baby unit at the hospital for eight weeks. She had made a lot of progress and on their visits to see her and Charlotte, she seemed back to her old self and was being a lot more positive and confident about the future.

She would settle in at home for a few weeks and then she was starting sixth form college to get her A levels. Sally was going to look after Charlotte three times a week and take her to the local toddler group, then she was going to the onsite creche for the other two days. Sarah would be with other young mothers in similar situations.

When they had left Sarah and Charlotte at the unit, the boys were upset that they had been admitted and wouldn't be home for a long while, however the two months had flown by.

Rick had decorated their bedroom ready for her home-coming. He thought that fresh paint and wallpaper would help her settle in and put the business with Harry and what he had put her through to one side. Sally had been into town and bought new soft furnishings. They had just got the room finished the day before. They had hung new curtains and pictures put a matching duvet on the bed and placed scatter cushions on it, making it homely for Sarah and Charlotte. They had bought a new comfortable chair and a baby chair for Charlotte.

They wanted her to feel safe and independent. The room was quite large, and Rick had set up a quiet area with a desk and chair and also a bookcase, so Sarah could study. She was doing A levels in Health and Social care, Human Biology and Nutrition and dietetics. Sarah had always wanted to go to medical school to train to be a doctor. Now she had gained a lot more confidence, her parents hoped she was ready to pursue her dream.

Rick arrived home an hour later with Sarah and Charlotte. He helped them into the house and emptied the boot of their things. The boys and Sally were excited to see them. Sarah walked through the door carrying a bigger charlotte, who had grown a lot in the two months she had been away. She was starting to walk and was now a thriving toddler. There were hugs all round.

"Hey, Charlotte, you gonna give Maxie a cuddle? Ah there we are, hello gorgeous," said Max hugging his niece. Charlotte grabbed his bottom lip and gently pulled. "Ow, ow, you little rotter." Charlotte giggled, and he tickled her tummy.

David picked her up and gave her kiss. "Hello baby, I've missed you being here, yes I have," he cooed at her.

She toddled over to Sally and put out her chubby little arms for a cuddle. "Monma, Momma," she said, trying to say 'Grandma'.

Rick gave her her favourite cuddly tiger and she pressed it's tummy and it made a tiger cry. She kissed it and showed it to Rick. "Daddad, Daddad, ki, ki it."

Rick gave the tiger a kiss and brought both Charlotte and Sarah in for a hug.

"Welcome home you two."

"Thanks Dad, it's good to be back at home and not seeing you all at the unit."

"Ah welcome home love," said Sally, joining in.

"Oh, is this a group hug?" asked David, also joining in and pulling Max with him.

"Hoy, you idiot, I fell over," said Max, laughing. "Welcome home sis," he said, getting up and giving his sister a hug.

"Ah, Maxie. Thank you little brother," she said, ruffling his longish hair which was immaculate.

"Mind the hair," he said.

"God, some things never change, poser," she said, smiling at him.

"Do you want to see your room love. Your dad has redecorated it and we have made it right homely for you and Charlotte."

"Yeah, all right, thanks."

They all climbed the stairs and Sally opened the door to Sarah's room.

"Oh, Mam, Dad it's brilliant, thank you, both of you."

Charlotte started trying to climb up onto the bed.

"Good job I put those stair gates up," he said.

"Right, we'll leave you both to settle. I'll go and bring your things up," said Rick. "The boys can help me and then time for a brew."

"That would be nice, I'm dying for one," said Sarah, looking around at their new room. She eyed the bookcase.

"Ah Mam, Dad, you've got me some books on health and anatomy and physiology. Thcy are great, just what I need to get started, thank you."

"That's okay. I like this new Sarah, feisty! It's great to see you so confident and eager, back to how you were," said Sally.

"Well, she's gone now and hopefully she won't come back. I'm sorry to have caused you all so much trouble and stress."

"Don't you do that, you have nothing to be sorry for," said Rick. "You've done brilliantly these last couple of months."

"You, have been through a traumatic time love, it's hard for anyone to go through but you seemed to have turned a corner now," said Sally. "Well done," she added.

"Yes, well that's all in the past and it is going to stay there. Now, how about that brew."

"Mam, can I go round to Shireen's for a bit? She wants us to listen to some music and Aadi has got a new game, please, pretty please," asked David, with his hands in a praying position.

"Son, your sister has only just got back. See your friends another night," said Rick.

"I'll be an hour tops, promise."

"Go on then, but no longer and if you are longer, I'm sending your Dad round for you," said Sally. "Those three are inseparable at the moment, especially he and Shireen."

"So, it's still goin' well with them two then?" asked Sarah.

"Oh, he's always mooning over her," said Rick. "Right bags, Max give me a hand please."

"It must be love, obvs! Soppy get," said Max.

"Obviously, why do you abbreviate everything? Anyway, I think it's nice, she's good for him," added Sally.

He shrugged, walking down the stairs.

"I saw all the trailers for the film, gonna be good isn't it?"

"Yeah, our Max has got a non-speaking part," said Sally proudly. "He has to load a delivery truck at the farm. He's very excited about it."

"Ah, sounds good," said Sarah.

Later on, the family had their meal which was an Indian curry, onion bhajis, naan bread, poppadums' and pickles. Sally had cooked the meal and Rick had made a strawberry sorbet for afters.

Sarah had taken Charlotte upstairs for her bath. She was glad she was back and had enjoyed having a meal again with her family. Now, she wanted to settle in upstairs; just her and Charlotte. She was glad that they had decorated the bedroom and she realised then how lucky she was to have two supportive parents.

She felt that she could move on now and was looking forward to starting college and making some new friends.

Over at the Hadrian, Caitlin had her feet up and was taking a long earned rest. She was now seven months pregnant. The baby was due in September. They were very excited about becoming new parents.

Matthew had started decorating the nursery, ready for the baby's arrival. It was going to be a lemon colour. They did not want to know the sex of the baby, until it's arrival and stuck to soft neutral colours.

They hadn't heard any unusual noises the last couple of months, but when going to bed the night before, Caitlin said she had heard a baby crying.

Matthew had been busy painting and popped into the sitting room to see if Caitlin wanted a brew.

"I'll get it. You've been busy painting all afternoon."

"No, I will, you just relax. It's my turn to look after you."

"I'm not an invalid and besides, I feel guilty with you having the pub to run."

"Let me worry about that, you just concentrate on resting, you need to look after you and the baby."

Caitlin started to get up off the settee. "Ooh."

"What's wrong," asked Matthew.

"Nothing, I just felt a kick that's all, feel there."

"He has a proper kick doesn't he?"

"How do you know it's a boy?"

"Just a feeling, now tea, you sit there," said Matthew, standing up.

After they had had tea and biscuits Matthew said he was going up to the attic to get the pasting table.

He walked up towards the stairs; it was always a bit dark up there. He was about to turn on the light when he thought he saw the figure of a little boy sitting on the steps, opening a bar of chocolate. He did a double take, and asked himself, was he imagining things? He peered around the corner and took in the faint outline of the boy's features and clothing. He wore grey school shorts, with a blue flannel shirt and a woollen patterned V-necked jumper. He wore grey socks and black boots. The boy had shiny black hair and looked about six years old. He could have been Jewish. When Matthew looked back again, there was no one there.

'Bloody hell, I must be hallucinating.'

He turned on the light and walked towards the attic. He looked at his hands and realised they were shaking when he turned the doorknob and entered the attic. He quickly turned on the attic light and scanned right round the room; no sign of anyone. He quickly got everything he needed, making enough noise to wake the dead and clattered downstairs with everything.

"Matthew? Are you okay, you're as white as a sheet, you look like a ghost?"

"Erm, fine don't you worry about me," he said shakily.

He went into the kitchen and took out a bottle of whisky and poured a small amount into a glass. Caitlin waddled into the kitchen.

"Are you going to tell me what's going on? You don't normally drink that stuff in the afternoon. You barely drink alcohol."

"I… I, oh it doesn't matter, you don't need the stress."

"What stress, you have me worried now. Hey sit down, you look ready to drop."

He sat down at the kitchen table; his eyes wide.

"Well, you have to tell me now. We always said no secrets."

"Are you sure?"

"Yes, tell me."

"Okay, try not to freak out. You know you said I looked like a ghost, well I think I have just seen one, on the attic steps. He was faint but I could make him out. He was opening a bar of chocolate. He looked about six years old with black hair. He looked almost Jewish." He went on to describe the boy's clothing.

Caitlin looked wide eyed. She sat with her finger on her mouth and pondered … "This sounds familiar, hang on …"

She stood up and went into the dining room, where she took out the punishment book for the orphanage. She walked back into the kitchen and placed it on the table.

"What are you doing, that's the punishment book."

All of a sudden, the book started opening by itself.

"What's happening?" cried Matthew.

"Arrrrgh!" screamed Caitlin, putting her hands over her eyes. When she dared open them, she looked down at the book. Underlined was the name Jakob Schmidt, crime – stealing chocolate – infliction the strap.

"It can't have been, you have to be kidding me?" said Matthew, looking at the book.

"You, you've seen his ghost! Matt! He's the German boy who was Jewish. He was taken in by the orphanage. He wasn't treated as fairly as the others, because of his origin."

"Well, I'll be damned," he said, looking wide eyed. "What do you want to do? We can't have ghosts wandering about."

"We already know it is haunted and we have never come to any harm. If something bad was going to happen it would have happened before now."

"It's starting again isn't it."

"Yes, it may be because I am nearly due."

"Yeah, well you could do without that stress. I think you should go and stay with your parents for a while."

"No way! Is that what you want?"

"Well, no, of course not. I want you here, but I don't want you and the baby distressed."

"Matthew, I am fine. I got a fright when the book did that. It's something we really can't explain as to why these things happen every few months, but we've known that since the early days."

"And what if it gets worse? We have a baby coming for Christ's sake."

"Let's just try to put it at the back of our minds."

"Easier said than done, that's the first time I've seen one and I don't believe in ghosts."

Matthew went and finished off his decorating for the day while Caitlin made their dinner. They washed up and he went downstairs to help out for a bit in the bar.

Later that night when they were in bed, Matthew couldn't settle. He closed his eyes, and he was a little boy again, about six years old. He was sitting at a small wooden desk and was practising his writing on a slate. He wrote his name in cursive handwriting. Then he rubbed it out and copied the spellings down that were on the blackboard.

He looked to the right of him, and the little German boy was sitting at his desk, trying to copy the words down. He didn't speak a lot of English and was struggling to understand what was going on around him. He must have felt very lonely.

Matthew tried to make friends with him and although they had a language barrier, Jakob realised he was the one person he could trust.

One of the girls who was a 'miss know it all' looked at Jakob's shirt cuffs.

"Miss, Jakob has chocolate all over his cuffs!"

"No shouting out Miss Nancy!"

"But Miss!"

"Head down and write down these spellings please."

The teacher walked over to Jakob.

"Where have you got chocolate from?"

"Ich verstehen nicht."

"In English please."

"Bitte."

"You have chocolate on your shirt."

"Ich verstehen nicht."

"Turn out your pockets," she said, prompting him to stand.

"Ich habe nicht."

She put her hand in his little jacket pocket and took out a half-eaten slab of chocolate. She took great pleasure in showing it around the class. "Ah and what do we have here?"

"Ich fand es in meiner tasche."

"Come with me Master Jakob," she said leading him to the front of the class, she lifted down the strap. Jakob looked at her in horror.

"Miss Jeffreys, excuse me but I saw Laurence put that in Jakob's pocket yesterday," said Matthew.

"Don't tell tales Master Matthew."

"It's not his fault."

"I'd be quiet unless you want to join your little German friend. He still ate half of it. Lift up your hand Jakob."

"Bitte hör auf." He held his hand up and closed his eyes, he felt the strap come down hard on his little hand.

"Aah!" he said, holding his hand. He looked down and bright red welts appeared on his hand. Jakob ran out of the classroom holding his hand and then sat in the boys' toilets and sobbed.

Back in the classroom, everyone looked shocked, but most were too frightened to say anything. Laurence sat looking smug. Matthew felt sorry for his little friend.

"Miss, it really wasn't his fault. He didn't deserve that."

Caitlin prodded him from behind. "Matthew shush."

"I would listen to your little friend if I was you."

"But you hurt him," he said warily.

"Right up here now, come on."

"I haven't done anything."

"You are answering back and speaking out of turn. Now please."

Matthew stood up and went to the front of the class.

"It's not a good idea to make friends with him, he came from the enemy. Hold out your hand."

"No."

"Do as I say."

Instead, she put the strap back and Matthew thought that he wasn't going to be inflicted. A look of relief swept across his face.

"Take down your shorts and underpants."

"No!" he cried.

She bent down and pulled them down and turned him to face the wall, so everyone could see his bare bottom. She brought the cane down hard on his buttocks.

The pain was unbearable. At first, Matthew never made a sound and then he let out a loud scream. He knelt down, rubbing his sore bottom, the tears rolling down his little cheeks. He scrabbled up, pulling up his little shorts, very red in the face and ran out of the classroom, screaming.

He was tossing and turning, and tears were streaming down his face. Caitlin looked over at him in bed and he was holding his bottom.

"Matthew, darling what on earth is the matter, are you in pain."

"Yes, she gave me the cane. You told me to be quiet, but I wouldn't listen, look at my bum please."

"Sorry?"

"She hit me across the bottom in front of the whole class."

She pulled down his boxer shorts to look.

"Matthew, there isn't anything there. You had a bad dream that's all."

"Jakob got the strap for eating the chocolate Laurence planted in his pocket, I was sticking up for him." He had a wild look in his eyes. He looked around and realised he was in his twenty-first century home with his wife.

"I thought I was asleep in the dormitory," he said, sniffing.

"Come here and snuggle in. You got a shock this afternoon, it's your mind playing tricks with you."

"Seeing Jakob wasn't a figment of my imagination you know; you do believe me don't you?"

"Yes, hush babes, come on, go to sleep."

Matthew snuggled into his wife and put his arm lightly around her and his baby. He closed his eyes and fell into a sound sleep.

The next morning, he awoke to Caitlin's side of the bed being cold and empty. He sat up and looked around. He looked at the clock it was nine a.m. 'How had he slept so long?' He quickly pulled on his jeans, shouting to Caitlin about the delivery.

"Why didn't you wake me? What happened about the delivery?"

"Hello, sleepy head. You looked so peaceful and needed some rest, the driver has stacked it all up in the bar and put the barrels in the cellar for us."

"Oh, thank God for that, he's a good un."

"Yeah."

"Right, I had better get on."

"Not till you have some breakfast and Simon and Adam have just come in; they will see to it."

"How long have you been up?"

"Since seven, I've had my breakfast and I started doing some work that I need to catch up on. I'll make you a bacon buttie."

"I wish you would slow down; you don't get enough rest."

"I'm fine Matt. Are you okay after yesterday?"

"Yes, that was quite a dream."

"Try and forget about it."

"Yes, you're probably right."

"I always am."

"Oh, really?"

"Well, most of the time."

"I know better than to argue with you."

Matthew and Caitlin got on with their day and tried to put what had happened behind them. They were both looking forward to the arrival of their child and didn't want anything else to spoil that; besides, ghosts couldn't hurt them could they?

Chapter 38

The summer had passed quickly, and it was now September. Life in the village was busy and as chaotic as ever. Filming had started and the sports field was filled with lorries, trailers and caravans.

The weather was still quite warm, and it had been a hot summer. The park had been especially busy, with people wanting to sunbathe. The village was far busier than it normally was because of the film crew and actors.

Emily walked into the bakery and joined the queue.

"Yeah, can I have a Cornish pasty please pet. Sarah, what do you want?"

"Oh, I'll have a cheese pasty please. You have some lovely looking cakes here," remarked Sarah.

"Can I tempt you both?"

"Yes, I'll have a chocolate éclair please?" said Robson.

"Make that two please and I'll get these."

"You sure?"

"Yes, Robson."

"I wouldn't hear of it, it's on the house."

"Oh, no, we should pay," said Sarah.

"You two are doing a good thing for the village."

"You have a living to make pet but thank you anyway. How much is it?"

"£8.50 please."

Sarah passed over the money.

Emily was wide eyed as she watched the pair in front of her it was Robson Dean and Sarah Lancaster who were the lead parts in the film 'The Hamilton's'. They smiled at her on their way out and said, "Hello."

They stopped just outside the shop and started talking to a man with short dark hair and a distinctive Lancashire accent.

"Hi Lee, how are you?"

"Great, thanks Sarah."

"Good to see you Robson," he said, patting him on the back.

"Have you just arrived for the filming?" asked Sarah.

"Yes, I just thought I'd get something to eat before we start. We're filming up on Brookfield Farm today."

"Oh, you are playing the farmer, aren't you? Err … 'Jack' …

"That's right. I'm just getting something to eat from the bakers. Is it all right if I join you both."

"Yes, we were just going over to the park," said Robson.

"I won't be long, wait for me?"

"Yes."

Emily was getting served when Lee Ingham entered the shop. He had just been on television in a drama series on BBC called 'The Spectrum'. It was about a young girl who was on the Autistic Spectrum. The drama was about how she fitted into society and how she showed enormous courage and determination despite her many disabilities and obstacles.

Emily turned to go out of the shop, smiling shyly at Lee.

Lee saw that she felt a little awkward.

"Hello there, nice day isn't it," he said.

"Yeah, it's been quite hot lately."

She left the shop and went past Sarah and Robson.

"Oh, sorry pet, didn't see you there," said Robson.

"You're right in the way, sorry love," said Sarah.

"It's okay," said Emily, smiling at them both and walking past them.

She was on her lunch break. She hoped the park wasn't too crowded, so she could sit down and eat her sandwich.

She found a park bench and sat down in the shade next to the trees. She stretched out her legs and sighed with relief at having five minutes to herself. She couldn't wait to tell everybody about who she had just seen and talked to.

'Then again, I suppose I should get used to it,' she thought.

The filming would be continuing for three months and it was due to be broadcast the following year on BBC.

She suddenly heard excited barking and Charlie her cocker spaniel sped up to her and jumped on the bench, licking her face.

"Charlie! Charlie boy where did you come from?" She looked around and couldn't see Tom anywhere. She suddenly got worried thinking that he had got out of the house.

"Charlie! Charlie! Where are you, you daft dog!"

Tom came into sight and was relieved to see him with Emily. He was still a young dog and was prone to running off out of sight.

"Hello, Ems! This is a nice surprise. I thought you'd be in the office?"

"Oh, I needed some fresh air and time away from writing up my notes."

She was still in her nurses uniform and didn't want to go back covered in mud. She still had patients to see that afternoon. She gently pushed Charlie off her knee onto the ground.

"Get down please Charlie," she said, brushing dried mud off her trousers.

Tom sat down and kissed his wife. "I had a spare half hour and thought I'd bring trouble out for a walk."

"You got a busy afternoon?" asked Emily.

"Yes, I have to call on two parishioners and I have some paperwork to do."

"Have you had lunch?" asked Emily, eating her sandwich.

"Yes, a little bit, these older ladies insist on filling me up. They say I look skinny and need a good meal inside me."

"With the amount you eat and being a strapping rugby player?" remarked Emily.

"The village is so busy at the moment," said Tom.

"Yes," she said smiling, and went on to tell him who she had seen in the bakery.

"So, Lee is going up to the farm for filming, he's playing a farmer called Jack."

"Oh, Lee is it?" he teased. 'Jack, that's a coincidence,' he thought, thinking of James's Dad.

"Yeah, well what do you want me to refer to him as?"

"You've been listening to their conversations?"

"I couldn't help but hear, the size of the bakery …"

"Come to think of it, James and Rachael did mention they were getting someone well known to come to the farm," said Tom, thoughtfully.

"I'll have to tell Rachael when I get back to work, and, speaking of which, I will have to get back soon," she said, halfway through her sandwich.

"How long have you got left of your lunch hour?"

"About fifteen minutes. We only get half an hour; it isn't long."

"Those are the joys of working for the health service."

"Yeah well, I love it really, no matter how challenging."

"Yes," sighed Tom. "I know what that's like, we always seem to be rushing about these days, we seem to have a few snatched minutes here and there."

"Well, we've just been busy with work that's all. Tell you what, why don't we go into town for a meal on Saturday night?"

"Yeah, that would be nice. Shall we ask Rachael and James to come?"

"Well, I could mention it to her when I get back, or just the two of us could go?"

"Well, see what she says, but maybe it would be nice just the two of us."

"Yeah, we'll see, I have to go now. See you later Tom," she said, giving him a kiss and stroking Charlie.

"Yes, see you later sweetheart, love you."

"Love you too," she said, walking away with a pang of guilt.

She looked back to where they had just been sitting. It was where she and James had sat a few months ago and had ended up kissing passionately. She loved Tom with all her heart and had put the event behind her, but when they were away for a weekend with James and Rachael, the same thing had happened again when they had been left alone in the woods.

Little did she realise was that Tom and Rachael had had a couple of near liaisons, just like she and James had. It had never gone further than kissing between the four of them, but there were obviously attractions there. The four of them had a lot of history between them and weren't about to risk everything because of a couple of foolish episodes.

Anyway, that had been a good while ago and she was happy with Tom and Rachael was happy with James. That was how it was meant to be and how it would stay. There had not been any more episodes and the four of them had put it all behind them.

'Still,' she mused to herself. 'I still get guilty at times. If Tom and Rachael found out, it would destroy everything.'

She took one final look back and saw Tom walking away with Charlie on his lead.

Tom walked away, thinking how lucky he was to have a lovely family with Emily, the boys and Charlie. His job was very important to him, and a beautiful home came with it.

He had felt guilty when he nearly ended up kissing Rachael when she got upset about James trying to end it all and also on New Year's eve, outside their house when he and Rachael had gone outside to fetch some logs from the shed for the wood burner. On both occasions, Rachael was feeling vulnerable and was under a great deal of stress and before they knew what was happening they had ended up in each other's arms.

The four friends cared deeply for each other, and they would never cross the boundaries, even though it had nearly happened a couple of times. Since then, they had all remained very good friends and what had happened with each other's partners was buried safely in the past.

It was a hot day and Patrick, and Philip were enjoying a well-deserved break from work. They had booked the week off and were spending a few days at their lodge, which was at the holiday park in Berwick, on the Northumberland Coast. The park was situated in a pretty little fishing village with the beach just a few minutes' walk away. The holiday park was quiet, and family orientated with many amenities and even had a fantastic fish restaurant which served up produce from the North Sea, which was caught right near the village.

The park was clothes optional at certain times of the year and they had gone for an event organised by British Nudism. There was to be a barbecue, disco, yoga, water sports, and some team sports had been organised, with the chance to win some prizes.

They had just been to the yoga session and were walking through the park carrying their mats and water bottles when they saw a sign for body painting.

"Here Phil let's go and get some body art done."

"Oh, I am not sure."

"Ah, come on it'll be good."

"What if it doesn't wash off."

"Course it will, come on," said Patrick, dragging him across to have a closer look.

There was a poster showing some of the work the artist had done previously.

"Think I would like the dragon done," said Patrick enthusiastically. "What about you?"

"Erm, I don't know."

The artist had just finished painting a butterfly on a woman's back. Her partner had had all over body paint done and he had been painted like a spider. He saw Patrick and Philip and wandered over.

"All right lads, see anything you like?"

"Yes, can I have a dragon done please?"

"Do you want it all over or just your top half?"

"Well, I was going to have just my back done, but why not all over please."

"And how about your friend?"

"He's worried it won't wash off."

"It will last for about a day and then will start to wash off. It is plant based paint and doesn't have any harmful chemicals in it."

"Go on Phil."

"Well yeah okay. I'll just have my back and chest done though. Can I have the tiger?"

"Yes sure, the tail will go partly down your leg, is that all right?"

"That's okay," said Philip, who was feeling a little nervous about having someone quite literally paint his body. 'Oh, why am I being nervy, what harm can it do,' he thought.

"Right, who is going first?"

"Okay then, I will," said Philip bravely.

"If you step behind this curtain, for some privacy, you can put your things down."

He handed his mat and water bottle to Patrick and went behind the curtain. Forty five minutes later, he came out and gave Patrick a surprise. He had decided to go the whole hog and have an all over body paint.

"Wow! Look at you!" remarked Patrick. "I thought you were just going to get your top half done?"

"Well, I decided to stop being a wuss and just go for it."

"Don't sit down yet though. It is quick drying but just give it ten minutes or so to be sure," said the artist.

After another forty five minutes Patrick was done and emerged from behind the curtain. They took some photos with their phones and the artist also took some.

He gave them both a leaflet about a body painting gallery, which was being held at the Northern Gallery in Newcastle. They would be paid for showcasing his work.

"Just if you're interested, no pressure. I will pay you a fee of course."

"How much?" asked Patrick.

"Patrick!"

"Sorry."

"No, it's all right. I didn't expect you to do it for nothing. It's £200 plus refreshments, which includes a drink and a buffet."

"Can we think about it," asked Philip.

"Yes, take your time. No rush, it isn't until the end of next month. My number is on the back of the leaflet if you do decide to take part."

"Thank you very much," said Patrick giving the man his money for their body painting.

They walked away, looking at the leaflets.

"I'm not sure about this Patrick. I mean getting this done is one thing but being gawked at like an exhibit is another."

"Well, people can see you now."

"Yeah, but the majority of people here are in the buff, and it is a relaxed holiday village. It's a different matter in town."

"I know what you mean. Still, think of the money."

"Well, there is that we'll have to give it more thought."

"Are we going to the disco tonight?"

"Yes, why not, we could show off our artwork."

"Well, there's no point in having all of this done and then to cover it up with clothes is there," laughed Patrick.

"No, I suppose not. I am starving. The barbecue will be starting soon, let's head over there."

"Yeah, we won't be able to go for a swim now though."

"No, we'll leave it until tomorrow afternoon," said Patrick, grabbing his hand.

Philip looked down and smiled. He felt totally relaxed here, no work to worry about, just total relaxation with a man he loved dearly.

"You enjoying yourself Philip?"

"I always do when I am with you," he said, stopping to give him a kiss.

He put his arm around him and pulled him close as they walked along the road. They dropped their yoga mats off at the lodge and went over to the barbecue.

They had a very enjoyable afternoon. They had burgers, sausages, spare ribs, chips, which was all cooked by one of the restaurant's chefs. The food was delicious and cooked to a high standard. There were also vegetarian and fish options.

After the barbecue, they sat around a campfire. Someone had brought a guitar and there was singing and dancing, and Philip and Patrick joined in.

The time had passed quickly, and they decided to go back to the lodge for a rest before going to the disco.

They both sat down on the deck chairs by the lodge. The family opposite were also sitting outside and waved when they saw Philip and Patrick. They had set up a paddling pool for their two small children who were having a whale of a time filling plastic little buckets with water and jumping in and out of the water.

Patrick smiled as he watched the two children, it reminded him of when he and his brother Steve were little, playing in their back garden in the paddling pool. They each had a sun hat on to protect them from the sun as they were both fair skinned. The boy and girl must have only been about three and four.

Philip was watching the look on Patrick's face.

"Takes you back, doesn't it?"

"Yes, they have no inhibitions at that age."

"I don't think you ever had any inhibitions about nudism."

"No, I don't. I'm happy in my own skin aren't I?"

"Yes, and that is why I love you. I must admit I feel more relaxed in the Summer when we don't have to worry about wrapping up like in winter."

"Well, when the trees drop their leaves in the autumn, we put our clothes on," said Patrick, watching the two children playing.

"Well said."

"Phil?"

"Yes?"

"You ever think about kids?"

"Any particular kids or kids in general?"

"Having kids, starting a family?"

"Well yeah, I suppose I would like to be a dad someday, why do you ask?"

"I love you and I would like us to have kids together some day."

"What? Fostering?"

"Well, there is that, but I was thinking more of our own."

"It may have escaped your notice but we both have the same equipment, something is missing."

"I meant artificial Insemination. We would have to find someone willing to carry a child for us."

"That can cost thousands."

"Yeah, but we might be lucky enough to have it work first time."

"Just think our own kids, it would be nice. Do you think we'd make good dads?"

"Yeah, why not? We've as much chance as anyone else. We manage Tabitha?"

"Patrick, Tabitha is a cat."

"Can't be that much different."

"It is, and until now, we have had only ourselves to see to. All that will change, once kids come along."

"Why, do you not think we are up to it."

"I didn't say that. There is nothing I would like more. All I am saying is that there is a lot to think about, and yes, I think we should look into it."

"Well, we looked after your nephew before and that was all right."

"Yes, and then he went home. All I am saying is it's not like we can take them back if we've had enough. We have to be fully committed, and yes, I think we are ready and would make great parents."

"Great, look I know what we'd be taking on and I know there will be a lot of planning and saving money, but we could possibly do it."

"We would have to reduce our hours at work and possibly take time off when they are very young," said Phil.

"Can we look into it?"

"Of course, Patrick; I am just saying we need to be realistic."

"I realise that."

They discussed a plan of action before going over to the disco and it was decided that they would look into surrogacy and adoption.

Jack Macalister left his house at Haydon Bridge and set off along the road with his shepherd's crook in his hand which he was using as a walking stick. He was headed in the direction of the southbound side of the dual carriageway. He was headed for Brookfield Farm.

Elsie was at a hospital appointment and the taxi had come early for her. A care assistant was due to come and sit with Jack but had been delayed, so Elsie phoned one of the neighbours to keep an eye out, just in case he went wandering, which he was prone to do.

'I need to get the sheep in for clipping, best get a move on,' he thought. 'There's a lot to do; and we'll have to make some haybales ready for winter, and there's the feeds to organise. Got held up this morning. Dad won't be happy, I promised I'd help out in the school holidays.'

He walked along the path that led up to the bypass.

'Traffic's bad this morning. Normally at this time, the milk float comes. I need to cross this road.'

He was standing at the side of the bypass, ready to cross. He stepped out, but a car was headed in his direction and had to slam on the brakes and they blew their horn. The driver couldn't stop and as soon as he could, he pulled over and alerted the police.

Jack stood by the side of the road in a world of his own. All he could see in his mind's eye was the farm back in the day when he was growing up. In his mind he was out in the fields tending to his sheep.

A police car pulled up and the officer got out of the car and approached Jack.

"Good afternoon sir. Do you realise that you aren't meant to be walking on this busy road?"

"Eh?"

"Come on, get in the car and I'll take you somewhere safe. Where were you headed?"

"Back home, I need to go and get the sheep sorted. I promised me dad that I'd help him in the holidays; only me and a pal were on a bike ride. I'll get into trouble now for being late."

The policeman steered him towards the car and got him safely into the front seat. He looked down at Jack's feet and realised that he had his slippers on. He carefully went around to the other side of the car and got in. He fastened Jack's seatbelt drove the car down the slip road and parked just by the village of Haydon Bridge

"So, what's your name then?"

"Jack, Jack Macalister."

"Date of birth sir?"

"28 June 1934. I am fifteen next birthday."

"Really, and what year are we in Jack."

"1949."

"Right."

"Do you know where you are?"

"Course I do, I've lived here since I was born. I am at Sleathwaite, our farm is here."

"Would that be Brookfield Farm?"

"That's right, you know it then."

"Yes, yes I do."

He spoke into his radio. "Hello, yes this is tango 445, can you please run a check on a Jack Macalister, date of birth 28 June 1934. I found him wandering on the bypass that runs over Haydon Bridge."

He turned to Jack. "So do you live at the farm now."

"Yes, I told you I'm late. Are you going to take me home."

"Yes, I am."

"Dad'll be cross. He might give me the belt for being so late."

"No need to worry sir, we'll have you back where you need to be."

His radio crackled and a voice said, "Yeah, Mark, he lives at 6 The Meadows, Haydon Bridge."

"Thanks a lot."

"Right, let's get you home then." He did a three point turn and headed back toward the village. The policeman pulled up outside a pretty bungalow.

"I don't know this place, I don't live here, I said I live on the farm. Look, I've got my crook ready for herding cattle."

"Just wait here a moment please sir."

He walked up the drive to the front door and rang the bell. There was no one home, so he went and called on both sets of neighbours. The first one was out but the second one said that Elsie needed to go out for a medical appointment and that the care assistant had been delayed. "I was about to go and check on him, only I got an important phone call."

"Do you have a mobile number for his wife?"

"No, she hasn't got a mobile phone. It would make things easier, what with old Jack wandering. He can wait here with me if you like."

"Does he have any family near here?"

"Yes, his son, James Macalister lives at Brookfield Farm."

"Ah, that's where he was headed, I found him on the bypass."

"Oh, my God!"

"Well, luckily he is safe now."

"Do you want to bring him into my house?"

"He's confused enough as it is. Do you have a number for his son?"

"No, sorry. I had his old one but then he changed his number, and he didn't get around to giving me the new one."

"I'll take him up to the farm. there should be someone there."

Mark got back in the police car. "Right Mr Macalister, let's get you home, shall we?"

"I told you it wasn't there. Will you have a word with my dad for me; explain why I am so late."

"Of course."

Fifteen minutes later, PC Mark pulled into the farm. He stopped the car and helped Jack out.

"Now, I'm home, but it's changed. That big tractor weren't there when I left this morning. Dad must have bought a new one, the Fergie was on its last legs. Dad! Dad, it's me Jack. A policeman gave me a lift home! Where are you?"

James was walking up the road with Sammy and Kim and was surprised to see his dad there with a policeman.

"Hello, has something happened?"

"Are you James Macalister sir?"

"Yes."

"I found your dad wandering on the bypass near Haydon Bridge."

"Oh, my God, are you okay?"

"Yes Dad. I was on my way to help you with the sheep, sorry I'm late. This nice policeman gave me a lift home. Sorry I was on the bike ride with Jack Wil…"

"Dad?"

"I think he's a little confused, a driver nearly hit him. He alerted us almost immediately."

"Dad, you've got your slippers on. Weren't you supposed to be waiting with the care assistant till mam got back?"

"Is my mam not here, at home?"

"No."

"The care assistant got delayed and the neighbour was going to keep an eye out, but he left before she had a chance to check on him. Can we go in the house and get him sitting down?"

"Of course, yeah, I'll put the kettle on," said James feeling in his pocket for his house keys.

They went in through the back door and got Jack sitting down. James filled the kettle.

Jack looked up. To him, James looked just like his Dad did when he was growing up.

"Dad, can I have a glass of milk please."

"Dad, it's James your son. You don't work or live here anymore. I'll make you a nice cup of tea."

"Okay."

"Is your father prone to having strokes or does he have Dementia?"

"Both," said James, sadly.

"He was in a world of his own when I found him, he thought it was 1949."

"I'll ring the doctor. He may have had another TIA," said James.

They finished their drinks and after seeing that Jack was settled, the policeman left.

Jack went and sat by the fire which James had lit. It was a warm afternoon, but Jack was feeling cold. He sat back and closed his eyes, pleased to be home.

When he opened his eyes, he was still in the farmhouse kitchen. He was sitting by the fire with a couple of baby lambs. His mother was at the kitchen table making bread. Jack was six years old again with curly blond hair, just like James and Cameron's.

"Jack, you can go and help your Dad collect the eggs when he gets home."

"Is he seeing to the sheep?"

"Yes, you were at school then. He needed to bring them in for shearing. Have you got homework?"

"Yes, just spelling and some arithmetic."

The door to the farmhouse opened and in stepped Daniel Macalister.

"Right lad, now you're back from school, you can help me with the hens. You had a good day?"

"Yeah, we played tag at lunchtime and they had the hoops out. This afternoon we had lessons outside, but they brought us in when a bomber flew across, just in case. Luckily, it was an English one. Miss said to get in in case we got hit by the Jerries." It was 1940 and in the middle of the second world war.

"I had my gas mask just in case."

"Good, make me a brew would yer our lass, then we'll go over to the hens."

"Aye I will do that. Sit next towor Jack at the fireside; only tek those mucky boots off first."

Jack looked around the kitchen and smiled, glad at last to be at home. He felt safe here even if it was wartime. They were safer out in the countryside than in the towns in the Blitz.

Brookfield Farm had had just had one previous tenant, Jack's grandfather Ali Macalister. It was in the days when a lot of the work was done by hand. They grew a lot of their own produce, which they sold to the villagers of Sleathwaite, as well as for their own use.

Time would tell how successful the farm would be in the future and how long it would stay in the Macalister family. Farming methods were improving and set for revolutionary change.

The author

Katharine Wilson was born as Katharine Davison
in Ryton, Tyne valley in 1971, when the village
came under County Durham in the U.K. She was
educated at Ryton Comprehensive school and left
in 1987. She has worked in various support roles
including early years and health and social care.
She worked for one of the leading hospital trusts
at Royal Victoria Infirmary where she worked a
health care assistant on the Cardiology Ward until
2019. She has two grown up sons.
Her hobbies are walking, reading, writing, watching T.V. dramas, yoga and cooking.

This is her first novel she has submitted for publi-
cation.

The publisher

He who stops getting better stops being good.

This is the motto of novum publishing, and our focus is on finding new manuscripts, publishing them and offering long-term support to the authors.
Our publishing house was founded in 1997, and since then it has become THE expert for new authors and has won numerous awards.

Our editorial team will peruse each manuscript within a few weeks free of charge and without obligation.

You will find more information about
novum publishing and our books on the internet:

w w w . n o v u m - p u b l i s h i n g . c o . u k